YULE BE SORRY

A BEAUFORT SCALES MYSTERY - BOOK 2

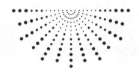

KIM M. WATT

Copyright © 2018 by Kim M. Watt.

All rights reserved. No part of this book/ebook may be used or reproduced in any manner whatsoever, including scanning, uploading or electronic sharing, without written permission except in the case of brief quotations embodied in critical articles or reviews.

Seriously, don't steal books. Share them. Talk about them. Review them. Tell your friends about them. Writers *love* that. But book thieves will be fed to dragons.

This book is a work of fiction. Names, characters, businesses, organisations, places, events and incidents either are the product of the author's imagination or are used fictitiously. Any resemblance to actual persons, living or dead, events, or locales is entirely coincidental.

For further information contact: www.kmwatt.com

Cover design: Monika McFarland, www.ampersandbookcovers.com

Editor: Lynda Dietz, www.easyreaderediting.com

Logo design by www.imaginarybeast.com

ISBN: 978-1-9993037-6-1

First Edition: December 2018

10 9 8 7 6 5 4 3 2 1

For Mick,
who always believes.
And who gives proper consideration to questions
regarding Yorkshire, baking,
and dragons.

CONTENTS

1

MORTIMER

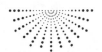

The air was crisp and still, sparkling with the promise of frost, and the stars pocked across the sky were dim beyond the Christmas lights. The scent of mulled wine and roasting chestnuts rolled across the cobbled streets, and yellow light spilled from the steamed windows of the pubs (both the nice one with foodie aspirations, and the other one, where the carpet was always sticky and it still smelt of cigarettes from the 90s). The smattering of shops and businesses that crowded the little village square had fairy lights and decorations and fake snow in their windows, and even the butcher's empty display cases with their dubious plastic holly managed to look grudgingly festive.

But no one was window-shopping tonight. All eyes were on the tented market stalls blossoming across the square, crowded by shoppers with red noses and heavy jackets, while the stall holders chattered through their spiels and breathed mist onto the night.

The fairy lights and lanterns of the stalls shone on hand-tooled leather bags and knitted beanies, paintings in small frames and bird houses waiting for a distant summer. There was jewellery with hand-lettered labels, and cakes wrapped clumsily in clingfilm, cupcakes with towering domes of wintry frosting and novelty T-shirts with flashing lights and tinsel. There were toys and puzzles, journals and pickles and nougat and gingerbread. There were wreaths and trees and brightly coloured soaps, wooden toys and dried flowers and bacon sizzling on a grill and a stall selling hot chocolate and spiced cider. It was, in short, a wonderland, the sort of place that required immediate exploration, and Mortimer was more than a little worried that was exactly what was on Beaufort's mind. The old dragon had wriggled his scaly head out under the canvas at the back of the Women's Institute stall and was peering around eagerly.

"Um, Beaufort?" Mortimer said. "No one can see you, can they?"

"Of course not, lad," he said. "We're dragons. No one sees dragons unless they're expecting to see dragons."

Mortimer could think of at least half a dozen occasions in the last year alone where humans had seen dragons whether they expected to or not. It was one thing spending time with the Toot Hansell Women's Institute, who were not only remarkably well-disposed to see dragons, but were very indisposed to share that knowledge with anyone else. It was quite another being in the middle of a crowded market place where anyone Sensitive enough could see them. All they needed was some reporter over from Skipton, writing a story on the Christmas market for the local paper and being all *observant*.

"Beaufort, do come back in," Alice said, not looking up from restocking the mince pie plate. Mortimer watched carefully to make sure she didn't drop any. Although, with Alice, that was unlikely.

Beaufort gave a very pointed sigh and retreated, bumping into Miriam's legs.

"Oh! Sorry, Beaufort. Are you alright?" Miriam was pink-cheeked in the soft light, hair escaping in all directions from under a misshapen wool hat.

"Just keeping an eye on things. It's terribly busy out there, isn't it?"

"Yes." Miriam checked for eavesdropping customers before she kept talking. "I don't think anything needs keeping an eye on, though. And you do need to be careful – we don't want a repeat of the first Christmas market."

Beaufort Scales, High Lord of the Cloverly dragons, veteran of more battles than he cared to remember and possessor of a most impressive set of age-yellowed teeth, looked suitably chastened. He sat down next to Mortimer, out of the way of the two women selling Christmas cake and chutney and hot drinks, and Mortimer's own enchanted dragon-scale baubles and magical boats.

"That market was more fun, though, don't you think?" he said to the younger dragon.

Mortimer snorted. "You made us wear dog suits, Amelia almost *ate* a dog, and then you caught fire. I guess it depends on your definition of fun."

"It was more fun than sitting behind the counter, not being allowed to talk to anyone."

Mortimer inspected him for a moment, then held out a plate. "Christmas cake?"

"May as well."

MORTIMER HAD NEVER IMAGINED what would come from such a little thing as suggesting to the High Lord that time spent searching for treasure troves would be better used collecting barbecues and gas bottles for dragons to sleep on. Beaufort had abruptly transformed from a bored old dragon to a very *interested* old dragon. Interested in *everything*, and once Mortimer had met Miriam and come up with the idea of restarting the dragon-scale trade (only instead of selling scales to knights for armour, he made magical baubles that unfolded into flowers and floated in mid-air when lit, or boats that blossomed into intricate sailing ships once they touched water, or gliders that were delicate and beautiful and near enough unbreakable. He felt it was an improvement), Beaufort had gone from interested to *involved*. It still made Mortimer shudder, thinking of the old dragon crashing the Women's Institute meeting almost two years ago. Although that was nothing compared to the murder investigation they'd crashed this last summer.

Miriam held out a jug of mulled wine to the dragons. "Beaufort?"

"Don't mind if I do."

"Mortimer?"

He took a paper cup with a wary glance at Beaufort. "Not too much."

"Mortimer, the wine had nothing to do with last time."

Mortimer had his own thoughts regarding that. He still distinctly remembered Beaufort, in a dog costume, wandering off to buy mulled wine from a very confused stall holder. He had nightmares about it, in fact. "Well. Just – it's for the customers, isn't it?"

"We always make extra," Miriam said, pouring some for Alice, who took it with a smile and wrapped her hands around the cup.

Mortimer sighed. Beaufort had already finished his wine and was looking at the tureen expectantly. The High Lord was bored. It never did for the High Lord to get bored. He'd start Thinking About Things, and that never ended well.

Alice tipped her mug to the dragons in a gap between customers, white hair falling in neat lines to her chin from under her rather fetching felt hat. "The baubles are selling very well, Mortimer. I hope you have more."

"I do. And the boats?"

"Not as well, but they're still popular." Alice leaned forward to watch the dragon-scale baubles bobbing softly at the ends of their tethers, like gently lit balloons. Some of them looked like birds, others like stars or butterflies or flowers, others just globes with fanciful patterns carved in their sides. They burned without using fuel or releasing heat, and had proved so popular that Miriam had introduced the dragons to something called the Etsy. The income was handy for things like gas bottles and barbecues, which the Cloverly dragons had embraced eagerly. But Mortimer felt that was only the start. He was currently trying to figure out whether to invest in AGAs, or if the logistics of underfloor heating in the caverns was a possibility. There were many options available for a modern dragon.

Miriam sat down on a folding chair next to the dragons, and Mortimer shuffled a little closer to her, letting the heat of his breath warm her hands. Beaufort sat by the counter, watching the passage of customers with old gold eyes while their gaze passed unseeing over the dragons, draped in fireproof blankets and half-hidden in the shadows.

"I feel like a horse," he grumbled, shaking his wings so violently that the blanket almost fell off.

"Well, you don't look like one," Alice said, stooping to pull the blanket up again and patting him on the shoulder. "Not to me, anyway."

"It's better than looking like a dog," Mortimer said under his breath, and Miriam snorted.

Beaufort looked back at them both and grinned suddenly, exposing those fearsome teeth. "Never mind, lad," he said. "I'm sure something exciting will happen soon."

Mortimer fervently hoped not.

🐉

IT WAS GETTING LATE, the customers dwindling, heading home to firesides and warm beds. The mulled wine was almost finished, the boxes of chutneys and cakes and baubles under the counter all but empty. It had been a good night for the Women's Institute, and Alice and Miriam were the last ones to take their turn standing in the cold (relative cold, thanks to the dragons, who radiated a lot more heat than the gas heaters some of the other stallholders were using). Gert and Jasmine had stayed to help them pack up, but it was mostly just empty boxes. The stall was rented and would be collected the next day.

"I think that's the last of them," Alice said, handing Gert a shopping bag full of flattened boxes.

"How did my cordial sell?" Gert had an enormous scarf on over a puffy coat, and bore a startling resemblance to a large purple bear.

"All gone. I think telling people that it might be a teeny bit alcoholic and that they shouldn't serve it to kids was actually a selling point."

"Of course it was." Gert tucked the bag under one arm and picked up the empty mulled wine urn with the other. "You ready?"

"Oh, no. You go on. We'll pack up the rubbish then walk back. No sense all of us hanging around."

"Are you sure?"

"The walk'll be nice," Miriam said.

"If you prefer, then," Gert said. "Come on, Jas. Let's get out of the cold." The younger woman nodded and picked up a storage crate full of paper plates and mugs and napkins.

"Lovely sandwiches, Jasmine," Beaufort said from the shadows.

"Oh, really?" She gave the old dragon an enormous smile. "You really liked them?"

"They were wonderful," Beaufort assured her, while Miriam

and Alice made agreeable noises. Mortimer nodded vigorously. Fire breathing doesn't lend itself to a very refined palate, so he hadn't minded the sandwiches, although somehow they'd been both soggy *and* dry, and while the filling had looked like turkey and cranberry, it had tasted more like some sort of foam insulation. He imagined that was why Alice had asked Jasmine to be in charge of transport rather than, well, anything else. The younger woman had made some lovely wreaths for the stall, but so many bits had fallen off on the way here that they'd had to just use them for decoration at the back, where no one could see the gaps.

"Well, I'm so glad you liked them." Jasmine's cheeks had flushed a rather pretty shade of pink, and she was still grinning. "Okay – 'night everyone!" She all but skipped off toward the van, leaving a trail of paper cups behind her.

"I'll get them." Miriam hurried off in a swirl of bright skirts and multi-coloured thermal tights, collecting the spilled cups and calling to Jasmine to slow down. Alice smiled, and went back to wiping off the counters.

Beaufort stretched, and brushed Christmas cake crumbs off his snout. "Is there any mulled wine left?"

Alice raised her eyebrows, tucking the cash box into her bag. "There is."

"It will keep, you know," Mortimer pointed out, although he supposed the danger was past. They were one of the last stalls still packing up. Even if Beaufort got it in his head to start wandering around, hopefully anyone perceptive enough to see him would be coming out of the pub and would either think they were hallucinating or that he was a very odd, slightly oversized Shetland pony.

"But I thought this market was a one night only thing," Beaufort said.

"We could take it to the W.I. meeting next week." Alice sounded as if she was smiling, although she didn't look up from what she was doing.

"Well. Of course. That's right. We should do that. You, I mean." Beaufort had a disappointed little droop to his shoulders.

"That seems like a good idea," Mortimer said, trying to help Alice by taking the bin bag out but only succeeding in puncturing it with his claws. "Oh. Sorry."

Alice took the bag off him. "Leave that, and do try to relax a little, Mortimer. It all went perfectly, no one looked twice at either of you, and there's just enough mulled wine for four good glasses. A perfect evening, in other words. There's no reason for you to fuss so much."

Mortimer felt his scales flush a slightly ashamed yellow. Alice hadn't even raised her voice, but it was worse than being shouted at by Lord Margery.

❧

"TOO LATE, AM I?" A man leaned over the stall counter and peered into the shadows beyond, smelling of beer and chips and some undefined hunger that made Mortimer's stomach tighten. The young dragon froze where he was, taking on the pale, murky colours of the tent canvas and the cobbled street underfoot, feeling Beaufort doing the same. The man felt *aware,* and combined with that hungry smell, it didn't seem like a good thing.

"You are, I'm afraid," Alice said pleasantly. "I've just sent the last of the stock off. Not that there was much left."

"Those baubles," the man said, straightening up to look at her. "Pretty good craftsmanship."

"Excellent," Alice agreed, re-bagging the rubbish bag that Mortimer had torn.

"Make them yourself?"

"No, but we buy them direct from the artisan."

"The *arti*san, now. That's fancy." The man grinned, and Alice left the bag of rubbish on the ground, folding her arms.

"Well, he is an artist. They don't come from a factory, if that's what you're asking."

Mortimer considered the fact that Amelia and even her little brother Gilbert were helping him now, and wondered what, exactly, constituted a factory.

"I'm quite interested in the technique," the man said. "I'm a bit of an artisan myself."

Mortimer and Beaufort exchanged uneasy glances. The man's hungry scent had deepened. Dragons can catch the whiff of emotions the way dogs can physical smells, and this one was ugly.

"I'm afraid I can't help you with that," Alice said, not moving. "He's a very private individual."

Mortimer rather wished he was somewhere more private right now.

The man put his hands on the counter, leaning forward again as if he wanted to grab Alice and drag her out. "I can keep a secret," he said, and his eyes went to the dragons. Mortimer stared back at him in horror, not sure if the man could actually *see* him, or if he was just looking in their direction by chance.

For a moment no one moved, then Alice stepped deliberately in front of the dragons and leaned over the counter until her forehead almost touched the man's. He pulled back in surprise, and she said, "If one shares a secret, it's no longer much of a secret, is it?"

They glared at each other, and Mortimer couldn't have said who was going to look away first, or what the man might do. Then Miriam appeared, hurrying down the rows of stalls, a bright apparition in the night.

"Oh, hello," she said. "Are you after Gert's cordial? Only it all sold out."

The man glared at her. "No, of course I'm not after *cordial*."

She frowned. "Well, there's no need to be rude about it."

"He was just leaving," Alice said. "Weren't you?"

"I—"

"Yeah, we're leaving," a new voice said, and Mortimer risked shifting a little so that he could see the marketplace better. A big man in a new jacket of the sort that's designed to look old was coming across the cobbles, swinging a paper bag from his finger-tips. "Come on, Bill. Don't hassle the nice ladies."

Bill grumbled something about them not being very nice, and Alice gave him a disapproving look. "I was just asking about the baubles," he said aloud.

"It's late. I'm sure the ladies want to go home." The new man grabbed Bill's arm. "Let's go."

Bill glared at Alice and gave a little feint like he was going to grab her. Mortimer felt a growl forming at the back of his throat, and Miriam squeaked, but Alice just raised an eyebrow and smiled. There was a moment of still, frost-speckled silence, then Bill walked away, muttering under his breath. His friend – or maybe brother, Mortimer thought. They did look quite similar, and wasn't there a whiff of that same hungry scent? – touched a finger to his flat cap in mock salute, and followed him.

"Is – is everything okay?" Miriam asked.

"I'm sure it will be," Alice said, and Mortimer looked at Beau-fort, raising his eyebrow ridges.

The bigger dragon shrugged, but his voice was a rumble at the back of his throat when he said, "Well, then. Shall we go?"

"I think we should finish the wine and give them a head start," Alice said. "He was a little agitated."

And observant, Mortimer thought. *He seemed terribly* observant.

IT DIDN'T TAKE LONG to finish the wine, but by the time they had, the rest of the stalls were empty, some of them even broken down and taken away already. Lights still shone in the pub windows, but the marketplace was silent and still and full of the scents of Christmas. The two women and the dragons walked together across the cobbles and toward the quiet streets beyond, the dragons taking on the colours of the night. If anyone had been watching, they'd have looked like shadows in the corner of the eye, something not quite seen. Dragons aren't invisible, but they are *faint*, which is quite effective when no one expects to see dragons. They were perfectly clear to Alice and Miriam, however, contented green smoke drifting from their nostrils. There had been no more sign of the men, and the extra glass of mulled wine had gone a long way to making Mortimer feel better about things.

They walked in quiet companionship, Miriam carrying the last boxes of homemade mince pies, the scent of brandy and icing sugar drifting about them in the night. The women's breath made dragons of their own in the chill air.

They came to Alice's house first, and Beaufort insisted on waiting until she was inside, the light rolling out of the hallway and lighting the neat path between the dormant flowerbeds.

"Satisfied?" she said.

"He was a very unpleasant man," Beaufort said. "Can't be too careful with these things."

"He was just drunk. And the day I can't handle a drunk man is the day I resign as W.I. chair." She gave them a little finger-wave and shut the door firmly, leaving them alone in the night.

"I knew he wasn't a customer," Miriam said, looking around nervously.

"I rather think Alice is right about him," Beaufort said. "I'm quite sure he's nothing to worry about."

Mortimer thought of the man looking straight at him in the shadows of the stall, his blue eyes sharp in the night, and shivered. The mulled wine seemed to be wearing off.

BEAUFORT AND MORTIMER left Miriam in the friendly chaos of her kitchen, minus the mince pies, which she insisted they take with them. Not that either dragon had argued particularly hard against it. They ambled together down the path that crossed the stream behind her house and snaked up through the woods beyond to a small rise, walking shoulder to shoulder, pupils wide in the night. Away from the lights of the stream-girt village, the stars hung low and heavy above the trees, and as they breasted the little hill the fields beyond the woods unwound below them, multi-coloured green and cross-stitched with stone walls.

"Beautiful, isn't it, lad?" Beaufort asked, pausing at the top and sitting down with his tail hooked around his feet.

Mortimer looked at him curiously. The High Lord had been around to see St George murder his predecessor (it was hardly a fair fight, considering High Lord Catherine, although large by the standards of today's Cloverly dragons, had been half the size of the daring knight's horse and was snoozing on her back in her favourite bramble-berry patch at the time), and he'd not been a young dragon then. He'd kept the clan safe and hidden as the humans spread and the old Folk faded, had seen kings and queens rise and fall, had watched the steady march of trains and cars and planes and cities, and still those golden eyes, glazed like old pottery, saw wonder in the world. Mortimer couldn't even begin to comprehend how he managed it. Sometimes just the thought of getting Beaufort through another winter market unnoticed was enough to start him stress-shedding, let alone imagining all those centuries protecting a whole clan. He didn't know how the old dragon had the energy. And not only that, but being so terribly *enthusiastic* about everything. He sighed, and Beaufort gave him an amused look.

"Are you alright there, lad?"

"I think so." He scratched his chin. "Do you think that man – that Bill – actually saw us?"

"I doubt it." Beaufort tipped his head up to the stars.

"He looked like he saw us."

"He was just looking to make trouble. Some people are like that. In all species. I don't think we should worry about it."

"But he was quite unpleasant to Alice," Mortimer pointed out. "And didn't you smell him?"

Beaufort looked back at the slow roll of land below them. "It's no good jumping to conclusions, lad. You do worry yourself unnecessarily."

Mortimer sighed. He supposed he did, at times. But often he was right to worry, particularly when it came to the High Lord. "I thought you might have scared him off, though. So Alice wouldn't worry."

"Not everyone needs saving, you know. Plenty of people are very good at saving themselves."

"But you must be a bit worried about him. You made Alice check the house before we left." Mortimer couldn't shake the feeling that something about the whole encounter had been *wrong*. Off. As if it wasn't an accident that Alice had been in the stall alone (or apparently so) when Bill showed up.

Beaufort's lips hitched up to show yellow teeth. "There's a difference between being able to save yourself and feeling safe." He unfolded his wings, shaking them out with a snap. "But I'm not worried about him. He was just a man who'd had a bit too much beer. Things are good, Mortimer. Our friends are safe. Our clan is coming out of hiding again. Your trinkets are selling so well, and everyone's *smiling*. People love them. You give them something to take home that makes their hearts sing."

Mortimer nodded, then asked the question that had been rattling around in his head since the first day Beaufort had trotted up to the W.I. and managed to get himself invited in for tea. "Can this last, though, Beaufort? Us and the humans?"

"Why shouldn't it?"

"It didn't before. People blamed us for things. We spent centuries in hiding. Most of the clans are hiding still."

"We're not exactly on the national news."

Sometimes it feels like it's not for lack of trying, Mortimer thought, but just said, "What about the Watch, then? What if they find out we're trading with humans? Or if something goes wrong?"

"There's no point worrying about that until it happens. Coexistence can work, Mortimer. It's good for everyone."

"We can see that. But not everyone does. Not even all the Cloverlies."

"It has to start somewhere. Why not with us?" Beaufort gave him an enormous grin, then took two lumbering strides forward and leaped, wings catching at the air and pulling him aloft, suddenly graceful against the night sky. Mortimer watched him go, torn between the High Lord's unshakable confidence and his own heartfelt conviction that this was too simple, too perfect. That anything this good couldn't last. Then he shook his wings out and followed the old dragon into the sky, the boxes of mince pies clutched firmly to his chest and leaking warm sweet spices across the darkness.

2
DI ADAMS

Detective Inspector Adams was glaring at the station coffeepot when Detective Constable James Hamilton appeared in the staffroom door, tall enough to fill it but nowhere near wide enough. She turned her glare from the hapless pot to him.

"Why does no one – *no one* – fill this thing up when it's empty? Or at least switch it off? Smells like a car yard fire in here."

"Well. Yes." He looked more amused than worried, and she scowled at him.

"'Oh, just go get a coffee across the road,' everyone says. I *do*. I *always* do, but one day I would like to be able to buy a flat, and if I get all my coffee across the road, that will never happen."

"That is a problem," he said agreeably. "I like a nice cup of tea, myself."

DI Adams snorted, and flicked the kettle on. "It's not the same. But, fine. Tea it is. Want one?"

"I won't say no. Two sugars, please."

She doled sugar into the mugs, then leaned against the counter as they waited for the kettle to boil, rubbing her fingertips through the base of her tightly bound hair. She'd tried straightening it, but nothing took, and short hair was almost as much trouble to maintain, what with having to go for haircuts all the time. So she wrestled it into a bun every morning and put up with the headaches. She'd take it down to a number one again, but that seemed to make people nervous. Plus it was cold up here. She was sure London had never been this cold. And there had always been coffee in the station. Of course, there had also been *things* under the bridges that she was now reasonably sure she hadn't imagined. There didn't seem to be any up here. Bridges, that was. She wasn't so sure about the rest.

"What's going on, then, James?" she asked the detective constable.

"Right, yes. I was coming to tell you, actually. You know you said to keep an eye out for anything happening around that village with the funny name? The one where the vicar was murdered last spring? Tool Handle, or something?"

"Toot Hansell?" DI Adams asked, her back stiffening so quickly it was almost a spasm. She winced.

"Yeah, that's the one." James looked expectantly at the kettle as it clicked off.

"What about Toot Hansell?"

"It's nothing huge. Just their postman's disappeared." He took half a step forward, and DI Adams stared at him, kettle forgotten.

"Disappeared how?"

"Gone. Poof. Done a runner, I guess." He stretched a hand out toward the kettle, but the DI was in the way, so he dropped it again with a sigh.

"But gone *how*, James?" she demanded impatiently, trying to keep the unease out of her voice. The postman. That couldn't have anything to do with the bloody Women's Institute, could it? Well, not the W.I. exactly. More their rather unusual associates. "Details, please."

"I don't have the full details. It's Skipton's case at the moment, unless the postman turns up dead or kidnapped. I just know the van's been found, but not him or the presents." He looked longingly at the empty mugs. DI Adams ignored him.

"So maybe he just did a runner?" Not an everyday story, but still pretty routine. That was okay. She'd once thought that routine was boring, but that was before Toot Hansell. Before London, for that matter.

"Maybe, but it seems he'd been on the same round for about twenty years, and never missed a day. Pretty old-school."

The inspector wondered vaguely when turning up for work daily had become old-school, and said, "Anything else?"

"One other thing, which is a little weird. The van was all scorched, like someone had tried to firebomb it, and there were some weird scratch marks on the top. No theories on that yet. Might be that it's unrelated – DI Adams? Inspector?"

But she was already out the staffroom door and heading for her desk to grab her jacket and her keys. Scratches and firebombing and Toot Hansell. She didn't like the sound of that. She didn't like the sound of that at all.

DI ADAMS HURRIED into the Skipton police station and leaned over the front desk. The constable behind it stared at her in alarm. "DI Adams? What are— I mean, how can I help you?"

"PC McLeod, isn't it?" She tried for a reassuring smile, but judging by the look on the young man's face she didn't do a very good job of it. It wasn't like she'd even been that sharp with him last time she was here. Not that she remembered, anyway. "Good to see you again. Who's in charge of the missing postman case?"

"Um. DI Collins?"

"Any chance I can talk to him?" The famous Skipton DI, off on holiday in Corfu when the vicar had been murdered. He was probably going to be all put out because she'd solved his crime while he was away eating calamari and getting sunburnt.

"I – I suppose so. He just came in." PC McLeod punched something into the phone, then gave DI Adams an anxious smile. "You can wait over there if you want."

The inspector looked at the row of plastic chairs and grimaced. She didn't want to sit down. She shouldn't even be here. She should be minding her own business. Or going straight to Toot Hansell. To the root of the problem, as it were. If it was a problem. She paced in an irritated circle in front of the desk, waiting. And hoped he wasn't so put out that he'd leave her here until tea time.

"DI ADAMS?"

She jumped up, shoving her phone back in her pocket. It hadn't been that long – long enough to make a point, short enough not to be rude. "DI Collins."

He gave her a surprisingly genuine smile, a big man with big hands, looking like he spent a lot of time out in the weather. "How can I help?"

"Well. Just wondering about that missing postman."

"What about him?"

"Any ideas?"

He shrugged. "Still considering the possibility he just did a runner, although it doesn't seem likely at this point. Techs are going over the van, looking for trace."

"What about the, uh, fire damage?"

He was still smiling, but his eyes were sharp. "Leeds, you say. What's your interest?"

"Possible connection to a cold case." Which was tenuous. Okay, which was a lie, if she was going to be entirely honest with herself. But DI Collins nodded as if the answer satisfied him.

"Not sure yet. Maybe they tried to torch the van to make sure there was no evidence left, but it didn't take. That's the working theory for now."

"Accelerants?"

"Like I say, the techs are looking at it now."

The inspector found a card in her jacket pocket and handed it to him. "Can you let me know what they find? It's sort of a personal interest thing. The case isn't active."

DI Collins took the card and examined it as if it held the answer to his deepest questions. "So I take it you don't want it going through the office."

"You know what it's like. They'll say it's taking me away from my active cases." She gave him a smile that felt fairly unconvincing.

"Is it?"

"No." Not yet, anyway.

He pocketed the card and clasped his hands in front of him like the world's biggest schoolboy, waiting to be excused. "You want to give me any clues on this? Because it's a beggar of a case. We've nothing at the moment, not even a tyre print."

"I don't even know if it's related or not. If it is, then of course." *All the bits that aren't to do with dragons, anyway.*

"Hmm." He examined her thoughtfully. "I guess that'll have to do, then."

"Thanks." She shook hands with him awkwardly then retreated, far too aware that he was watching her go with that same patient gaze. Dammit, it had to be someone who actually knew what he was doing, didn't it? Couldn't be some old country boy just going through the motions. Although, if her last experience had been anything to go by, he wouldn't feel like he knew what he was doing for long once he got involved with Toot Hansell.

She hurried back outside, jingling her car keys impatiently.

THE ROAD to Toot Hansell felt familiar, even if she hadn't driven it since the early days of summer, when the fields had been brilliant green and wildflowers had bloomed along the dry-stone walls that flanked the lanes. Now the greens were mixed with bare earth and frozen mud, and the low light was cold and clear, outlining the fells with a bleak and savage clarity that made her turn the car's heating up. The sky was high and pale and thin, and she felt as if she were driving across the far reaches of a world that didn't much care if she survived it or not. It was indifferent. Say what you want about cities, but they're never *indifferent*. Angry, yes. Usually, in fact. But this was something else. She had the sudden, irrational fear that she'd get a flat and find out she had no spare, and freeze to death out here before anyone came along. Then an ancient green Land Rover creaked past her in the opposite direction, the driver with a woolly pink hat pulled down over his ears, and DI Adams took a deep breath. She wasn't in some Siberian wasteland. Honestly, it was less than an hour from Skipton. It wasn't the end of the world. It just felt like it.

Just as she was wondering if she'd forgotten the way after all, the village unfolded itself under the fells. Some trick of the winter light made it luminous, more in focus than the fields that surrounded it, the grey stone of the houses less dreary and more plucky, bearing up brightly under the winter chill. There had been no snow yet, and the lawns were stubbornly green among the leafless trees and the empty flowerbeds. Lights were on in houses, Christmas trees visible through windows, and the roads were strung with both standard decorations and wreaths that looked like the work of the Women's Institute. Streams clattered everywhere, catching the doubtful sun and splintering it into glittering shards. Little waterways circled the village and ran through it, burrowing under roads and popping up in gardens, turning it into a place built on water and magic. DI Adams scowled at it all suspiciously and headed for Miriam's house. If there was trouble, that was where she'd find it.

☙

DI ADAMS PARKED outside Miriam's little cottage and examined it. There were no lights on in the living room except for those of a Christmas tree, but there was smoke coming from the chimney. She'd probably be in the kitchen. She rubbed her face with both hands, a small anxiety uncurling in her stomach. In the summer, Toot Hansell had proved some things to her, such as the fact that what she'd seen in London had been real, not some stress-related glitch in her perception. Also that women of a certain age were horrifyingly determined, and very disinclined to act sensibly. But it was hard, when she was back in Leeds, to reconcile these things with what she saw to be true all around her. It wasn't like there were gnomes marching through the city streets or unicorns prancing across the midtown rooftops. She knew what had happened *had* happened, but it was harder to believe the longer she was away.

She thought of DI Collins looking for firebombing postmen, and grimaced. The last thing the dragons needed were more police poking around the place. And anyway, it might have nothing to do with them.

She checked for dead rabbits (it had become somewhat of a habit after her first encounter with Toot Hansell), got out of the car and marched up the path before she could change her mind. Eliminating suspects. That's all she was doing. Nothing out of the ordinary at all.

☙

MIRIAM ANSWERED the door with a smile on her face, gasped, and slammed it shut. DI Adams blinked at the door. That she hadn't expected. She should really learn not to expect *anything* around here. She raised her hand to knock again, and the door opened.

"Detective Inspector," Miriam said, her cheeks pink and her smile on crooked. "Sorry. You surprised me."

"Evidently," DI Adams said, and found herself peering past Miriam, looking for signs of a looted postal van. She dragged her attention back to the woman in front of her. "I hope this isn't a bad time."

"Oh! Oh, no. Come in, please." Miriam pulled the door wide, and the inspector wiped her boots carefully as she came in, smelling candles and wood smoke and baking. "We're just in the kitchen."

We. DI Adams braced herself, and followed the older woman down the short, dim hall and into an oasis of golden light and warmth. Alice was sitting at the kitchen table with a cup of tea, and looked entirely unsurprised by the unexpected visitor.

"Good afternoon," the inspector said, her vision swirling with migraine-like dots and the room feeling far too hot. "Lovely to see you all again." She looked hard at the spot on the floor that made her eyes water, and a headache-y, vertigo-ish feeling washed over her. It lingered for a moment, then retreated as the corner resolved itself into the large rug in front of the AGA, and the two dragons sitting on it. Beaufort was grinning enormously, an oversized mug of tea in his paws, and Mortimer had a mince pie halfway to his mouth. He looked less than enthralled. The room settled around her, the migraine spots retreating, and DI Adams' shoulders sagged in relief. She realised that she *had* almost thought she'd imagined the dragons, that there was something Not Right with her. They also looked friendlier than how she'd started to remember them. They didn't look like they'd go around attacking postmen, but she had to admit that she was somewhat of a novice when it came to dragons.

"Good afternoon, Detective Inspector," Alice said. "Can we offer you a mince pie?" She was watching DI Adams curiously, and the inspector was suddenly certain that the older woman could tell she was wearing her most ancient bra, the one that had gone a funny grey in the wash and which didn't match her knickers at all.

She smoothed her hair and pulled a chair out, reminding herself that she was the officer of the law here. "That'd be lovely."

"And tea!" Miriam had been standing awkwardly by the door, and now she lunged toward the counter, suddenly animated. "Tea, yes?"

"Ah, yes, please." DI Adams watched, bemused, as Miriam dropped the tea pot in the sink, squeaking at a small tidal wave of sudsy water, and searched for a reasonably intact mug. Alice got up to find a plate, and served up a mince pie next to a neatly folded paper napkin, with a tarnished fork on the side.

"Cream?" Alice offered, as Miriam over-filled the kettle and almost dropped it on her own foot.

"No thanks – is she okay?"

"Figures of authority make her nervous. You must remember from last time."

"Well, yes, but last time she was a suspect. She's not a suspect now."

Miriam managed to get the kettle on top of the AGA, but not before she trod on Mortimer's tail, eliciting an outraged yelp.

"I don't think it matters. Even I make her nervous. Can you imagine?"

DI Adams met Alice's amused gaze, and thought, *yes, actually*. And also thought that Alice knew it perfectly well. Aloud, she said, "So, Beaufort, Mortimer. How are things?"

Beaufort tucked his tail safely out of danger and gave that

alarmingly toothy smile. "Marvellous, Detective Inspector. Yourself?"

"Not bad, not bad at all. Tell me, what've you been up to recently?"

The dragons stared at her, Mortimer's eyebrow ridges pulled up in an anxious line. "Why?" Beaufort asked. "What's happened?"

DI Adams sighed. She'd never been good at the whole casual, just-making-conversation thing. She'd never been good at conversation, full stop. It just seemed like an awful lot of wasted effort. "Any trouble? Any *issues*?"

"What sort of issues?"

Between Beaufort's fierce golden gaze and Alice watching with her fingers steepled under her chin, DI Adams was starting to feel like she was the one under interrogation. Not that this was an interrogation. No. She wasn't even on duty. Well, not in this jurisdiction, anyway.

She sighed. "Postmen. Well, postman. And missing post."

"*Our* postman?" Alice demanded. "I waited in all morning for him! Our Christmas boxes should have been arriving today."

"Christmas boxes?"

"Christmas boxes!" Miriam hefted the kettle off the AGA, aiming it vaguely in the direction of the teapot on the table. The DI regarded the wandering spout in alarm, then grabbed Miriam's arm.

"Milk?"

"*Milk!*" Miriam dropped the kettle on the table and rushed to the fridge. Alice picked the milk jug up from next to the mince pies and added some to the DI's mug.

"*This* nervous?"

"Even the meter reader makes her nervous. Misspent youth, I imagine," Alice replied, and filled the teapot. "Miriam, come sit down, dear."

"Should I make sandwiches?"

"It's 3 p.m. We don't need sandwiches."

"Right." Miriam sat down and examined her own mug with interest.

"The Christmas boxes are for our charity dinner," Alice said. "The dinner is a fundraiser itself, but we also ask people to donate little items to the boxes, books and toys and so on. They can either bring them to the dinner, or we have some for sale. Then the boxes are collected and go out to children who might not get a Christmas otherwise."

"Right," the DI said. She remembered her mum doing something similar at one stage. Although they might have been being sent overseas. She just knew that she'd had to grudgingly give up her favourite book to someone less fortunate, and therefore hadn't thought it was a great Christmas. "So there were presents in the post, too?"

"Only the boxes, as far as I know. I have some book and toy orders coming next week."

"Anyone else know you had these orders in?"

"The W.I., yes. But these are children's books and toys. Nothing expensive. Why would anyone steal them?"

"And why have you come to see us?" Beaufort asked quietly. "I rather feel that this isn't entirely a social call, although we're very happy to see you, of course."

There was a silence in the kitchen, full of the soft purr of the fridge and the tickings of the AGA, and the DI reached for the teapot to give herself a moment to think. What on earth was she doing? She was away from work without any sort of authorisation, treading on another department's toes for the sake of something that might not even be a case. And she was talking to dragons about it. Not only that, she was kinda-sorta suggesting to said dragons that they'd been kidnapping postmen and stealing the Christmas mail. Assuming she really wasn't imagining dragons, which she didn't seem to be, this was possibly a little silly.

She could get herself singed for her troubles. Or eaten. They weren't big dragons, but they did have plenty of teeth. And she couldn't quite forget how terrified the cupcake murderer had been when he'd turned himself in. Well, been convinced by certain meddlesome members of the W.I. to turn himself in. His only concern had been that the cells were dragon-proof, which had the whole station laughing at him. Except the DI, of course. She poured tea into her mug and picked it up, wrapping both hands around it despite the heat. It had a worn Peter Rabbit design on it.

"Whoever took the postman," she said, looking straight at Beaufort, "left some rather *dragon-y* traces behind. Which isn't to say it was dragons, but, well."

The silence came back, heavier and louder.

Beaufort nodded thoughtfully, then said, "Well. We can't be having that."

"No, no, no," DI Adams said. "This was not a suggestion that you should go off investigating. I'm the detective here." How did she even need to point that out? Again?

"Well, if it's dragons," Beaufort said, "I rather think that this is our territory."

"I'm not saying it was dragons. It was probably just someone doing a terrible job at burning the evidence." She paused, then added curiously, "Do you actually breathe fire?"

Beaufort puffed his cheeks out and spat a little fireball into the centre of the kitchen. It floated for a moment, then drifted to the floor, where Mortimer swiped it hastily off the rug and patted it out on the stone flags.

"Okay. So, yes, it could have been a dragon. But I'm not saying it was."

"Well, it wasn't a Cloverly dragon," Beaufort said. "No one would do that."

"I just wanted to make sure you didn't know anything about it," the DI said. "I'm sure it's going to turn out to be kids or something."

"They tried to burn the van?" Alice asked.

"Yes. It didn't take, but it was pretty scorched, apparently."

"And straight away you thought of us?" Beaufort asked, looking offended.

"Well, no, not exactly. But it was a factor."

"And the other factors?" Alice was sitting very straight, and looked alarmingly disapproving.

"I think I've shared enough for now."

"I think if you're suspecting dragons you should tell us why," Alice said sharply. "Six months ago you didn't even know they existed."

The DI pinched the bridge of her nose and swallowed a sigh.

"Are you alright?" Miriam asked. "Do you want a sandwich? I knew I should have made sandwiches."

"*No*. No," she managed more calmly. "I'm fine. I'm not hungry."

"Are you sure?" Beaufort asked. "You seem quite small, even for a human. I can get you a rabbit."

"*I don't want a rabbit.*" She clutched the table with both hands and tried to remember what, exactly, she'd thought she was going to find here. It certainly hadn't been straight answers. She should have remembered that there were never straight answers in Toot Hansell.

"What sort of person doesn't want a rabbit?" Beaufort whispered to Mortimer, rather loudly.

Mortimer shushed him, and said, "How can we help, Inspector? Can we help?"

She stared at him and wondered why the only creature acting reasonably in here had scales and wings. "No. Well, yes, actually. You can stay out of the human side of things, and let me know about anything from your end. I'm sure it's nothing to do with you, but just ... if you hear anything." *Let me know and I'll go arrest some dragons?* She took a hurried gulp of tea to smother a laugh that was trying to make its way out. This place was not good for her.

"It won't be a Cloverly dragon," Beaufort said again.

Mortimer looked doubtful, and said, "We'll see what we can find out."

"Thank you. That'd be great." The inspector looked at her half-finished tea, and decided she'd had as much of the W.I. and dragons as she could manage in one sitting. "You still have my card?"

"We do," Alice said. She sounded unimpressed. "Am I to take it our boxes are missing, then?"

"I'd say so, yes."

"Most unfortunate. I'll have to order more." She stood and extended a hand across the table. "Are you sure we can't do more, Detective Inspector? We can't have the dragons being implicated."

Beaufort gave a snort that threatened to scorch the tablecloth. "A dragon will not be responsible for this. What would we do with a postman?"

The DI looked at the few crumbs of mince pie left on her plate and said, "What do you eat, exactly?"

There was a sudden, shocked silence, broken by Miriam taking a nervous slurp of tea and promptly choking on it. Alice patted her on the back, and the dragons stared at the inspector in horror.

"You're not suggesting—" Mortimer began, then was cut off by Beaufort.

"That is *preposterous*," the High Lord spluttered. "*Eating* people? Even in my younger days we didn't *eat* people. I know some clans carried on like that in the Middle Ages, but, honestly. What do you take us for? Savages?"

"Dragons," the DI said. "Which is a little outside my area of expertise."

Beaufort gave DI Adams a look that reminded her of her mother. "Inspector, I am disappointed in you."

"That's not fair! I've never met dragons before."

"All the more reason to do your research."

She rubbed her face. There was a headache cranking up behind one eye. "I watched *Game of Thrones*. Does that count?"

"Oh, no, no," Alice said hurriedly. "No, that's very fictional. Very."

"*Game of Thrones?* Is that on the television?" Beaufort pronounced the last word with care, and possibly an extra syllable.

"You have TV?"

"We've been watching a few shows here," Miriam said, her face red. "*Midsomer Murders* and *Poirot*, mostly."

"Oh, fantastic," the DI muttered.

"It's very clever," the old dragon said. "We've been learning a lot."

The inspector wondered if she had any painkillers in the car. "Wonderful. That's just wonderful."

"We eat rabbits, mostly," Mortimer said quietly, apparently the only one paying attention.

"We learnt a long time ago that livestock are missed," Beaufort said. "And even if we actually liked the idea of eating something that talked to us, humans apparently don't taste particularly nice. A bit stringy and dirty was what I was told, but that was a long time ago. Before running water and indoor plumbing, certainly."

"Well," DI Adams said. "That's good to know." She pushed her chair back and got up. "I'm going now. But you'll stay out of the human stuff, right?"

"It's just dragons you're interested in?"

"Just dragons, Beaufort."

He sighed. "Fine."

DI Adams turned to go, and paused at the kitchen door. "When you say just dragons – you mean just dragons and not humans, right?"

Beaufort exposed his teeth in that alarming grin. "Not humans. Or gnomes, or dwarfs, or gargoyles, among others."

The DI stared at him for a long moment before she said, "Vampires?"

"Don't be silly. Vampires don't exist."

"Oh." She relaxed a little. "So, no werewolves, then, either."

"Plenty of those. Some of them are quite good sorts."

Her headache was actually quite bad now.

3
MIRIAM

I t was a sombre little group that was left behind in the kitchen. Miriam clutched her tea, thinking about what the inspector *hadn't* said. She wouldn't have come here just because a van was set alight, surely? She wouldn't jump to conclusions like that without evidence. So what was the evidence? Was it something to do with them, with the W.I.? Maybe even her? Oh, God, she wasn't a suspect *again*, was she? She didn't think she could take being a suspect all over again. Just the thought made her stomach roll over.

"Sandwiches?" she suggested, slightly desperately.

Alice gave her one of those severe looks she was so good at. "Miriam, it's the middle of December. Why on earth would we want sandwiches at four in the afternoon?"

"But I don't know what to do," Miriam whispered. "What should I do if I don't make sandwiches?"

"Just sit here and calm down," Alice said, and patted her shoulder reassuringly.

"I wouldn't mind a sandwich," Beaufort said, then when Alice glared at him he added quickly, "The inspector wasn't looking at the W.I., Miriam. I'm sure it'll all be fine."

"She still makes me nervous. She's very… efficient."

"So am I," Alice pointed out.

"Yes. You're making me nervous too. You're going to want to do something, aren't you?"

Beaufort looked very *interested* at that, and Mortimer buried his snout in his paws.

Alice screwed her face up like she was trying not to say something sharp. "Well, at least I'm not going to arrest you."

"You think she might *arrest* me?" Miriam heard the waver in her voice, but she couldn't help it. This just got worse and worse.

"Of course not, Miriam. I was only joking. Why don't we all go into the living room and have a nice sit down?"

Miriam shot out of her chair. "I haven't checked the fire! I have to check the fire!"

"I'll do that," Mortimer said, and padded out into the hall. Miriam watched him go anxiously. He didn't look much happier than she felt. Beaufort had lapsed back into uncharacteristic silence, the tip of his tail scraping the floor restlessly.

"And we could have some whisky, if you have it?" Alice suggested.

"Whisky?" Miriam looked at the dark already pressing in against the windows, hiding the winter garden from view and disguising the misdeeds of van torchers and postal thieves. "Yes, actually. That sounds rather good." She got up and went to rummage in the pantry.

As it turned out, she didn't have any whisky, but after some scuffling she found a bottle of Metaxa with a dubious, lopsided label that her sister had brought back from Greece. She poured generous measures into four mismatched glasses, although Mortimer made a face and nudged his over to Beaufort.

The High Lord took it in his front paws and examined the contents with his eyebrow ridges drawn down low and worried. "Who would kidnap a postman?" he asked.

"And who would make it look like dragons?" Alice added.

"She didn't tell us everything," Mortimer said. "I'm sure there's something more. Why was she asking about what we ate?"

"Probably just because he's missing," Beaufort said. "If they'd actually found a half-eaten body, she'd have told us."

Miriam gave a little squeak at that and took a healthy gulp of Metaxa, then started coughing wildly. It was quite horrible stuff.

"But she was sure enough that it could be dragons that she came to ask us about it," Alice said, ignoring Miriam. "Beaufort, can we really be sure it wasn't a dragon?"

Beaufort still had that worried look on his face, and now he swallowed Mortimer's Metaxa, releasing a puff of bright blue steam. "I suppose we can't, really. I'd like to think no one would do such a foolish thing, but, well. Maybe I'm wrong. Young dragons can be very silly at times."

"It would endanger all of you," Alice said. "It seems more than silly."

"Not everyone's happy with how things are," Mortimer said, not quite looking at Beaufort, who snorted.

"Unhappy's one thing. No one would do something like this deliberately."

Mortimer looked like he had more to say, but he only poked a log into the centre of the fire, sending a little cascade of sparks onto the hearth.

Miriam had somehow finished her Metaxa, although she didn't remember drinking it all. She topped her glass up, her face feeling tight and hot in the heat of the fire. "Maybe someone's framing you."

"Framing us?" Beaufort looked dubious.

"Sure." She took another sip of the Metaxa. It wasn't so bad, once you got over the initial sensation that your throat was on fire, and your nose stopped running. It had made the nervous, sick feeling in her belly fade, at least. "Maybe it's another dragon clan out to get you, or – or – I don't know. Sea serpents, or something."

"It wouldn't actually be possible for sea serpents—" Mortimer began, and Miriam gave a startled hiccough. She hadn't really meant sea serpents, but everything else seemed to be real, so why not? She examined her glass, bemused to find it empty again.

"No, she's right." Beaufort scratched his chin. "It makes more sense than one of our own doing it. Maybe it's the Bellerby clan. They still live in the bottom of that slate quarry up near Hawes. Absolutely refuse to move, despite the fact that they have to keep digging new caverns every few weeks when the old ones collapse. They despise anything new, but I'm quite sure they're horribly jealous of our barbecues."

"How would they even know about the barbecues?" Mortimer asked. "They never come out."

Beaufort snorted impatiently. "Well, if not them, then the Kettlesmorgs."

"The Kettlesmorgs? They're the size of hamsters."

"Mortimer, you're not being very helpful."

"It just seems unlikely, is all. It'd take fifty of them to even singe a van."

Beaufort glared at him. "It won't be a Cloverly dragon, so it must be another clan. They'll be trying to scare us back into hiding."

"It seems an odd way to go about it," Alice said. "By drawing attention to you, I mean."

"It's a warning," Beaufort said. "They're telling us to stop associating with humans, or they'll make it impossible for us to do so."

Mortimer still looked dubious. "Why haven't they just reported us to the Watch, then?"

"This is dragon business. We've always dealt with our own matters. Not even Skintboggles would go to the Watch, and they're always grovelling about the place pretending they're not even dragons."

"Well, technically," Mortimer began, then ducked when Beaufort glared at him, the High Lord's ears starting to turn a threatening puce colour. "That's quite right, is all I was going to say."

"Who are the Watch?" Miriam asked. She glanced at everyone's glasses, but hers was the only one empty. That didn't seem very fair.

"They're a very ancient order," Beaufort said. "They keep the humans and the old Folk like us apart. Nosy little busybodies they are, too."

"So this could be a matter for them," Alice suggested.

"Not if it's dragons," Beaufort said firmly. "The Watch and dragons tolerate each other, that's all."

"Plus, no matter who's responsible, they'd ban us from seeing you on pain of exile," Mortimer said. "They're very strict. I hope they haven't heard about the post van."

"Yes, they don't believe in mitigating circumstances. If they investigate there could be all sorts of trouble." Beaufort frowned at his glass as if not sure what to do with it, and Miriam leaned forward to top it up, using the opportunity to fill her own as well.

"It doesn't sound like there's much we can do, then," she said. "We should probably just stay out of it."

"Well, we did rather well last time," Beaufort said. "And I've been studying those television shows very closely. I've picked up a lot of tips on investigating. I'm sure we can handle this."

Mortimer stared at his paws. "Beaufort, I don't think that's the best idea."

"Why ever not? The DI came to us for help, didn't she?"

"No, I think she came to see if we might be suspects."

"Rubbish. Anyone can see we're not suspects."

Mortimer closed his eyes, and Miriam thought from his pained expression that he might be counting to ten. She probably shouldn't have given Beaufort more Metaxa. She took a careful sip, spilling some on her fingers. She appeared to have put a little too much in the glass.

"Mortimer? Mortimer!" The High Lord sounded annoyed. "Are you listening?"

He opened his eyes again. "Beaufort, sir, she thinks dragons did it. We're the only dragons she knows. We're suspects."

"We might be persons of interest, but suspects is pushing it."

"Well, either way, we can't go rushing off investigating."

"She asked us to."

"No, she asked us if we could look into dragons. That is not the same thing as *investigating*."

Alice took the Metaxa bottle off Miriam with a rather unnecessarily firm expression, the younger woman felt. "Seems to me that the best way to show you're innocent is to find out who's guilty."

Mortimer clapped his paws over his snout, his scales taking on a sickly grey that didn't match anything in the room as Beaufort agreed heartily.

"Are you sure?" Miriam asked, trying unsuccessfully to reclaim the bottle. "That seems pretty much exactly the opposite of what the inspector told us to do. Plus there's these Watch people to think about."

"Yes," Alice said thoughtfully. "But we don't know that the Watch have heard anything yet, and if we can get it resolved quickly enough, they won't have to. Plus, this is rather out of the DI's jurisdiction, from the sounds of things. Both in the sense that it may be dragons, and in the sense that she doesn't actually work up here. So whoever's in charge of this case won't even know about dragons. They'll be completely at a loss, as well as being a risk if they start noticing dragon-y traces. Beaufort, you and Mortimer – all the Cloverlies, in fact – need to keep a very low profile. Even stay away for a while, particularly if this Watch might come sniffing around as well as the police."

Mortimer let out a small puff of relieved pink smoke, and started to take on his own colours again, purples and blues creeping back. "That seems very sensible," he said. "Is there Christmas cake, by any chance? I could really go for a piece of Christmas cake."

Alice waved him to silence. "In a moment, Mortimer. Look, the only thing for it is that Miriam and I will undertake some investigation on this side, with a little help from the W.I. Pre-empt any police poking around. You two can eliminate the Cloverly dragons as suspects, then canvas the – what did you call them? The Folk? The ones you can trust, anyway. We'll get to the bottom of this in no time with a bit of sensible division of labour."

Mortimer stared at her, colour running out of his scales with alarming rapidity. Miriam wondered vaguely if dragons could faint. She didn't feel so good herself, come to think of it.

"That seems reasonable," Beaufort said. "We'll have to be careful though, all of us. This attack could well have raised a few flags at the Watch already. If they're investigating, they can't fail to notice that there are a few dragonish things around." He gestured at the baubles drifting silently across the low beams of the ceiling, glowing with yellow light and alive with soft movement.

"We'll get them stashed away," Alice said. "Miriam, are we in agreement?"

Miriam put her face in her hands, feeling really quite unwell. "I don't think I want to be an investigator. It all went a bit wrong last time."

"Nonsense, you were a wonderful investigator. Besides, it's not like you'll be doing it on your own."

"What if you get arrested again? What if *I* get arrested?"

"That was nothing but a ploy by the detective inspector," Alice said firmly. "And no one's going to suspect you of firebombing vans."

Miriam tried to think of another reason that they shouldn't investigate, other than just the fact that it was a Really Bad Idea and that the inspector had specifically told them not to, which apparently counted for nothing. Or it certainly seemed to count for nothing when it came to the High Lord of the Cloverly dragons and Alice Martin, RAF Wing Commander (retired). Miriam supposed it was just in their natures. It certainly wasn't in hers. "I don't feel very well," she said aloud, straightening up. "I think I'm getting the flu."

"That's the Metaxa," Alice said, rather unsympathetically.

"That's settled, then," Beaufort said, and nudged Mortimer, who almost fell over. "Good plan, yes, lad?"

"I don't think—" Mortimer began, but Beaufort wasn't listening.

"We'll head back to the caverns, then. No time like the present to get started."

Alice stood up, straightening her cardigan. "Quite. We'll sleep on it and get started tomorrow." She picked up the Metaxa bottle, then added, "Just so we know, what do these Watch people look like?"

"Oh, that's easy," Beaufort said cheerily. "They're cats."

"Cats?"

"Cats. There's one Watch cat in the village, but he turns a blind eye because I found him in the river when he was a kitten a couple of his lives back. Pulled him out and warmed him up, then dropped him on a friendly doorstep. He's been quite decent with us since then."

"I don't like cats very much," Miriam whispered. "I'm allergic."

Alice looked like she had a lot of questions, but eventually she just said, "Good to know. We'll keep an eye out for any unfamiliar cats, then."

"Good, good. Mortimer?"

"Coming," Mortimer said, sounding rather miserable. Miriam knew how he felt. The day had started out so well. They'd been totting up all their earnings from the night before, and there had been plenty for both the W.I. and the dragons, and Mortimer had been talking about buying AGAs for the caverns, and Beaufort had thought it was undragonish until he realised it meant he didn't have to worry about sliding off the top of the barbecue in his sleep, and they'd all laughed, and it had all just been so *nice*.

And now the dragons were sneaking out into the early night like they'd done something wrong, and she felt ill. And yes, some of it was probably from the Metaxa, but she had a feeling that an awful lot of it was from the fact that they were going *investigating*. Again.

"Alice," she said uncertainly, when the older woman came back from seeing the dragons off. "I'm really not very good at this."

"You're much better at everything than you think you are," Alice said. "And it'll all seem a lot clearer in the morning. You pop off to bed and I'll bring you a cuppa."

Miriam made a small noise that could have been agreement or disagreement, and did as she was told. It was easier than thinking about things too much.

MIRIAM WOKE in the morning with a nasty taste in her mouth and a horrible headache. She pushed herself up in bed and, peering blearily around the dim room, discovered a cold mug of tea and a half-eaten sandwich on her bedside table. She thought she remembered eating the sandwich, but she wasn't quite sure. She might have dreamed it.

She pushed the covers back and climbed out of bed, looking down at her old flannel nightie with the ragged hem, printed with the pink bunny rabbits. She was almost one hundred per cent sure that Alice went to bed in perfectly ironed silk pyjamas, but she couldn't muster the energy to feel embarrassed. Not just yet, anyway. She had a feeling that might come later.

She staggered into the bathroom, turned the shower as cool as she could stand it and jumped in, squeaking loudly and splashing soap all over the tub. *Serves you right*, she told herself, but she didn't quite believe it. Getting a little drunk on ancient souvenir Metaxa seemed like the most reasonable response she could imagine to the prospect of undertaking another dragonish investigation.

MIRIAM TRAILED down the road after Alice, feeling damp and unhappy. She had an idea the day was going to prove to be a long one. She'd told Alice that she was sure she really did have a touch of the flu, but Alice had said tartly that, as far as she knew, you couldn't buy the flu bottled from Greece. So that had been her excuse to spend a rather miserable December day sitting on the sofa feeling sorry for herself completely ruined.

Now she wondered if her Paracetamol were out of date, and if scrambled eggs had been the best thing for breakfast. She still felt distinctly queasy, and her pink rain jacket was making her eyes hurt. It seemed an inauspicious start to the investigation.

Alice let them in the little gate to Gert's house. It was a small, squat cottage with sunken windows that looked like it was folding in on itself, but the light inside was bright and warm.

"Alice, I really don't feel well," Miriam whispered.

"Being out and about will be good for you, then." Alice knocked sharply on the door. Rat-*tat*-a-tat-tat. Miriam winced. It felt like someone was knocking on her skull.

Gert answered the door in half-glasses and an enormous

purple jumper with cows embroidered on it. Miriam closed her eyes. The cows looked like they were moving.

"Alice! Miriam!" Gert exclaimed, and her voice was far too loud. They should have started with someone quieter, like Rose. Rose always talked as if she was in a library. "How lovely! Come in, come in. Mind the mess." She stepped back into a narrow hall, cluttered with a rack of coats and bags and muddy wellies, and padded into the shadowed depths beyond.

"Who 'tis, Gertie?" a raspy voice called from one of the rooms beyond the hall, and Alice and Miriam exchanged glances as they took their boots off. Husbands were rather extraneous to W.I. business. Especially when it was dragonish W.I. business.

"Just a couple of the girls. Don't fuss yourself. I'll bring you a cuppa in a moment."

"Right you are. Hello, ladies."

"Hello," Alice and Miriam called back dutifully, glancing into the living room as they went past. There was a fire on, and the Christmas tree was heaped with lopsided tinsel and flickering lights. Miriam spotted a slipper-clad foot hanging off one end of the sofa and felt faintly envious.

Gert led them into a low-ceilinged kitchen and waved at the table. "Sit, sit. Tea? Or mulled wine? We could treat ourselves, couldn't we? It is almost Christmas!"

Miriam made a small, panicked noise at the back of her throat, and Alice said, "No, tea would be wonderful, Gert. Thank you."

They made themselves comfortable at the table while their host busied herself with cups and teabags, and Miriam examined the pile of neat labels and curls of ribbon at the end of the table. 'Homemade Damson Gin', the labels said, and she swallowed against a nasty stickiness in her throat.

"Gert," Alice said, once a tea had been taken through to the living room and the three women were sat at the table together. "Did you hear about the postman?"

"I did. It was on Facebook this morning. Terrible, isn't it?"

"Yes," Alice said, and Miriam knew the older woman was looking at her expectantly, but she was concentrating on not spilling her tea. Alice was going to have to do this one on her own. Who ever thought tea-drinking could be so difficult?

"Well," Alice continued, when it was clear Miriam had nothing to add, "remember the terrible incident with the vicar, and the detective inspector who came around?"

"Of course. It was very sad, that, but the new vicar seems nice."

"She does," Alice said, and Miriam made some agreeable sound at the back of her throat. She wasn't sure if an extra teaspoon of sugar would make her feel better or worse. It was probably worth a shot. She wasn't actually certain that feeling worse was even possible. She pulled the sugar bowl toward her and added a spoonful, moving carefully. Alice tutted slightly, and Miriam had the feeling that if it hadn't been such an impolite thing to do, Alice probably would have rolled her eyes.

"Well, the inspector visited us the other day," Alice said.

"What for?" Gert demanded. "Has there been another murder?"

"No, no murder—"

"Oh, thank God for that. Imagine being linked to another murder! No one would ever join the W.I. again." Gert opened a Tupperware full of mince pies and pushed them into the centre of the table.

"Well, yes—"

"Never mind what it could do to property values." Gert leaned forward conspiratorially. "Have I told you our Dani's gone into real estate?"

"No, you hadn't. That's nice."

"So if you need your house valued or anything, she's only in Leeds. She can come out."

Alice frowned. "I have no intention of selling my house, Gert."

"No, of course. But just so you know."

Miriam hid a smile behind her mug, quite glad that she wasn't in any state to take part and wondering if Gert had been the best place to start their questioning. But the reigning arm-wrestling champion of Toot Hansell was the repository for all village gossip, if not all gossip in the county, so it had seemed reasonable at the time. Plus, it was common knowledge that Gert Knew People, and quite often Knew Things, too (including, according to local rumour, how to Make Problems Go Away). It was just terribly easy to get sidetracked by her very extended and very tangled family.

Alice took a sip of tea and pushed on. "The inspector came to see us about the missing postman."

"The missing postman? She doesn't think we had anything to do with it?"

"No, nothing like that." There seemed to be a silent *yet* at the end of the sentence. "The inspector did want to know if we'd heard anything about it, though. Particularly as certain aspects of it seemed, well, dragon-y."

"Dragon-y?" Gert put a mince pie on her plate, scowling. "In what way?"

"There was a certain fire-related element to it."

"Oh, my." Gert pushed the Tupperware toward Miriam, who caught a whiff of brandy and swallowed hard. "And the dragons …?"

"Well, of course they had nothing to do with it," Alice said sharply. "This is Beaufort and Mortimer we're talking about. But that's not to say that other, ah, parties might not have had a hand in it."

"Other parties? Well, that is intriguing! What sort of other parties?"

Alice sighed. "We don't know yet. Look, Gert, have you heard anything? Rumours about the postman, perhaps, or anyone suddenly having lots of spare presents to sell or anything like that?"

Gert ate her mince pie while she thought about it, her gaze fixed on some inner distance far beyond the warmth of the kitchen, chewing slowly. Miriam took another sip of tea. The sugar was definitely helping, but it didn't make the tea taste very nice.

Finally, Gert wiped her fingers on a paper towel and dusted crumbs off the front of her jumper, then said, "I can't think of anything out of the ordinary right now, but let me make some calls. I know a few old girls with their ears to the ground."

"Wonderful," Alice said. "But discreetly, yes? I don't think the inspector will really appreciate our getting involved."

"Obviously."

The two women nodded at each other and smiled while Miriam examined the Tupperware, wondering if a mince pie might actually help. More sugar, plus a little hair of the dog. It seemed reasonable, and she was feeling marginally less sick with the tea inside her. She reached out a hesitant hand while Alice and Gert moved on to discuss the market takings, then jerked back with a yelp as a large, smoky grey tabby with a kink in his tail and one ragged ear appeared on the table. The cat stared at them with flat, amused green eyes, his ears pricked with interest.

"Tom! You know you're not allowed on the table." Gert clapped her hands at him, but he ignored her, examining Alice and Miriam with that unblinking gaze.

"Yours, Gert?" Alice asked, not looking away from the cat.

"Oh, he comes and goes." Gert picked the cat up and put him on the floor. "I'm not sure he belongs to anyone at all, but at least half the street feeds him."

Miriam peered under the table, but the cat was already gone. "We should probably head off," she said to Alice.

"Oh, you can talk, then?" Gert said. "You look a little peaky."

"Flu," Miriam mumbled, and Alice gave an unladylike snort.

They called goodbye as they walked through the little hall, and a disembodied voice floated back to them from the living room. At the door, Gert watched with her arms crossed as they put their jackets on.

"I'll find out what I can," she said.

"Thank you." Alice steadied Miriam as she stumbled, one boot half-on. "You know the dragons would never do anything like this. And they helped us when we were implicated."

"For the dragons," Gert said, and grinned.

"Exactly."

✿

OUTSIDE, it was still raining, and Miriam pulled her hood up with a shiver. Gert waved as they started down the path then shut the door, leaving the day a little greyer than it had been.

"Where now?" Miriam asked Alice.

"Jasmine's, I think. See if that husband of hers has shared any police gossip with her."

"Okay." Miriam opened the low gate, and added, "Alice? Remind me to never, ever drink Metaxa again."

"I honestly thought anyone over the age of twenty had already learnt that lesson."

"My youth was obviously not as misspent as you think."

Alice laughed, and turned to shut the gate behind her. A ripple of grey movement in the damp bushes caught their eyes and they both jumped back, Miriam grabbing Alice's arm. The big grey tomcat appeared on the gate post, sheltered by the small arch above, and looked at them with that expression of eternal amusement.

"*Alice*," Miriam hissed, "*Do you think—?*"

"Of course not. He's just a cat." She glared at him. "Aren't you?"

The cat looked even more amused, if possible, and yawned, exposing sharp white teeth and neat pink gums.

"Let's go," Alice said. "We can't be distracted by every cat that comes along." She turned and walked away.

Miriam hesitated, still watching the cat, not sure what she expected it to do, but oddly sure that there'd be *something*. So when the cat winked, Miriam winked back. It seemed only reasonable.

4
MORTIMER

"This is a bad idea," Mortimer whispered to Amelia.

"Well, what did you think he was going to do?"

"Not this."

The Grand Cavern was packed. Well, as packed as it got. The Cloverly dragons were not only small dragons, they were a small clan these days. It was one of the reasons they'd survived the expansion of humans and adapted so well to life in the small patches of wilderness left to them. Mortimer counted about sixty dragons gathered in the warmth of the big fire that always burned in the centre of the Grand Cavern, even in these modern days of barbecues and gas bottles. They sat in little huddles on the worn rock floor, muttering to each other, or perched on ledges along the walls, waiting expectantly. A little deeper into the cavern than the fire rose the tall rock of the High Lord's ancient seat. Not long ago, there was a rough bed of broken swords and rusting shields atop the outcropping, but now it was crowned proudly with a gleaming Weber barbecue. One of the top-of-the-range ones, with shelves and a pot warmer, and a temperature gauge on the lid. Beaufort appeared to be snoozing on the rounded top, but Mortimer could see the gleam of one gold eye, cracked open and watching the newcomers.

Apparently, the High Lord had not been as certain that his clan was above suspicion as he had made out to the inspector, a position Mortimer agreed with wholeheartedly. Not all dragons thought their forays into the modern world were a good idea, no matter how comfortable the barbecues or how tasty the mince pies. There were certain dragons who thought some things were best left well alone, and that going back to living in the shadows was a better option. There were days Mortimer thought that himself, especially when Beaufort was being excessively *enthusiastic*, and Mortimer's stress-shedding was playing up. But still, to eat a postman – that took a pretty high level of determination. And now he wasn't quite sure what the High Lord was thinking of, calling a full Furnace of dragons. He scratched at a loose scale and waited.

Beaufort let the muttering and shifting build, let the questions and whispers be passed from one to the other among the waiting dragons. Furnaces, a gathering of all members of the clan, weren't called often, and usually only for matters of succession or war. There hadn't even been one regarding the transition from gold to more modern treasure, or the question of whether selling dragon-scale trinkets to humans was a good idea. Those had been the High Lord's decisions, and news of them had spread quietly outward, to be participated in or not as each dragon preferred. Dragons, for the most part, run their own lives with little interference from each other, or indeed the High Lord. This meeting was unusual, to say the least, and Mortimer could see Lord Margery (all high-ranking dragons were Lords, gender being a rather fluid term to them. And titles weren't hereditary, but hard-earned through bravery or cleverness. It was quite a satisfactory system) watching the gathered dragons with a disapproving look on her face. She wasn't entirely delighted that Beaufort had found a new lease on life with all the human interaction. She'd been fairly certain she was going to make High Lord within the next century or so, but now … well, since Mortimer had first introduced Beaufort to the concept of barbecues, the old dragon had shed all his patchy scales, grown lovely new ones, and was spending very little time snoozing by the fire, as would befit a very ancient dragon. He didn't look like he'd be dropping dead of old age any time soon, and as that was the only way a High Lord left office without losing in a fight to the death with a challenger, Lord Margery had some waiting ahead of her.

Beaufort finally sat up and cleared his throat. A hush fell over the assembled dragons, and sharp eyes turned expectantly to the High Lord on his sleek silver throne. He cut an impressive figure, Mortimer had to admit, perched there broad and barrel-chested, with the firelight running off the golds and greens of his scales and his head lifted high above them. He shook out his wings, making himself appear larger still, then folded them back into place with a snap.

"Fellow Cloverlies," he said, his deep voice booming off the walls. "Thank you for coming. I appreciate this was all on short notice, and I hope it won't take too long."

"What are we doing here, Beaufort?" Lord Margery asked. She was perched on the highest ledge in the cavern, so that he had to look up at her. "Are we going to talk about this human nonsense you keep dragging us into?"

Beaufort regarded her with the same sort of smile he gave young dragons learning to fly, which made her puff angry yellow smoke, then he said, "Not exactly, no."

"Well, we should be! All this bauble rubbish. It's undragonish!"

Mortimer huffed. Bauble *rubbish?* Well, that was just rude. He'd like to see Lord Margery make one.

"It's merely a matter of shifting focus," Beaufort said. "Rather than scrabbling in the dirt for leftover treasure, of which there is very little, we're creating our own. It's very innovative—"

"It's very *risky*," Lord Margery said. Her wings were half-open, flushed a deep and angry purple-red against the grey stone walls. There was a rumble of agreement from some of the assembled dragons, and Mortimer saw Rockford in the middle of it. He would be. He was only about Mortimer's age, but he was so big he was like a throwback to the days when dragons had still been known to steal sheep and burn the odd farmhouse. And he was always on about wanting to go back to the "glory days of dragons", whatever that was meant to mean. When they'd been hunted for their scales, maybe?

"It's how we will move into this age of humans," Beaufort was saying. "Rather than trying to cling to something long gone."

"It's how we'll bring the humans down on our heads. Again."

A louder murmur drifted through the Furnace, and Rockford snapped his wings out, knocking over a smaller dragon who looked like he wanted to say something but didn't dare. The other dragons who always seemed to stick with Rockford, scaring the hatchlings and talking a lot about some mysterious training but never actually doing much, laughed. Other than them, though, Mortimer couldn't see who was speaking. Except for Lord Margery and the little group, no one seemed too keen to oppose the High Lord.

"We can survive in fear or we can thrive in courage," Beaufort said. "Which do you prefer?"

Silence answered him, and Lord Margery growled something at the back of her throat, then folded her wings and sat down, taking on her usual rather fetching colours of silver and blue. Mortimer grinned, hearing Amelia give a little snort of amusement next to him. If all else fails, suggest a lack of courage and suddenly every dragon in the place is behind you.

"Now then," Beaufort said. "If anyone has any more objections before we get started?"

No one answered, not even Rockford, and Mortimer sighed. He'd half-hoped the whole thing would be derailed, whatever the whole thing was. Calling a Furnace was serious, and he hoped it was just to tell everyone to keep extra-low profiles.

"Yesterday," Beaufort said in a grave tone, "a postman was kidnapped and the mail stolen. All signs point to the involvement of dragons, and no one is leaving until we find the culprit!"

Indignant chatter erupted across the cavern, everyone protesting at once, and Mortimer sighed. So that was what the High Lord was thinking. Never mind *Cloverly dragons would never do such a thing*. No, let's just accuse everyone, all at once. He shook his head.

"Did he really think that would work?" Amelia asked, a note of wonder in her voice.

"He's been watching too much TV." Mortimer sat down wearily. "May as well make yourself comfortable. It's going to be a long day."

ODDLY ENOUGH, attempting to simultaneously interrogate sixty-odd dragons was not working out so well. Even Beaufort looked a little dispirited, and Mortimer had shed five scales in the last hour. *Five.* He was carrying them around with him until he could take them to his workshop, because Beaufort was making good on his threat not to let anyone leave.

"Beaufort, sir," he said, as the High Lord demanded to know, for the fourth time, where a somewhat round and very annoyed-looking dragon called Wendy had acquired a large pink blanket for her barbecue. It featured a cat sleeping by the fire while mice played around it. "There's too many dragons. It just doesn't work."

Wendy nodded vigorously. "Just silly, this."

Beaufort huffed frustrated red steam. "It always works for Hercule Poirot."

"Yes, but he's usually got half a dozen humans, not sixty dragons," Mortimer pointed out.

"It's the same principle."

"Principle, yes. But all that's happening is everyone's getting annoyed, and no one's going to help even if they can. Plus Lord Margery's already made Gilbert cry."

Beaufort followed Mortimer's gaze to where Amelia was standing in front of her little brother, and looked to be exchanging some rather sharp words with Lord Margery. Gilbert had both paws clutched to his chest and had flushed a murky mix of anxious grey and embarrassed lilac. It had been his job to stop anyone leaving, which on reflection wasn't the best idea, considering he was both young and a little on the sensitive side.

Beaufort sighed. "You may be right, lad. But this is most disappointing. I even have a notepad." He showed the younger dragon a large yellow pad, somewhat singed on one corner following a heated exchange with Lord Pamela.

Wendy snorted. "That's a waste of trading scales, that is. A *notepad*."

"All the best detectives have them," Beaufort said, sounding offended.

"You're a *dragon*."

"You're wearing a purple beanie," the High Lord snapped back.

She adjusted it with a frown. "Still better than your notepad."

"I'm sure the notepad'll come in handy for something." Mortimer supposed he should just be happy Beaufort hadn't managed to find an overcoat and a Homburg hat from somewhere.

Beaufort huffed yellow smoke. "I would suggest, Mortimer, that rather than offering platitudes, you come up with some ideas yourself."

"Oh. I mean, yes. Sorry." Mortimer attempted a smile, but it came out goofy and lopsided. Beaufort never snapped. Beaufort was positive and upbeat to the point of it being infuriating, and he never, ever snapped. Which meant that the High Lord was more worried than he let on.

Beaufort sighed slightly, shook his head, then turned back to Wendy and said, "I'm sorry. That blanket is truly charming." He waved a paw. "Plus the beanie is very fetching. Brings out your scales."

"It *is* fetching," she said sharply. "And I'll tell you again, I got it from one of those W.I. ladies. You can ask Amelia. She arranged the whole thing in exchange for a few scales."

"Amelia traded scales?" Mortimer asked.

"Yes, she can get most anything for a couple of scales." Wendy folded her blanket carefully and clutched it to her chest, as if worried they might try to snatch it off her. "Now, Beaufort, are we quite finished here? Only it's well past morning tea time."

Beaufort scratched his chin. "Yes. I think we may as well be. I do believe a different approach is called for."

Wendy huffed and turned her back on them, and Mortimer followed the High Lord back to his seat. The old dragon was moving slowly, and Mortimer's belly twisted with a stab of panic. "Umm – Beaufort, sir?"

"Yes, Mortimer." Beaufort looked up at his Weber as if it was going to take an awful effort to climb onto it.

"I'm sorry."

"Don't be sorry, lad, you were right. This was a silly idea." The old dragon sighed. "It's so hard to believe that a Cloverly could have done this. Yet here we are, and with no more idea who's behind it than before."

"It might not be a Cloverly," Mortimer said, worrying at his tail. "And this could still work. Maybe if we had fewer dragons …?"

Beaufort gave him a look that was far more his usual self.

"When I said come up with ideas, Mortimer, I meant *new* ideas." He scrambled up onto his barbecue. "Now, quiet. I need to settle this lot down."

🐌

"WHAT DO YOU MEAN, 'A SIDELINE'?" Mortimer asked. He was trying to stay calm, but, honestly. Trading scales for blankets? And *beanies?* Trailed by Gilbert, who was slowly recovering his russet colours, he'd dragged Amelia into a quiet corner as the Grand Cavern emptied. Beaufort had apologised for the inconvenience but not the accusation, and Lord Margery had been muttering mutinously. She wasn't the only one. There had been shouting, and arguing, and even a few snapping teeth and stray fireballs. Mortimer was fairly sure that Rockford and his silly lot had been behind most of that, but Lord Margery had been particularly angry because Amelia had called her a cruel old lizard for upsetting Gilbert. But even she had finally left, and now the cavern was almost empty again, everyone wandering off to their own caves and grumbling about being held up for the morning. Beaufort had refrained from telling everyone not to leave town, although it had taken a mid-speech interruption and all of Mortimer's best diplomacy to convince him not to.

"Mortimer, have you *seen* how many baubles and boats we've been making?" Amelia asked. "We honestly can't keep up with demand when we only use our own scales, or what we can find."

"But I don't understand. We use the proceeds to benefit the whole clan. Why isn't everyone just giving us their scales, like we asked them to?"

Amelia rolled her eyes and looked at Gilbert, who shrugged. "Look," she said, "it's all very well, the whole clan pulling together idea, but we're *dragons*. We like having our own treasure, and sometimes we need a little incentive to do the all for one and one for all thing."

"Well. Well, I think that's very shortsighted."

"You've been spending too much time with Beaufort," Gilbert said. "You're getting all into lofty ideals and forgetting the fact that we're all individuals who just aren't very good at that sort of thing."

"I never forget that you're an individual, lad," Beaufort said from a ledge above them, making Gilbert yelp. "In fact, I can't." Gilbert had recently added a second piercing to his tail, and today his claws were purple with yellow spots. Mortimer wasn't sure if that meant something or was just a style choice. And he was wondering for the first time where the young dragon got his paint.

"Sorry," Gilbert mumbled. "I didn't mean anything by it."

"It's quite alright," Beaufort said.

"It's *not*," Mortimer said. "This whole project was about ensuring we all had access to barbecues and gas bottles, so everyone could be comfortable through the winter, and keep the eggs warm, and not be constantly hunting for fuel. Don't you remember? Five years ago, it was such a bad winter that we spent all our time trying to find enough fuel to keep from freezing. And that was before the time we spent hunting for animals that weren't even around, it was so cold. Some weeks it was eat or be warm, we didn't have time for both. We lost three eggs, and they're rare enough as it is. I'm trying to fix that. I'm trying to make our lives better, and dragons are more interested in, in *blankets*? And *beanies*?"

It was quiet for a moment, and now Mortimer couldn't decide if he was more furious or hungry or just plain tired. He'd been working twenty hours a day in the lead-up to the market, trying to make enough baubles to ensure they'd be able to afford all the gas they needed to see them through winter. Stealing gas bottles had proved risky, given the number of garages with CCTV or that

were open 24 hours, and there had been that explosion when a few
of the younger dragons got careless and decided to play catch with
the bottles on the way home. Not to mention that Cedric, who was
maybe not the brightest dragon, kept coming back with bottles of
cream, for some inexplicable reason, and no one could convince
him he couldn't run his barbecue on it. All in all, it was best to get
Miriam to refill the ones that they had, and he'd organised a way
to make that work. For everyone. And now this. A black market in
scales, going on right under his snout, for cat blankets and purple
beanies. He snorted anxious orange smoke.

"Mortimer," Beaufort said, his voice deep and serious. "You're a
wonderful young dragon. And all of these things you've done have
been terribly clever, and I appreciate it enormously. You're making
all our lives better."

Mortimer didn't say anything, but he could feel his scales
flushing an embarrassed lilac.

"However," Beaufort continued, "dragons will be dragons. We
all crave our own treasure."

"But aren't the barbecues enough? And the gas bottles?"

"No," Amelia said quietly. "Everyone wants something that's
just theirs. Like in the old days, how everyone used to want a
crown, or a sword that no one else had. A dragon's hoard is always
their own."

"Old days," Beaufort grumbled. "It wasn't *that* long ago."

"So, how does it work, then?" Mortimer demanded. "How've
you been getting these things?"

"Gert," Amelia said. "She gets whatever we need, and in return
I've made her a few dragon-scale toys, and even turned some old
rings into a necklace for her. The rest of the scales go straight to
the workshop."

"Very enterprising," Beaufort said approvingly, shooting
Mortimer a cautious glance.

"Yes," Mortimer said. "I'm sure it is." He dusted his paws off. "I better go do some work. Especially as it seems we have no shortage of scales."

He marched out of the cavern and into the rain without looking back.

MORTIMER STARED around his workshop bleakly. It had taken him months to get it set up just the way he liked, with solid stone benches lit by prisms that collected the light from outside, and the new addition of bright gas lamps. There were chimeneas in the corners, and specially adapted metal clamps and tweezers and hammers and other tools that he'd commissioned from the local dwarfs, and hooks on the walls where they lived when they weren't in use. There was a deep basket full of glittering scales by one bench, and more baskets of completed baubles and water-activated boats waiting to be taken down to Miriam and boxed up for orders. But what was the point now? No one needed it. No one *wanted* it. They all thought they could just do this stuff themselves, although doubtless no one was thinking about practical things like gas bottles. No, everyone just wanted beanies.

He hunkered down next to the scale bin and tucked his paws under his belly. Dragons will be dragons. *Pah*. Well, he'd show them. He wouldn't get *anyone* any gas bottles. He'd stop making baubles. He'd just be a selfish old dragon like the rest of them. He'd go to Miriam's and eat mince pies and be warm, and bollocks to everyone else. He'd watch TV, and drink tea, and make baubles just for her, and sleep on the floor in front of her AGA. He'd – he lowered his chin to the ground and tucked his tail around him, closing his eyes. He'd carry on just as before, because he didn't want to see even grumpy old Lord Walter shivering in the drafts of the Grand Cavern. He didn't want to see another dragon crying tears that steamed in the cold embers of their empty nest. He didn't want to see hatchlings sleeping through the day rather than making nuisances of themselves, because they were too cold and hungry to play. But he was going to sulk for a while first.

"MORTIMER?"

Mortimer shook himself, startled to find that he'd fallen asleep. He was more tired than he'd thought. And with the chimeneas out it was *cold* in here. His tail had gone numb, and his breath hung in the air.

"Lad? Are you in there?" Beaufort's bulk shut out the weak daylight in the entry tunnel, and Mortimer could hear the old dragon's claws scratching on the hard stone as he padded in. He wrinkled his nose and held his breath. He couldn't stand the High Lord's endless optimism now any more than he'd been able to stand his disappointment earlier.

"Mortimer?"

The younger dragon still didn't reply, tucking his paws in a little tighter and dropping his snout toward his chest as if that would make him invisible. He was already the anxious grey of the stone. He seemed to spend a lot of time that colour, he thought gloomily.

"I brought you some mince pies. I still had a couple left from the other night."

Mortimer twitched, but didn't look up.

"You have wonderful ideas, lad. Wonderful talents. You just have to learn a little about dragon nature. Nature in general, really."

There was the scraping of scaled skin on the floor, then a clatter as Beaufort bumped into one of the baskets. Half a dozen baubles rolled across the workshop, and Mortimer swallowed a sigh.

"Dragons are individuals. We always have been. Do you know what happens when you try to stop dragons being individuals?" Beaufort paused, giving Mortimer a chance to reply. He didn't. "They rebel. And the more you try to stop individuality, the more it comes out. So, no matter that you were doing all this for the greater good, once everyone had time again, once they'd stopped having to spend every moment searching for fuel or food, once they didn't have to spend all their time just *surviving*, they were always going to go back to finding the things that matter to them, whether it was allowed or not. And because there's not exactly a whole lot of jewels and swords out there for the taking, it's going to be blankets and beanies and cushions and – well, I'm not sure, but I've heard that Lord Pamela has a whole collection of sheep-skins, all dyed a different colour."

"But how can they not care?" Mortimer blurted, finally lifting his head. "How can they not care if *everyone's* okay, not just them?"

"They do. If it was watch the other Cloverlies starve or give up their beanies, they'd hand them over in an instant. But it's not. You've given them freedom to have both."

"But it's *sneaky!*"

"We are dragons, lad."

"But," Mortimer sat up properly and glared at the old dragon. "But why didn't they just say? We could have handled it all, done it through Miriam, not risked other human/dragon contact."

"Dragons, remember. There's a proper way, and the dragon way."

"You *knew*. You knew this was going on. Am I the only one who didn't know?" His chest was hot. How could be so stupid? He was meant to be smart. Everyone said he was smart!

"I didn't know exactly, but I do know dragons. I've been one for an awfully long time."

"Why didn't you tell me? Warn me to look out for it, at least?"

"Because these things need to happen. Anything I stopped

would have started up again differently, and maybe more riskily. Sometimes it's best to let things happen and see where it goes. As it turns out, Amelia did rather wonderfully. She's a clever one. She saw the demand, and rather than letting dragons run off trying to trade scales any old place, she channelled it to make sure you had all the scales you could ever need, and that there weren't half a dozen dragons trawling around the village peeking in shop windows on a Monday morning."

Mortimer sighed. He still felt foolish for not realising, and was trying to decide if he felt more admiration for Amelia, or resentment that he hadn't been included. "You still could have told me that you suspected something was going on," he said, knowing he sounded peevish but not really caring. He had a right to feel peevish. He'd started the whole trade agreement, and now everyone was just jumping on board like it was a, a, well – one of those sale things he'd seen on Miriam's TV.

"I could have. But I didn't like to get involved when it seemed that whatever was happening was working rather well."

Mortimer spluttered, his scales starting to take on their usual purples and blues. "*You* didn't like to get involved?"

Beaufort grinned. He'd turned a gas lamp on, flooding the little cavern with light, and it shone off his teeth rather dramatically. "I choose what I involve myself in, Mortimer. Young dragons figuring out how the economics of the clan are going to work is not something I want to be in the middle of."

Mortimer thought of about half a dozen possible retorts, then gave up. "Fine. I guess I get it. It doesn't mean I like it, though."

"We don't get to like everything, but if it works and doesn't hurt anyone, we need to accept it."

Mortimer made a face. "Do you have those mince pies?"

Beaufort handed the box over, and Mortimer took it, then reluctantly gave the second tart back. "How do you know?"

"Know what?"

"What to get involved in. What to turn a blind eye to."

"That, lad, is centuries of practise. You'll get the hang of it."

Beaufort ate his mince pie with evident enjoyment, and Mortimer nibbled at his own, thinking that the High Lord's words had sounded a little ominous. He wasn't at all sure he wanted to get the hang of those sort of things. It all seemed very … Lord-ish.

5
ALICE

Alice knew she wasn't the most patient person in the world, but Miriam was being impossible today. It was all very well having a few drinks to get through a stressful situation. She had even been known to do it herself at times, such as back in those rather unpleasant days when her unsatisfactory husband was still recently missing and the police were asking all their questions. But if you were going to drink, you really had best be able to handle yourself.

"For goodness' sake, Miriam, what are you doing?" Alice asked, as the younger woman tripped over the kerb for the third time. She seemed to be spending more time looking over her shoulder than at where she was going as they trudged through the damp, empty streets. They really should have taken the car, but it hadn't been raining this heavily when they'd set off.

"I'm looking for that cat," Miriam said. She finally had some colour back in her cheeks, but her eyes were anxious.

"I rather doubt, even if it was one of those Watch cats, that it'd be following us in this weather."

"But it did come out after us. What if it overheard us?"

"Then it did. We can't be paralysed by the fear a cat's watching us. That's just ridiculous."

"It's not. Beaufort said this Watch might be looking into the attack on the postman."

Alice sighed. Miriam was right, of course, but there wasn't much they could do if the cat *had* overheard them. Sneaky things. And what a peculiar world it had become since meeting Mortimer and Beaufort. On the whole, she rather liked it, but this worrying about cats was no good.

"Is there a name for it?" Miriam was saying.

"A name for what, dear?"

"For the fear that a cat's watching you. There's one for ducks. Ana-something. Anatiddly? Anantiduck?"

Alice stopped. "What on earth are you talking about?"

"Anatidaephobia. That's it."

"Miriam, do you want to go home?" Alice regarded her with some concern. There was rain dripping off Miriam's nose, and her hair was even frizzier than normal.

"*Hmm?* Oh, um, no. I'm okay. But that's a real thing, you know. The duck thing."

"I rather doubt it. Look, I can do this on my own. If you're going to spend the whole time worried about cats, there's really no point."

"No, I want to help." Miriam sounded offended, and wiped rain out of her eyes. "I'm just not feeling a hundred percent."

"Yes. That we've gathered." Alice headed off again, the rain slicking off her wax jacket and running down her arms. She was glad she'd invested in some new Hunter wellies this year. They really were most comfortable. She looked sideways at Miriam's paisley print boots. They had a hole in the toe, which wouldn't be helping matters.

JASMINE'S HOUSE was a new and rather pretty semi-detached close to the Skipton edge of town, with big front windows that showed off a Christmas tree tilting somewhat dangerously over the living room sofa. They trooped up to the door and Alice rang the bell with cold, rain-wrinkled fingers, setting off hysterical barking inside. She made a face.

"Ugh. Primrose," Miriam said.

"I know. I hate that horrible dog. It yaps constantly, and I'm sure it wee'd on my geraniums last time Jasmine came by. They've not been the same since."

Miriam made a small noise of commiseration as the door opened, unleashing a rush of warmth, the smell of burned coffee, and a wave of high-pitched yapping that drilled into Alice's skull. She saw Miriam wince and felt a moment's sympathy for her. It was not what one needed on a hangover.

"Oh!" Jasmine exclaimed, looking anxiously from one woman to the other. "Is there a meeting? Is it here? Did I forget? Oh, God, I *always* forget—"

"No, Jasmine, just us," Alice said, scowling at the hysterically bouncing fluff-ball that was pawing at Miriam's sodden skirt. "Just popping by for a chat."

"Oh." Jasmine looked at the sky doubtfully. "And you walked?"

"It's just a bit of rain. Never hurt anyone." Alice looked at her expectantly, and after a moment the young woman gave a distressed squeak and jerked the door open.

"I'm *so* sorry. Honestly, I'm terrible. Come in, come in out of the rain."

They came in, shaking rain off their coats and trying to avoid Primrose. The dog nipped Alice's heel, and she muttered darkly about pounds and dog catchers as they followed Jasmine through to the kitchen. It was sleek and modern, post piled on the big kitchen island and a bunch of drooping, waterless lilies competing with the smell of cooking that hadn't gone quite right. There was a recipe book out on the counter and a pile of haphazardly chopped vegetables next to a slow cooker.

"I'll put the kettle on," Jasmine said, fussing over trying to find mugs and sugar and milk. She opened the wrong cupboard twice, which Alice rather thought should be impossible in one's own kitchen, certainly after seven years in it. "But I don't have any biscuits! Oh, no – Ben took all of the last lot into the station!"

Alice quietly thanked whatever small gods looked after kitchens and visitors. It was entirely possible, of course, that Ben really had taken the biscuits to the station, if he bore someone there a grudge. But he was quite a nice young man, so the odds were good that those biscuits were in a bin somewhere.

"It's quite alright," she said aloud. "We just had mince pies at Gert's."

"Oh! I did make some mince pies the other day—"

"No, no," Alice and Miriam said together, and Miriam added, "You can only eat so many mince pies in a day."

"I suppose," Jasmine said, a little disconsolately, and turned back to the kettle. "So, is everything okay?"

Alice exchanged a glance with Miriam, then pulled out a barstool at the island. "Have you heard about the postman?"

JASMINE ONLY OVER-FILLED one cup of tea, splashing water across the counter, and Alice caught her before she used the salt instead of sugar.

"Sorry about that," Jasmine said, wriggling onto one of the stools. "I don't know how I get through life sometimes."

Alice silently agreed, and took a sip of tea. It was actually quite good, and she wrapped her fingers around the mug, trying to chase the chill from them. There was a twinge in her knuckles that she didn't much like. Toot Hansell had an astonishingly healthy population, considering the mean age was rather well north of forty, but it apparently didn't keep her entirely exempt from the small degradations of age.

"So, Jasmine," she said. "What's Ben told you?"

"Well, I'm not really supposed to say. I mean, he's not even meant to tell me, which is silly."

"Entirely."

"And he's a really good policeman. He wouldn't tell me anything if it could affect the investigation. Like when the vicar was murdered. I didn't even know you'd been arrested until after you got back!"

Alice winced slightly. Most people chose not to mention that little matter, but it was impossible to be annoyed with Jasmine. She meant well. "That was very restrained of him."

"But this is different. It's not to do with *us*."

"Of course not."

"So I guess I could tell you."

"It won't go any further," Alice said, and took another sip of tea.

"Well," Jasmine said, leaning forward as if to make sure they weren't overheard. "Apparently the whole van was scorched, and there were enormous scratch marks on the roof and the driver's door, like a wild animal had tried to get in!"

Alice mentally scaled the description down a few notches, considering Ben was still very into that Monsters and Basements game, or whatever it was called, but it still didn't sound good for the postman. "Do they have any leads?" she asked.

"No, although they're watching all the markets for stolen goods. The presents and things."

"And what are they saying about the scratch marks?" Miriam asked. She was looking positively perky now, although her skirt was dripping on the wood floor.

"I don't know. Ben didn't say." Jasmine looked suddenly doubtful. "It wasn't – it couldn't have been dragons, could it?"

"Of course not," Alice said. "Can you imagine Beaufort or Mortimer doing that?"

"No," she agreed. "But what if there were other dragons?"

"Well, that is a possibility. But they're looking into it now. And it's best you don't mention that sort of thing to Ben."

"Umm."

"Oh, Jasmine. You *haven't*." Alice's voice was full of horror, and Miriam covered her mouth, suddenly pale again.

"Well, not *really*. I just said, you know, wow, that sounds like dragons! And he laughed. He always laughs." There was a tremble of upset in Jasmine's voice, and the older women exchanged glances.

"I'm sure he doesn't always laugh," Miriam said.

"He does. And I'm not *stupid*. I mean, I know I'm a bit ditsy, and I have trouble with some things, but I'm not stupid."

"We never thought you were," Alice said. "And I'm sure Ben doesn't either."

"But – well, he may as well have patted me on the head! He was so condescending about it."

"You have to be ready to believe in dragons. And I don't think Ben's there yet." Ben was a nice, *solid* young man, and a very good policeman. But for all his Monsters and Basements games, no one could accuse him of being terribly perceptive. Unlike certain detective inspectors.

"Well, I guess it doesn't matter." Jasmine picked up Primrose, who had been pawing at the legs of the stool, and buried her face in the dog's fur. The dog gave Alice a startlingly evil glare. "He thought I was joking, so that's it."

Alice returned Primrose's glare and said, "Well. I think it's best if you don't mention them again anyway. Just in case. As it happens, the inspector's already paid us a visit. We don't want any more interest than that."

"I won't say anything," Jasmine said, her words muffled by

Primrose's fur. The dog bared her teeth at Alice, and she bared hers back. The dog whimpered and looked away, and Alice gave a satisfied smile.

Miriam got up and went to rub Jasmine's back, careful to avoid Primrose. "It'll be okay," she said. "It really is okay. You're lovely, Jasmine, and no one thinks you're stupid. No one who knows you, anyway."

Jasmine snuffled, and lifted her head, looking at Miriam with red-rimmed eyes. "Have you been on the mulled wine?" she asked. "Only you smell quite boozy."

Miriam left Jasmine and the dog and went to sit down again.

THE RAIN HAD EASED by the time they left, and Jasmine had cheered up enough to offer them lunch, which they declined as tactfully as they could. She stood in the hall watching them pull their boots on, still sniffling a bit. Alice wondered if there was something more wrong than just Ben laughing at her, and made a mental note to come by more often. Jasmine was a good deal younger than the rest of the W.I., but the meetings seemed to make up much of her social life, and Alice wondered if that was enough. Being happy in one's own company wasn't a natural thing for everyone. It hadn't occurred to her that Jasmine might be lonely, but she looked it now, hugging her elbows in the hall, wearing a sweatshirt that was at least three sizes too big and had a cartoon reindeer on it.

Miriam peered out the door, and said, "No cats."

"That's, um, good?" Jasmine said, sounding confused.

"Too much festive spirit," Alice whispered, and was relieved when Jasmine gave a delighted snort of laughter.

"Nothing festive about it," Miriam said darkly, but she was smiling.

"Oh," Jasmine said suddenly. "I forgot. Who's doing the eBay listings for the baubles? Only the pictures aren't very good. I'm sure I could do better ones."

"Etsy," Alice said, fastening the top button of her coat.

"No, eBay. And have we dropped the prices? Or is it like an eBay special?"

Alice gave Miriam a quizzical look, and the other woman frowned. "I did the Etsy listing. I already had an account for my herbal creams and dreamcatchers. I've never even used eBay."

"Are you sure it was eBay?" Alice asked Jasmine.

Her mouth tightened in annoyance. "Yes."

"Well. I think we better take a look." Alice pulled her boots off again, and behind her Miriam sighed and struggled out of her coat.

⁊

ALICE TOOK a cautious sip of soup. It actually wasn't bad. Admittedly, it was Marks & Spencer's Thai something or other, so it should be edible. But it was always hard to know what Jasmine did to food. It was an anti-talent.

"There," Jasmine said, pointing at the screen of her tablet. She'd insisted she was hungry and that they all needed to have a little lunch while she found the listing, and Alice and Miriam had felt too uncomfortable to refuse. It was hard to tell if Jasmine actually realised how bad her cooking was, and now certainly wasn't the time to tell her.

Miriam leaned over the younger woman's shoulder, peering at the little screen. Alice kept her distance. Primrose was back on Jasmine's lap, and she bared her teeth if Alice came too close. Alice wasn't at all sure what she'd done to deserve such vitriol, but she was starting to return it quite passionately.

"Well," Miriam said. "They do look a bit like our baubles, don't they?"

In the small images on the screen, the baubles floated against a

YULE BE SORRY | 71

dark background, softly glossy and lit from within by warm yellow light. As far as Alice could see, they had the same intricate markings and delicate folds as Mortimer's, and she couldn't see any strings holding them suspended from hidden hooks.

"An awful lot like it," she said.

"The photos aren't very good," Jasmine said. "If you blow them up they get all pixelated. But listen to the description: *The perfect gift for someone who has everything! Quixotic Christmas baubles float and fly! They'll burn forever without needing fuel! Special high-technical material never gets hot! Buy yours before stocks run out!*"

"'Quixotic'?" Alice asked.

"Yes," Miriam said, peering a little closer at the screen. "That's an odd word choice, isn't it?"

"Sounds like someone got carried away with a thesaurus. 'High-technical', too."

"That's odd as well."

"Who's selling them? Jasmine, can you tell?"

"Umm." Jasmine tapped the screen. "They call themselves 'Modern World Enchantments'. It gives an address in Huddersfield, but it's just a postbox."

Alice got up and braved the silently snarling dog, leaning over the screen with Miriam between her and Primrose. She hoped the silly mutt wouldn't get it in her head to bite Miriam instead. She scanned the listing.

"They're selling them terribly cheaply. Ten pounds! For all that work – honestly, they must be plastic or something."

"We should order one," Jasmine said. "Then we can get a proper look."

"Good idea." Alice retreated to her chair, the dog's gaze never leaving her. "Use my card. We'll factor it into the market expenses. We need to see what's going on with this. We can't have Mortimer's baubles being copied. He puts so much work into them."

Jasmine took Alice's card and leaned over the screen, and Alice folded her hands together under her chin, thinking. *I'm an artisan myself*, the man had said at the market. And hadn't his friend been carrying an unmarked paper bag, one that could easily have come from their very own stall?

She rather thought he had.

THEY LEFT Jasmine looking much more cheerful now that she'd discovered the baubles and made them lunch. Alice decided that she would ask if Miriam would give up the internet side of things to the younger woman. She wasn't sure it would help, but it couldn't hurt. Unless, of course, Jasmine was as inclined to mishaps in that area as she was in everything else. Still, it was probably worth the risk.

The day hadn't improved, and even Alice was starting to feel a little damp and miserable as they trekked through the rain to Priya's house (Earl Grey tea and Christmas cake), then Rosemary's (chai tea and buttery shortbread), and Rose's (strong Yorkshire tea and apple slices, while being lightly slobbered on by her enormous Great Dane, who was much less nippy than Primrose), and finally Carlotta's (coffee spiked with brandy, and cranberry biscotti). No one had anything of interest to add, although they'd all been very concerned that the dragons might be implicated. Rose, who was some undefined age past eighty and not much bigger than a ten-year-old, had become very excited, dropping her library voice and shouting about hiring private investigators and top lawyers, and the Great Dane had started barking and running all over the house, knocking tables over and tripping over its own enormous feet. It had taken a while to calm everyone down, and to clean up the slobber and spilt tea afterward.

Now they trudged toward Miriam's, the houses along the lanes turned inward against the early grey dusk. Alice felt like all the tea was going to start slopping out her ears, and she was so full of cake that she had no intention of eating dinner. Possibly for days. Miriam looked much more cheerful than she had earlier, although her nose was bright red and her hair was a tight mess of brown and silver curls.

"Ooh, I'm glad that day's done," the younger woman said, letting them in the gate.

"*Hmm*," Alice said, not really listening. She followed Miriam in, pulling her boots off for what felt like the thousandth time today. She couldn't wait to get home, but she had to get her thoughts in order first, and she wanted to hear what Miriam might say.

"Tea?" Miriam asked, as they padded in their thick socks into the warmth of the kitchen. Miriam left a trail of damp left foot-prints behind her.

"Oh, no," Alice said. "I'm awash." She sat at the kitchen table, running her fingers through her hair absently.

"Can I get you anything else, then?" Miriam asked, sounding puzzled.

"No. Sit down for a moment."

Miriam sat, lines of concern wrinkling her forehead.

"What do we know now?" Alice asked.

"Nothing more, really. The postman's gone missing with all the post, and there were scorch marks on the van."

"And someone's selling baubles that look oddly like Mortimer's."

"Oh. Oh, do you think—"

"I don't know what I think," Alice said. "We didn't lose any baubles yesterday?"

"No, I was going to send the first lot of Etsy orders today, but we were investigating instead."

"Of course. Are you sending them tomorrow?"

"Yes, I need to go to the post office first thing."

Alice drummed her fingertips on the table lightly. "Well. Let's see how it goes. Send the parcels, as per normal." She got up abruptly. "I need to look at a few things. Thank you for your help today, Miriam. I appreciate it." Miriam started to get up, and Alice waved her back down. "I can see myself out. Have a good evening."

"You too," Miriam said, looking relieved as she sank back into her chair.

Alice pulled her boots on at the door and set off once more into the dreary day.

SHE WALKED HOME deep in her own thoughts, the village quiet around her. Few places are more desolate and empty than a small village on a rainy afternoon in December. The Christmas lights on the lamp posts burned bravely, but the persistent drizzle seemed to wash the brightness from them. She liked walking when she needed to think, rain or not. It tended to shake more things loose than just sitting at home or pottering around the house.

A fancy-looking silver Audi purred past her, too close for the empty streets, and she jumped sideways to avoid the wake it pulled behind it. She put her hands on her hips, glaring after it pointedly, and announced, "Idiots." Then she stood there frowning as it vanished around the next corner. She'd been too busy trying to keep dry to see into the dim interior and maybe spot the driver or even a passenger, but hadn't she seen that same silver Audi around earlier? Maybe more than once. She tried to think. Outside Miriam's, at the start of the day, maybe? Maybe even outside Gert's? She couldn't be sure. She could just be jumping at shadows, too worried about cats and missing postmen. She sighed and adjusted her hood, then kept walking.

All else was quiet.

She was already jingling her house keys when she walked up

the path to the front door, looking forward to a hot shower and some dry clothes. Even if she hadn't actually got all that wet, the whole day had made her feel damp. She pulled her boots off under the shelter of the little porch roof, the door already ajar, and straightened up to see the grey cat sitting on her outside mat.

"Well, hello," she said. "What do you want?"

The cat didn't answer, just blinked lazily.

"Are you following me?"

The cat got up and nosed his way around the door.

"Oh, no. No, I do not have animals in my house."

The cat glanced over his shoulder, then trotted down the hall while Alice called him something rather unladylike and hung her coat up. She followed him to the kitchen in her socks, shivering as rain slipped off her hair and down her collar. The cat was sitting expectantly by the fridge, his amused green eyes watching her.

"What are you after, then? I'm not a cat person. You should go back to Gert."

The cat jumped onto a chair at the little kitchen table and settled down on his haunches, yawning.

"Do *not* get comfortable." She glared at the tom and flicked the kettle on. "I'm going to get changed. You just—" She glanced out the window, where the rain had become heavier, streaking the glass, then back at the cat, his fur matted in damp clumps. "Ugh." She went upstairs.

The cat had moved to the mat in front of the AGA by the time she came back down, her hair dried and her comfortable clothes on. She doubted she'd have any company this afternoon, so she'd dug out some fluffy trousers and a big green jumper with holes in the elbows that might have once belonged to her missing husband. Her hands were still aching faintly, and she sighed as she looked at the cat. He paused his grooming and looked back at her with interest. It was still raining, even heavier than before.

"Fine. But don't think this is going to become a regular occurrence." She found a tin of tuna in the pantry and spooned some into a bowl. "And if you're a spy, you're a terribly obvious one."

The cat investigated the bowl, then nibbled the tuna, purring loudly.

"Although, I suppose you're only obvious if one realises there are such things as feline spies." She rubbed her forehead, and decided a hot toddy was in order. If the weather weren't enough, the possibility of harbouring furry enemy agents would do it.

She started up her laptop on the kitchen table while she waited for her drink to cool. The cat jumped up on her lap and she scowled at him. He purred placidly, and started to bed into her trousers, claws working rhythmically.

"How on earth is that comfortable for anyone involved?" she demanded.

The cat rubbed his head on her arm and settled himself where he could keep an eye on the screen.

"Bloody animal," she muttered, although she had to admit that he was reassuringly heavy and warm. After a couple of false starts, she found eBay and searched for Modern World Enchantments. They had a new listing, this one titled *Magically Aggrandising Model Boats!*

"There's that thesaurus again," Alice murmured, taking a sip of hot toddy and making a face. It was still too hot, and rather stronger than she'd intended.

Be amazed! Be awed! Highly technical materials combine to create a boat that not only floats, it grows! Order yours today before stocks run out!

Alice followed their advice and ordered one. Then she opened another tab and started a new search, with more confidence this time. She didn't much like computers, but certain things she was quite familiar with. The cat looked on with interest. "How's this for spy stuff, kitty?" she said to him. "Learning anything?"

The cat just purred.

6

MIRIAM

M iriam staggered into the dusty little post office/village shop, carting two enormous shopping bags full of carefully packed baubles and boats.

"Am I in time?" she asked the big-bellied man behind the counter. "The post hasn't gone yet?"

"No, you're good." He glanced at his watch, then winked at her. "Just."

"Oof, that was lucky." She pushed the boxes over the counter, watching him weighing them up and entering details on the computer. "So someone's covering the route, then?"

"Yes, Royal Mail got someone sorted." The shopkeeper shook his head. "I've heard nothing else about Sam, though. You know, the usual postman. Terrible happenings, really."

"Oh, it is," Miriam agreed. "Awful." She checked the date on some milk in the little display fridge and put it back again. She always tried to buy a few things as well as do the post here, but it was a risky business. The last lot of digestives she'd bought without checking had a family of moths living in the bottom of the packet. She hadn't even realised until she'd eaten two.

"And Christmas time, too," the shopkeeper said. "As if we're not stretched enough as it is." He ran a hand over his thin hair, looking mournful, and Miriam glanced around the empty shop. The tinsel that had been pinned up over the door had escaped and was hanging down one side of the frame like a furry anaconda waiting for a victim, and the only other concession to the season was a display of biscuits in faded souvenir tins that she was sure had been out every year she'd lived here. She smiled encouragingly.

"It must be quite a worry."

"It is. People'll take their custom elsewhere, if they can't rely on the post here." He dropped the last of the boxes into the sack behind his chair and pushed the card machine toward her. "Don't know what I'll do then."

"I'm sure it'll all work out," Miriam said, wondering if she should buy a tin of biscuits just to cheer him up. The total on the machine soon changed her mind.

"Well, you know what the police are like. More important things to do, I imagine."

"There's a missing person. That seems quite important to me."

"We'll see." He retrieved the machine, tore off the receipts and handed one to her. "Season's greetings and all that."

IT WAS another grey and rather unpleasant day, and Miriam had built the fire up in the living room before she left. It was comforting to come home and see the smoke curling from the chimney, and to know she'd be inside in the warm and dry in just a few moments. She loved Bessie, her old Volkswagen Beetle, even with all her temperamental behaviours, but it had to be said that she wasn't wonderful in the winter. The heater might manage to blow some tepid air, but it was more than overwhelmed by all the freezing draughts coming in around the doors and windows.

Never mind that every puddle she drove through came up through the floorboards, and Miriam had to wear wellies so her feet didn't get wet.

She let herself in and pottered through to the kitchen, carrying some fresh bread from the bakery and a bag of veggies from the greengrocer, humming as she went. Her hangover was completely gone after a good night's sleep, no doubt helped by a large serving of shepherd's pie the night before, and the fact that everything seemed to be running as usual with the post made the missing postman seem rather remote and unlikely. There had to be an explanation, and it wasn't going to have anything to do with dragons or the W.I. She just knew it.

A rather fierce face popped up at the window as she dropped the carrots in the sink to rinse them, and she jumped back with a squeak. The face split in a terrifying grin, and Beaufort waved, breathing hot dragon breath all over the window and steaming it up.

"There you are, Miriam," he bellowed. "We were just about to leave."

A smaller face appeared next to him, looking apologetic, and Miriam thought she should have bought more bread. Or maybe even some of the moth-eaten digestives. Dragon appetites were every bit as prodigious as legend suggested.

She went to the door to let them in.

"So, you see," Mortimer said, "I'm not being unreasonable, am I?"

Miriam looked at the empty plate on the coffee table and said, "Shall I make more sandwiches?"

"You think I'm being unreasonable," Mortimer said, flushing an ashamed yellow. "But I'm *not!*"

Alice, who had arrived not long after the dragons, bearing a large apple cake (which was almost gone, as Mortimer appeared to be comfort eating), chuckled softly. "I don't know much about dragon nature, Mortimer. But humans are quite like that, too. It's not even necessarily about having something *better* than everyone else, although some are like that. Mostly it's just about not being the same as everyone else."

"You see, lad?" Beaufort said. "It's just people."

"I don't think I much like people," Mortimer muttered, squeezing his wings against his back in annoyance. "Scaled or otherwise."

"Why don't I make some hot chocolate?" Miriam suggested. "That would be nice, right?"

"Maybe," Mortimer mumbled, and Beaufort tweaked his tail. "*Ow.* Sorry. I'm sorry. I'm being really horrible, aren't I?"

"It happens to the best of us," Alice said. "But the key is not to wallow around in it. Have a bit of a complain, then get on with things. Otherwise you just sit there being grey and grumpy until no one wants to talk to you ever again."

Mortimer looked thoroughly alarmed, the yellow rushing away and being overtaken by a very solid grey indeed, and Miriam said, "Are you sure no one wants hot chocolate?" She rather fancied one herself, but guaranteed if she went and made one, everyone else would want one five minutes later. Or two of her current guests would.

Alice's phone rang, a business-like little trill. She gave a humph of annoyance and left the room to answer it.

"Yes?" Miriam heard her saying. Then, "I see. Oh. One moment, please. I'm just going to put you on speaker phone." She came back into the lounge and set the phone on the coffee table, motioning the dragons to silence. "Frank," she said, "My friend Miriam is here with me – she's helping me arrange the charity dinner. Can you tell me again what's happened, please?"

"Ah, yes. Hello?" the disembodied voice on the phone said.

"Hello," Miriam replied dutifully.

"Sorry about this, ladies, I really am. I know you were relying on my turkeys for the dinner, seeing as they're local and free-range and all the rest. But, well. I've been robbed."

Four variations of "you've *what?*" came back to him, and he said, "Uh, hello?"

"I'm sorry, Frank. There seems to be a bit of an echo," Alice said, glaring at the dragons. "When you said the turkeys were missing I hadn't appreciated that they'd been stolen. I thought it was maybe foxes."

"Oh, no. No feathers, no blood, no broken latches. The pens were opened neat as you please, sometime last night. I've reported it to the police, but they said it was probably PETA or some such, even though I've never had any complaints or threats. The police seem to think the birds have just been released and will come back on their own, but I don't think so. If that were the case they'd be home already." He sounded very concerned considering he was raising the birds to kill them, but Miriam supposed the sudden loss of Christmas income likely had at least a little to do with that.

"Well, Frank, I'm very sorry this has happened," Alice said. "Thank you for letting us know."

"No problems, Ms Martin. I'll be in touch if they come back."

"Wonderful." Alice tapped the speaker off and walked back into the hall. "Now, about our deposit ..."

The dragons and Miriam looked at each other.

"It can't be Gilbert," Mortimer said. "Not after last time, when he took all those chickens from the rescue. He knows he has to leave well enough alone."

"*Hmm*," Beaufort said.

"Well. It can't be related, anyway, can it?" Miriam asked. "I mean, no one goes about stealing the post *and* poultry."

"I'd like to say no," Beaufort said, "but I'm not sure. If it's not Gilbert, it's a very odd coincidence."

Alice walked back into the room, frowning. "Well, that does put a spanner in the works. I don't know where we're going to get another half-dozen nice turkeys at such short notice."

"At least this morning's baubles got off okay," Miriam said brightly. "And you should get that counterfeit one soon—" She stopped, wincing. By silent agreement, she and Alice hadn't mentioned the strange eBay listing. Not with Mortimer so emotional about Amelia's little side trade already.

"What?" he said now, his eyes wide.

"I'm going to put that hot chocolate on," Miriam said, and scuttled out the door.

&.

"THIS REALLY ISN'T the end of the world, Mortimer," Alice said. He was an ashen grey, lying flat on his belly with his paws pressed over his snout.

"Well, no," he said, his voice muffled by the carpet. His hot chocolate was now a tepid chocolate, an unpleasant skin forming on top of it. "Uncontrolled scale distribution and counterfeit baubles, not to mention missing postmen and stolen turkeys. Of course it could be worse. I'm just not sure how."

"We have no reason to think any of this is linked," Miriam said.

"Hmm," Beaufort said again, and she glared at him, mouthing not helping. He looked faintly surprised, but cleared his throat and said, "See here, Mortimer. We're going to get to the bottom of all of this. It'll be absolutely fine."

"I see no way that this can be absolutely fine."

"That's not the attitude, lad."

Mortimer growled at the carpet. "I bet none of this would have happened if there hadn't been a black market in scales going on."

"And I bet none of this would have happened if you'd just stayed in your caves like good little dragons," Alice said. "Honestly,

Mortimer. Pull yourself together, or I'll have to come over there and tweak your silly tail."

Mortimer stared at her with wide eyes, then sat up.

"That's better. Now drink your hot chocolate, and we'll talk about this like the grown-ups we are."

Mortimer picked it up and made a face. "It's—"

"*Drink it.*"

Mortimer squeaked, and drank the cold chocolate in one hurried gulp.

"Good man. Dragon. Now, let's—" Alice was interrupted by her phone again, and she gave a small, rather dragonish growl that make Mortimer squeak again. Miriam didn't blame him. She was just glad Alice wasn't angry at her for mentioning the baubles. Or not yet.

Alice poked the phone irritably, and said, "Yes? Oh, hello, Jasmine, love." She listened, then said, "I see. Well. That puts a rather interesting light on things."

Miriam shivered. She didn't like the sound of *interesting*.

"Right. Call Priya, Rose, and Gert, would you? I want everyone who's available here at Miriam's within the hour. Thanks, Jasmine." She hung the phone up decisively, looking like she wished it were an old-fashioned one she could slam into a cradle. Mobile phones were rather less satisfying, Miriam thought.

"What's happening?" Beaufort asked. He was the only one other than Alice who looked, if not happy, at least energised. Of course they were. They both loved *interesting*.

"We're calling an emergency meeting," Alice announced, standing up.

"Now?" Miriam asked, confused.

"Yes. Right now. Immediately. We need to get as many of the W.I. to meet here as can manage it, and we'll spread the word to the others afterward. This may be a direct attack on either the

Toot Hansell Women's Institute or the Cloverly dragons." She paused, thinking. "Or both. Either way, I. Am. Not. Having it!"

Miriam looked at Alice with something close to awe. She looked furious, standing ramrod straight next to the windows with her hands on her hips, and it occurred to Miriam that she was rather happy not to have known Alice in her RAF days. Civilian Alice was more than enough.

"Wonderful," Beaufort said happily.

Miriam sighed. This was sounding awfully like investigating on a grand scale. "Shall I make sandwiches?" she suggested.

Alice stared out the window, frowning and tapping her phone against her leg. "Not right now," she said. "Miriam, do your neighbours have a silver Audi, by any chance?"

Miriam frowned. "I don't think so. Why?"

"It's probably not important." She stared into the grey day for a moment longer, then shook her head and started scrolling through her phone. "Can you call Rosemary and Teresa? I'll deal with everyone else."

Miriam looked at Mortimer. His colour had come back a little with the tepid chocolate, but he was still very subdued. "Beaufort," he whispered, "should we go?"

"Of course not, lad." The old dragon's eyes were bright and eager. "It's time for some action!"

Miriam thought that, with any luck, there would be more cake and tea than action, but said nothing. She had a horrible feeling that once the W.I. were involved, she and Mortimer would be very much in the minority when it came to wanting to stay out of things.

THERE CERTAINLY WAS a lot of tea and cake, and Gert had turned up carting a catering box of mugs as well as some of her fearsome cordial. Carlotta had brought mulled wine, and the house was overflowing with mince pies and Christmas cookies, turning the emergency meeting somewhat festive as the ten available members of the Toot Hansell Women's Institute (which also happened to be all current members of the Toot Hansell W.I.) crowded into Miriam's little living room. They perched on dining chairs brought through from the kitchen and crammed together on the sofa and the window seat, while the more flexible women (including Rose) sat on the floor with the dragons. The combination of fire and mulled wine and bodies made the room hot and a little stuffy, and everyone looked flushed and excited. Primrose alternated between barking at the dragons and snarling at Alice until she shoved the yappy little thing into the hall and closed the door on her. Miriam nibbled on her thumbnail and tried to enter in the spirit of things. She couldn't. She was pretty sure they were about to – once again – embark on Obstructing a Police Investigation and Withholding Evidence. She felt a little ill.

Alice clapped her hands together sharply, silencing the clamour of excited conversation and drawing all eyes to her. "Ladies," she said gravely. "We have a situation." No one answered, and she examined each person as if she were divining their commitment before she continued. "We believe that the missing post may have something to do with the W.I. as well as the dragons."

A ripple of surprise passed through the group, and she waited it out patiently.

"Yesterday, a van was taken on its way to Toot Hansell. I think that may have been a miscalculation on the part of the attackers. Jasmine has told me that a second van has just been attacked, and the driver has gone missing, this time leaving Toot Hansell."

The exclamations of surprise were louder this time, and Jasmine went pink as Teresa patted her shoulder admiringly.

Alice continued. "Today's van would have been carrying – Miriam?"

Miriam started to speak, stopped, cleared her throat and tried again. "Ah, twelve baubles and seven boats."

Mortimer gave an angry little whimper.

Alice nodded. "It's a lot to lose. A lot of work for Mortimer, and income for both the W.I.'s charitable concerns and the dragons. It has also come to our attention that someone is selling baubles and boats that look very much like Mortimer's on eBay. They are significantly undercutting us, but we don't know if these are counterfeits or stolen. It has to be one of the two, as no one else has access to the genuine article."

Miriam examined Gert, but she looked just as shocked as everyone else. Not that she'd really suspected Gert of robbing vans either, but, well. Gert Knew People, and she had access to scales. It wasn't like they had many other suspects. Any, actually.

"On top of that, someone has stolen Frank's turkeys."

There was a moment's stunned silence, then Rose burst out laughing, surprisingly loud and infectious, setting everyone else off. Alice let it go, smiling slightly.

"That can't be connected, can it?" Pearl asked finally, still grinning. "I mean, stealing baubles is one thing. But *turkeys?*"

"This is why I feel it's rather targeted," Alice said. "Those were our turkeys."

Everyone considered this for a moment, the mood in the room growing sombre. It wouldn't be the first time the Toot Hansell W.I. had come under attack. Last time the vicar had died over it. Miriam shivered, and hoped the postmen were alright.

Jasmine put her hand up shyly from where she sat on the floor by the fire, still very pink and looking a little overheated in her Christmas penguin T-shirt.

Alice smiled at her "Yes, Jasmine?"

"Um. Well." The younger woman took a sip of mulled wine at the same time as she spoke, and the cup slipped, splashing spicy red wine all over her T-shirt and the carpet. She yelped, and there was a sudden rush of movement and a general call for cloths and club soda and salt, and Rosemary and Carlotta started arguing over which was the best to use. Miriam hurried to the kitchen, glad of the reprieve, ignoring the rather unproductive argument as she cleaned the old carpet and told Jasmine to go borrow a top from her bedroom. Jasmine hurried off, mumbling apologies, and by the time she came back in the wine was cleaned away and everyone was settled again. Primrose followed Jasmine in and climbed into her lap, where she sat growling steadily at Alice.

"I'm *so* sorry," Jasmine said.

"It's quite alright," Miriam replied. The old, garishly patterned carpet was threadbare in places and somewhat stained already. It was most forgiving.

"You were saying?" Alice said.

"Oh! Oh, yes. Um. The baubles? The ones on eBay?" Jasmine coughed and took sip of wine, and Miriam decided to keep a cloth close by. Just in case.

"Yes?" Alice nodded encouragingly.

"I've sort of been keeping an eye on them, and there were two reviews yesterday that said they were dangerous. Someone had one shoot out their living room window, right through the double-glazing, and someone else had one *explode!* They said they just heard a bang and came downstairs to find pieces of it all over the place."

"Oh, dear," Alice murmured, looking at the dragons. "Is that possible?"

"Not with Mortimer's," Beaufort said firmly, before the younger dragon could reply. "Is it, lad?"

"Well, it shouldn't be," Mortimer said, tucking his tail tighter over his toes. His shoulders were hunched up around his ears, and he hadn't even touched the assorted mince pies the ladies had piled in front of him. "We test them really thoroughly. I leave them in the work shop alight for at least two weeks before I bring them down here, and light them and put them out twenty or so times to make sure they're consistent. If they're not, I start again."

"And mine have been up since last Christmas," Miriam said. "They were too nice to put away."

"Well," Alice said. "I think it's safe to assume these are counterfeits, then."

"But how? You need dragon scales, and the right charms – how could anyone ..." Mortimer trailed off, and Miriam peeked at Gert again. She still looked as confused as the rest of them.

"There's other Folk who can get access to scales, and know how to cast charms," Beaufort said. "Someone must have rumbled us, and now they're stealing your ideas." He shook his head. "We should have copyrighted them."

Mortimer stared at him. "How, Beaufort? I can't exactly send a magical item off to the local patent office, can I?"

Beaufort waved a paw dismissively. "You could have put one of those little C's in a circle on them. That would have made them think twice, at least."

Mortimer buried his snout in his paws. "This is terrible. Someone's going to get hurt. I have to stop making them. We have to stop *selling* them!"

"We won't be beaten by these horrid people," Priya said, leaning forward on the sofa and shaking a finger at the young dragon, who looked at her with some alarm. "We can start by all complaining to eBay that they're counterfeit products and shouldn't be being sold. That should at least slow them down."

"If they're not trademarked, they can't be counterfeited," Jasmine said with surprising authority, then whispered, "I'm sorry, Mortimer."

"It's okay," he said. "I should have seen this coming. I should have known it wouldn't work. We should have just stuck to the market stalls. Or I should never have made them at all. I *knew* it."

"Rubbish," Beaufort said. "There is one answer, and one answer only to this. We get to the bottom of it. We find the missing post-men, and we find the culprits. No one steals from the Cloverly dragons or the Toot Hansell W.I.!"

The women looked at each other doubtfully, then Gert said, "That's more *like* it!" and a ragged cheer went around the room. Excited chatter started up, and Gert waved them to silence. "Where do you want us to start?" she asked Beaufort.

"Ah. Well. Finding the spot where the postmen were taken from would be good. Mortimer and I could have a sniff around, see what we come up with."

"Excellent idea," Alice said.

"I could ask Ben," Jasmine said, "but I don't know if he'll say. If I start asking questions he might not tell me anything more at all."

"Have you checked Twitter?" Miriam blurted, then wondered what on earth she was doing. What was *wrong* with her? She shouldn't be encouraging this. Mortimer was staring at her in horror. After all, they were meant to be the sensible ones. But Beaufort's enthusiasm really was terribly contagious.

Alice looked at her like she was speaking another language. "How will that help? Isn't that just a lot of people insulting each other?"

"No, it's great." Jasmine had her phone out already. "And that's a fantastic idea. Someone will've driven past and put a photo up."

"What on earth for?" Alice still looked mystified.

"Human curiosity," Rose said. "We can't help ourselves."

"Well, maybe *some* of us can't—"

"Here!" Jasmine said triumphantly. "Look, it even says, 'What's happened up at the start of High Fell walk? Cops everywhere and a burned-out van. #skipton #dales #news.'"

"*Hashtag?*"

"Are they those nice potato things you made once?" Beaufort asked.

"Um, no—"

"Never mind, Jasmine," Alice said. "That's wonderful. Well done, you."

Jasmine went an even deeper pink, and Carlotta topped up her mug of wine.

"Well, then," Beaufort said. "Show me where that is on a map. Mortimer and I'll head over there now."

"We will?" Mortimer asked.

"No time like the present."

"We should drive," Alice said. "You can lie down in the back, then if it's safe we'll stop."

"Flying's quicker."

"Someone may notice two dragons flitting about the place."

"We don't *flit*."

"Um, Alice?" Teresa said.

"We're not discussing this, Beaufort. You will be riding in the car."

The High Lord looked obstinate, and Alice glared at him.

"Alice?" Teresa said again.

"On a day like this, no one will ever notice us," Beaufort said.

"No."

"Alice," Teresa repeated, a little louder.

"Look," Miriam said. "Alice is right—"

"*Alice*," Teresa said, and everyone finally looked at her. "The police are here."

In the sudden stillness that fell over the room, they all clearly heard the rat-tat-tat of the knocker, but the dog was the only one that reacted, yapping hysterically as she raced out of the room.

"We're not meant to know anything about this, are we?" Gert asked, looking at Alice and Miriam.

"Not as such," Alice admitted, and Miriam covered her face with her hands.

Rat-*tat*-a-tat.

7
DI ADAMS

D I Adams was not having a good morning. She blamed it on Toot Hansell in general and the Women's Institute in particular, although they probably weren't to blame for the fact that yet again no one had filled the coffee machine, or that she'd dropped the coffee she bought from across the road and splattered her new grey suit trousers with it. Nor were they technically the reason Detective Chief Inspector Temple (often known as The Temper) was glaring at her as she tried to creep out the door without being seen.

"Adams!"

"Sir."

"Where are you off to?"

"Follow-up on that smash and grab in Chapel Allerton last week."

He gave her a suspicious look. "Spending a lot of time out and about."

"Well, that's where the crime is, sir." She cringed inwardly as she said it. He already acted like he was doing her a favour, letting some London cop come and join his precious team.

He frowned, then snorted laughter. "Fine, you want to freeze your toes off, go for it. We've got proper cold up here, not your balmy London winters."

She sighed. "It is pretty chilly."

"Just don't go catching the flu and wanting signing off on sick leave. Soft southerners." He laughed again, apparently feeling this was quite witty, and DI Adams pulled a smile from somewhere then headed out the door.

SHE HADN'T ENTIRELY LIED. She had every intention of swinging by Chapel Allerton on the way. Or maybe on the way back. Probably that. But one of the reasons she was having a bad morning was that she'd barely slept last night, and what sleep she'd had was peopled with enormous, fire-breathing dragons of the *Game of Thrones* variety, furiously attacking London while she ran after them waving a scone and shouting, "Let's all have a nice cup of tea and talk about it." Which was a phrase she had never uttered in her life, and didn't imagine she'd have any need to in the future.

Nightmares aside, she'd spent most of the night thinking about missing postmen. DI Collins had that whole salt-of-the-earth, hale-and-hearty thing going, but she doubted he had any first-hand knowledge of dragons, or any on his contact list. There was a protective little part of her that wanted to make sure it stayed that way. For all the horror that she'd seen in London – the things that had stolen the kids, the things that were terrible and hungry and had just about broken her – the dragons were the other side of a world she hadn't even known existed. They were light and magic and beauty. Alright, they were *frustrating* light and magic and beauty, but they made her feel a little like that time she'd discovered a butterfly had built a chrysalis in the wilting bamboo plant in her bedroom at home. She hadn't even told her mother, and certainly not her little brothers. They'd have poked it, and peered at it, and cheapened its magic with a lot of talk. Plus her youngest brother probably would have pulled it apart to see what was inside. He'd been that sort of kid. Now he was in elder care and exceptionally good at it, which precisely no one had expected.

So she had to figure out the missing postman before DI Collins got too close to the truth behind the case, whatever that might be. Which meant going to Skipton to find out what he knew, and then probably braving another visit to Toot Hansell. No one had called her, of course, but she had about as much confidence in Alice and Miriam telling her what was going on as she had in DCI Temple inviting her home to meet the missus. Or mister.

"MORE IMPORTANT THINGS?" DI Adams asked, bewildered. She was sitting across a messy desk from DI Collins, holding a mug of tea that read You Can't Get Owt For Nowt, which she supposed was some Yorkshire witticism. He hadn't come out to meet her this time, just told PC McLeod to let her in and make them both a cuppa while he finished a report. He'd waved her to the chair with that same friendly smile, then ignored her while he typed with surprising efficiency. She had the uneasy feeling that he was probably better at keeping up with paperwork than she was. And now he'd just told her that the case wasn't a priority, because, to quote, he had more important things to do. She tried to keep the disbelief from showing on her face. In a place like this? More important things to do than find the occupant of a fire-bombed van?

"Look," DI Collins said. "We're a small outfit. We're stretched as it is going into Christmas, and to be honest, it looks like the postman did do a runner with the contents of the van after all. He had a girlfriend his wife knew nothing about, and apparently had been looking at flights to Majorca. He's probably out there somewhere right now, flogging the lot. We've put alerts on all ports and borders, and that's all we can do for the moment."

"A man is missing. His van was *torched*." She couldn't quite get her head around how casual he was. Although she supposed she should be happy she hadn't sat down to hear him say, *I think it was dragons.*

"Well, maybe Leeds can take it on then, since you're obviously not busy enough."

DI Adams gave him a tight smile. "I have a full caseload myself."

"And yet here you are, sticking your nose in." The big inspector pushed a pile of folders toward her. "I have two runaway kids. A stabbing. A brawl in the town centre that we're still rounding up. A whole bunch of domestics, as per the usual Christmas spirit. A couple of break-ins. A fifty-two-year-old man who says his mother's been abducted by aliens and a pod person returned in her place. Car thefts. Plus a load of bloody turkeys gone missing. All of which need attention just as much as a van full of missing post, if not more. The techs found nothing. There weren't even signs of a struggle. So, really, if you're so bored in Leeds that you have to keep coming out here to hassle us, please take your pick."

DI Adams sighed. "I don't mean to hassle you."

"Yet here you sit." She scowled, and he gave her a smile that suggested he wasn't as put out as he sounded. "Just stating the facts, DI Adams. And, speaking of such tricky things, why aren't you talking to my boss, if Leeds is so interested?"

DI Adams took a sip of tea, then said, "Do you always ask questions you know the answer to?"

"Only when it amuses me. On your own time, are you?"

"I am." Now that *was* an out-and-out lie, but she was here now.

"Missing postmen a special interest of yours?"

"Something like that."

"You need better hobbies."

"I don't have hobbies."

"Maybe you should get some."

"Are you going to let me take a look at that file?"

He shrugged. "Sure. If it'll make you happy. Merry Christmas." He fished it out from between the other folders. "You can use an interview room. I expect it back on my desk by afternoon tea."

"It will be." She grabbed the file and retreated before he could ask her anything else.

⚓

"DI ADAMS, you still on your own time?"

"Yes – wait, it's not anywhere near afternoon tea time!" she protested as DI Collins scooped up the folder. To be fair, she'd finished reading it half an hour ago, but she'd been doodling on her notepad in the peace of the interview room, looking up dragons on her mobile so she could tell Beaufort that yes, actually, she had done her research. Although none of the dragons she was finding on Wikipedia or even more dubious sites seemed to support the existence of tea-drinking dragons. If she was honest with herself, she was mostly putting off getting in the car. It wasn't often you could find a quiet spot to sit for a while, and Toot Hansell was unlikely to offer anything in the way of peacefulness, for all its rural English idyll.

"New developments, Adams." DI Collins looked at her expectantly. "Are you coming?"

"Coming where?" she asked, already shrugging into her coat and dropping her paper water cup in the bin.

DI Collins regarded the cup with interest. The edge had been chewed ragged. "You have a rabbit in here, or just dubious stress management techniques?"

She scowled at him. "What new developments? And where?"

"Another missing mail van, same spot, just outside Toot Hansell. Coming?"

She just about stepped on his heels as she grabbed her bag and hurried out of the room after him.

"WHAT'S YOUR NAME?" DI Collins asked. He didn't have the dashboard light on, but he was taking the corners fast, and DI Adams was clinging to the door handle, regarding the dry-stone walls hemming them in with some distrust. She could smell farm-yard smells, even with the windows closed. This was why she never wanted a country post. Farm smells and silly narrow lanes with walls on them rather than nice wide kerbs. She swallowed a protest as DI Collins hit the accelerator, swung them around a tractor, and roared down a small straight.

"Adams," she said, trying to see the speedometer.

"Really? That's what your friends call you?"

"Sometimes."

"You don't sound posh."

"What?"

"Only posh people call their friends by their last names."

She snorted. "I'm definitely not posh." She wasn't anything in particular, really. Sometimes people assumed that since she came from London and had the heritage she did, she'd have grown up in some rough council flat, all drug users on the stairs and single mums with twelve kids. She hadn't. She'd had her own room, even if her brothers had shared, and although there had been a few years where any clothes that didn't come from the market had come from charity shops, it hadn't lasted. And there had always been food on the table and new shoes before they outgrew the old ones. They'd even had a tiny backyard in their terraced house, big enough to play hopscotch in.

"So what's your name?" DI Collins repeated.

"Adams."

He gave her an amused, evaluating look, and she resisted the urge to tell him to watch the damn road. "That bad, huh?"

"I don't love it." It was Jeanette. It wasn't *bad*, but it wasn't her, either. Only her mum really used it.

He grinned. "You want bad names? Mine's Colin."

DI Adams tried to stop pumping the imaginary brake pedal on her side of the car. "Colin Collins?"

"Yeah. Family legend says that Dad was celebrating a little too hard, and when he went to register the name he wrote the same thing in both boxes."

"Really?"

Collins shrugged. "Maybe. Maybe he was too tipsy to remember what Mum wanted to call me. Either way, that's me. Colin Collins."

"No middle name?"

"Nope."

"Okay. Yeah, that's pretty bad."

"Ah, could be worse. They could have called me Moonchild or something. It was an option, apparently." They were briefly airborne as they came over a rise, and narrowly avoided a truck coming the other way that was, DI Adams considered, far too big for the road. "But alright then, Adams. What's got you so interested in missing postmen that you're wasting your days off sitting in interview rooms in strange police stations? I know we've already established that you don't have hobbies, and no friends close enough to use your first name, but it's still a little over-dedicated."

She considered telling him it wasn't a day off, but that would only seem more suspicious. And the truth wasn't going to work. Well, I'm pretty sure it has something to do with dragons? Or, failing that, it might be the ladies of the Toot Hansell Women's Institute that we should be looking at? And most likely it involves both the W.I. *and* dragons, and, as far as she knew, that was no one's area of expertise but her own?

"I told you last time," she said. "Cold case. Tenuous connection, but you never know."

"Tell me about this cold case, then."

She scowled at him. "Shouldn't you be concentrating on driving?"

"I'm a right good multitasker, me."

"Well, that's just bloody fantastic," she mumbled, and braced herself against the dashboard as the DI braked for a couple of sheep ambling across the road.

SHE WAS SAVED from concocting a plausible cold case by the fact that just past the wandering sheep they encountered a whole sea of woolly backs blocking the road. There was a small red car on the far side, with a confused-looking young man behind the wheel and a woman leaning out the window taking photos. The young man kept trying to nudge his way into the increasingly anxious flock, and DI Collins put the window down, waving and bellowing at him to stop. The young man apparently took that as an indication to hurry, so he leaned on his horn, setting it off in long blats. The sheep panicked, surging and jostling between the two cars, and DI Collins said a few choice words about tourists, then turned the engine off and opened the door.

"What're you doing?" DI Adams asked.

"Need to get the silly animals off the road before anyone drives into them." He opened the boot and she watched him in the rear-view mirror as he pulled a pair of old and very dirty wellies on.

"You've got to be kidding me," she muttered, and settled back to watch. A moment later there was a knock on the window. She glared at him as he beckoned her out. "No. Absolutely not." He beckoned again, looking impatient. "No! I've only got my normal shoes!" She pointed at them.

He opened the door. "I'm not going to make you wade through a bloody lake, Adams. I just need you to walk back to the top of the rise and flag down anyone before they run into this lot. There's a high vis jacket on the back seat."

"Oh. Right." She climbed out, grabbed the jacket and picked her way through the sheep droppings up the little hill. She stood there shivering in the cold grey day, half watching for cars and half watching DI Collins pushing his way through the sheep to scold the driver of the red car. Country policing. Couldn't pay her enough.

ALL OF WHICH meant that it took them rather longer to get to the crime scene than either DI was particularly happy with, but eventually the sheep were back in a field (DI Collins grumbling that he really didn't care whose field it was, so long as the bloody road was clear), and they were moving again. This time DI Collins did have the dashboard light on, and he was driving fast enough to have no desire for conversation. DI Adams didn't think she could have talked anyway. She was too busy trying not to get whiplash.

They pulled into the side of the road just before a lay-by, tucking the car in tight to the dry-stone wall. DI Adams had to climb out the driver's side. The tech van and the marked car belonging to the officers that had been first on the scene were parked beyond the lay-by itself, and the lights on the marked car painted blue and red swathes across the dim day. Cars slowed to a crawl as they went past, occupants gawping at the black and yellow crime scene tape. The Royal Mail van huddled alone in the little gravel parking area, the doors open as the techs crawled through it. The back was empty, devoid of parcels and letters, and there were scorch marks across the doors and the roof where the paint was raised in tight, burned blisters. There were long, angry scratches on the doors that looked like they'd been done by a knife. Or claws. Beyond the stone walls, fields ran green and muddy under the fells, and sheep watched them incuriously. Across the road, the hills climbed up toward a broken-down stone hut and a copse of trees made ghostly by the rain. There was no village nearby, no farmhouse spying on them. Just fields and sheep and damp greyness, and it felt unutterably lonely. DI Adams shivered, then went to inspect the van more closely.

"Any of this ringing any bells with your cold case?" DI Collins asked, making her jump. She'd been taking photos of the scratches with her phone.

"I'm not sure."

"Come on, Adams. Give me a hint. Was your case about missing postmen? Or is it the failed fire-bombings and the Freddy Kruger marks there that've got you interested?"

She stepped away from the van hurriedly, pocketing her phone. "Some elements are kind of related."

He frowned at her. "I'm letting you ride along from the goodness of my heart here."

"No, you're letting me ride along because you have no idea what's going on."

He spluttered as if he was going to make an excuse, then gave her a startlingly infectious grin, opening his arms wide to take in the damp day. "Go on, then. Give me something. Anything!"

DI Adams grinned back. She couldn't help it. But the smile faded as she looked at the van again. "I really don't think I can help. This is the same place the other van was found, right?"

"The very one."

"No signs of struggle in either case."

He said, "None," even though it wasn't a question.

She paced around the van, examining the muddy gravel, then crouched down. "Someone had a cigarette. Look, ash."

"We got a sample," one of the techs said, and she felt heat rise in her cheeks. Great. Now she looked like the big city cop telling the locals how to do their jobs.

"Of course. Sorry."

The tech shrugged and went back to photographing the interior of the van, in case anything shifted when it was towed. Not that there was much in there to shift, unless some mail materialised out of the headlining.

"There was no ash last time," DI Collins said.

"No. So I imagine it was the postman who stopped for a smoke. Which means it's not connected to the kidnappers. Attackers. Whatever." She rubbed the back of her neck and sighed. "I've got nothing. I'm sorry." And she meant it, too. Not just because she wanted to point the suspicion away from dragons. Because it was a case, an *interesting* case, and it felt good to be looking at something beyond the typical robberies and assaults and domestics that lay on her desk in Leeds.

"Well, we've got a pattern," DI Collins said. "And we'll make sure tomorrow's van has an escort."

"They won't take it, then."

"Which is something." He rubbed his hands together, huffing white breath on the cold air. "Come on. We'll go chat to the good people of Toot Hansell, see if that gets us anywhere."

"We will?"

"We will, Adams. You've got nothing else to do, right? No sewing circle or clay-pigeon shooting meet to get to?"

"Um. Right." *Bollocks.*

"You know Toot Hansell, then," DI Collins said. He was driving more slowly now, which was something. She had enough to worry about with the spotty rural phone reception out here, meaning she had a missed a presumably angry call from DCI Temple which would need dealing with at some point, as well as the fact that she was going to have to face Toot Hansell in the company of an inspector who had no idea what was really going on. She didn't need to worry about the possibility of a head-on collision with a tractor as well.

"A little. Just from the case in the summer."

"Of course, the poisoned vicar. Yes, it sounded like it was all very exciting."

"I guess I stepped on your toes a bit there."

"I was in Corfu, sipping cocktails and swimming in crystal clear waters. No toes were stepped on. Although, my aunt was one of your main suspects for a while."

"Oh, you're kidding me." That was just spectacular, that was.

"Not even slightly. Miriam Ellis."

DI Adams pinched the bridge of her nose. At least it wasn't Alice Martin. "I see."

"Yeah, it's a small world up here." The car came up over a rise, and Toot Hansell unrolled before them, glittering with light in the greyness of the day. "Shall we see if she's home? She makes a mean mince pie."

DI Adams tried to think of any reason that would make sense as to why a mean mince pie sounded like a terrible idea right about now, and she couldn't come up with a single one. Other than the fact that it came accompanied by at least one member of the Toot Hansell W.I., and possibly dragons.

❦

THEY PULLED up outside Miriam's, behind a Smart car and an ancient, rust-pocked Rover, and DI Adams got out carefully. There was a good head of smoke coming from the chimney and warm light painting the rose bushes outside the living room windows. Miriam was home, then. That was unfortunate.

DI Collins ambled up the path with a long, slouching stride, and gave the front door a cheery knock. An explosion of yapping greeted it, and DI Adams had flashbacks of last summer and that horrendous scene in the churchyard.

DI Collins frowned. "I wonder when she got a dog?"

"I don't know, but it doesn't sound very happy."

They waited. The dog kept barking.

DI Collins knocked again. "Maybe she's gone out."

"We should go, then."

"Give her a chance to answer. That dog sounds completely hysterical."

DI Adams didn't feel entirely calm herself. "She might be hiding. I got the feeling that I made her rather nervous."

"Surely not. Such a friendly person as yourself."

DI Adams scowled, and reached past him to knock on the door again. The dog sounded like it was having conniptions.

"It *looks* like she's home," DI Collins said. "She wouldn't go out and leave the lights on like that." He stepped off the path and stopped. "Adams," he said.

The concern in his voice seized her chest, squeezing. Was it the dragons? Had he seen them? Worse, had they *done* something? Was Miriam bleeding out in a scorched armchair as théy pounded on her door? Had she been wrong? Were the dragons really no different than the creatures in London? She hurried to stand next to him, her mouth horribly dry.

The living room window was crowded with women of a certain age, all peering out at them with varying levels of alarm on their faces. There were also two rather scaly faces, one looking much more worried than the other. DI Adams let out a shivering breath and glanced at DI Collins, who had raised one hand in a nervous sort of greeting.

"Looks like we've interrupted a W.I. party," she said cautiously.

"Bloody hell," he said. "It's like stumbling into a nest of tea-bearing squirrels. You never want to deal with all of them at once. They're so hopped up on cake and biscuits that they can't focus on anything."

DI Adams snorted. "Unless you're Alice Martin."

"Oh, God. Alice Martin. Don't leave me alone in there, Adams." He walked back to the door, and DI Adams took a moment to compose herself. Since he had neither screamed nor mentioned anything more – or less – terrifying than the chair of the W.I., he probably hadn't seen the dragons. He probably thought the glass was a bit misted up, hard to see, and it probably even made his eyes hurt if he looked at it for too long. That was how it had been for her before she realised she was seeing dragons. She stole a look at DI Collins. On the other hand, he could be pretending he didn't see them, thinking that she couldn't see them. She sighed. No wonder this place gave her a headache.

The window was emptying, and Miriam had vanished. DI Adams went to wait by the door, while the dog's barking grew even more hysterical.

8

MIRIAM

"Oh, it's Colin," Miriam said.

"And Detective Inspector Adams," Alice pointed out.

Mortimer hoped Beaufort wouldn't offer the inspector a rabbit again. She hadn't seemed to appreciate it very much last time. He looked up at the women crowded above him and the High Lord, all peering out the living room window at the visitors waiting by the door. He had a feeling that none of this was going to be appreciated by the inspector, actually.

"Well, it can't be an official visit," Miriam said, fiddling with the curtain. "Why would it be an official visit?"

"Miriam, it's *Detective Inspector Adams*, who has specifically told us to stay out of things," Alice said.

"Ah. Yes. That's a good point."

"We should go," Mortimer said, trying to see past his own breath, which was steaming up the window, then wondering why he was worried about seeing out. He was probably best not to. He certainly didn't want the rather large man Miriam had called Colin seeing in.

"We should all go," Priya said.

"How?" Gert demanded. "Out the bathroom window?"

Rat-a-tat, rat-a-tat. The knocks sounded impatient, and Primrose was barking herself hoarse. Mortimer could hear her clawing the door frantically.

"I was thinking more out through the kitchen, if Miriam brings them straight in here," Priya said. The ten women and the dragons turned to look at the cups scattered across the coffee table and collected on side tables, the napkins and cakes and biscuits, cardigans and handbags and scarves. "Or we wait really quietly in here with the door shut and Miriam takes *them* to the kitchen."

"That might work," Miriam said dubiously.

"Of course it won't work," Alice said. "They're police officers, not vacuum cleaner salespeople. Jasmine, is your dog ever going to stop barking?"

"Primrose is a very good guard dog," Jasmine said.

Alice muttered something unfriendly under her breath.

"Well, we can't just leave them out there," Beaufort said. "It looks suspicious. Mortimer and I'll lay low, and you can just say you're having a meeting. A perfectly normal, Christmas meeting."

"It's the only way," Alice agreed. "Go answer the door, Miriam."

"Oh, can't you? DI Adams makes me so *nervous*."

"It's your house. And your nephew, for that matter. Go answer the door."

"Oh, Alice—"

"Miriam, pull yourself together, honestly."

"Now, there's no need for arguing," Beaufort began.

"Beaufort, shush," Alice said sternly, and Beaufort stopped mid-breath.

"Beaufort, I really think we should go, at least," Mortimer said. "It's too risky."

"Mortimer, calm down. We may learn something if we stay, and it's highly unlikely this other police officer will even notice we're here."

Mortimer thought, rather gloomily, that knowing his luck this Colin would not only notice, but arrest him for making exploding baubles that weren't even his. He sighed heavily, then hurriedly patted out the smouldering bit on the bottom of the curtains.

"Is *someone* going to answer the door?" Teresa asked. "It's getting awkward now."

"Well, I guess anyone can answer it now," Mortimer said, and raised a paw to DI Adams and Colin as they stood on the path, staring in the living room window.

Outside, Colin raised his hand in response, a bemused look on his face, and Mortimer went the grey of cold porridge.

💩

"JASMINE, please get your dog under control," Alice said from the hallway, and Mortimer poked his head around the living room door anxiously. He was starting to think Colin hadn't actually seen him, as the big inspector hadn't started shouting or reacted at all, but had just gone back to the door to wait. So either he wasn't going to make a fuss about dragons, or he had just been waving at everyone in general. Hopefully the latter.

"Oh, she's fine," Jasmine said, coming out into the hall. "She wouldn't hurt anyone, would you, Primmy?"

The dog was still on the doormat, and she paused her furious yapping to snarl at Miriam as she reached for the door handle.

Miriam jerked her hand back. "Are you sure?"

"Of course. Primrose! Primrose, come here! Come to Mummy!"

Primrose looked back at Jasmine, then snapped at Alice's ankles as she joined Miriam at the door.

"Primrose! Don't be naughty!"

Alice muttered something under her breath that Mortimer couldn't quite hear, and she and Miriam glared at Primrose. The dog was a furious ball of tan and white fluffiness, legs wide as she obstinately held her position in front of the door. There were also quite a few rather sharp teeth in among the fluff, which Mortimer didn't much like the look of. The dog seemed to be positively looking for trouble, and Beaufort huffed next to his ear.

"Horrible little thing," the High Lord said. "Caused all sorts of trouble last time, too."

The horrible little thing had indeed caused all sorts of trouble for the dragons last time, and seemed to be making a point of doing it again.

"Ooh, look," Miriam said, and held up a shortbread biscuit. "Amazing the things you find in your pockets." She waved the biscuit at the dog. "Here you go, pup. Biscuit, look."

"That's a waste of a good biscuit," Beaufort said. "She won't appreciate it."

Primrose tipped her head to one side and stopped snarling. She whined instead.

"*Mmm*, yum. Nice biscuit!" Miriam waved it encouragingly.

"Miriam, how long have you had that shortbread biscuit in your pocket?" Alice asked.

"No idea. But I obviously knew it'd come in handy." She waved the biscuit again, the dog's eyes following it eagerly. A thin thread of drool descended from her teeth.

"*Such* an uncouth animal," Beaufort said, and Mortimer decided not to tell him he had Christmas cake on his ears.

"Oh, Miriam, she shouldn't really have sweet stuff—" Jasmine stopped as Miriam, Alice, the dragons, and Gert, who had stepped out of the living room to see what the fuss was about, glared at her. "But that's fine. One won't hurt."

"Come on." Miriam backed away from the door, still holding the biscuit out. "Good dog. *Good doggy.*"

Primrose's tail was wagging, bright brown eyes still fixed on the shortbread, but she didn't move.

"Here we go," Miriam stepped closer to her again, waving the biscuit in front of the dog's nose so she could catch the scent. "Lovely biscuit. All for you."

Primrose took a small step forward, then there was another sharp rap on the door. Miriam gave a squeak of surprise and jumped, and the dog lunged.

"*Ow!*"

"*Horrid monster!*" Beaufort bellowed, and Mortimer shushed him in alarm.

"You little—" Alice grabbed Primrose around the belly and lifted her off the floor. The dog was firmly attached to Miriam's finger, and Miriam was swearing quite fluently between yelps of pain. "Jasmine! Sort this dog out!"

"Oh, no! Oh, I'm so sorry, this isn't like her at all!" Jasmine had both hands pressed to her chest and couldn't seem to move.

"I don't care!" Miriam shouted. "Get it off me!"

"Aunt Miriam? Are you okay?" The man's voice was muffled by the door, and when no one answered he knocked again, hard enough to shake the wood panels. "Aunt Miriam!"

"Ms Ellis? Miriam? What's going on?" DI Adams' voice now, sharp with warning.

"*Jasmine!*" Alice snapped, as the dog wriggled in her grip, still refusing to let go of Miriam. "Come *here!*"

The younger woman took a timid step forward, then yelped as Beaufort cantered past her, tail whipping wildly into the walls. He slid on the stone-flagged floor and crashed into a side table, sending a vase flying. It missed the rug and shattered on the stone floor, making someone in the living room scream.

"*Beaufort!*" Mortimer hissed, trying to shout without actually being loud about it. How was this happening? How was this kind of thing *always* happening?

"Aunt Miriam," Colin shouted from outside, "Stand clear of the door! *Stand clear of the door!*"

"Beaufort, *no!*" There were quite a few voices shouting this time, and Mortimer was suddenly aware that the ladies of the Women's Institute were leaning over him, crammed together in the doorway.

"*Beaufort!*" Mortimer shout-whispered again. "*Stop!*"

Beaufort ignored them all. He recovered from his slide and charged straight for Miriam, eyes fixed on the dog. He was snorting angry yellow steam, and Primrose let go of Miriam with a howl, wriggling wildly as she flung herself out of Alice's hands.

Beaufort pounced, trapping the dog under one taloned paw, and Jasmine screamed, "*Primrose!*" The High Lord spun his body away from the door as it flew open and pressed himself tight along the wall, fading to an off-white that matched the plaster admirably.

Colin had obviously expected more resistance from the door, and his momentum sent him stumbling into the hall, arms wind-milling for balance. He almost recovered, then one boot hooked the rug that Beaufort had rucked up in his headlong flight down the hall, and the inspector went sprawling onto his belly, catching himself with one hand in the broken vase.

"You b—" He looked up to see the ladies of the Toot Hansell Women's Institute staring down at him from the living room doorway. "Ow," he amended, and sat up, blinking and rubbing his eyes. Mortimer held his breath. If he breathed out now, he'd singe a police officer, which seemed like a Very Bad Thing.

Colin twisted to look at Miriam, who was holding her injured finger up so that the blood ran down her hand and didn't drip on the floor. "Aunt Miriam?" he said cautiously. DI Adams was standing in the doorway, looking like she didn't know who to glare at first. She finally settled on Beaufort, who let his lips hitch up in a small smile, but otherwise didn't move.

"Hello, dear," Miriam said brightly. "Lovely to see you."

"What—" Colin looked from her to Alice to Jasmine frozen in the hallway and back to the faces jostling for position at the living room door, but, Mortimer was relieved to note, not at either him or Beaufort. "What on earth are you lot up to?"

⁂

ALICE USHERED Miriam and her nephew into the kitchen so that she could peroxide Miriam's bite and Colin's vase injury, Rosemary and Carlotta following and arguing over the best thing to do with dog bites. Colin was still rubbing his eyes and looking faintly bewildered, and neither dragon moved until he was out of sight beyond the kitchen door. Then Mortimer scuttled rapidly back to the hearth, and Beaufort released Primrose then followed, looking rather pleased with himself.

DI Adams crouched next to them as they took on the reddish shades of the patterned carpet, while about her the W.I. fussed with making more tea and finding more plates for mince pies.

"What are you *doing?*" she hissed at them. Mortimer made a doubtful little sound, and concentrated on trying to stay red. The inspector looked *very* unhappy, and it was making him want to go the colour of porridge again.

"It's a meeting," Beaufort whispered back. "Regarding Christmas."

"Do I look stupid?"

"You look lovely. A little tired, maybe—"

"Shut. Up." DI Adams rubbed her forehead, hard, and Mortimer rather sympathised. Beaufort had the same effect on him sometimes. The inspector looked up at the women perched on the chairs and sofa, all watching her nervously. "Well, talk among yourselves," she snapped, and they looked at each other doubtfully.

"We're terribly sorry," Mortimer whispered, his voice a little wobbly. "We really haven't been poking around."

"Is that just because you haven't had time to yet?" she demanded, and Mortimer promptly lost all his colour. He shuffled onto the stone flags in front of the hearth and hoped he'd blend in a little better there. Beaufort made a little noise that suggested he either had indigestion or was trying not to laugh. "This is *not* funny," DI Adams hissed. "There are two people missing."

"And you have reason to believe dragons are involved," Beaufort said. "Yet you're telling the only two dragons you know to stay out of it?"

"I don't know for sure that it involves dragons. And it's not even my case. I'm tagging along with DI Colin bloody Collins there, and you're prancing around calling attention to yourself."

"We hardly *prance*," Beaufort sniffed.

"Colin Collins?" Mortimer said, and his nose went lilac with embarrassment when the High Lord and the DI both stared at him. "Sorry. I know. Not important."

DI Adams looked back at Beaufort. "Can't you just do what I asked, and stay out of the human side?"

Mortimer snorted, and covered his snout in horror. "Not funny. I know. Sorry again." He looked to see if there was anything lilac in the room that he could sit on, and wondered if he might be hysterical. He never had been before, but there was a first for everything. Especially around Beaufort and the W.I.

"Detective Inspector," Beaufort said, finally looking away from Mortimer. "Whether or not the culprits *are* dragons, if they're making it *look* like they're dragons, they're doing it deliberately. That means they're trying to stir up anti-dragon sentiment, and possibly frame us. Therefore, you need our expertise, unless your dragon knowledge has improved considerably in the last two days."

DI Adams scowled at him, looking like she wanted to disagree.

"And if there are dragons or other Folk involved, I don't think you're going to get too far without us."

The inspector started to say something, but Pearl said suddenly, "They're coming!"

Immediately everyone tried to look everywhere but at the two dragons taking up a considerable amount of space in front of the fire, and the inspector got up, brushing her trousers off. Mortimer discovered that he could do grey rather easily, after all.

DI Collins came in with a frighteningly neat bandage on his left hand, carrying an enormous tea pot in the other. He looked anxious, and Mortimer felt an immediate sympathy with the man. It was bad enough when you knew there were dragons involved. The whole situation must be twice as confusing when you didn't realise that. Alice followed him in with another pot, and there was general fussing with cups and milk and sugar. Mulled wine was poured and cakes were sliced, and Carlotta and Gert wedged DI Collins between them on the sofa. He sat there trying to make himself smaller, with his knees pressed together and his elbows tucked into his sides. DI Adams sat back down on the floor in front of the dragons, clutching a cup of tea that Jasmine had almost dropped on her.

"Well, then," Miriam said, smiling at her nephew, "it's so lovely of you to drop in, and I'm terribly sorry about all the fuss. And your poor hand."

"S'alright," he said around a mouthful of mince pie. "It's not that bad. And we're sorry to interrupt, really."

"Oh, that's fine," Gert said, patting his knee and making him jump violently enough to knock a mince pie to the carpet. "Always nice to have young folk around."

"Absolutely," Carlotta agreed, squeezing his arm. "Always time for the police."

"We're not here in an official capacity," DI Adams said, taking a slice of Christmas cake from Priya.

DI Collins frowned. "Speak for yourself."

"Well, I mean, we're not here to accuse the ladies of hijacking a postal van. Ha. Haha." No one else laughed, and DI Adams busied herself with her cake. Mortimer was astonished to smell something anxious and embarrassed on her.

"Ye-es," DI Collins said. "That is quite true." He finished his mince pie, and no one spoke. Mortimer could clearly hear the horrible little dog grumbling from her place in Jasmine's lap, and wondered why she hadn't been put in the garden. Or preferably the cellar.

DI Collins wiped his fingers on a napkin and said, "Well, you're a chatty lot. I feel like we interrupted something. You plotting to overthrow the government or something?"

This time *everyone* laughed a little wildly, except DI Adams who muttered something that sounded an awful lot like *wouldn't put it past them*.

DI Collins took a sip of tea. "You still sending your Etsy stuff out, Auntie Miriam?"

"Oh, yes. We've been quite busy, really. Me. I've been. I mean—" Miriam gulped tea, choking a little as Alice stared at her with frown lines dividing her forehead. She recovered and patted her mouth with a napkin, then said, "We as in the W.I. We've been selling through my account. Very busy. Yes."

"That's great," her nephew said, helping himself to a piece of gingerbread. "Did you have anything in those vans?"

"Oh. Well, yes. We did, unfortunately."

Mortimer looked sideways at DI Adams, and caught her eye. She gave a very small shrug, and looked at Beaufort. He was watching the other inspector with great interest, and Mortimer only hoped he didn't forget that not only were they not meant to be getting involved, but also not actually meant to exist, as far as DI Collins knew.

"I hope you didn't lose too much," DI Collins said.

"Well, it was a shame, definitely. But we can try again tomorrow." Miriam smiled at him more easily, the lines of her shoulders relaxing.

DI Collins nodded, then said to Jasmine, "Ben been telling tales?"

Jasmine gave a little gasp of horror as the room froze, cups halfway to lips and biscuits half chewed. All eyes were on the big inspector, and Miriam hiccoughed, slapping a hand over her mouth and slopping tea onto her skirt. Then Primrose flung herself out of Jasmine's grip and bolted toward Beaufort, yapping.

"*No!*" Jasmine cried out, and DI Adams grabbed for the dog, then jerked back as the horrid thing snapped at her, bumping into Mortimer and making him squeak. Primrose turned her attention back to the High Lord, growling and baring her tiny teeth. Beaufort bared his teeth back, and the dog promptly rolled on her back, all four legs in the air, trembling in fright.

"Is that dog alright?" DI Collins asked.

"She's epileptic," Alice said, before Jasmine could reply. "And, to answer your question, yes. We did know of the second van before you got here."

Jasmine buried her face in her hands, her shoulders trembling, and DI Collins looked uncomfortable. Well, *more* uncomfortable, Mortimer thought. He hadn't really looked comfortable since he and DI Adams had crashed through the door. Miriam hiccoughed again, rather loudly.

"Now, look," DI Collins said to Jasmine. "Don't take on. I'm not going to get him in trouble. We all bring stories home now and then. But this is an active investigation, and it's just not acceptable. If he really can't help telling you, you need to keep it quiet, alright?"

Jasmine looked up, her eyes red-rimmed and hectic patches on her cheeks. "You really won't get him in trouble?"

"Not this time. But one day it'll come back to bite him. Remember that. Now," he looked around the room. "You ladies know everything that goes on in this place. Anything you want to share with me?"

Nervous mutterings spread around the room, and various unrelated titbits of gossip were hesitantly offered up, everyone looking like they were picking their words very carefully indeed. Mortimer took a deep breath, taking the chance while the inspector was distracted to shift his legs a little. He seemed to have been trying to grab the stone floor, and he had cramp in his paws. As the discomfort eased, he became aware that Beaufort was trembling next to him. He tried to carefully peer around to see the High Lord's face without letting his firmly grey snout drift over the red carpet. Beaufort scuffled a bit, still shaking, and now Mortimer could see that Primrose was licking the old dragon's face eagerly, head butting him as he tried to stay out of range. He couldn't be shaking with rage, could he? Was he trying to resist incinerating the silly thing, or eating it? That wasn't like Beaufort at all, but the dog truly was a horribly annoying creature— The High Lord sniffled, and suddenly Mortimer was back in the dark of the Christmas market two years ago, watching Beaufort's dog costume go up in flames.

"Oh, *no*," he whispered, and DI Adams glanced over her shoulder, giving him a fierce shushing look. "*Allergic*," he hissed, tipping his head toward Beaufort, and she dropped her plate and lunged for the dog, sending her cup spinning across the carpet in a spray of tea.

She grabbed Primrose and scooped her up (rather fearlessly, Mortimer thought) while the dog whined and wriggled and strained to get back to the dragons.

"Adams?" DI Collins said, and Mortimer felt Beaufort take a shuddering breath.

"Loo," DI Adams said. "The dog. I think it needs the loo. To go out, I mean."

"Oh," he said, and she gave him an enormous and very unconvincing smile.

"Shall we take her out?" she asked.

"What?"

"Will you show me where the door to the back garden is?"

"Have you adopted that dog?"

"No, no, just if you come with me—"

"Adams, I rather think Mrs Shaw—"

There was a sudden burst of heat next to Mortimer, accompanied by a resounding "*AHHH-chooo!*"

THE ROOM WAS VERY, very still for a moment, then DI Adams said, "I'm terribly sorry. My hay fever seems to be playing up." She sniffed pointedly, but in Mortimer's opinion she didn't sound like she could carry off a dragon sneeze. Miriam gave another strangled hiccough, one hand still over her mouth.

"It's December," DI Collins said slowly. He still had a Christmas cookie halfway to his mouth and was looking at DI Adams with something like wonder.

"It's the Christmas tree?"

"Jasmine, please take Primrose out before she bites the detective inspector," Alice said, and DI Adams looked down at the dog in alarm. Primrose had her teeth bared, and was regarding the inspector's arm rather hungrily. Jasmine rushed to DI Adams, and the inspector shoved the dog at her. Mortimer watched as the DI carefully wiped her hands on her legs, taking a moment to investigate the back of her trousers. As far as he could see, they seemed to be intact. Beaufort had his paws over his nose, and his shoulders were hitching as he tried to hold another sneeze in.

"Are you sure you're alright?" DI Collins asked.

"Yes, fine." DI Adams picked up her discarded cup. "Ah, what time does the post office shut? We should really head over there. Don't want to miss it."

"I guess."

She sidled out of the room, as if still not entirely sure she wasn't missing half her trousers. Alice looked at DI Collins and said, "Why don't you get the car started? If she's coming down with a cold it's going to be no good her getting into a chilly car."

"Well—" he looked at his half-finished tea.

Gert hauled herself off the sofa and took DI Collins' plate, which still had a piece of Christmas cake on it. He clutched his cookie and watched it go mournfully.

"Off you go," she said. "We'll send her out with a Tupperware."

"Um," DI Collins said, then Carlotta did something that Mortimer didn't quite see, but which sent the inspector lunging out of his seat. "Yes," he said, while Carlotta grinned broadly and Gert scowled at her. "Yes, we'll be off, then. Thanks for the hospitality, ladies. Let me know if anything comes up, Auntie Miriam?"

"Of course," she said, and padded out into the hall with him in tow, hiccoughing regularly.

There was a long, thin moment, while they waited to hear the door close, then Teresa, who'd been peering out the window, said, "He's gone!"

Beaufort let his breath out in an agonised whoosh that set an abandoned paper napkin alight, and Mortimer scampered to grab it before Miriam's poor abused carpet suffered any more damage. The High Lord rubbed his snout wildly with both paws, then sat back on his haunches and grinned.

"Well," he said. "Nicely handled, ladies."

Mortimer didn't want to know what a badly handled encounter with the police would look like. Plus Beaufort seemed to have forgotten that there was a possibly singed detective inspector still in the house somewhere.

He picked up DI Adams' abandoned mince pie with a heavy sigh and sat back down on the hearth to eat it. Well, no point it going to waste.

9

ALICE

"All in one piece," Alice announced. She'd found DI Adams in the kitchen, trying to examine the back of her trousers without taking them off. "Although the hem does look a little charred."

"Fantastic," DI Adams muttered. "I just bought these."

Alice looked at the coffee stains splattering the lower legs and said, "It looks like they've had a bad day."

"You could say that." The inspector sighed, rather deeply for such small matters as stained trousers, in Alice's opinion. "Look, do you have anything to tell me? Do I need to come back?"

"No, Detective Inspector. At the moment we have nothing." Except maybe the silver Audi, but she still wasn't entirely sure that had actually been the car she'd glimpsed through Miriam's window earlier. It had been vanishing around the corner when she spotted it. Plus, it was a small village. Anyone could have bought a new car, and she just happened to keep spotting it.

DI Adams put her hands in her trouser pockets and gave Alice a look that was designed to extract confessions. "Look," she said, keeping her voice low. "I have said that if the dragons find out anything from their side – i.e. the not-human side – that's fine. But I don't want them or you poking around in anything else. I don't want to find myself looking for missing W.I. members as well as missing postmen."

"Understood," Alice said, returning the look calmly. The thing with lying, she had always believed, is that you must be absolutely sure it's for a good cause, and entirely necessary. And you must know all your tells. Alice knew hers, and not one of them showed.

"I'm serious," DI Adams said.

"I do understand, Detective Inspector."

"I will not hesitate to charge you with either withholding evidence or obstruction of justice, particularly if it's the only way to keep you safely out of this case."

Alice just raised her eyebrows slightly. She had plucked them only that morning, and DI Adams frowned and patted her own as if to make sure they hadn't become suddenly unruly.

"Both," the DI said. "I'll charge you with *both* if I have to."

"I'm sure you won't have to," Alice said. "Now, can I offer you and Colin some cake to take with you?"

"I don't want cake, I want to know I'm not going to get a call about you going missing."

"Oh, no danger of that," Alice said. "But I rather think Colin would like cake. I think Carlotta gave him a bit of a fright."

"Alice—"

"How about a coffee to go? That would be nice, wouldn't it? I'm sure there'll be some takeaway cups from the market lurking around somewhere."

DI Adams ran her hands over her tightly bound hair and shook her head. "I'm going to the loo. Then I'm leaving before anything else happens to my trousers." She stalked out of the kitchen, brushing past Miriam, who gave an alarmed *hic* and ducked away as if she thought the DI might grab her and shake her like a kitten.

"Miriam, dear, do you have any of those paper cups with the lids left over?" Alice asked.

From the hall rose a sudden volley of angry yaps, followed by a growl and some very broad and distinctly non-posh cursing.

"Someone get this bloody dog off my trousers!" DI Adams bellowed, and Alice winced.

PRIMROSE WAS EVENTUALLY REMOVED from the by-now very irate inspector's trousers, leaving behind several holes and a small tear. DI Adams stomped out the door with two Tupperwares of cake under her arm, joining a bemused-looking DI Collins in his car. Alice didn't think that the trip back to Skipton was going to be particularly pleasant. Neither of them looked very happy.

"Is your hand alright, Miriam?" Jasmine asked in a small voice. The W.I. had regrouped in the living room, cradling fresh cups of tea and, in a few cases, more mulled wine. The atmosphere was no longer festive, and the excited chatter had given way to an anxious quiet. Primrose had, by general agreement, been banished to the kitchen. Infuriated yaps drifted into the hall.

"It's fine," Miriam said, waving her bandaged finger in the air to prove it. She had finally stopped her nervous hiccoughing. "Just a little nip. It was the shock more than anything."

"I really do feel terrible."

"Oh, don't. She was just overexcited."

Alice raised her eyebrows but didn't comment, and looked at Beaufort to see what the High Lord thought of that. The High Lord, however, was occupied with licking out a bowl of eye-wateringly sweet and strong eggnog that Pearl had brought with her.

"Marvellous," he declared, setting the bowl down. "Just the ticket. So, ladies, what's next?"

"Next?" Miriam asked blankly.

"Next," Alice said. "The show must go on, yes?"

"The show?" Rosemary frowned at her cake. "I thought we were just doing a dinner. Last year's show wasn't terribly successful."

Alice grimaced. "Not terribly successful is the understatement of the year, if not the decade. I don't know what I was thinking, agreeing to a tap-pantomime of Les Misérables."

"It sounded good in principle," Miriam said, then gave an awkward little grin when everyone stared at her. "Well, maybe not, now I think about it."

"Anyway, we're not talking about that sort of show," Alice said. "We're talking about finding the missing postmen and tracking down these monsters who are counterfeiting Mortimer's baubles."

"Oh, we should have told the police about the baubles!" Jasmine exclaimed. "I'll tell Ben."

"You will not," Alice said, then sighed when Jasmine looked down at her cup with colour rising in her cheeks. "I mean, it's best not to."

"But why not?" the younger woman ventured, not looking up.

"Because if there are dragons or other Folk involved, then we can't be tattling to the police or drawing attention to it. It's too risky."

"Plus there's the Watch to consider," Beaufort said. "If they get wind of it, there'll be all sorts of trouble. And if the police know, the Watch will know. They've got spies everywhere."

Jasmine looked up finally. She was still a little pink, but her voice was firm. "But Detective Inspector Adams knows. And she hasn't told anyone else."

"DI Adams isn't necessarily an illustration of the police as a whole," Alice said. "Nor is Ben," she added quickly, when Jasmine opened her mouth to protest. "Others may be rather quicker to talk about things, and the next thing you know there'll be reporters and all sorts sticking their noses in." *And not long after that will come the government authorities,* she thought. *And that will be the end of everything.*

"Anyway," Beaufort said. "The inspector told us to stick to Folk stuff while she sticks to human stuff, and baubles are Folk stuff. She can't argue with that."

"Besides, she'll be all tied up with paperwork," Gert added. "The police are always all about the whole paperwork thing."

Carlotta circled the room with the mulled wine. "We'll keep this in the family," she said. "Just like in the old country."

Rosemary snorted. "You're from Manchester."

Carlotta glared at her, and ignored her empty glass. "My heart is Italian."

"Did you get it at the corner shop?"

"Just because you don't care about your heritage—"

"Ladies," Alice said, and they subsided. "Listen, Jasmine and I have ordered a bauble and a boat, respectively. Mail still seems to be getting to us, it's just getting out that's the issue. Hopefully we'll get them in the next day or so, then maybe we'll know a little more."

"It's just not right," Mortimer said. He'd shed two scales on the hearth and seemed to have got his appetite back. Having finished his mince pies, he was steadily eating his way through a plate of overcooked brownies that Alice assumed were Jasmine's. Even given the fact that they were dark chocolate, they looked somewhat scorched. "Stealing designs like that. We should report *them* to the Watch. Or get Detective Inspector Adams to lock them up. Or throw them in the duck pond and let the geese attack them." He took another brownie.

"That's the spirit, lad," Beaufort said cheerfully.

"What about the other orders?" Miriam asked. "I've got eighteen orders to fill tomorrow, and I need to replace the ones that were stolen today. Where do I send them from? *Do* I send them?"

"Of course we send them," Alice said. "We can't let our

customers down. Mortimer, do you have enough boats and baubles to replace the ones we've lost?"

"Yes," he said, around a mouthful of brownie. "I'll just need to check we have the right ones."

"Alright. I'll arrange a DHL pickup for tomorrow afternoon, and we'll send out all the orders at once. It's the safest option. The way things are going, who knows if Royal Mail will even be able to get someone to come collect post tomorrow."

"I know I wouldn't do it," Gert said. "Damn risky business, being a postman around here."

"It's not right," Mortimer said again, to no one in particular. "All that work, and people just take them without even a by-your-leave. Stolen goods and black-market scales, and it shouldn't be allowed. It shouldn't!" He frowned at the empty plate. "And now I've gone and eaten all the brownies. I'm so sorry!"

Rose patted his shoulder. "It's quite alright, Mortimer. You need to keep your strength up."

"I suppose," he said, and huddled down with his chin on his paws.

Carlotta found a plate with a few pieces of shortbread left on it and placed it in front of Mortimer, then said, "So what do the rest of us do?"

"What you're good at," Alice said. "Talk to people. Find out anything you can about anyone who's been maybe a little too interested in the baubles, or might suddenly have a lot of presents to dispose of. Anything out of the ordinary." She paused, considering, then added, "This may be nothing, but has anyone noticed a new silver Audi about the place?"

The women exchanged glances. Beaufort was watching her with interest, and Mortimer was nibbling a shortbread disconsolately.

"Can't say I have," Gert said. "You notice the plates? My

nephew's sister-in-law's cousin's partner works at the DVLA. I could run it past him."

Alice could never understand how Gert kept all these in-laws and cousins straight. She shook her head. "YC18, but I didn't get the rest."

"New, then, with the 18," Gert said.

"And local," Jasmine said, plucking at the carpet. "Y is Yorkshire, C is Leeds."

"Is that so," Alice said, smiling. "Well done, Jasmine. As I say, it may just be a visitor, or someone's got a new car. But I've seen it a few times, I think."

There was a quiet moment while everyone considered this, then Pearl said, "Right, then. When do we meet up again?"

"Let's say 10 a.m., day after tomorrow. Any volunteers to host?"

"Come to mine," Priya said. "But you can leave that dog behind, Jasmine. I don't want it frightening my cats."

"She wouldn't—"

"Nowhere with cats," Beaufort said. "Anyone who doesn't have cats?"

"Alice, you don't," Miriam said.

"I seem to have acquired one," she replied.

"Why would you do that *now?*" Miriam demanded.

"I didn't really seem to have much choice in the matter."

"No one ever has a choice when it comes to cats," Mortimer said. He'd eaten three biscuits and was trying not to look at the others.

"What's wrong with cats?" Priya demanded. "My cats are perfectly lovely."

"I'm sure they are," Alice said, "but it seems they're not to be trusted."

"They're really not," Beaufort said, and launched into an explanation of the Watch while the ladies of the Women's Institute listened with rapt attention, *ooh*-ing in all the right places. Alice half-listened, but it was nothing more than Beaufort had said before, about the cats being the police force of the Folk, so to speak. Or the border guards might be more accurate. Mostly she watched Gert. She didn't suspect her, exactly, but the big woman hadn't volunteered anything about the side market she had going with Amelia. Alice didn't want to come out and ask her in front of everyone else, but she decided she'd have a little talk with Gert, sooner rather than later. Mortimer said that Amelia was supplying Gert with baubles and jewellery, which was harmless enough, but maybe someone in Gert's complicated and occasionally shady family had got wind of it and decided to get themselves involved.

Although that didn't explain the exploding baubles. That suggested someone was making their own. For which you needed some sort of magical, and likely dragonish, partner.

THE MEETING BROKE up not long after, the women making their way home through the darkening streets with their depleted plates of goodies, sharing cars or walking, and all of them checking warily for spying cats and lurking silver Audis. Priya had been very upset, and even when Beaufort had assured her that not all cats belonged to the Watch it hadn't helped. She appeared to be most bothered by the idea that her cats tended to follow her into the loo.

"But what are they *doing?* How does that help their intelligence efforts?" She paused, then added, "And I clean their litter box. How are they so smart but still need the litter box?"

Alice thought of having to go outside for the loo in winter, and thought that cats were likely just as smart as they feared. "It's probably best if you don't let on you know," she said. "We don't want them wondering how you found out."

"I'll never look at them the same way," Priya said, pulling her coat on. "And I'm never letting them in the loo with me again."

Pearl, waiting for her on the path, smiled and said, "It doesn't surprise me. They always look like they're up to something, cats."

Alice agreed and waved them off, then went back to the living room. As was befitting of a Women's Institute gathering, the cups were already gathered and washed, the plates put away, the crumbs swept up. Only the two dragons and a very anxious-looking Miriam remained. Mortimer looked faintly queasy, and had gone a strange yellowish green colour. Alice clapped her hands together briskly.

"Well? Shall we go?"

"Go?" Miriam repeated blankly. "Go where?"

"To have a look at the place the van was found," Alice said, frowning at her. "Jasmine found it, remember?"

"But it's a crime scene."

"The police will be long gone by now."

"I still think Mortimer and I should just fly over," Beaufort said. "There's no sense you ladies going out in the cold and damp."

"We won't melt," Miriam said, looking like she'd rather not disagree, but unable to help herself. "We *ladies* are just fine."

Beaufort frowned. "I have a feeling I said something wrong."

"I don't feel very well," Mortimer whispered. "Could *I* stay here, out of the cold and damp?"

"Nonsense," Alice said. "You'll feel much better with a bit of fresh air. And Beaufort, I know you mean well, but we can decide what's best for us ourselves."

"I don't think the car is such a good idea," Mortimer said. "I really feel quite poorly."

"Those brownies were a bit iffy," Beaufort said. "Even for me."

Mortimer groaned, holding his stomach, and Alice sighed. She wasn't quite sure what dragon vomit would do to the upholstery of her car, and she didn't really want to find out.

"Come on," she said. "I'll open a window and you can stick your head out. Just tell me if you think you're going to be sick, alright?"

Mortimer nodded miserably, and she led them out into the chilly day, Miriam wrapped in an enormous red and orange woollen poncho and not looking much happier than Mortimer.

ALICE TRIED to drive a little more conservatively than usual, taking bends gently and not accelerating quite so hard on the occasional straight. Even so, Miriam was clutching the door handle with white knuckles, and Mortimer was hanging half out of the window making uncomfortable groans. He ducked every time they saw another car, then scrambled to shove his head into the fresh air again. It wasn't an auspicious start to the investigation.

"Not far now," Alice said, as Mortimer puddled back onto the seat while they passed a mud-splattered van going in the opposite direction.

"That's okay," Mortimer said. A little blue had crept back onto his snout, displacing the sickly yellow-green. "I think I'm feeling a bit better."

"That's the ticket," Beaufort said cheerfully. "Some fresh air always helps."

"I suppose." Mortimer burped loudly, and covered his snout with his paws, the blue draining away again. "I'm *so* sorry!"

Miriam laughed. "It's okay, Mortimer. Shows you enjoyed your meal."

"It does? That's a little odd."

Alice snorted, and flicked the indicator on. "That's one explanation. The other is that Jasmine put about a cup of baking soda in those brownies, from the bit I tasted."

Beaufort leaned between the seats and peered out the windscreen as the car started to slow. "Is this it? Where the postmen were taken?"

"Somewhere around here," Alice said, and a moment later they saw yellow and black tape flashing bright against the grey stone walls of the lane. She pulled in just beyond the lay-by, and stopped to let Miriam climb out before she nestled the car in as close to the wall as she could. She didn't put the hazards on. It was quiet enough around here, and she didn't want to draw any attention to them.

The dragons tumbled out, Mortimer looking better but still burping with painful regularity. Alice wasn't too sure she liked that. Dragon burps seemed a little fiery, and she hoped he'd be done with them by the time they got back in the car.

"It's empty," Miriam announced, from the edge of the crime tape.

"Did you think they'd leave the van here for everyone to gawk at?" Alice asked.

"Well, no." Miriam's nose was pink in the fading light. "I just thought there'd be – something."

They stared at the empty gravel of the lay-by, too rough for tyre tracks, and Alice patted Miriam's shoulder. "You're absolutely right," she said quietly, wondering where the postmen were now, and who had them, and if they were even alive. "It does feel like there should be something."

"Well," Beaufort said. "We'd best take a look." He slipped under the tape with his wings close to his back and padded across the rough gravel, heavy head swinging and golden eyes collecting the last light of the day. Mortimer gave a final burp then followed him, and they circled the area like scaly bloodhounds, peering over the wall into the field beyond, splashing through small puddles and examining the weeds.

Alice beckoned Miriam to follow her, and they went to lean against the wall at the edge of the lay-by, watching the dragons work. Alice was cold all the way through. She hadn't been dressed to be outdoors when she arrived at Miriam's that morning, and driving all the way here with the window open hadn't helped. She hugged her arms around her, trying to ignore the gnawing discomfort in her knuckles, and they waited. A car flashed past without slowing, and the dragons didn't look up. They were faint enough when people were standing still. It would be terrible luck indeed if someone managed to see them from a car.

She was almost ready to admit defeat and suggest to Miriam that they get in the car and turn the heater on when Beaufort and Mortimer came back, a dispirited droop to their wings.

"No luck?"

"It's too muddled," Beaufort said. "There's fear, from when the postman was attacked, and the excitement of the police that found the van. I think one was Jasmine's husband. He always smells a little puzzled, like burned eggs."

Alice wondered why puzzlement would smell of burned eggs, but put it aside for now. "Nothing off the attackers?"

"Nothing. Just excitement and fear."

"If they were flying," Mortimer said with a hesitant look at Beaufort, "the smell would disperse quickly. It wouldn't have a chance to sink into the ground."

Beaufort *humph*-ed, and looked at his paws. "Quite true, lad. Quite true."

No one said anything for a moment, then Alice said, "Well. We've found out all we can here. Let's get everyone home."

It was a quiet ride back to Toot Hansell, and Alice dropped the dragons at the edge of the village, pulling into a gap in front of a farm gate, where they could take flight unnoticed. It was already all but full dark, and she uncharacteristically wished the winter would hurry up and be done. The long nights seemed too full of unpleasant possibilities.

"We'll find them," she said to the dragons. "I have a plan for the DHL delivery."

Beaufort perked up immediately. "A plan?"

"Yes. I'll show you tomorrow when you bring the baubles down." She waved them off, Mortimer not looking very comforted, and pulled back onto the road.

"A plan?" Miriam said.

"Of course. One must always have a plan."

She took by Miriam's silence that the younger woman didn't entirely agree.

SHE DROPPED Miriam off before she went to Gert's. She both wanted to be able to talk to Gert alone, and to give Miriam a little break. The younger woman did try, but she was maybe not the best at the careful art of informal interrogation.

Gert didn't look surprised when she opened the door in purple jogging bottoms and an ancient sweatshirt advertising an AC/DC tour. She just said, "Come on in," and led Alice through to the kitchen.

The same voice called from the living room, "Who 'tis, Gertie?"

"Just one of the girls."

"Right you are." The volume on the TV went up, and Gert closed the kitchen door behind them.

"Drink?" she said.

"It feels like that sort of day," Alice said. She was only just starting to feel warm again, and Gert's kitchen was delightfully cosy and full of the smell of curry. Gert took two tumblers from a corner cupboard and a whisky bottle from a shelf crowded with chipped porcelain figurines and tacky souvenirs. She sat down across the table from Alice and poured them both a generous measure, and they clinked glasses solemnly.

"You want to know about Amelia's baubles, I take it," Gert said.

"It's the only other source of scales we know of."

"That's fair." Gert took a sip of whisky and rolled it in her mouth for a moment before swallowing. "I don't get any unworked ones. Amelia wanted to keep it all quiet, but she was worried that if there wasn't some outlet, dragons would start getting ideas about trying to set up their own trade. So I buy blankets or cushions or piercings or whatever they want, and she makes me baubles and boats and gliders and so on for the kids and grandkids. I've got fourteen grandkids now, you know? We're all getting together on Boxing Day. Rented a hall down Manchester and everything. It's going to be wonderful."

Alice thought it sounded horrifying, but she made a pleased expression and said, "No one could have got hold of the baubles and passed them on to someone?" *Or gone into business themselves,* she added to herself. Gert's family had some interesting elements.

"Not unless they've been under my tree. I mean, I wouldn't put it past Angie, but no. No one's been up here. And that Amelia's got her head on straight. I don't think she's dealing with anyone else."

Alice didn't think so either, and she sipped her whisky with a sigh, letting the heat spread in her chest. "Piercings?" she said after a moment.

"Quite the market for it among the younger dragons, apparently. Nail polish, too."

"Well. The things you learn." Alice finished her drink and got up. "You'll let me know if you hear anything?"

"You know I will."

Alice nodded, and made her way out. She hadn't really thought Gert had anything to do with it, but sometimes you had to tick all the boxes, just so you knew they were ticked.

THERE WAS no silver Audi outside Gert's, or on the roads home, but the cat was sitting at her door when she walked up the path. He examined her critically.

"You could go back to Gert's, you know," she said, opening the door. "I'm sure you'll learn just as much there."

He trotted in with his kinked tail held high, heading straight for the kitchen. Alice watched him go, then shook her head and pulled the door closed again. She didn't have any tuna left. She was going to have to go to the shop. She trudged back to the car, wondering why she was going shopping for an unwelcome cat that wasn't even hers.

She figured it had something to do with the powers of the Watch.

10
MIRIAM

The next day dawned clear, the clouds finally lifted, the thin winter sun not offering much heat but flushing the fells, painting the fields gold, and sparkling on the waterways of Toot Hansell. Miriam was glad to see the sun back. Somehow kidnappings and exploding baubles felt much less likely, much less *immediate* with the sun out. She put a fresh batch of mince pies in the oven (the trick was to make the pastry ahead of time and keep it in the freezer, then doctor up some bought mincemeat so that it tasted like homemade. It was the only way to keep up with a dragonish appetite for mince pies) and mixed up a ginger cake. That done, she started assembling boxes for the baubles, checking the windows impatiently, and wondering when exactly the dragons were going to turn up.

MIRIAM HAD COOKED four batches of mince pies and the ginger cake was cooling on the rack and spicing the air by the time Alice arrived. There were brown boxes and recycled packing paper strewn across the kitchen table, and a sticky flower of tangled tape hanging from the counter, plus her pen jar had been knocked over and there were markers and pencils and leaking Bics all over the floor. She'd also somehow forgotten to do the breakfast dishes. She felt the tops of her ears grow hot as she led Alice in.

"I thought I'd get ahead."

"How many boxes have you made up?" Alice asked, surveying the mess.

"Um. I think about fifty." Which was a small untruth. She'd stopped counting at fifty. There was something deeply comforting about putting the boxes together, and she'd just kept going. They were stacked six deep around the table, and Miriam's skirt had caught them as she went to answer the door, strewing a dozen or more across the floor. She collected them hurriedly, the heat spreading to her cheeks.

"How many do we have going out today?" Alice asked.

"Maybe thirty altogether," Miriam mumbled, trying to stack the escaped boxes and knocking more over.

"Well, then. We're ahead for next time." Alice put the kettle on and took some mugs from the cupboard. "Where shall we store them?"

"Spare room?"

"Excellent." Alice collected an armload of boxes and headed into the hall just as Miriam spied three scaly heads bobbing a little awkwardly up the garden path. Beaufort led the way with Amelia and Mortimer trailing behind him, all of them walking carefully on their hind legs with big baskets clasped to their chests, straps hooked over their shoulders where they wouldn't interfere with their wings.

"They're here!" Miriam shouted, dropping the boxes and rushing to open the door. "Oh, I was so worried you weren't going to arrive in time! The van's meant to be here in an hour!"

"Do calm down, Miriam," Alice said, coming back into the

kitchen and picking up more boxes. "There's plenty of time. We'll make short work of it with two of us."

"Five," Amelia pointed out as she staggered in the door, using her tail for balance and leaving muddy footprints across the stone flags. Miriam and Alice exchanged glances.

"Two with hands," Alice clarified, carrying the boxes out of the kitchen, and Amelia shrugged.

"Up to you," she said, and put her basket down, helping herself to a mince pie.

"Morning, morning," Beaufort said, struggling to get out of his basket. "Blasted thing. I think it's caught."

Miriam pulled the big teapot down while Mortimer helped the High Lord out of the basket. A shoulder strap had somehow got caught over one of his spines, and now he had a paw trapped in it and was looking slightly panicked.

"Mortimer!"

"I'm doing it, just hold still."

Beaufort grumbled something about High Lords not being pack horses, but held still as Mortimer fiddled with the straps. The younger dragon looked tired, and his scales had a distinctly grey cast to them.

"Did you find anything at home, Beaufort?" Miriam asked.

"No, nothing our end," he said, finally escaping from the straps. "Thanks, lad. Horrible contraptions, those things."

"S'okay," Mortimer mumbled.

"Are you alright, Mortimer?" Miriam asked.

"Fine," he said, and started unpacking the basket with a weary slump to his shoulders.

Amelia eyed the cake. "This looks nice. Mortimer, have you seen this? And all the mince pies?"

"I guess." He was frowning at the baskets as if he'd forgotten something.

Amelia stuck her tongue out at him, but he still wasn't looking.

Alice raised her eyebrows at Miriam as she came back into the room, and Miriam shrugged.

"So, anything new down here?" Beaufort asked

"Nothing so far," Alice said, handing Amelia a plate and shooing her away before she could try cutting the cake. "But hopefully we'll know more tomorrow. The scouts are out."

Miriam sat down at the table and started lighting the baubles while the tea brewed, setting them floating about the kitchen. It was their final quality check, which had become part of the routine ever since that one bauble that Mortimer had thought blossomed into a perfectly nice floral design, but which had made Miriam blush and giggle so much that she'd had to call Alice for a second opinion. Alice hadn't blushed or giggled (Miriam couldn't imagine Alice doing either of those things, actually), but she'd given a surprisingly deep, rusty chuckle and suggested that there was probably a special market for such things, but it wasn't one the W.I. could really be a part of. There hadn't been any more with problematic shapes since, but it wasn't worth sending them away unchecked. Besides, Miriam had to admit that this was her favourite part. She loved the magic of it, setting one bauble after another free to dance softly across the room, blooming into exotic flowers and butterflies and birds of paradise. It made a bright day even brighter.

Alice had filled the sink, and now she floated the boats in it one by one. Dry, they looked like paper boats or little hats folded from the hard, glossy dragon scales. As soon as the water surrounded them, though, they unfurled masts and sails, growing and transforming into sloops and ketches, schooners and barquentines, strung about with the fine threads of their rigging and flying pennants from their masts. Miriam thought they were some of Mortimer's finest work.

"It's most frustrating," Beaufort said. "None of the Cloverlies know anything about it, obviously, and last night I even tried talking to a few dwarfs, as well as the tiddy uns at the lake. They couldn't help, and I'm not certain what our next move should be. We've got to be quite careful about our investigations. We don't want to tip the wrong Folk to what we're doing here."

"That makes it sound rather sinister," Miriam said, watching a bauble bloom into a collection of hummingbirds. "Oh, this is lovely!"

"I'm sure we'll find some leads," Alice said. "We'll just have to be persistent." She retrieved a boat from the sink, shaking off the last few water droplets while it shrank, then tucked it into a box and fetched another.

"Well, we did find out about the whole black market in scales thing," Mortimer said. "So that's always good to know."

"It's not exactly a *black market*," Amelia protested. "It's more of a, um, *side* market."

"Oh, well, that's fine then. If it's a *side* market."

She glared at him. "You're just sore because you didn't think of it yourself."

"I'm *not!* That's so unfair. I taught you how to make everything, and you just—"

"Oh, stop being so ridiculous! We'd never have enough scales if it wasn't for me! We wouldn't have enough *baubles* if it wasn't for me!" Amelia had gone a dangerous puce colour, and Miriam moved a couple of boxes out of the way, just in case.

Mortimer was still pointedly not looking at Amelia, but his colour wasn't right, either. "Oh, really? You think I couldn't do just as well on my own?"

"Now, you two," Beaufort said. "We've been over this more than enough."

"Beaufort, you know it's not that simple," Mortimer snapped. "We've already said that this *side market* could be connected to the missing postmen and the counterfeit baubles."

"Mortimer!" Miriam exclaimed. "You're not accusing Amelia—"

"No! No, Amelia, I'm not—" Mortimer flushed yellow, his front paws raised. "No, I really didn't mean that!"

But Amelia had gone very pale, blending into the stone flags as she stared at Mortimer with wide eyes.

"Well, that was a bit off, lad," Beaufort said.

"Mortimer, apologise!" Miriam exclaimed, dropping the baubles and hurrying over to crouch next to Amelia. She put one hand awkwardly on the young dragon's shoulder, discovering that it was quite hard to comfort a dragon. They were very *spiny*.

"Amelia," Mortimer said, clutching his paws to his chest. "Amelia, I – I haven't slept, and I know it's no excuse, and …" He trailed off, looking around the kitchen desperately.

Amelia just shook her head and looked at the floor.

"Well, now." Alice had been pouring tea and ignoring the drama, and now she turned around with the teapot still in her hand. "No one's accusing Amelia of any wrongdoing, other than maybe going a little bit behind Mortimer's back, are they?"

"No! No, exactly." Mortimer still had his paws up, looking not unlike a large scaly meerkat. "I just – it came out all wrong. I'm so sorry, Amelia, really."

"But it is exactly what's happened, isn't it?" Alice said, going back to pouring the tea. Miriam stared at her, the kitchen suddenly far too hot. Was Alice actually accusing the Cloverlies of being behind all this? "I don't mean that Amelia has done anything wrong," Alice continued. "But someone else has." She set two mugs down on the table and looked at the others. "We're not really looking for other, non-Cloverly dragons, are we, Beaufort?"

"Well, now. That's a little hasty." But he didn't quite look at her.

"Dragon-scale baubles, scorched van, no scent because the attackers were flying. Beaufort, I know you don't want to think badly of your clan, but if you've been so secretive about our little trade agreement that none of the other Folk – none of the other dragons – know, I don't think we can get away from it being an inside job. At least partly, anyway. I imagine they need some human help for the eBay listing and so on." She handed Miriam a cup of tea, and Miriam took it with wide eyes. Alice made it sound so reasonable!

"I didn't like to admit to you that it was possible," Beaufort admitted. There was a softly ashamed yellow tinge to his scales. "The idea that a Cloverly dragon could be involved is just intolerable. But you're right. They're really the only ones who know."

There was a little, uncomfortable silence, then Miriam finally found her voice. "You do always say that Folk are just people, Beaufort. People do intolerable things all the time."

"This is true." Beaufort examined his mug. "But dragons are terribly old compared to most people. We should know better."

"I don't think age has got anything to do with it," Miriam said. "Anyone can be quite foolish or very wise."

There was another small silence, an easier one this time, and Alice handed out mince pies. Amelia didn't move.

"But the baubles," Mortimer said. "That's what I don't understand. Not the fact that they're stealing them, because that makes sense in a nasty way. But why are they making their own? They're not easy, you know. You need special tools, you need to get the charms just right—"

"Yes," Alice said. "And evidently they aren't getting them just right. I checked that eBay listing again, and they've had half a dozen more bad reviews. Someone's boat blew up so big that it smashed the bathtub. Who knows how many people haven't even tested them. It could be chaos on Christmas morning."

"I know I've already talked to the Cloverlies," Beaufort said, taking another mince pie. He'd regained his normal colours. "But it wasn't a proper interrogation. It didn't work very well. I think I should try a proper one."

"Beaufort, no," Mortimer and Amelia said together, and exchanged embarrassed looks. Mortimer hesitated, then slid his mince pies onto Amelia's plate. She gave him a most unpleasant stare, which made him flush an even deeper yellow. Her own pretty, deep red colour was starting to come back again though, which Miriam thought was good in more ways than one. She didn't like seeing the dragons falling out, and it was unnerving having a ghost dragon in your kitchen. She gave Amelia a final pat on the shoulder and sat down again.

"Why on earth shouldn't I?" Beaufort demanded. "If we're saying that it has to be a Cloverly, we need to deal with this!"

"Because it didn't go – it didn't go entirely well last time," Mortimer said cautiously.

"I admit the results weren't particularly useful, but I don't think I pushed hard enough." He scratched his chin. "Yes. I should have been firmer."

Miriam exchanged glances with Alice, wondering what a dragon interrogation looked like, and Mortimer said, "I'm not *quite* sure that was the problem."

"Well, I intend to resume my investigation," Beaufort said, sounding enormously satisfied. "I still don't think a Cloverly would be deliberately hurting anyone, but it's time to take this seriously. Someone must know something."

Mortimer took a mouthful of tea and helped himself to a new mince pie, chewing carefully before he took a deep breath. "Alright. Yes. I think we do need to try again. But can we do it subtly this time?"

"Well, I wasn't rude last time, if that's what you mean," Beaufort said. "I don't know what more I can do."

Mortimer sighed, and took two more mince pies. Miriam went back to lighting baubles, since the immediate crisis seemed to be over. Dragons investigating dragons felt rather safer than her investigating anyone. And less likely to result in arrest.

"So what do I do?" Amelia asked. "Should I stop with the scales?

Only I'm not sure that's a good idea. There's a real demand for blankets at the moment."

"You should carry on as normal, Amelia," Alice said. "But maybe see if you're not getting as many scales, or if there are certain dragons who aren't trading with you who were before."

"I still don't know how the group interrogation went wrong," Beaufort said. "I'm very disappointed in that Poirot fellow."

"I don't think it's meant to be an instructional show," Miriam observed. "Ooh, this is a new design." She cupped the bottom of a bauble that had just unfolded into something like a pirate galleon, all square sails on the mainmasts and little trysails on the bow. It was even adorned with a dragon figurehead.

"Ugh, that one shouldn't be in there," Mortimer said. "It doesn't work."

"It's lovely."

"It goes upside down as soon as you let it go. I couldn't get it quite right."

"That's a shame." Miriam released the bauble, and it bobbed in a stately manner across the kitchen, perfectly stable. It was so perfect and lifelike that she half-expected to see a swarm of tiny sailors scrambling up the rigging. "It looks like it works."

Mortimer blinked at it in surprise. "It kept capsizing."

"I fixed it," Amelia said, her eyes on the ship. "It was too pretty to throw away. It just needed ballast."

Mortimer's shoulders slumped, and the yellow rushed back, deepening to ochre as he muttered a thank you.

ANOTHER POT of tea and most of a ginger cake later (Miriam didn't even count the mince pies, just noted with some wonder how rapidly they were vanishing), the boxes were packed.

"Now, just to hope these ones don't go missing, right?" she said cheerfully. Things still felt a little unreal in the warmth of the kitchen, with the sun collecting in the windows.

"Don't even joke about it," Mortimer said. "I'll never catch up if we lose these ones too."

"We won't," Alice said, and lifted her handbag onto the table. She dug inside for a moment, then waved a little plastic packet at them. "This is going with them."

"What is it?" Beaufort asked, squinting.

"A GPS tracker. I'll attach it to one of the parcels, and if it goes anywhere it shouldn't, we'll know."

"A what, exactly?"

"It's like an electronic scent," Mortimer said, looking impressed. "Alice can follow it from her computer."

"My phone, actually," Alice said, and popped the tiny device out of its packaging. It was barely the size of her little fingernail. "Apparently, the battery should last for at least a week, so we'll have plenty of time to track it down."

"Where on earth did you get that?" Miriam asked.

"It's a good thing the post is still coming in," Alice replied, as she taped the tracking device carefully to one of the packages, hiding it in a fold in the paper where, Miriam imagined, no one would even notice it. "I ordered it online. Nasty little website, all full of things you can use to spy on your spouse. Seems rather a waste of time bothering if the relationship's at that point."

Miriam watched her smooth the paper down carefully and tape it in place, and wondered if she'd ever actually have the courage to ask Alice about her missing maybe-dead-maybe-not husband. She didn't think so.

"There," Alice said, giving the box a final pat. "Never even know it was there."

"Very clever," Miriam agreed, just as there was a sharp knock at the front door. She jumped up and hurried down the hall, already spying the yellow and red van blurred through the glass door panes. "It's DHL!"

"Perfect timing," Beaufort said cheerfully, then tucked his tail out of the way as Alice and Miriam hurried back and forth with the boxes, stacking them at the door while the driver ferried them out to the van. He accepted a mince pie and a slice of ginger cake happily, and drove off with his mouth full and one hand on the wheel. It was all over and done within five minutes, leaving the kitchen suddenly empty and full of drifting wisps of tape and packing paper.

Alice pulled her phone out and set it on the table, opening the tracking app while the others gathered around her. Amelia looked quite like herself again now, and Miriam noticed that Mortimer kept passing her mince pies and cake, so that was alright. She wasn't sure how dragons settled grievances, but she felt it was probably best that they weren't allowed to escalate. Certainly not in her kitchen.

"There we go," Alice said. "Look, he's off into town." Sure enough, a little green dot moved steadily down the map of the main road, then stopped outside the bakery.

"Well. After we gave him cake, too," Miriam said, hands on her hips, and they stared at the phone and the unmoving dot until the screen turned itself off.

"Well, that's not very exciting, is it?" Beaufort said.

"It does do the job, though." Alice turned the phone back on. The dot still sat outside the bakery.

"Maybe he stopped for coffee," Miriam said. The bakery doubled as a small deli, and there were a couple of little tables tucked in one corner. It had better coffee than the bookshop, but not such a nice smell.

"Following him would do the job, too," Beaufort said.

"Beaufort, we are not discussing this." Alice gave the High Lord a look that made Miriam squirm, and he puffed red smoke. "You're not running around the place following people. And on such a clear day, too. Absolute foolishness. Anyway, look. He's off again." The green dot moved down the road, then stopped in front of the butcher's.

"Well, that was enthralling."

Alice glared at Beaufort, but this time he just grinned, and after a moment she smiled back. "Alright. So it's not that exciting. But it does work. If anything happens to the parcels, we'll know."

"What're we going to do if it does go off-route?" Miriam asked.

"And how do we know what his route is?" Mortimer added.

Alice opened her mouth, then shut it again, looking very uncharacteristically at a loss. "Well. I don't exactly know what his route is," she admitted. "But we can find out where the DHL hub is, and if it doesn't go to that address for sorting, we'll know it's gone missing."

"And then?" Amelia asked.

"And then we see where it goes. We can go take a look at where it ends up from a distance, and decide whether to tell DI Adams or deal with it ourselves. It's the best we can do." Alice seemed to have recovered herself, and Miriam relaxed. She didn't like Alice looking doubtful. It was like waking up in the middle of the night to find your bedroom had been completely turned around, and now you were sleeping with your feet where your head should be and the dresser on the ceiling.

"More tea?" she suggested.

"More tea is always a good idea," Alice said.

"Let me know if it moves," Beaufort said, and curled himself up on the rug in front of the AGA, tucking his paws and tail in neatly like a large green cat, albeit a winged one that was smoking slightly. A moment later his breathing settled into soft, rumbling snores.

"I wish I could do that," Mortimer said sadly. "It takes me an hour and three meditation exercises to get off."

"There's your problem, then," Alice said. "Skip the meditation and have a hot toddy instead. Works for me every time."

"I'm not sure that's the healthiest advice," Miriam said, and collected the mugs. "Who's for more mince pies?"

MIRIAM SUPPOSED THAT, if you were actually driving the van, the life of a DHL driver was probably reasonably interesting. At least you weren't in an office or something, which had always seemed to her to be a most miserable way to pass the time. However, watching a DHL driver as represented by a little green blip on a phone screen was entirely uninteresting. Alice had plugged her charger in and put the screen to permanently on, leaving it propped up against the fruit bowl on the kitchen table. Once they'd stared at it for long enough that Miriam was starting to see floating green ghosts in her eyes even when she looked away, she went to find the playing cards. While Beaufort snoozed she and Alice tried to teach the two younger dragons how to play gin rummy, but quickly gave that up in favour of last card, which entailed less explanation. It still wasn't an entirely easy prospect given that the dragon's claws weren't ideal for holding cards, and they kept singeing them when they got overexcited. However, they caught on rather quickly, and there were already some quite literally heated exchanges going on.

"*Ha!* Pick up five, Mortimer."

"No – reverse!"

"Reverse back 'atcha!"

"Aw, Amelia!"

Miriam glanced at Alice, and they both smiled. The dragons seemed to have got past the side market problem, for the moment at least. Miriam supposed that there were always going to be problems, trying to bring a clan of old creatures into a modern world, one so soundly ruled by humans that the very existence of dragons wasn't even considered. But it was good for Mortimer to remember that he was neither the one controlling it, nor the one who had to *try* to control it. She sorted through her cards. "Pick up two, Amelia."

"Ha, no – pick up four, Mortimer."

"Where are you *getting* these?"

Miriam laughed as Mortimer struggled to pick up the cards, her gaze straying to their DHL blip.

"Miriam, your turn."

"Umm." She blinked, trying to be sure her eyes weren't just tired and playing tricks on her.

"Miriam?"

"Is it meant to be doing that?"

Alice jumped to her feet and snatched the phone up, giving it a quick shake as if she thought it might be a mistake. "Beaufort," she said sharply, and the old dragon uncurled with a scraping of scales, his eyes bright and wide awake. "I think we have something."

On the screen, the green blip had left the road and was racing across open country, heading west.

11

DI ADAMS

D I Adams made her escape from the nippy little dog, the dragons, and the ladies of the W.I., and wedged herself into the passenger seat of DI Collins' car, setting two Tupperware containers crammed with assorted cakes and biscuits on her lap. Her head was pounding. She wasn't sure if the headaches were due to the fact that she was still getting used to dragons, her brain and her eyes arguing over what they were seeing, or some sort of stress reaction to the Women's Institute, but she was going to start taking painkillers before she got here from now on. She dropped the cake boxes unceremoniously in the back seat, then fished in her bag for some Paracetamol. She swilled two of them down with a gulp of coffee from one of the paper takeaway cups Alice had handed her, burning the roof of her mouth.

"Alright?" DI Collins asked, taking a more cautious sip from his cup. It wasn't the best coffee DI Adams had tasted, but it made up for it by being impossibly hot. "There's water in the back."

"I'm fine." Or she would be once the painkillers kicked in.

"Big antihistamines."

"What?"

"Those tablets."

"Paracetamol. Bit of a headache."

"Not antihistamines?"

"No. Why?" Honestly, this was no better than being back with the W.I. Things really should have started making sense once they left Miriam's, shouldn't they?

"For your hay fever."

Oh. Right. "Once I'm away from whatever triggered it, I'm usually okay."

"Must make it hard at this time of year, being allergic to Christmas trees," DI Collins said, pulling out from between the parked cars and heading toward the centre of the village.

"Sometimes. It depends on the tree. They're not all as bad as that. And it might have been the incense. Or the candles."

"Allergic to a lot of things, aren't you?"

"I have sensitive nasal passages," she said, and wished she hadn't.

He snorted. "Whatever you say. Look, my aunt's a bit ditsy – she reckons she's some sort of psychic, and makes all these mad concoctions and so on – but she's pretty harmless."

"That was rather the conclusion I came to as well."

"The thing is, something seemed off. Did you notice that?"

Well, there were the two dragons in the room, she thought, and had to swallow an unexpected bubble of laughter. "I wouldn't have said so. Like I said, Ms Ellis always seems a bit nervous around me."

"Understandable," he said solemnly, then grinned. "No, more than that. Like they were all up to something."

The smile came easily this time. "Do you mean your special friends on the sofa, or just in general?"

He laughed. "Well, I think Carlotta did actually grab my bum to make me get up, but I can't prove it."

"It must be terrible for you, being plied with cake and adored."

"You didn't do badly on the cake yourself."

DI Adams glanced in the back seat at the well-packed Tupperwares. "Alright. Yes. The cake is wonderful."

"Bet you never got that in London."

"True." But she'd never had to deal with the Women's Institute
in London, either. Or dragons. Although there had been worse
things than dragons in London. She rubbed her forehead and
wondered how many things she hadn't seen, how many *creatures*
had watched her pass from the shadows, and she'd never even
imagined they existed. It wasn't a nice thought. It made the skin
crawl on the back of her neck.

"Sure you're alright, Adams?"

"Yeah." She dropped her hand, and watched the houses slipping
past, quiet and grey and lit from within like Christmas lanterns.

"It's probably a W.I. headache," DI Collins said. "I get them too."

THE VILLAGE SHOP/POST office smelt of microwaved soup and gave
them nothing further to go on. All the proprietor could tell them
was that the mail had been collected as usual, even though it had
been done by someone new, and no, the new driver hadn't seemed
worried or nervous.

"She was very nice," he said, rocking back in his creaking chair
behind the counter. He had tomato soup on his shirt. Well, hopefully it was tomato soup. DI Adams still harboured suspicions that
this place was far too nice. It was the sort of village where people
probably made sacrifices to ancient gods in their back gardens and
danced naked under the moon to ensure a good harvest. "I even
offered her a cup of tea, but she said she'd better not. I guess she
was worried about keeping to the schedule."

Or creeped out by you, DI Adams thought, examining the patchy
shelves and the Christmas decorations that had seen many better
days. He was probably harmless, but she couldn't help imagining

he did things like stir the tea with his finger, then lick it clean. He had that look.

Toot Hansell had held nothing back on the decorations for the cobbled village square. The little well in the centre was decked with sprays of holly and pine, and Christmas lights glittered on every lamp post. Someone had obviously ordered broad red ribbon in bulk, because even the rubbish bins were festooned with it. There was a big Christmas tree in the corner by the bookshop, daubed liberally with fake snow and crowded with oversized baubles and small Santa Clauses and faded rocking horses and tin men. It was also crowned with a bright red Wellington boot, for no reason DI Adams could see. She quite liked it.

They circled the village square clockwise, checking in at the hairdresser's, where the young man dyeing an elderly woman's hair purple, the elderly woman herself, and the woman playing solitaire on the front desk computer giggled a lot and were very eager to help DI Collins, if not DI Adams. He smirked all the way to the bakery with its little deli section, where DI Adams was given the last gingerbread man, which had a slightly wonky smile. He seemed slightly put out that he wasn't offered anything, so she broke it in two and handed him half wordlessly as they went to try the greengrocer's. There, they spoke to a big man with bright eyes and chapped red hands, who laughed on every second word. DI Adams thought he only needed a beard to be able to play Santa quite believably. But as friendly as everyone was, no one had seen anything out of the ordinary. No one thought either the usual postman nor his replacement had been acting odd.

In the dodgy pub, which looked almost appealing with a fire going and Christmas lights twinkling among the threadbare tinsel, they finally found some CCTV cameras. Well, one, overlooking the village square. The odds that it might show someone following the post van were ridiculously slim, but they didn't have anything else to go on. However, a few questions put to the owner, who looked like he sampled his wares thoroughly and regularly, soon determined that the camera wasn't actually connected to anything. So that was the end of that.

"I can't believe there aren't more cameras," DI Adams said as they left the pub and walked to a small tea shop with faded yellow gingham curtains in the windows. They clashed wildly with a jumble of red and green decorations piled on the sills. "None even in the square."

"Not exactly crime central around here," DI Collins said, opening the tea shop door and setting a little bell jangling. "I can't even remember the last time I was out here for work." It was hot and stuffy inside the tea room, and smelt of boiled beef and cabbage. DI Adams wrinkled her nose. He sounded so *happy* about it. God, but it must be boring. What had he been worried about earlier – stolen turkeys? I mean, what sort of job was that, looking for stolen turkeys? She sighed and took a moment to check her phone while he spoke to the small lady in enormous glasses behind the counter. She had a pile of crochet in her lap, and it looked a lot to DI Adams as if she'd crocheted not just all the chair cushions, but most of the decor in the place.

She had another missed call from DCI Temple, and there was a voicemail this time. She went outside to listen to it.

THERE WAS nothing more to be found in the bookshop, the butcher's, or the second pub, which was much nicer than the first. The menu sounded like it didn't come out of the freezer, either.

"Is that everywhere?" she asked DI Collins.

"There's another pub over by the church, and a little school on the way out of town."

"This place has three pubs but no chemist?"

"They've got the fountain of youth over there," he said, nodding to the little well. DI Adams knew there was a wooden winch system under its neat tiled roof, but it was hard to see much of anything beneath the weight of Christmas decorations it was wearing.

She looked pointedly at a very tall, very skinny man in an enormous puffer jacket tottering down the sidewalk in the company of a very small, very round man in an overcoat. Neither of them looked like they'd see their eighties again. "You sure about that?"

"Well, fountain of good health, then." He beeped the car open. "We'll drive the post route back, then you can go do something exciting with the rest of your day off. Like count paperclips or alphabetise your emails."

Day off. Yep. If she wasn't careful, she was going to have a lot of those. DCI Temple had wanted to know where the hell she was, because a patrol car had nabbed someone with a trunk full of electronics from the smash and grab. She was lead investigator on the case, and he needed her in the interview room. She'd put on a poorly voice and called him back, making up something about being hit with a stomach bug on her way to Chapel Allerton, and said that she was waiting to see a doctor, but couldn't really go far from the nearest loo. It made her cheeks hot even thinking about it, but it was the first thing she'd thought of. He'd *humph*-ed and told her to get in first thing in the morning, and she'd thought she was in the clear. Then he'd told her to bring a sick note from the doctor. So she wasn't quite sure how she was going to deal with that.

She took a last look around the village square, willing something to jump out at her, some place she hadn't seen before, even just an upstairs window with some local busybody leaning out of it and watching everything. Cases had been broken open on less than that. Instead, she found herself staring at the Christmas tree at the other side of the square. It seemed to have grown legs.

She squeezed the bridge of her nose and looked again. Yes.

There were five pairs of legs just visible under the lower limbs of the tree, and, as she watched, the branches at what would have been around eye level started to move. Was someone *climbing* the damn tree? But no - the legs hadn't moved. The branches stilled, then moved a little on the other side of the tree, where more of the legs were, knocking a bauble to the ground. She narrowed her eyes at the legs. They were very sensibly clad, and the feet sported a mix of hiking boots and wellies in cheerful colours.

"You've got to be kidding me," she mumbled.

"Are you getting in, Adams?" DI Collins demanded. "Only the heater's not doing much good while you've got the door open."

She shut the door and started across the square toward the tree, setting off a sudden flurry of movement in the branches. She stopped and watched as Priya, Teresa, Rose, Carlotta and Pearl scattered, waving to each other and calling out goodbyes rather too brightly, Priya stopping to grab the fallen bauble and shove it somewhat haphazardly back into the branches before hurrying off. They were all walking with great determination, and Carlotta almost bowled Rose to the ground as they collided trying to go down a side street at the same time.

DI Adams considered grabbing at least one of them to find out what they were up to, but her head gave a warning throb at the thought of it. She turned back and climbed into the warmth of Collins' silver Audi instead.

SHE WATCHED the slow roll of the farmland unfurl around them as they left Toot Hansell, the fells turning deep purples and greens as the last of the light faded. DI Collins hummed to himself, tapping his fingers on the wheel, and the car was warm and peaceful, an insulated pocket in the world protected from interfering dragons and problematic, tree-spying civilians and suspicious chief inspectors. DI Adams drifted, not quite dozing, lulled by the purr of the car and the warmth of her seat.

"You want to keep working this?"

"Sorry?" She blinked herself upright.

"You seem to be the only person who might have a bit of insight, so it works for me." He pointed at his phone, nestled in a cradle on the dash. "Put your number in there."

"You've got my card."

"Adams, I've got eight hundred and twenty-three cards at last count, and they're all in my desk drawer. I'll never find yours, and I don't want to go back to the W.I. alone. Please don't make me do that. Give me your phone number."

She snorted. "You accuse me of having boring hobbies, and you count business cards?"

"Fine, don't give me your number. But don't expect me to call you with updates when I can't find your card." He grinned. "And you won't have mine for when you have to deal with the W.I. again."

"I can handle the W.I.," she said, and picked up his phone. It wasn't entirely a lie. But she still didn't want him poking around this case without her about to run interference in the matter of dragons.

She looked up as she hit save, just in time to glimpse the lay-by flashing past, strung about with crime tape and looking dreary and uninviting.

"What the hell?" She twisted in her seat to look back, the damp and dying day making it hard to make much out.

"Ah, just walkers or busybodies," DI Collins said, not slowing. "We've got plenty of both. But the techs have been through, and if they missed anything the rain'll do for it tonight anyway. There's nothing for anyone to mess up."

"Right," she said. "Of course." And wished she'd been able to see just a little better, because it had looked awfully like the slim figure of Alice leaning against the wall, Miriam in some bizarre red and orange swaddling next to her, while two dragons prowled the shadows, barely glancing up at the car as it passed.

DI ADAMS LEANED back in her chair and regarded the man on the other side of the interview table. Interviews were rarely as interesting as they looked on TV or in books. She'd never had the chance to match wits with a master criminal, and she had a sneaking suspicion that most police never did. The majority of criminals she'd dealt with were either belligerent or taciturn or overconfident, but always uncooperative, and often with a poor grasp of just how much trouble they were in. And usually fairly scared underneath. This one was ticking each box in turn.

"So you have no idea how the stolen goods got in your car?"

"Nah. S'not mine."

"Even though your fingerprints are all over it."

"Well, I, like, looked at it when I found it, right?"

"Right." She sighed and checked her mug. It was empty. She'd told DCI Temple that she hadn't seen a doctor in the end, but had gone home and self-medicated with over-the-counter stuff, which had sort of got her around the sick note problem. He hadn't said anything, just scowled at her and muttered something about soft southerners as he walked away. She didn't know if that meant he believed her or not.

"You know, if you told me who else helped you with the smash, I could probably get the charges down to possession of stolen property."

She waited while he worked it out. His lips were moving like he was playing her words back to figure out what they meant. She checked her phone, but there was nothing from DI Collins. Which was a good thing, of course. She was struggling to keep her mind on things today. She was sure it had been Alice and Miriam and the dragons in the lay-by the afternoon before. Of course, it could also have been walkers out with two big dogs, given the poor light and the rain, and the fact that she had *expressly told* the W.I. and the dragons to stay out of things. Because that had worked so damn well last time.

"But," the man said, "I didn't know it was stolen. So, like, how can I be guilty if I didn't know it was stolen?" He grinned triumphantly, revealing startlingly white teeth.

"That will not work in court."

"Well, but, like, it might have been a present."

"Of tens of thousands of pounds of electronics?"

"I got friends."

"Sure you do," she said. "What're their names?"

"There's, like, Mike, and—" he stopped. "Hey. You're trying to trick me!"

"And somehow failing, which does not bode well for my day." She got up. "I'll let you think on it a bit longer. Decide by this afternoon, or I'll charge you with the whole damn lot."

"That's not *fair!*" he wailed as she walked out and nodded to the uniformed sergeant.

"Pop him back, can you?"

"Will do."

"Cheers." She checked her phone again as she walked back to her desk. One message from DC James Hamilton, asking her if she knew anything about voodoo, because he'd just found chicken feathers and bones all over a garage where he was looking for witnesses on an assault case. Then a second message saying to ignore the first, as it seemed the guy kept snakes. Then a third in all caps asking her to call animal control, followed by a fourth that was quite unfriendly, and said that she should keep her volume up, else what was the use her having a phone? It ended by saying he was going to A&E to get his hand seen to.

She flicked the computer on and stared at the emails waiting to be answered and the files waiting to be completed, and decided she needed coffee. Paperwork might be easier than people — and certainly easier than dragons — but she still couldn't face it without coffee.

HER PHONE VIBRATED as she picked up her coffee, nodding to the barista. She checked the display and pushed out the doors onto the street before she hit answer, her stomach tight but her shoulders suddenly looser. Here it was. She'd been waiting for the call without even realising it. It had been inevitable.

"Adams," she said.

"Hello, Adams. How's big city life?"

"Fantastic. How's the country treating you, DI Collins?"

"Call me Colin, it's fine. Or Collins, since you have such an aversion to first names."

"And did you have a reason for calling me, Collins?"

"I did, as it happens – oh, move over, you numpty."

DI Adams regarded the hurrying winter crowds on the streets, piled with shopping bags and flushed by Christmas lights, not a sheep in sight, and thought she was rather happy being where she was. "You alright there?"

"Yeah, yeah. Bloody tractors."

"And your reason for calling?"

"Ah, yes. Of course. No more missing postmen today."

"You're calling to tell me no postmen have gone missing today?"

"Well, it's a change from the last two days."

"That's super. Shall I expect a call tomorrow for another thrilling update?"

"It's a possibility, Adams. It's a possibility."

He sounded far too amused with himself, and DI Adams sighed. "Well, thank you for that. Valuable info."

"Ah, but I haven't got to the good bit yet."

"There's a good bit? What, the milkmen are still all there as well?"

"Oh, haha. A nice little jab at country living."

"Collins, I'm working." Or should be.

"Alright, alright. Just received a call that someone's found an empty DHL van parked at the start of a footpath about a kilometre from our favourite lay-by. Doors open, no cargo, no driver. Scorch marks on the roof."

DI Adams felt her heart give that familiar, welcome uptick as the adrenaline kicked in. "I'm on the way."

"I thought you were working."

"I'll call you when I'm closer." She ended the call without waiting for a response and checked her pockets. Good thing she kept her car keys in her jacket instead of in her bag. She wouldn't be able to use the sick stomach thing twice.

"ADAMS! WHAT'S KEEPING YOU?" DI Collins' voice was hollow over the Bluetooth.

"Your damn country roads. Far too many sheep and horses and what have you."

"Don't know about the what have yous, but we do have plenty of the others. Where are you?"

"Not far from the lay-by where the postmen were taken, coming in from the A59."

"Right, then. Straight on past it, turn left at the next lane you see, next right, and you'll see us in no time."

"Got it."

"Don't get lost. I know it's tough without street signs."

"I imagine I'll just about – what the *hell?*"

"Adams? Are you alright there?" Concern spiked through his voice.

"Yes. Yes, fine. Just some idiot speeding."

"Ah. Yes, we have plenty of those, too."

"Anyway. Left, then right."

"Yes. If you come to the old oak tree, you've gone too far."

"On which road?"

"I'm joking, Adams."

DI Collins was still chuckling when she cut him off, peering at the road ahead of her. It might be a nice day, but that didn't make the driving all that much easier. The low sun was right in her eyes, and it was hard to see anything *stationary* around here, let alone anything moving. And that car had gone by so bloody fast it was pretty much impossible to be sure what she'd seen. Actually impossible, really. And she was tired and skiving off her own work to go chasing around in the middle of nowhere on a case that wasn't even anywhere near her jurisdiction, so it wasn't surprising that her mind was making connections where there were none, convincing herself she was seeing things she wasn't.

That had to be it.

Because the idea that she'd just seen a familiar pale green Toyota Prius tearing past her in the direction of Toot Hansell, driven by an older woman and packed with three dragons and another woman of a certain age, was impossible. Although the fact that everyone seemed to be shouting and at least two scaly paws and one human hand had been jabbing wildly at the overhead light seemed like an oddly accurate detail.

12
ALICE

"Let's go," Beaufort said, his old gold eyes luminous in the warm light of the kitchen. They were watching the green blip speed across the fields, not as fast as it had been on the roads, but faster than anyone could walk or even run. Anyone human, anyway, Alice amended.

"We don't know where they're going to end up," she said. "We need to wait."

"That driver could be in danger," Beaufort replied, tapping his claws on the table.

"So could we if we go rushing after them without knowing where they're going."

Beaufort cocked his head at her. "When I said 'let's', I meant let us as in let us dragons go."

"And can you drive my phone, clever clogs?"

"*Drive* it? What, it transports you?" Beaufort looked at the phone with rather more interest than he had before.

Alice waved her hand impatiently. "Operate it."

"Oh. Well, no, but—"

"Then we go together." She glared at him, and Beaufort opened his mouth as if he was going to argue, took another look at her, and subsided.

"Fine. We go together. But you have to stay back and let *us dragons* deal with whatever we find."

Alice raised her eyebrows.

Beaufort fidgeted.

Miriam said, "It's stopped."

They turned to look at the phone.

"Car, now," Alice said, and there was a general rush for the door.

·

As it turned out, a Toyota Prius might be perfect for transporting the chair of the Women's Institute and whatever items she has cause to lug around, and might even be suitable for a small family, but it was not built for two women and three dragons. After five minutes of pushing and arguing, while tails and wings fell out of doors and someone managed to put the hazard lights on, Alice stepped back and said, "Enough! Beaufort, get out."

"I'm in now," he said, peering over the roof of the car at her. He had his head out the window and Mortimer was trying to coil his tail into the footwell. Amelia was buried somewhere beneath both of them, having claimed a spot before anyone could suggest that she should stay behind.

"You're not really in, though, are you?" Miriam said. "And I think you're standing on Mortimer's wing."

There was a strangled squeak of agreement from the car.

"Oh, sorry, lad!" Beaufort changed his position, earning a yelp from Mortimer and some rather unfriendly language from Amelia. "Sorry!"

"Beaufort, get in the front," Alice said, marching around the car to peer over the High Lord's shoulder. "There's no room here."

"No, no. You two get in the front. We'll be fine."

Amelia's language became even less friendly, and Mortimer sounded like he was agreeing with her, but his words were too muffled for Alice to be sure.

"You're the biggest one here," Miriam said. "We'll have a better chance of fitting with me in back."

"It doesn't seem right," Beaufort began, and Alice opened the door. The big dragon's body and tail spilled out onto the road, leaving him clinging to the window with his front paws, his chin resting on the frame. "Well, that was just uncalled for."

"We really do need to get going," Alice said, getting in now that she was in no immediate danger of being hit by a flailing wing. "Beaufort, up front with me."

"We should have flown," he muttered, but picked himself up and climbed in.

Alice drove sedately enough through the village, but as soon as they were over the last stream she accelerated rapidly, ignoring a little "*oooh*" from Miriam in the back. They didn't have the luxury of time that they'd had last night, and as far as she knew no one was likely to vomit on her back seat, so she took the corners tight and fast, her fingers light on the wheel, humming a half-remembered tune to herself. Beaufort had his snout almost pressed to the windscreen, his paws on the dashboard, and behind her she was vaguely aware of Miriam sliding first into Amelia, then into Mortimer, while the dragons clung to the doors. She hoped no one got carsick. She couldn't stop if they did. Anything could be happening to the DHL driver already. Plus, she wanted to get there before the police did.

Her phone was nestled in a cradle on the dashboard, a blue arrow showing them speeding their way toward the green dot. She was going to park as close to it as she could get, even if they didn't see the van. She was pretty sure the parcels wouldn't be in it any more, anyway. A DHL van was no match for the soggy fields at this time of year.

"Is it near the same lay-by?" Beaufort asked. His nose had an excited red tinge. He was terribly fond of car trips, Alice was realising.

"Looks like it's close to it," she said, braking hard as they came around a corner and met four horses plodding docilely down the road. Amelia plunged into the back of Beaufort's seat with a squeak, and Mortimer ended up wedged so tightly in the footwell behind Alice that he gave up trying to get out after a couple of attempts. They crept past the horses, giving them a wide berth, then once they were clear Alice hit the accelerator, making Miriam squeak again. Beaufort was grinning hugely.

THE LITTLE GREEN dot was at its closest point to any road that Alice could see, and she found a spot to park in front of a locked wooden gate with well-rusted hinges and a National Trust stile next to it. They sat there for a moment, looking out at the afternoon. The sun was fading already.

"I don't see a van," Beaufort said.

"No," Alice agreed, and got out of the car with her phone. "But the signal's that way." She pointed across the stile, and Amelia scrambled out of the car and onto the top of the gate, deep red wings spread for balance.

"I don't see anything," she said.

"Then *let's* go," Alice said, with a meaningful glare at Beaufort. He gave her a toothy grin in return, then followed Amelia over the gate and into the field beyond, Mortimer shaking the cramp out of his tail as he trailed after them. Alice and Miriam climbed over the stile and set off in the dragons' footsteps.

They marched across the field, following the curve of the

muddy National Trust footpath that led away from the wall and avoiding the sheep droppings wherever they could. Miriam was wearing pink clogs, and she kept slipping off them into the mud.

"Miriam, do you want to wait for us?" Alice asked, the third time it happened.

"No, no. I'm fine." One of the clogs got stuck and she stepped straight out of it into the mud in her socks. "Oops."

"Indeed. Not the best footwear, maybe." Alice was wearing her hiking boots and a heavy jacket, and had a rain hat pulled down over her ears. She'd come prepared this time.

"They're very comfy," Miriam said, then gave up and took the clogs off entirely, padding after the dragons in her stocking feet. "Is it much further?"

"It looks like it's in that copse," Alice said, examining her phone. "Or just beyond it."

"I wonder where they left the van," Mortimer said. "It'd be good to try and get a look at that, too, wouldn't it?" He looked quite happy as he trotted across the field, taking on the bright winter greens of the grass.

Beaufort took to the air briefly, keeping low. They hadn't seen anyone around, and the last car they passed had been not long after leaving Toot Hansell, but there was no point taking any risks. He landed lightly. "No tyre tracks anywhere that I can see."

"They couldn't have driven across here without getting stuck," Alice said. "There are plenty of little lanes with passing bays around here, though. They could have moved it after they offloaded the baubles, hidden it somewhere."

"They didn't move the other two," Miriam said.

"Maybe they're getting more careful."

THE GROUND GREW stonier as they approached the trees, and Miriam started making little squeaks of distress as she stubbed her toes or stepped on rocks disguised in the mud.

"You can wait here, you know," Alice said again as Miriam hopped away from a thistle with a yelp.

"No, no. I'm good."

Alice hoped they didn't encounter anything that required running away from. She wasn't going to be able to give Miriam a piggyback.

The dragons became grey and wraithlike as they picked their way into the trees. It was a young copse, all skinny silver trunks and leafless heads, and a small breeze whispered secrets through the branches. The sun was all but gone, and under the trees the ground was close to freezing, pocked with rabbit holes that Amelia investigated with interest.

"We're almost there," Alice whispered. "About a hundred metres."

"Right," Beaufort said. "You—" He stopped as Alice looked at him. "—come with me," he continued. "Everyone else stay here. It'll be quieter with just two of us." He padded off into the gloom, and Alice fell into step with him, the hard ground absorbing her footfalls. It was desperately silent in here without the breathing of the other dragons and Miriam's mutterings. She glanced back to see the younger woman perched on a rock, rubbing feeling back into her toes, then checked her phone. They were almost there.

They didn't speak, the dragon's footsteps silent on the hard earth, Alice treading as lightly as she could. Fifty metres, now. The phone screen was bright in the failing light, and she couldn't see that well when she looked away from it. The after-image painted ghosts among the trees, and she wished she'd thought to bring her cane from the car. Not to help her walk – just in case of unfriendly bauble thieves. Beaufort was tipping his head this way and that, searching for scents and sounds, scanning the deepening shadows.

"Anything?" she whispered, and he shook his head. They crept on.

The phone was showing them that they should be right on top of the tracker, and Alice supposed it must be fairly accurate, if it was meant for tracking cheating partners. But still they'd seen no one, heard nothing. And it was rapidly getting dark now that the sun was lost behind the hills, and she hadn't brought a torch, either. Very ill-prepared of her, just like the way she hadn't thought about how they'd know if the van went off-route. In the end it had been very obvious, but still. It wasn't like her. She blamed the cat. Something about his amused gaze and ragged ears was making it very hard for her to kick him out, and he'd come into her bedroom last night and purred so loudly about being on the bed that she hadn't wanted to push him off. Which meant she'd had to sleep on the wrong side, ending up with a horrible night's sleep. Why on earth did people have the sneaky animals around?

She pushed the phone into her pocket and stood still, waiting for her eyes to get used to the dim light. The torch on the phone wouldn't be good enough to help her out here, and she found that after a moment she could see reasonably well. Certainly well enough to spot parcels and missing delivery drivers.

"I can't smell anything at all," Beaufort told her as she caught up to him. "Just sheep and rabbits." His belly growled dangerously and he added, "Excuse me."

"Not at all." Alice shuffled around in a half-crouch, hands on her knees as she peered owlishly at the ground, but it was movement in the corner of her eye that caught her attention. She straightened up, frowning, and spotted something fluttering in the chilly breeze. She picked her way over to it, checking where she put her feet in case she stepped on something important, and retrieved a scrap of brown paper from where it was caught in a bush, struggling to break free. She fished her phone out and switched on the light, using it to examine the paper. It was as big as her palm, scuffed by movement and tape, and there was half a postcode printed on one side in familiar, curly handwriting. She sighed.

"Beaufort?" she called, and heard the rapid pad of feet approach her from outside the little pool of light. A scaly head loomed into view, thrown in rather alarming contrasts by the harsh light of the phone. "They're not here."

He looked at the paper, then up at her. "They found the tracking thingy?"

"I don't know. Maybe the packing just tore. Maybe they took all the wrapping off. But either way, it didn't work." She crumpled the paper and went to throw it away, then stopped herself and put it back in her pocket. The tracker was gone. No doubt it was somewhere around, probably trodden into the dirt by their own silly feet, and their hope of finding the culprits with it.

Beaufort looked around carefully, his pupils wide as they drank in the light. "There's more paper."

"Can you smell anything?"

He circled the area slowly, finding more scraps caught in the bushes and trapped by mud. "Not really," he said. "Humans and cars and dragons."

"Dragons?"

"It was packaging for dragon-scale baubles, and the scales came from any number of dragons. It could mean everything, or it could mean nothing."

Alice sighed, and rubbed her forehead. "Beaufort, we're not doing very well. We just seem to be going in circles."

"I know it feels like that. But we always come through, don't we?"

She smiled at him. "That's a lovely thought."

"And a true one. Let's go back." He waited as she adjusted her hat and squared her shoulders, then they walked together through the trees as the night bred quiet and secretive life around them.

IT WAS a subdued drive back to Toot Hansell, broken only by a momentary excitement when Amelia hit the overhead light with her tail, and neither the dragons nor Miriam seemed to be able to figure out how to switch it off again. Alice tried to ignore the commotion, squeezing past an oncoming car as she said, "It's just a little slide button. If you'd all stop poking it at once, I'm sure *one* of you can switch it off."

As it was it went on and off several times before Mortimer managed to get it firmly off, by which time Alice had decided she'd had more than enough of them all for the evening. She dropped the dragons off in the same place as the day before, thinking wearily that unproductive car trips were becoming a habit, then took Miriam home.

"Um, do we have a plan for tomorrow?" Miriam asked timidly as she got out of the car. She was holding both her shoes and her sodden, filthy socks, and her toes looked terribly cold.

"Just the meeting in the morning at Jasmine's," Alice said. "And with any luck the counterfeit baubles will have arrived while we've been out today."

"You think the post got through?"

"I understand it had a police escort from Skipton to here and back."

"But they got the poor DHL driver."

"Baubles are dangerous things, it seems," Alice said, and smiled at Miriam. The younger woman looked bedraggled and unhappy. "Don't worry, Miriam. We'll get to the bottom of this. Get some sleep."

Miriam waved uncertainly, and Alice waited until she'd gone inside and shut the door before she put the car back in gear and went home, checking for the silver Audi almost reflexively but not seeing it. She was tired and annoyed both by the lost tracker and the fact that she didn't know what to do next. She should know what to do. That was who she was.

THE CAT WAS WAITING at the front door again, his tail twitching as if annoyed by her tardiness. She'd taken to calling him Thompson, because it seemed to suit him more than just plain Tom.

"Back again, are you?" she said. "The tuna's not going to last forever, you know." Although she'd bought cat food yesterday, Thompson had looked at it in disgust before turning and walking away to lie down in the furthest point of the kitchen from the bowl. She'd ended up sharing the chicken from her own dinner with him, and found herself back at the shop buying tuna this morning. It was evidently mind control.

Thompson narrowed his eyes at her, then wandered inside and pawed his way through the post lying on the mat.

"Don't you damage any of that."

He gave her a scornful look, turned over a couple of cards with a paw, then sat down again, seemingly satisfied.

"Nothing for you?" she asked, collecting the letters and pulling the door shut behind her. "I can't imagine why not."

He gave her a purring mewl and led the way into the kitchen, and she wondered if she was now, in fact, a cat person. She wasn't sure she liked the sound of that.

ALICE WOKE LATE the next day. She hadn't slept well, between Thompson taking up half the bed again and breathing tuna on her face, and her mind shuffling through different possibilities for the bauble thieves and kidnappers. While it seemed that it could only be dragons, she couldn't get the man at the Christmas market out of her head, or the silver Audi that had appeared on the streets so soon after. Could that be him as well? It seemed to her that he'd been too curious, too pushy. And hadn't he looked at the dragons instead of just into the shadows of the stall? Just as if he knew to expect dragons? She wasn't sure, but she needed to ask Beaufort about him, see if he'd smelt anything strange on the man. Although she supposed Beaufort would be busy with his own interrogations this morning.

She pushed the covers aside, careful not to disturb the cat, who yawned and rolled onto his back, looking like he'd had a wonderful sleep. She pulled her dressing gown over her pyjamas and padded downstairs barefoot to put the kettle on. She was measuring tea into the teapot – teabags were fine for later in the day, but not for that first cup – when a warm body snaked around her ankles and she jumped, almost spilling the tea leaves.

She frowned at him. "Sneaky little monster."

He gave her his flat green gaze and mewled softly, then rubbed his head on her legs again. She wondered why she hadn't just kicked him out, as he obviously made his home anywhere that was happy to feed him. It wasn't like she'd have been doing him any hardship. And especially after what Beaufort and Mortimer had said about the cats of the Watch. But then again, there was always that theory about keeping your enemies close.

She took the tuna out of the fridge.

ALICE CHECKED the street behind her for the cat, but she couldn't see him. Or a silver Audi. She pulled her scarf up tighter to her chin and marched down the road to Jasmine's, a Tupperware of mini quiches under one arm and a bag over her other shoulder. Thompson had followed her out when she left home but had stayed on the doorstep watching her like some forlorn puppy whose mistress had left him behind for the first time. She supposed that if he was actually following her she'd never even know it, but that bloody Primrose would keep him out of the meeting. She was good enough for that, at least.

She went up the two little steps to Jasmine's door and knocked sharply. A moment later it swung open, releasing warm air heavy with the scents of scorched coffee and small dogs. She managed not to wrinkle her nose and smiled at Jasmine instead.

"Hello, dear. How are you?"

"Morning, Alice. Come in." The younger woman returned her smile and swung the door wide, revealing Primrose with her teeth bared in a silent snarl. Alice waited until Jasmine turned away, then snarled back.

Inside, the living room was already full, warm with bodies and the flickering gas fire, and awash in the scents of tea and coffee and perfume and cake, overwhelming the dog smell. Alice found a spare folding chair and settled herself down, feet crossed neatly at the ankles, to wait for everyone to arrive. She'd learnt a long time ago that patience paid off better than irritation, particularly in the civilian world.

Miriam was the last to arrive, looking pale and anxious and with her woolly hat spilling curly hair everywhere. She squeezed in next to Alice and hissed, "I have news!"

Alice smiled at her. "Me, too." Then she cleared her throat and said, "Ladies? Are we ready?" The chatter dropped away almost instantly, all eyes on her. Everyone was strung too tightly, by the feel of things, and it wasn't surprising. "Thank you all for managing to make this rather last-minute meeting," she said. "We'll get right down to business, because I know the weeks before Christmas are busy for all of us, and we don't need any more complications. Firstly—"

"Can I?" Jasmine blurted. "Alice, look – the bauble arrived!" She held out a box that looked as if it had been wrapped by an eight-year-old buzzing on energy drinks and Mars bars. Brown packing tape was strung across it haphazardly, one corner looked as if Primrose had been gnawing on it, and the address label was smudged with dirt and attached at an angle that made Alice feel faintly twitchy.

"Wonderful," she said aloud. "Let's take a look. Make sure we keep the packaging, though. Beaufort will want to examine it."

Jasmine nodded and crouched down at the coffee table to unwrap the box while the ladies of the W.I. gathered around to peer over her shoulders.

"Shocking wrapping," Miriam said, as bits of paper fell away with torn edges and uneven shapes. It looked as if someone had just grabbed any old scrap of packing paper they could find, and bound it together with so much tape that Jasmine was having to attack it with the knife they'd been using to cut the parkin.

"And what's that smell?" Rosemary asked. "It's like the whole thing's been sitting in a pub basement for six months."

"The paper feels weird, too," Jasmine said. "Greasy."

Alice reached out and rubbed it between her fingers. Maybe not greasy exactly, but slick. Dirty-feeling. She wiped her hands on her trousers as Jasmine opened the box inside the wrapping (it was held together with even more tape and appeared to be assembled from three or more mismatched boxes) and lifted the bauble out of a bed of dirty, crumpled newspaper, old brochures, and what looked an awful lot like used tissues.

"Well, that's taking recycling a bit far," Gert said, as Jasmine fished the bauble out, trying not to touch the tissues. They had a nasty, crusty look to them.

"It's not as nice as Mortimer's," she said, holding the bauble up to inspect it. It wasn't – the seams were rough, and the design carved on the outside consisted of the sort of stars a five-year-old might draw.

"It's nothing like Mortimer's," Alice said, and went back to her

176 | KIM M. WATT

seat to pull out the newspapers. "And look at this. Apparently it's more than just the odd one misbehaving. They're lethal, all of them, soon as they're lit. There's a huge story on them in the paper."

"Oh," Jasmine said in a very small voice.

"We'll see what Beaufort says," Alice added, turning around with the papers in her hand. "Have a look at – *Jasmine!*"

"You didn't say not to light it," Jasmine whispered, and there was a nervous murmur of agreement, as well as a general movement away from her. She was still holding the ugly bauble in one hand and a lighter in the other.

"Put it out," Alice said. "Put it out *now!*"

As if hearing her, the bauble blossomed abruptly with sharp-edged petals, making Jasmine squeak and jerk her hand away. The thing dropped to the floor, and for a moment Alice hoped it was a dud, even thought she could see it trembling, and there was a nasty smell starting up that suggested it was burning the carpet. She took a careful step toward it, and the bauble shot straight up, eliciting a small scream from Jasmine, then it retreated to a corner of the living room ceiling. It hovered there while the women exchanged worried glances, then without warning it roared toward the door, banked, and barrelled straight for the sofa and the women standing in front of it, sparking with fury and belching fiery light.

13

MORTIMER

"I will never catch up," Mortimer said. "Never, ever, ever."

"Mortimer, don't take on," Beaufort said. "We won't be sending any more until we clear this up, anyway."

"But then what? Then there'll be a massive backlog, and everything will have to be done at the last minute, and I can't. I just can't!" Mortimer wrung his tail, and a little shower of scales pattered onto the floor of his workshop. "And I'm stress-shedding *horribly!*"

"We'll do it," Amelia said from the entrance to the little cavern. Gilbert was peering around her shoulder. "Gilbert and I aren't tired at all. We'll get started while you get some rest – you worked all night last night. We'll do tonight, and then we'll all just keep going in shifts until we're caught up. This is going to be okay."

"How *can* it be?" Mortimer wailed. "We can't even *send* them!" The calm of the field had vanished entirely. For a little while there, hunting for scents in the crisp late afternoon with the cold dome of the sky high above them, he'd almost forgotten that there were kidnappers and bauble thieves to deal with, and possible traitors within their ranks. It had all felt rather exciting, like he was a character in a TV show, completely sure of himself and not at all worried about High Lords and black markets and exploding baubles. He'd certainly forgotten that he'd lost about two weeks' worth of work.

"Well, we're not going to let this sort of thing continue," Beaufort said. "We will deal with the situation, and by the time we're ready to start posting them out again you'll be all caught up. Say thank you to Amelia and Gilbert."

"But I haven't even finished teaching Gilbert yet—"

"I have," Amelia said. "Enough to be going on with, anyway. I'll keep an eye on him, and you can check everything tomorrow."

Mortimer looked at her with something close to despair. "But—"

"Mortimer, say thank you to Amelia and Gilbert, then straight to your cave."

"But—"

"Mortimer." Beaufort's voice carried a note of warning that cut through the younger dragon's exhaustion and made his tail twitch.

"Thank you, Amelia and Gilbert."

"It's okay." Amelia pointed at the workbench. "You can start on flattening the scales, Gil."

"That's so lame. I want to make the actual stuff."

"Get flattening or I'll *make* you lame."

"Right you are." The small dragon went to grab an armload of scales from the basket in the corner.

Mortimer trailed after Beaufort as they headed down the tunnel to the mouth of the cave, then paused. "Amelia?"

"Yeah?"

"Sorry I was so horrible. And thank you for fixing the sailing ship bauble."

"S'cool." She already had a dragon scale clamped to the bench in front of her. "Get some sleep, M."

"Okay." He padded after Beaufort, his eyes scratchy and his limbs suddenly leaden. "I think maybe I will."

❧

MORTIMER DIDN'T EVEN BOTHER to find any dinner, just went straight to his own cavern, curled up in a nest of fireproof blankets on top of his barbecue and promptly fell asleep. If he had dreams he didn't remember them, and when he woke to a dark winter morning his stomach was rumbling and he had the sort of stiffness that comes from sleeping the whole night without stirring once.

He slid off the barbecue and stretched, shaking his wings out, then sat where he was for a while, taking his time to wake up, and considering things. It was astonishing how much easier it was to think after a decent sleep. And astonishing just how hard it was to get such a sleep sometimes. He yawned and scratched his chin.

He was going to have to get used to this black-market situation. And it was a black market. It had to be, considering dragons are, at heart, scaly pirates. He understood that, even if he didn't want to. He was going to have to pretend he knew nothing about it, so everyone could keep right on thinking that they were getting away with it. At least there was no chance of running out of scales. He poked his patchy tail and sighed. He was keeping them pretty well supplied, too. And maybe with Gilbert helping and it not just being him and Amelia he'd feel a little less under pressure. That would be rather nice.

Then he thought of Beaufort and his terrible enthusiasm, and shuddered. Yes, more help with the baubles would alleviate a certain amount of stress, but definitely not all of it. He yawned again and padded out into the pre-dawn dark, heading for the workshop.

Amelia and Gilbert were arguing loudly enough that he heard them before he even reached the cavern entrance, somewhat shattering a rather pleasant daydream of them all working together in calm companionship, possibly accompanied by tea, sunshine, and maybe even a little nice music, if he could figure out how to get a radio to pick up a signal inside the workshop.

"It's a *statement*," Gilbert insisted, as Mortimer padded down the short tunnel to the cavern itself.

"It's a mess," Amelia snapped.

"It's modern."

"It's ugly."

"It's got attitude."

"It looks like something I saw a ghost vomit up once."

They glared at each other, and after a moment Mortimer coughed politely. They both turned their glares on him, and he waved awkwardly. "Morning."

"Morning, Mortimer," Gilbert said, his shoulders relaxing.

"Well? What do you think, M?" Amelia demanded.

Mortimer pottered over to peer at the bauble floating softly above Gilbert's workbench. Technically, the young dragon had a flair for it. No rough seams, delicate, fine lines in the detailed pattern he'd embossed on it, and not a single instability causing it to roll over or bob about the place. It would be quite wonderful, if it wasn't quite so ... so ... "It's unusual," he said, patting Gilbert's shoulder. "Good blending of the scale shades."

"Thanks," the young dragon said, giving Amelia a smug look. She rolled her eyes.

"It's just not very festive," Mortimer continued. "Humans love the whole Christmas theme at this time of year. Maybe we can do some more, um, non-traditional designs for midsummer. Or maybe Halloween."

"Told you," Amelia said. "Snowflakes and birds and stuff. Not whatever that is."

"And ships," Gilbert pointed out. "You're making ships. And I've seen the Christmas books. *Ships* aren't very Christmassy."

"Yes. Quite right. That was an experiment," Mortimer said. "From now on, let's stick to traditional Christmas designs, shall we?"

Gilbert gave a slightly dramatic sigh but took his bauble and went back to his bench, tail piercings clattering on the stone floor.

"Sorry," Amelia said to Mortimer. "He's really good at this sort of stuff, so I got him making some on his own. I didn't think I needed to tell him to keep it Christmassy."

"He is good at it," Mortimer said. "Just more good will to all and less death head stares on the details, I think." He paused. "Was there a sea serpent fighting a unicorn skeleton on that?"

Amelia snorted. "So you didn't spot the zombie centaurs trampling the pixies? Ugh. He'll grow out of it. I hope."

Mortimer supposed it was possible – Gilbert wasn't even eighty yet – but he didn't think it was that likely. "Maybe. There's probably a market for his work, anyway, just not a Christmas one." He yawned. "Have you two slept?"

"We're good for a few more hours yet."

"Alright. I'll be back as soon as I've had some breakfast."

Winter was always slimmer pickings for dragons, the rabbits skinny and wary, the trees offering no cover for daytime hunting. Regardless of the time of year, however, a few of the clan were tasked with collecting extra food each day for those that either couldn't or didn't have the time to get their own. As the bauble business had become busier, Beaufort had ordered Mortimer to help himself to the clan food – ordered, because Mortimer still felt a little awkward and uncomfortable about the whole thing. The clan food was usually reserved for the High Lord, old dragons, and treasure hunters, but he supposed that he was, in a way, the treasure *supplier*. No one had to go off searching for anything other than rabbits and the occasional fat pigeon now. And he wasn't a bad hunter, but he had noticed that there was something rather nice about not having to look in the eyes of the creature you were about to eat. He secretly thought that Gilbert had a point with the whole vegetarianism thing, but he wasn't quite sure if that was more a matter for younger dragons. Would it seem silly for a dragon of his age to suddenly go vegetarian? Well, more so than any other dragons, since as far as he knew Gilbert was the only vegetarian dragon in existence. He wasn't entirely sure about it, but he'd tried Miriam's vegetable chili and he thought it was possible. Maybe.

Beaufort was in a corner of the Grand Cavern, talking in low tones with Lord Walter, a dragon who was possibly even older than the High Lord himself, and who, unlike Beaufort, looked it. Mortimer could hear the old dragon's quavery voice drifting over as he took his pick of the rabbits laid out neatly by the fire in the centre of the stone floor.

"Eh?" Lord Walter was saying. "Scales? Lad, I can't keep my scales on for trying."

Mortimer grinned at the idea of anyone calling Beaufort "lad", and singed the fur off a rabbit with a neatly controlled blast of flame.

"A *blanket?* I'm telling you, Beaufort, I don't take with these modern notions. I've been through this with you before. Trading with humans and gallivanting about villages. It's not dragonish!"

Mortimer pushed his rabbit about a bit, trying to hear what Beaufort was saying.

"I'm the last person who'd be trading with damn humans. Nasty creatures. You watch. This will all end in fire and death and dragons' heads on stakes again, you mark my words. You should know better." The ancient dragon turned and stalked stiff-legged away from the High Lord. "Humans. *Pah!*" He spat a stream of greenish flame into the fire as he passed, making Mortimer jump back with a squeak.

Beaufort ambled over to the fire, not looking particularly perturbed, and Mortimer busied himself with his rabbit.

"Morning, lad," the High Lord said.

"Morning, Beaufort, sir."

"Sleep well?"

"Yes, thanks. Ah – was that about the stolen baubles?"

"Yes, I'm taking your advice and being more subtle about it. I'm questioning everyone one at a time," Beaufort said, brandishing his singed pad. The top three names, printed in large spindly letters, were crossed off, and he'd only been able to fit three more on the page. Writing wasn't a natural activity for dragons.

"And Lord Walter?" Mortimer asked.

Beaufort scratched his chin thoughtfully. "It's amazing how the anti-human sentiment lingers, Mortimer. How the hatred sticks."

"He must have seen terrible things."

"So have a lot of us, lad. We saw some bad times. Once, dragon-scale armour was the very height of fashion for the richest knights. Light, harder than steel, beautiful. Dragons very rarely had to steal gold back in those days. You could pretty much name your price for scales. Until the knights worked out that dead dragons got them an enormous amount of scales and a lot of popularity, particularly when it came to the rougher clans that liked stealing sheep and burning farms. The next thing we knew, dragon-killing had become a sport, and no one cared if you'd actually stolen so much as a hamster. Every knight wanted to be a saint, or to win some princess' heart by killing the dread monster. Most princesses were rather smarter than the knights gave them credit for, and thought it was a ridiculous idea, but no true knight ever let the facts get in the way of a good slaughtering. And finally the dragons who could, hid, and the ones who couldn't, died." Beaufort sighed. "It was a terrible way to live."

"I suppose I can kind of understand how he feels, then," Mortimer said. "You know, the danger of contact with humans."

"I can't," Beaufort said flatly. "Living in fear and hatred, living without joy or forgiveness for all those centuries? No, Mortimer. I can't understand it at all."

𝕒

MORTIMER DROPPED his rabbit bones into the fire, then sat back on his haunches to lick his paws clean with the fastidious concentration of a cat, his gaze wandering around the cavern. There were quite a lot of dragons in here for what was really a rather reasonable winter day. He spotted Rockford and his hangers-on huddled together in a corner, and wondered what they were up to. They didn't normally spend any time at all in the Grand Cavern. Beaufort tended to laugh at them when they were boasting about their fighting skills, and it made them a bit huffy.

The High Lord had wandered off again and cornered a harassed-looking dragon called Violet, who had some very patchy scales not just on her tail but everywhere else as well. Mortimer thought she might be the only dragon other than Lord Walter who was shedding more than he was. Beaufort was questioning her while she tried to keep track of two very small dragons that appeared to have only recently grasped the rudiments of flight.

"And where were you yesterday afternoon at approximately 4 p.m., Violet?"

"When, sir? *Rupert get off the ceiling right this instant you'll fall and crack your skull and I am not going to show you any sympathy!*"

"Around when it was getting dark."

"I really don't know. Probably trying to *Josie don't you dare bite the High Lord's tail if he doesn't skin you I will!*"

Beaufort twitched his tail out of reach of a small, gleefully red dragon, and said, "I imagine you had your paws full."

Violet gave him a disbelieving look. "I'd love to have my paws full. Having my paws full sounds wonderful. Harriet's meant to be sharing the parenting, but I don't even know when I last saw her. It might have been this morning. Or half an hour ago. But it feels like last summer and *gods love me you two if either of you leave this cavern I will let you freeze out there and the ghasts can eat your bones!*"

Mortimer blinked in alarm, and Beaufort patted Violet gently on her shoulder. "I think that's all fine. Let's see if we can maybe find some help for a spot of herding duty, shall we?"

Violet looked at him blankly. "Can we? I mean, *would* someone?"

"Of course," Beaufort said, and Mortimer could see him wincing slightly. The two young dragons, neither of them bigger than a cat, had run back from the cavern mouth and appeared to be having a tug-of-war with his tail. "Lovely little critters. Just lovely." He flicked his tail, and the hatchlings went flying backward, giggling and spitting half-formed flames.

Mortimer plucked Josie off the floor as she went scampering past, and saw an older dragon called Lydia snatch Rupert out of the air on his way to the ceiling. She beckoned Mortimer over imperiously, and he carried the wriggling Josie to her, depositing the little dragon next to her brother.

"Behave yourselves," he told them. Not that they'd have much choice, with Lydia. He still remembered being left with her as a very small dragon himself, and how much his tail had hurt after she'd caught him wearing one of her crowns and having a sword fight with his shadow. Yep. Good luck to them.

He turned to head back to the workshop and found himself snout to snout with Lord Margery. "Um, sorry," he muttered, scooting sideways while she gave him a look that suggested he still wasn't too old to have his tail thoroughly tweaked.

Lord Margery marched toward the seat of the High Lord, even though he wasn't on it. "Beaufort," she said, and her voice was hard and carrying. "We need to talk."

Mortimer suddenly decided that Amelia and Gilbert could manage on their own for a little longer, as the cavern grew quiet and the dozen or so dragons inside turned to watch. He had an idea that at least some of them had been waiting for just this. It explained why there were so many dragons here. Rockford was nudging a burly dragon called Lucille, who had piercings in all her spines, and they were both flushing an excited red, grinning broadly. Mortimer didn't like the look of that. Rockford would love to see Beaufort's changes revoked. The big dragon hated the idea of human contact as much as Lord Walter, but for different reasons. Lord Walter thought dragons were safer away from humans. Rockford, Mortimer suspected, thought dragons should be eating humans, as if it was something they'd ever done. He had some very strange ideas about what he termed the "glory days" of the Cloverlies, and didn't seem to have a great grip of history. In fact, he didn't have a great grip of much other than being big and loud, in Mortimer's humble opinion.

"Lord Margery," Beaufort said, his voice amiable, and suddenly Mortimer knew that, never mind anyone else, the High Lord himself had been expecting this. "How may I be of service?"

"You can drop this charade of human/dragon relations before we're chased from our homes, for a start. Or you can stand down so someone more responsible can take your place."

Mortimer heard his own quick intake of breath echoed around the chamber, and a few jeers from Rockford's corner. The High Lord faced his challenger with his eyebrow ridges raised slightly, his gaze warm and resigned.

"You know that I believe this is in the best interests of all of us, Margery," Beaufort said.

"Which is why I no longer think you are suitable to continue as the High Lord of the Cloverly dragons."

More gasps, and some rapidly hushed cheers, and all eyes were on Beaufort as he nodded thoughtfully. "A High Lord cannot just step down. Are you challenging me to a battle?"

"I'd prefer not to," she said, her voice steady and her wings high. "But since you're such a fan of new ways, why not be the first High Lord to give up his seat for the good of the clan?"

"Because I do not agree that going into hiding again is in anyone's best interests."

"You're wrong, Beaufort. This cannot continue. You'll expose us all, and the humans will tear us apart as they did our parents, our cousins, our friends, our children. I don't want to remove you, but I will if I have to."

"And if we fight and you lose?"

"Then so be it."

Beaufort sighed. "The old ways are really not the best, you know. The rule of the strongest is no longer the wisest choice. So, no, Margery, we won't fight. And I won't just step down either. We'll vote."

"We'll *what?*"

A rumble of noise washed around the cavern, and Rockford shouted, "Fight him, Lord Margery! Fight him!"

She glared at him, and he subsided into silence. She looked back at Beaufort, eyebrow ridges raised. "What on earth are you talking about?"

"A vote," Beaufort said. "It's when every member of the clan has a voice—"

"I know what it is, you imbecile. But when have dragons ever had their lives decided by a *vote?*"

"Well, maybe it's time they did." Beaufort flipped the cover down on his notebook, rather sadly, Mortimer thought. "Spread the word. This afternoon we call another Furnace. Every dragon shall have a voice in deciding the future of the clan."

"Boo!" Rockford bellowed. "Fight! Fight! Fight!" Lucille and a couple of others joined him, but not even Lord Margery looked at him this time, and after a few half-hearted shouts the little group fell silent again.

"This is ridiculous," Lord Margery said. She'd gone a strange mottled colour, partly her own silver blue, partly angry puce and a little alarmed pink. It wasn't a particularly nice shade.

Beaufort gave her a broad grin. "I don't know. It might be fun."

"Imbecile," Lord Margery muttered again, and padded off, shouldering past Mortimer with a baleful glare. Rockford hurried after her, trailed by a handful of dragons, and Mortimer scooted backward before anyone could "accidentally" step on his tail.

"Votes!" Rupert shrieked, barrelling across the middle of the cavern. Lydia must have dropped them both in her shock at the challenge. "Do the votes!"

"Votes!" his sister echoed as she flew after him, then crashed into the wall and bounced off a couple of outcroppings before coming to rest at Beaufort's feet. He looked at her indulgently.

"And who will you vote for?" he asked.

"Rupert," she said firmly, and her brother cheered.

Mortimer swallowed hard, the rabbit suddenly heavy in his belly, and stared at Beaufort. The old dragon had climbed onto his seat and was arranging the fireproof blanket over his barbecue as if he had nothing more important to do. Mortimer stumbled over to him, and the High Lord sat back on his haunches and regarded the younger dragon with his eyebrow ridges raised in mild interest.

"That's a funny grey you've gone, lad," he said.

"Beaufort, you *can't*," Mortimer said, his voice sounding strange and faraway.

"It's a better plan than rolling about the place trying to knock each other's teeth out. I quite like my teeth."

"Well, yes, but—" he stopped. He knew Beaufort couldn't just not answer the challenge. That wasn't how it worked.

"Do you think I might lose, lad?"

Mortimer gave an awkward little shrug.

"You may be right. But there's no use in going forward when

half the clan are dragging their feet and wishing you'd drop dead so they could go back to the old ways."

"But then we need to talk to them. We need to explain that this is good for everyone, that – that it's safe and everything ..." He trailed off, thinking of the bauble thieves.

"It's not, though, is it? *We* think it's better than the alternative, but that doesn't mean everyone does. That's my fault. I shouldn't have pushed ahead without making sure the whole clan was behind it."

"What if you don't win?" Mortimer could barely whisper the words. There weren't many dragons alive who could remember the days before Beaufort was High Lord. He couldn't even imagine it. It seemed like the world would be a much darker and more unfriendly place without the big dragon at its centre.

"Well, then. I shall take myself off somewhere and have a nice retirement." Beaufort patted him on the shoulder. "Now off you go. An old dragon needs his naps."

Mortimer watched him climb onto the barbecue and settle himself down with every evidence of enjoyment, then ran for the cavern entrance. He thought he might be about to lose his rabbit.

14

MIRIAM

M iriam passed a restless night, full of fractured dreams of baubles eating postmen and vans turning into dragons that promptly vanished, leaving behind nothing but wrapping paper. Eventually she gave up and went downstairs to sit at her kitchen table, peering blearily out at the heavy dark of a winter morning and wondering what she was going to make for the impromptu meeting at Jasmine's. Everyone had assured the younger woman that they'd bring a plate and she shouldn't cook anything at all, and hopefully she'd listened, otherwise they'd all be sitting there amid the fumes of an abused oven.

Miriam shook herself. That was a terribly unfair thought. Well, maybe not un*fair*, but certainly unkind. Being tired was no excuse. She got up and switched the radio on for some company, then pulled the butter out of the fridge. She had time to make some Christmas cookies, and get them decorated as well. No one could stay miserable when there were cookies to decorate. Or, indeed, to eat.

It was a very pleasant way in which to pass a winter morning. The kitchen filled rapidly with sweet, buttery scents, and Miriam

192 | KIM M. WATT

even dug out her winter spiced chai tea, still sweet-smelling after a year in the cupboard. The Christmas carols had been overplayed since the last week of November, so she swapped the radio for an old Tom Petty CD and danced happily in her slippers, scattering flour over every surface and singing badly but enthusiastically. There was frost shining in the garden as the sun crept up and wandered through the bare branches of the trees, the sky was a pale and fragile blue, and, missing postmen and counterfeit baubles aside, all was well with Miriam's world.

She headed for the door just before 10 a.m., cheeks pink from the shower, carrying a tray of cookies on which the icing was still drying and wondering where her favourite gloves were. There was a scattering of post on the mat, and she realised that she'd been playing the music so loud that she hadn't even heard it arrive. It seemed the police escort was working.

"Hopefully they couldn't hear me singing," she said to the quiet house, and put the cookies down to scoop up the mail. She shuffled through it, sorting the Christmas cards from the rubbishy things that companies send out disguised as real mail, then wrinkled her nose in startled disgust. Her fingers had slipped on paper that felt oddly greasy, like old menus in fast food cafes. She found it stuck to the back of a card by its own slickness, one ragged sheet that looked a little like that old fax paper that came on rolls and bleached in the sun, and a little like a receipt from somewhere terribly disreputable. There was either dried mud or chocolate smeared all over it. At least, she hoped it was dried mud or chocolate.

Do not trie to follow us agin.

The bubles ar ours.

Stop seling yors or else.

And no talking to polis.

Miriam read it twice, bewildered by the scratchy text and terrible spelling, like a ransom note written by a preschooler.

"Oh, dear," she murmured eventually. "Oh dear. This isn't good. This isn't good at all." She tucked the note carefully into her jacket pocket and wondered if she had time to break into her cheese puff stash. It seemed like the sort of situation that called for cheese puffs. But she was already late, so in the end she peered around the door, checked for chocolate-smeared note writers, and hurried out, locking the cottage up firmly behind her. She headed for Jasmine's house, coming back five minutes later to collect the forgotten cookies.

❧

ALL OF WHICH had seemed like rather urgent news to share, until now. Now she watched in open-mouthed astonishment as the counterfeit bauble bore down on the sofa like a small and furious comet. Carlotta was standing directly in its path, and she dropped into a squat with surprising agility, only ruined slightly by the fact that she immediately toppled backward onto the floor, crashing into Rose and sending her sprawling. Pearl grabbed Rose and tried to hold her up, and instead overbalanced and fell forward, landing on top of both Rose and Carlotta while the missile screamed over their heads. Teresa grabbed a cushion from the nearest chair and hurled it as hard as she could at the furious bauble, sending it careening back across the room toward Priya, who fielded it with a yelp and a glancing blow from the notebook she'd had on her lap. Miriam dived for cover as the ornament shot toward her at eye level, and Rosemary grabbed the poker from the fireplace and swung enthusiastically. She missed the bauble and smashed a wedding photo off the mantel instead, while the festive missile ricocheted off the wall and headed back toward the sofa. Rose had extricated herself from the pile-up, and she grabbed a coffee table book on steam trains and hit the thing hard enough to send it smashing into the windows. It bounced off with a painful crack, so loud that Miriam was astonished the glass didn't shatter. It was wobbling now, setting up an unhappy hum, and it had left a nasty smudge of soot behind on the window. Alice lunged, swatting the thing with her rolled-up newspapers like it was an overgrown and particularly bothersome fly, and it tumbled sideways across the room, ran into the wall (leaving an oily black mark this time), then spun away unsteadily and picked up speed again, the hum building into a tooth-rattling whine.

Alice raised her voice over the horrible noise. "We need to get it outside! If it explodes, it'll set fire to the whole place! Someone, open those windows!"

Primrose was barking hysterically, racing back and forth across the carpet, and as Gert rushed to open the windows she tripped over the dog and went face-first into the loveseat under the windowsill. Primrose fled, yelping in fright, and Jasmine scrambled over Gert to haul the windows open. The bauble was hovering near the top of the wall by the open double doors to the kitchen, and Priya grabbed the doors and slammed them, giving an alarmed squeak as the bauble dipped toward her. It seemed to rethink and wobbled into the centre of the room, staying high as if sensing it was in danger. Alice raised her newspapers like a tennis racket and jumped, swiping the bauble and sending it rolling across the ceiling, dragging a trail of soot and oil behind it. It hit the wall above the windows, dropped down as if it was going to pop neatly outside, then reversed and roared back toward Alice. She stepped back to give herself room to swing, tripped over Carlotta, who was still trying to get up, and they both went sprawling. The bauble thundered over them and headed for Miriam, buzzing so furiously it sounded like a horde of attacking hornets. She snatched her cookie tray off the table, gave what she felt to be a suitably Amazonian scream (although later she'd admit to herself that it was mostly just a scream), and swung.

The tray slammed into the bauble with a furious metallic clang, sending cookies and icing sugar scattering across the room, and the bauble flying toward the windows.

"Gert, *duck!*" Alice shouted from the floor, and the other woman, who'd just pulled herself out of the loveseat, dived back down with her arms clasped protectively over her head. The bauble shot outside, still screaming, and now trailing burning fragments that spun off and landed on the carpet, scorching it. The screaming rose to a crescendo, the light inside the ornament burning so brightly that Miriam could barely look at it. Then it blew apart like a mini-supernova, flames and shrapnel peppering the garden, and winked neatly out of existence, leaving the day feeling pale and somewhat empty.

No one moved for a long, fragile minute, then Gert lowered her arms and said in an aggrieved voice, "This was my favourite Christmas jumper. Look at that. Ruined!" She displayed a hole burned neatly into the sleeve from the debris the bauble had left behind.

Alice propped herself up on her elbows and said, "You could probably darn it."

"It'll never be the same," Gert said with a sigh.

"Never mind that," Teresa said. "What about poor Jasmine's living room?"

They looked silently at the soot-smeared walls and the burn marks on the carpet, the oily smudges on the ceiling and the cookies strewn across the floor. Someone's tea was overturned on the coffee table, and there was a pineapple upside down cake on the floor, upside down. A light dusting of icing sugar coated every surface. Smoke still drifted in the air.

"Can someone help me up?" Carlotta said.

A LIBERAL APPLICATION of soapy water, and an even more generous application of elbow grease later, and the living room was looking almost back to normal. Rosemary and Carlotta had managed to get most of the grease off the walls while arguing about the best way to do so, and Pearl and Teresa had dusted the icing sugar off everything. What biscuits hadn't been tidied up by Primrose while the Women's Institute had been otherwise engaged were tidied up more traditionally, and now there were only the scorch marks on the carpet left to show that they had recently been under attack. Miriam, Priya and Rose were still doing their best to make the marks presentable with the help of a pack of old razors Jasmine had found in the spare bathroom, but Miriam secretly thought that it was a lost cause. That was the problem with cream carpets. No forgiveness for the mishaps of life. Although, admittedly, exploding baubles were right up there with dragons for unexpected circumstances.

"Those things are *deadly*," Jasmine said, for about the twentieth time. She had finally stopped shaking, but her face was still a little pale, and Alice poured some Scotch into her tea while she was looking the other way. Gert had insisted that she needed some for medicinal purposes, to counteract the shock of having her favourite Christmas jumper so wantonly damaged, and most of the others had agreed it was a wonderful idea. Miriam had refrained. She still wasn't entirely sure she was over the Metaxa.

"They are terribly dangerous," Alice agreed. The newspapers she'd brought with her were spread on the coffee table, not that anyone needed any more proof after their first-hand encounter. Miriam had glanced over them while taking a break from scraping the carpet. They weren't quite what she'd term quality papers – one of them had a two-page spread featuring a woman who had apparently been kidnapped by mermen, and another featured several women who weren't wearing much more than mer*maids* – but they all featured the same story.

Christmas Baubles of Death!
My Christmas Baubles Burned My Gran!
Bauble Hell!

Miriam thought the last one might be a play on bloody hell, but she also thought that she might be giving the writers too much credit.

"So what do we do?" she said now, giving up on the carpet. It looked a lot better than it had, anyway. She got up and stretched, hands in the small of her back. "I checked my email before I came over, and we've had three order cancellations already. I've emailed back to explain that they aren't our baubles, but I don't think anyone cares."

"Would you risk it?" Pearl pointed out, and Miriam sighed.

"I suppose not. And it's not as if we can actually send any at the moment, anyway. But this is going to devastate Mortimer. And where are the dragons going to get money for gas bottles for the rest of the winter?"

"We'll cover it," Priya said. "Won't we?"

There was a general mutter of agreement, and Miriam inspected her cookies sadly. The icing was all smudged, giving the snowmen unfriendly leers and turning the stars into smeary sponges. There was also a generous amount of dog hair sticking to most of them, so she sighed and dumped them in the rubbish bag they were using for cleaning.

"Of course we'll look after the dragons," Alice said. "But by far the best thing we can do is to find out who's behind all this. This is most certainly personal now, with the DHL van going missing too."

"You don't think they sent that exploding bauble deliberately, do you?" Jasmine asked. "Oh, how awful!"

"No," Alice said. "I doubt they realised who had ordered it. I think they just can't actually make very good baubles." She patted

Jasmine's knee, then looked around expectantly. "Did anyone find out anything interesting?"

"Someone's growing pot in the library basement," Carlotta offered.

"That's Miss James," Rosemary said. "She's been doing that since the sixties."

"Mrs Ross, the wife of that bookkeeper type, seems to have quite a lot of gentlemen callers," Priya said. "I was chatting to her neighbour, and she said they're only ever there in the day, when Mr Ross is at work."

Gert snorted. "He's a book*binder*, not a book*keeper*, and she makes stained glass wind chimes. How do you think they afforded that fancy house?"

Everyone thought about that for a moment, then Pearl said, "Quite enterprising, really."

"Takes all sorts," Rose agreed. She was still scraping the carpet, peering at it a little short-sightedly. Miriam thought she might dig through to the floor beneath before too long, so she handed her a cup of tea and took away the razor. Rose accepted the tea and said, "We did see a silver Audi."

"Yes, but not the right one," Carlotta said hurriedly.

"How do you know it wasn't the right one?" Alice asked. "Where did you see it?"

"In the village square," Rose said. "It was a bit hard to see from behind the tree and all, though."

"Behind the tree?" Alice leaned forward, clasping her hands on her lap. "The Christmas tree? What were you doing?"

"We thought we should be a bit covert about things," Priya said, exchanging glances with Teresa. "But, um, it didn't work."

Alice frowned. "They saw you? Who was it?"

"Um. Detective Inspector Adams."

Alice stared at her for a moment, the corner of her mouth

twitching. "And you, Rose and Carlotta were hiding behind the tree?"

"And Pearl and Teresa," Priya admitted, twisting her cardigan through her fingers. "We may have looked a little suspicious."

"Detective—" Alice stopped, and laughed. "The poor woman must think we're all quite dotty. Well, serves me right for being so paranoid. There's probably half a dozen silver Audis in the area." She laughed again, not quite convincingly, in Miriam's opinion. She couldn't imagine Alice being paranoid. "Anything else?"

"Frank from the turkey farm was at the butchers," Teresa said. "He had all these sacks of grain and was throwing handfuls at Maisie, accusing her of stealing his turkeys so she'd get all the business."

"Ooh," Rosemary said. "Had he been on the sauce?"

"Probably. Maisie hit him with a leg of lamb and almost knocked him out, then got her boy and his friend to take him home to cool off."

"Well, that's all very interesting," Alice said. "But did anyone uncover anything that could be a lead?"

The women looked at each other, waiting.

"I think that's it, Alice," Rosemary said. "I'm very sorry."

"Don't be sorry," Alice said, although Miriam thought she actually looked quite sorry herself. "Process of elimination, isn't it? It's not like they're going to send us a note explaining themselves."

"Oh!" Miriam said, jumping up. "Oh, I can't believe I forgot!"

She rushed from the room and into the hall.

"Miriam," Alice called from the living room. "What on earth are you doing?"

"I got a note! I got a note!" She grabbed her coat and hurried back into the living room, digging in the pockets. Ugh, why were there so many pockets in this jacket? Of course, it was much better than not enough pockets, which was so often the problem with women's clothing, but it did make things hard to find.

"What note?" Alice asked.

"I was going to tell you, but then I forgot with the bauble and everything. It was like a threat! It told us to stop following them, and not to talk to the police. But it was all spelled terribly, and the writing was awful, too." Miriam moved on to the pockets in her trousers, frowning. "I did bring it." She glanced up at the windows as she searched, and froze.

"Miriam?" Alice said.

Miriam swallowed hard, feeling suddenly sick, and quite possibly like she was going to start hiccoughing again. "Um, are we sure about the silver Audi thing?"

"Why?" Alice got up quickly enough to knock the coffee table with her knee, spilling tea onto the newspapers.

"Because there's one right there."

The women scrambled to their feet and stared out the big bay windows to the little front garden and the street beyond. The silver Audi was at the kerb on the other side of the road, the heat of its exhaust smoke making plumes in the chilly air. It was liberally caked in mud, looking almost like one of those old two-toned cars, but there was no mistaking what was underneath.

"Well, I've had enough of this. I'm going to see what they're up to," Alice said, and grabbed the poker from the fireplace on her way to the door.

"Hold up," Gert said, and grabbed the coal shovel before anyone else could.

Rose armed herself with the fireplace tongs and rushed after them, and Miriam groaned. She didn't want to confront bauble thieves while armed with nothing more than household implements. But she couldn't stay here, either. She picked up her cookie tray (it was already badly dented, so there was no reason not to use it again) and hurried to the door.

The ladies of the Toot Hansell Women's Institute marched across the lawn, Alice leading with the poker swinging in one hand, flanked by Gert and her shovel and Miriam with her cookie tray. Following behind them came the seven other women, armed with umbrellas and golf clubs and saucepans and, in Jasmine's case, her phone. She was filming and giving an excited commentary as they went.

The silver Audi was parked between Gert's old Rover and Priya's 4x4, and as they approached it backed up rather urgently, crunching into the Rover.

"Hey!" Gert bellowed. "That's my car!" She broke into an ungainly jog, and the car lurched forward, almost making it out of the gap before nudging the 4x4 and stalling.

"My *car!*" Priya shrieked, and now everyone was running after Gert, who was brandishing the shovel over her head like a war club. The car gunned its engine, shot backward, hit the Rover again (eliciting an outraged howl from Gert), then shot forward and out of the gap just as the women charged across the road. Miriam hurled the cookie tray at the windscreen, and the car swerved wildly, the engine screaming in protest. Gert smashed a tail light with the coal shovel, and Alice got a glancing blow in that dented a side panel admirably, then the car was fishtailing down the road with Rose sprinting after it, spouting curses and gesticulating furiously with the fireplace tongs. She finally stopped as it revved around the corner, apparently still in first, and shouted, "That's right! You run! And don't come back!"

Miriam picked up her mangled baking tray, hoping she'd still be able to run like that in thirty years. Although, considering she didn't run now, the odds didn't seem good.

Alice shouldered the poker and looked at her thoughtfully. "Did you see them?"

Miriam tapped the tray against her leg. "Sort of."

"Was it the men from the marketplace?"

Miriam shook her head. "This sounds really silly, but I'm not even sure they were men. Or women." She looked at the other

202 | KIM M. WATT

women, standing in the street with their makeshift weapons. No one was laughing. "Did anyone see them properly?"

"They were wearing hats," Priya said, straightening up from inspecting the damage to her car. "I saw that."

"And scarves," Pearl offered.

"I saw the driver's hands," Gert said. She had patches of red high up on her cheeks. "Or maybe they were gloves. Weird gloves."

Alice smiled slightly. "I don't think so."

No one said anything for a moment, then Teresa said, "Their heads were too big."

Jasmine had been looking at her phone, and now she waved it at them. "It's all blurry. I mean, they are. Nothing else is. Just them."

"Like the dragons?" Miriam said, her stomach tight and uncomfortable. "The way they don't show up on camera?" Not that the strange occupants of the car had been dragons, no. But she was horribly certain that she'd been right to think that they weren't human, either.

Jasmine nodded without answering, and Alice sounded oddly breathless as she said, "Okay. Okay, so we know that now. Can you see the number plates?"

"No," Jasmine whispered. "It was too muddy."

Alice nodded as if she'd expected nothing else. "Well. No good staying out here freezing. Let's head back in."

MIRIAM FOUND the note lying on the hall floor under the coat rack as they trooped back into the house, and they gathered at the kitchen island to stare at it.

"Terrible writing," Carlotta said. "And spelling."

"It looks like they've never held a pen in their life," Pearl said, and Miriam thought of the hunched forms with their oversized heads, half-glimpsed in the speeding car. She shivered.

"And what's all this stuff?" Rose asked, rubbing some of the brown muck with her finger. It came off easily enough, and she sniffed it.

"Oh, don't do that," Miriam said. "It could be anything!"

"Yes, wash it off," Rosemary said. "You'll probably catch something."

"You do forget that I was a biologist," Rose said. "I've had my hands in worse." A shudder went around the table, and she grinned, then licked her finger. Miriam gagged, and there was a chorus of disgusted protest. "Chocolate," Rose said. "Not particularly good stuff, though."

"That is just awful," Teresa said. "Even if it is chocolate, where's it been?"

"Good for the immune system," Rose said, and Teresa flapped her hands.

"Well," Alice said. "I'm rather glad it is just chocolate, but it doesn't help us much."

"Unless it's the Easter bunny," Pearl suggested. Everyone looked at her. "What? We've got dragons and exploding baubles. Why not the Easter bunny?"

Alice shook her head. "Whoever – or *what*ever – is involved, this note is an overt threat, whether the bauble was or not. Whoever 'they' are, they may be dangerous."

"Bollocks to them," Gert said. "That damn bauble ruined my jumper. And they dented my bumper."

"And mine," Priya said.

"They can't get away with it," Miriam said, surprising herself. "Never mind dented cars or exploding baubles – they're endangering the dragons." Her chest felt hot with the injustice of it. When had the dragons ever done anything but make life better for people?

"Agreed," Carlotta said. "In the old country we wouldn't stand for such insults."

"Yeah, they're a proud lot in Manchester," Rosemary said, and for once Carlotta just snorted agreement.

"No one messes with the Toot Hansell Women's Institute," Priya said, and flicked the note off the table.

"Absolutely right," Gert agreed.

A ripple of nervous laughter crept around the room, and Miriam pressed her hands to her chest. It was warmer in here that it had any right to be, with the women standing shoulder to shoulder and smiling awkwardly at each other. But it was a good sort of warmth. The sort that started around the heart and could heat the whole world.

"Tea?" Jasmine said. She looked almost her normal colour again. "And I made some pigs in blankets. I just need to pop them in the oven."

There was a general rush for Tupperware as everyone insisted that Jasmine had done more than enough, and that they'd all brought plenty for everyone.

15

ALICE

Alice's house was on the way back to Miriam's, so they walked home together, full of sausage rolls and smoked salmon pinwheels and the beautiful little pastries Priya always made, not to mention all the cake and mince pies that had followed. Miriam was chattering nervously, and Alice listened with half an ear, still thinking about the men at the market. She was as near to certain as she could be that it hadn't been them in the car, but they still bothered her. None of the Women's Institute remembered selling them anything, and she had to admit that she couldn't swear she hadn't been the one to give them the baubles, either. They weren't local, that was all she was sure of. But plenty of people came to Toot Hansell for the Christmas markets and summer fetes. They were known for them. Everyone had promised to ask around, but Alice couldn't shake the feeling that they were running out of time. There were no more baubles going out. How long would the thieves keep their captives alive? Were they even still alive now, for that matter?

Her phone rang, startling her out of her thoughts, and she pulled it from the side pocket in her bag, checking the display. Her neighbour across the street. She frowned. He was a startlingly small old man whom she'd given her number to when she first moved in, in case he needed help. He'd used it to get her to the house half a dozen times in the first month, on the pretext of things like not being able to find his glasses, or not being able to reach something in the top of a cupboard, and after the third time he answered the door wearing nothing but a green velour dressing gown she'd had to tell him very severely that he was not to call her again unless he'd actually broken a bone. She still caught him staring at her from inside his house, his eyes level with the windowsill as he hid beneath it. She suspected that he wasn't even wearing the dressing gown when he did that.

"Hello, Pete," she said cautiously.

"Alice, you need to get back here quick," he said. "I've called the fire service, and we're doing what we can with the hoses, but hurry!"

Alice shoved the phone back in her bag without hanging up and broke into a run, ignoring Miriam's alarmed shout. *Her house.*

SHE WASN'T REALLY DRESSED for running, and it wasn't something she'd done much of for rather a long time, but she was still jogging when she came around the corner into her lane and saw the smoke. Miriam was struggling along behind her, doing her best to keep up, and Alice didn't wait. She ran down the lane to her poor, smoking house.

Every neighbour on the street, as far as she could tell, had their garden hoses out. There was only woodland to the right of her property, but her neighbours to the left had hoses running across the garden and coming out the windows, and more were set up in the gardens across the street. There was a chain of buckets going from Pete's house to her front door, and someone had found her own hose in the back garden and was using that, too. There was a terrible lot of excited shouting going on, and everything seemed desperately disorganised, but – and she dropped out of a jog to a hurried walk – there were no flames. Her front door was smoking, and the lower part of the ivy that climbed to the upstairs windows was a charred ruin, but there was no fire. Not anymore. Either her neighbours had been much more efficient than they appeared, or the bauble had failed to catch. And while she still rather thought that Jasmine's bauble had been an accident, she was quite certain that this hadn't been. No more than Miriam's note. Which meant it might not be the W.I. as a whole who were the targets, but just the two of them. The thought made her feel marginally better.

"Alice!" Pete shouted, tottering up to her. He wasn't wearing the bathrobe at least, she noted with some relief. "I think we've got it under control!" His trousers were drenched, and he dropped his bucket in the street and threw his arms around her. "We saved your house!"

Alice stood there rather uncomfortably and let him hug her, even though his fleece was quite as wet as his trousers, and his head was at a rather inconvenient height on her chest. She figured she could allow him that much, because it seemed that he was right. They had saved her house. Her home.

ALICE AND MIRIAM stood by the gate, looking at her front door. They had tried to call off the fire brigade, but the engine had been almost there already, so the firemen had insisted on coming. They had poked around and examined the door and asked a few questions, then declared her lucky. She rather agreed. It had been too cold and damp for the flames to catch, so other than the damaged ivy all she had was some bubbled paint on the window frames and a scorched front door with the paint peeling off it.

The fire captain, a stocky woman with dark hair, had said it looked like vandalism and that Alice should call the police. Alice had assured them she would do just that, and had made them all tea before packing them off again. Now the street was empty once more, the hoses rolled away and neighbours gone home. She'd even managed to get rid of Pete, although it hadn't been easy. He'd kept insisting that she needed companionship and affection after such a shock, and she was rather regretting letting him hug her. Apparently he was not the sort of man to miss the chance to capitalise on disaster.

"Are you sure you won't come back to mine?" Miriam asked, clutching her dented baking tray to her chest. Alice wondered what she was going to do with it.

"No," she said. "I'd rather stay here. And the hall needs mopping. Quite a bit of water got in."

"Do you want me to help you?"

"No, Miriam. You go home. I'll be fine."

"I'm not sure I will be," Miriam said, and Alice sighed. She didn't want company right now. In fact, at this very moment, she couldn't stand it.

"Nonsense, Miriam. You'll be absolutely fine. They've delivered their little messages, and that's all they wanted to do. We'll lie low for the rest of the day, let them think they've scared us."

"They have scared me."

Alice smiled, and it wasn't the friendly sort of smile she used as the chair of the Women's Institute. It was much older, and much harder, and Miriam didn't smile back. "There's nothing wrong with a little scare, Miriam. It reminds us we're still breathing. Off you go home now. I'll call you later." And she marched back inside, pausing to pull the mat out and lay it on the steps to dry. She locked the door behind her without checking if Miriam had gone or not, and walked from window to window, making sure that they were firmly shut. Only when she was certain that the house was secure did she retreat into the room that had once been a dining room. It was lined with bookshelves that reached all the way to the ceiling, with a fireplace on one wall and a set of rolling stairs waiting in the corner. There were deep chairs and soft cushions and mellow lights, and it was small and warm and quiet and *safe*. There, in the dim light, she sank into the grip of the chaise longue and finally let her smile fall away, leaving her face feeling vulnerable and unfamiliar. She lifted her hands and examined them, watching faint tremors dancing along her fingers. "Oh, dear," she said quietly, hearing the way the empty house swallowed the sound. "Oh, this is a right do."

ʁ

SHE STAYED there until the tremors had subsided, breathing the rich dusty scent of stacked books and listening to the silence. Her silence. She couldn't imagine losing this. The very thought of it made her stomach twist with horror and fury. She had worked very hard for this place, both in her career and in the way she'd shaped her life. She had created a haven, a place that was hers and that no one else could touch.

"I'm not having it," she announced to the empty room, and got up to light a fire in the wood-burner. "It just won't do at all."

Not that there was much else she could do today. Just as she had told Miriam, they needed to keep a low profile until they figured out what to do next. All their tracking efforts had failed. The silver Audi's number plates had been obscured. Pete said there might have been a car like that around earlier, but he was clearly angling for another hug, so she didn't quite trust him. Besides, he wouldn't have got the plates either, so even if he was telling the truth it didn't help them. And no one had seen anything unusual on the street before her door was fire-bombed. Or fire-baubled, most likely by the big-headed, weird-handed occupants of the Audi. Which left the dragons as their only hope for a lead.

She breathed life into the fire and rocked back on her heels, frowning. Where *were* the dragons? It was strange that they'd gone a whole day without checking in, especially in a time of crisis such as this. Maybe they were waiting at Miriam's. She picked her phone up from the side table, then stopped. In that case, Miriam would phone her. She needed to slow down. Rushing out into danger was just what the enemy wanted. What they always wanted. *Think before you act, Alice*, she reminded herself. Be calm. Be quiet. Be watchful. It had seen her through many complicated times in the past, and it wouldn't fail her now.

She selected a slim book on the lesser-known creatures of English mythology, and settled herself into the chaise longue, pulling a light blanket over her legs. So far she hadn't found anything at all about the Watch in any of her books, but there was time. There was always time.

IT WAS FULLY DARK OUTSIDE, the curtains pulled against the early night. The reading lamp cast a pool of soft light over the pages of Alice's book, and the fire was mumbling to itself contentedly. She had a tea on the side table and was reading about spriggans, small ugly creatures that can turn into giants at will and bring on storms as a distraction while they steal babies. They sounded most unpleasant, but seemed to be limited to Cornwall, which was a relief. She was wondering if there were any similar creatures roaming the Dales when there was a knock at the front door and she looked up, frowning. For a moment she wondered if it could be the dragons, then realised that they would have just slipped out of the woodland into the garden and come to the back door. Their continued absence was worrying her, although she doubted that any sort of Audi driver would really be any match for dragons.

The knock came again, and she put her book down, picking up the fire poker on her way to the door. Just in case.

She opened the damaged door warily, standing well back, then relaxed and pulled it all the way open. "Miriam? What's happened? Are you alright?"

Miriam raised a large pot, swathed in tea towels. Her ancient green VW Beetle huddled next to the fence. "I made too much, and I can't stand to be alone anyway. Every little noise is making me jump out of my skin. Can I come in?"

Alice frowned, not entirely sure she was ready for company yet. Then she looked at Miriam's pale, anxious face, and thought of the entire night stretching ahead, worrying about dragons and spriggans and exploding baubles, and she stepped back from the door. "Well. If it'll make you feel better."

Miriam eyed the poker nervously as she kicked off her boots, and Alice smiled.

"Just a precaution. I'm sure we're perfectly safe." But she locked the door firmly and took the poker with her as she led the way into the warmth of the kitchen, the curtains drawn tight against the night.

THE POT WAS BRIMMING with curry, seeping out from under the lid and staining the tea towels, and Miriam popped it on the stove while Alice found some rice and set it to soak. She also found a bottle of red wine in the pantry, and held it up for inspection.

"What do you think?"

Miriam shrugged. "The label's nice."

Alice shook her head. "You heathen." But she opened it and poured them both a generous glass, setting them on the kitchen table and leaving the bottle on the counter. "I'd say we should keep our wits about us, but I don't imagine there'll be any more trouble tonight. They'll be waiting to see if we back off."

"Are we going to back off?"

Alice pushed both hands back through her hair. "Quite honestly, I don't know. I'm not sure what else we can do. The dragons haven't been able to find any scents. Maybe they could get something from your note, but, well – they're not here. The tracker was discarded, quite deliberately I'm thinking now, and we have nothing else to go on. Nothing at all."

"Return address on the baubles?" Miriam offered, poking the curry with a spoon as if afraid it might jump out at her. It *gloop*ed reassuringly.

"No. The one on eBay is just that Huddersfield P.O. box. And if there was any postmark on the box that the bauble came in, it was impossible to see it, what with all the tape and so on."

Miriam tasted the curry and frowned, then added some salt from the grinder by the stove. "Almost all the bauble orders are cancelled now. Someone videoed one knocking over their Christmas tree and setting fire to the sofa. It's all over Facebook."

Alice nodded. "That was bound to happen. I suppose it's for the best. We can't even send anything out at the moment, since our mysterious counterfeiters keep intercepting them, and we certainly don't want *them* sending any out."

"But what about when we can start again? Poor Mortimer put so much effort in! What if this completely destroys his business?"

"I don't know, Miriam. One thing at a time. First, we need to find the missing drivers and make sure no one finds out about the dragons. That's what we need to concentrate on. After all that's sorted out, then we can worry about rebuilding the bauble business."

Miriam put a lid on the pot and sat down with a sigh. Alice pushed a glass of wine across the table to her, and Miriam stared at it as if reading her fortune in its dark surface. The curry was at a slow simmer, releasing spicy coconut scents into the kitchen, and it should have felt homey, comforting. Instead it felt like a candle against a darkness they had no hope of holding back. Everything was so out of reach. With all their leads gone, they were left relying on the dragons or the police to find the culprits, while they just waited here feeling useless and exposed.

They toasted each other silently, and Alice took a sip of wine with an appreciative nod. It was quite a good bottle, really. Movement at the door to the hall caught her eye, and she frowned. "Then there's that damn cat."

"What cat?"

"That one." She nodded at the scarred tomcat, standing in the doorway examining them. "How did you even get in? You were outside this morning, and I haven't seen you since."

The cat tipped them a wink, his tail sweeping low arcs across the floor.

Miriam stared at the cat. "Honestly, Alice, how can you let him stay? After all that talk about the Watch and so on?"

"I don't seem to have much choice in the matter. He just lets himself in." Although she probably shouldn't encourage him with tinned tuna.

The cat's gaze moved from one woman to the other, considering.

"I don't like the way he's looking at me," Miriam said. "Do you think he was listening to us?"

"Doubtless. Thompson's a nosy old cat."

"You've named him?"

Alice frowned, and took another sip of wine. "It just seemed to suit him. Gert called him Tom."

"But what if he did hear? What if he knows about – about our friends, and gets them in trouble?"

"You've already mentioned the Watch, Miriam. I imagine he knows we're onto him."

The cat glanced sideways and shook his head slightly, giving Alice the impression that he'd be rolling his eyes if he could. He crossed the kitchen to sit back on his hindquarters and put a paw on her knee.

"Hello. This is new, Thompson."

He dropped back to all fours and walked to the kitchen door, then stopped, looking over his shoulder at them expectantly. When they didn't move he huffed, and marched back to the table, glaring up at them.

"Alice," Miriam said nervously.

"What do you think he's going to do? Shed on us?"

The cat gave Alice a disapproving look and leaped onto the table.

"No! Bad cat! Down you go." Alice grabbed for him and he slipped away from her, body lithe under her hands. He swiped her wine glass with one soft paw, knocking it over and sending red wine swilling across the table as the glass rolled away, then lunged for Miriam's. She pushed back from the table with a yelp and knocked her own glass over, and Thompson narrowed his eyes with a distinctly satisfied air. Alice grabbed for him again and he leaped from the table, leaving her holding nothing more than a handful of shed fur.

"You horrid little animal," she told him, rescuing some unfinished Christmas cards as Miriam rushed to grab a cloth from the sink. "What on earth are you playing at?"

Wine was pooling across the wooden table and dripping onto the floor, and Alice shooed him away before he could cause any more trouble then grabbed the kitchen roll from under the sink. Thompson shook a little wine off one white-socked paw and retreated to the door to sit down, watching the women with interest.

"Honestly, this place is going to stink for days," Alice complained, bundling the sodden kitchen roll into the bin and going back to spray the table down with cleaner.

"Well, whether or not he's a Watch cat, he's a nuisance," Miriam said, rinsing out the cloth and passing it back to her.

"He is," Alice agreed, and they both turned to look disapprovingly at the cat.

He wasn't on the floor.

He was sitting on the kitchen counter, one paw resting against the bottle of wine. He'd already pushed it close enough to the edge that the base was hanging very slightly off. He purred.

"*Thompson*," Alice said warningly.

Thompson looked at the door, at the women, then back at the door, his eyes wide and bright and terribly expectant.

"Are we being ordered out of the house by a cat?" Miriam asked, soapy water dripping unnoticed from her hands.

"It appears so," Alice said. "As if dragons weren't enough to deal with."

THOMPSON WAITED IMPATIENTLY while they pulled on their coats and boots, then led the way out the front door with his tail high, not looking back to see if they were following.

"We could just shut the door and lock him out," Miriam whispered.

He stopped short in the middle of the path and looked back, his eyes narrowed. Miriam flinched.

"I don't think doors are much of an issue for him, somehow." Alice stepped out into the night, pushing Miriam gently ahead of her, and locked the door behind them. "He seems to come and go as he pleases. Anyway, we may as well see what he wants. We're not doing anything else."

"We *were* going to be eating curry and watching terrible Christmas specials."

"Well. This is a little more exciting, then, isn't it?"

Thompson stopped by Alice's car and put his paws on the door, and she fished the keys out of her handbag, then reached over him to open it. He jumped in and sat in the passenger seat.

"And where am I supposed to sit?" Miriam complained.

"He's only small. Stop complaining and get in."

Miriam did, apologising to the cat as she squeezed in next to him. He gave her an amused look, but didn't move to climb onto her lap. Instead, he waited until Alice had started the car then stood with his hind legs on the console between the front seats and rested his front paws on the dashboard, wrinkling his nose at the air rushing out of the vents. Alice turned the fan down and looked at him.

"Now what, Thompson?"

The cat looked at her, then pointed his nose forward, ears high and interested. Alice put the car in gear and they rolled off quietly, Thompson's eyes catching the lights of the dashboard and glowing a ghostly green.

At the end of the road, Thompson leaned left, still pointing with his nose. They went left. Then right, onto the main road. Then straight on, the cat as sure and fixed as a figurehead, guiding the car out of the village and into the empty winter night.

16
DI ADAMS

"Adams?"

DI Adams looked up, a sudden nervous sickness in her belly. Dammit, this was bound to happen, and she'd brought it on herself. She was really terrible with breaking rules. She hated doing it, and it was surprisingly problematic for a career in law enforcement.

"Yes, sir?" she said to Detective Chief Inspector Temple.

He sat down in the chair on the other side of her desk, the one usually reserved for witnesses or complainants, leaned forward, leaned back, then crossed his legs awkwardly. "Care to tell me what's going on? You were missing again yesterday, and rumour has it you've been up in Skipton."

Damn. "Well, not Skipton exactly. Toot Hansell. Where that murdered vicar case was last summer."

"Okay." He watched her, and she tried not to fidget. He wasn't huffing or growling or making any snide comments about southerners. That seemed ominous. "And?" he said finally.

"There were some things with the missing drivers' case that made me think there might be connections," she said carefully.

"I thought you closed the vicar's murder. You rethinking the guy?"

"No, no. That was the right guy. But there was some other, um, stuff, that I noticed when I was up there. I thought I might be helpful on the missing persons, since I already had connections in the village."

"Okay," DCI Temple said again, and shifted in his seat, uncrossing his legs and resting his hands on his knees, then staring at them like he didn't know what they were doing there. "So, are you, uh, settling in okay, Adams?"

Settling in okay? She'd been here ten months. "Um, yes, thanks. Fine."

"Right. Only your behaviour lately is, ah, a little erratic, and, ah, I've been told that I may be a bit harsh at times."

She started to answer, and he raised his hand.

"And, well, I know your transfer from London was due to work-related stress, and it has been brought to my attention that I may not be accommodating that as well as I could be."

"Sir—"

"No, Adams, it's fine. You lot have a different sense of humour, and I realise my jokes may have missed the mark at times."

"My lot?" She was fairly sure he didn't mean that as it sounded, but she still didn't like it.

"Southerners."

"Right."

They stared at each other, and DI Adams wondered what, exactly, was going on. Then he said, "Right. So. You know where the, ah, support officer for this sort of thing is."

"Yes."

"And if you need some personal time, I'm sure it can be arranged."

"Alright." Personal time? Really? What *was* this?

"Good." He nodded sharply, got up, took a step away then

stopped short and turned back. "Oh, God, Adams, when I said you lot, I didn't mean *women*. Christ. I'm not *sexist*." He started off again, froze, and revolved slowly on his heel. "I also didn't mean—"

This time she was the one who held her hand up, struggling to keep her voice level. The DCI had gone astonishingly red. "You meant soft southerners, sir. I know."

"Yes." He wiped his mouth. "Good." He seemed to be looking for something else to say, but gave up and walked away.

DI Adams stared after him, then turned to look at James as he set a tea down in front of her. He was wearing a bandage on his wrist, presumably from the snake incident the previous day. "Um," she said.

He shrugged. "I don't know what the hell's up with you and that village. But I had to tell him something, else you'd have been suspended."

He walked away again before she could decide whether to thank him for covering for her, or to shout at him for discussing her stress levels with the DCI. In the end she just sipped her tea, looking again at the text that had dinged in just as the chief inspector had sat down.

Adams.

There have been some interesting developments. Call me.

Collins.

She looked at the tea, then picked up her jacket and headed for the door, thinking that she'd prefer a coffee anyway. She'd give him a call while she waited and see what he had to say.

Twenty minutes later she was back in her car, winding her way out of the city, coffee jammed in the cup holder and half a sandwich in her free hand, wondering just how far this new sympathetic DCI thing could be stretched.

DI ADAMS PULLED into the car park of a National Trust centre, stopped next to DI Collins' car and got out. The dark was coming in fast, and there were no other cars around. The squat stone building of the centre huddled alone at the rear of the parking spaces, and she could see someone moving around under the yellow lights inside still. Otherwise, the place was empty, the rest of the village houses with their backs turned, as if shunning the walkers that must congregate here in better weather.

DI Collins was waiting for her, leaning against his car with his hands tucked into his pockets and his shoulders hunched against a nasty little wind.

"Collins," she said, folding her arms against the chill. Her city jacket wasn't made for the cold up here. It wound in around the seams and clawed at her face.

He didn't reply, watching her with an unnervingly sharp gaze, his usual smile absent.

"You said there were new developments? Some stuff I needed to see? Are you going to tell me about it, or have I driven all the way up here to get the silent treatment?"

He scratched his jaw. "What aren't you telling me, Adams?"

"Right now, you're the one who's holding back information."

"It's my case, remember? My prerogative."

"I know it's your case, Collins. But you called me here. And I'm trying to help, but I can't do that when I don't know all the details."

He watched her a little longer, and she uncrossed her arms, lifting her chin and scowling at him.

"I've had strange cases before," he said finally. "An artist spray-painting sheep as some sort of living art project. The old guy who decided the government was controlling everyone through milk and started putting food colouring in all the cattle troughs so the milk would come out green and it would have to be thrown away. The woman that kept stealing black cats and releasing them into the wild so that they could, apparently, grow up to be panthers.

There's still a whole colony of them up near Aysgarth. Then there were those UFO enthusiasts coming to blows over rocks. *Rocks.* Not even meteors. Plenty of weird stuff. But this one – missing postmen, a missing DHL driver, and some big city cop poking her nose in because she suddenly has some vested interest in a village she hadn't even heard of six months ago – nothing like this. So what gives?"

"What else has happened? You didn't drag me up here for this."

"Fire," he said. "The vans were fire-bombed. Or so we thought, although we couldn't find any accelerant."

"And now something else, too."

He hesitated, then sighed. "Now something else. Alice Martin's house."

"Alice? Is she okay?"

"She's fine. Didn't even call it in. The fire chief told us. Said Ms Martin made them all tea."

DI Adams smiled slightly. "That sounds about right."

"It does. But now tell me, Detective Inspector Adams, why you're concerned but not surprised, and why everyone was acting so strangely at my Aunt Miriam's house the other day. Including you."

DI Adams puffed out her cheeks and wondered how easy it actually was these days to find yourself sectioned.

"DRAGONS."

"Yes."

"Large, fire-breathing reptiles with wings."

"Well, not that large. Not these ones, anyway."

"Like *Game of Thrones*."

"Not so much. I get the feeling they may be perpetuating stereotypes, there."

DI Collins raised his eyebrows slightly. "Well, we can't have that, can we?"

DI Adams sighed and looked longingly at the warmly lit windows of the National Trust centre. "Do you think they have coffee in there?"

"It'll be closed," Collins said, and pushed himself off his car. "But there's a pub just down the road. Let's go get a drink. I think I could use one."

DI Adams rather thought that she could, too. She couldn't feel her fingers, and there was a low, throbbing band of cold settled around her ears. She retreated to her car and put the heater on full blast as she pulled into the road behind him.

☙

THE INSPECTORS PUSHED through two sets of heavy doors into the pub, the ceiling low above them and the old red carpet worn and not particularly clean-looking. DI Adams was having reservations about whether the coffee would be at all drinkable, but at least it was warm in here. There was an open fire burning and a rather ancient Labrador stretched out in front of it, belly up.

"Hi," the young woman behind the bar said.

"Two coffees," DI Collins said.

"Of course! Long black, flat white, latte, espresso …?" she trailed off, looking at him expectantly, and he made some small exasperated gesture.

"However it comes." He headed toward a booth, skirting the snoring dog.

The woman looked at DI Adams with an anxious smile.

"Make it two long blacks with milk on the side. Probably safest."

"Great! I'll bring it over." She rushed to what was, DI Adams had to admit, a rather impressive machine. Hopefully she was as good with it as she was enthusiastic about it.

She followed DI Collins to the booth, peeling off her jacket, and sat down, luxuriating in the heat of the fire. Her fingertips were icy to the touch, and she rubbed her hands together, blowing on them gently.

"Adams, I rather thought we had a certain rapport."

"Well, yes. We do. Of a professional sort."

He snorted. "Yes, of a professional sort, Adams. This is why I'm disappointed."

"I'm telling you the truth."

"Dragons. Like in *Game of Thrones*."

"Well—"

"Okay, fine. *Not* like in *Game of Thrones*. But dragons."

"Yes."

"I know I'm not some city cop, Adams, but for God's sake, you work in *Leeds* now, not bloody London. Is it really a thing there, taking the mickey out of the country plods?"

"I never—" she paused as the bartender arrived with a tray, and they sat in awkward silence, DI Adams nodding and mumbling thank you as each cup and each little jug of milk was placed down. As soon as the young woman turned away she started again. "I never took the mickey. You wanted to know the truth, and this is it."

"And you honestly expect me to believe there were two dragons sitting right in front of me in Aunt Miriam's living room?"

She sighed. "I know it sounds unbelievable."

"The problem is, I'm actually starting to think you believe it, which is even worse. Are you sure you're not on mental health leave?"

"That's really offensive."

"You know what, you're right. I'm sorry." He leaned back in the

224 | KIM M. WATT

booth, watching the sleeping dog rather than her. "That was uncalled for."

"It was." She stirred her coffee with more force than was necessary, slopping it onto the saucer.

"Which leads me to believe that you obviously are taking the mickey, and I've been wasting my time with you when I could have been following proper leads." He glared at her, then poured some milk into his cup. "God knows what that bit of poor judgement's going to have cost me."

DI Adams scowled at him. There was no point even talking to him. He'd made his mind up, and nothing she said was going to make any difference. And, okay, she'd questioned her own mental stability at times, both in London and in her first encounter with Toot Hansell. But he had no bloody right to do it.

They sat with their coffee in silence, and she wondered if she should just go. She'd head to Toot Hansell and check that Alice and Miriam were alright, take advantage of the fact that DCI Temple wasn't going to be checking up on her. Get the hell away from DI Collins and his sour face. Yes. That was the best option. She grabbed her coat and started to slide out of the booth, then Collins' phone rang, startling them both.

"Wait, please," he said, and she did, not quite sure why, perched on the edge of the bench while Collins answered.

"Yeah?" he said. Then, "*Another* one?" He dug in his jacket for his wallet, and DI Adams pulled her own out, dropping some money on the table.

"Where?" Collins asked. DI Adams followed him out the door and back toward their cars, shrugging into her jacket and turning the collar up against her neck. He said, "On the way," then hung up and stood staring at his phone, his coat still over one arm. It was cold and clear, and the last of the daylight had been chased away. It felt like frost, the grass already sparkling softly under the lights of the pub, and when DI Adams looked up, she caught a glimpse of stars.

"I hope you get them," she said, jingling her keys in her pocket.

Collins scratched his neck. "They took another van. M&S on flower delivery, coming back from Toot Hansell."

"Huh. Going for anyone now, are they?"

Collins sighed, and said, "Come in my car. You city drivers are worse than the tractors."

She gave him a measured look. "So you believe me?"

"Not even slightly. But the whole case is weird, so I don't know. Let's get your weird angle on it."

"Are you using weird because you don't want to say crazy?"

He groaned. "Adams, you're talking about *dragons*. Now are you coming or not?"

She opened the car door and got in, shivering and wishing she'd asked for a takeaway cup for the coffee.

THE M&S van sat with its back doors open, trapped by spotlights that bleached the trees of colour and made the night beyond the lay-by impenetrable. DI Adams, realising she needed either sleep or caffeine, had the unshakable feeling that at any moment a trio of tap dancers would come bobbing out into the light, feet clattering on the tarmac. She pinched her nose and got as close to the van as she could without getting in the way of the techs. She could see the now-familiar scrapes on the doors, although the black paint made the scorching harder to see. She could smell it, though.

DI Collins slouched out of the light, one hand raised to protect his eyes, and came to stand next to her. "Thoughts?"

She raised her eyebrows but didn't say anything.

"Dragons, huh?"

"Fire damage but no accelerants. Gouges on the doors inconsistent with any tools we're familiar with, unless we want to bring Wolverine into the equation. No fresh tyre tracks or other evidence of anyone being here but the driver."

"I thought your dragons were nice. What're they playing at?"

She studied him, trying to gauge if he was joking or not. She couldn't tell. "I don't think it's the dragons I know. But I imagine where there's one dragon there's others, and they might be less friendly."

DI Collins snorted. "Here be dragons." He left her and went to talk to the tech making notes by the front of the van.

DI Adams moved out of the way as a tech crouched by the back doors with a camera, and stood with her hands in her pockets and her feet planted solidly on the cold ground, rocking gently. She didn't know how to do this. She didn't know how you solved crimes with mythological beasts as suspects. You couldn't knock on doors, or fingerprint them, or put them in an interview room. You couldn't *arrest* them. She sighed. She fancied arresting someone. Anyone would do, it didn't have to be related. And if a chase was involved, even better. She sighed again and rolled her shoulders, listening to them creak and crack. Fat chance of that, for the moment.

A car purred up the lane, moving at a decent clip considering the flashing lights and spots and tape strung about the place. People normally slowed down for that sort of thing. The two inspectors turned to watch it pass, the light show flooding the interior, and after a moment DI Collins wandered over.

"Adams," he said, "Did that look like my Aunt Miriam in that car?"

"I rather think it did."

"And Alice Martin."

"I think so."

He rubbed his cheek. "Was there a cat?"

DI Adams smiled faintly. "At least it wasn't a dragon, right?"

Collins took his phone out and frowned at it. "Should I call her?"

"Why not? They might just be taking the cat for a drive, but it's worth asking."

He gave her a sharp look, and she shrugged. He was going to have to make his own mind up. She'd done all she could do. Although the cat was both new and intriguing.

He looked back at his phone, flicking through the contacts, and DI Adams heard the whine of another engine. It was revving wildly, running in far too low a gear, and DI Collins looked up as they heard the crunch of metal on stone, then the scream of a car sliding along a wall.

"That doesn't sound good," DI Adams said, taking a step back from the road. The scraping had stopped, the painfully shrieking engine approaching fast, and one high-beam light sprung at them out of the dark, the other presumably smashed. *"Run!"* she bellowed, and sprinted for the wall.

The van came careening into the lay-by, snapping the crime scene tape and skidding on the gravel. DI Adams, heart roaring in her ears, flung herself up and over the closest wall, hearing the snarl of metal on metal and the shouts of the others. A couple of the techs were crouching beside her, their breathing ragged and panicked, but neither of them seemed to be hurt. She motioned them to stay where they were and jumped up and back over the wall again, knocking a section of the loose stone on top flying and stumbling as she landed. She kept her feet, though, and ran for the van where it had come to rest after bouncing off the M&S vehicle, facing the wall with its remaining headlight dead. Adrenaline chased the cold and the weariness from her, leaving the night clear cut behind, every detail etched on her senses. The smell of burning rubber where the driver had tried, too late, to stop; the ever-present country scent of animal waste; the long shadows thrown by the one remaining spotlight; the still-moving back doors of the new van, hanging open; the glitter of broken glass; and DI Collins' voice, hard but not angry.

"Come out slowly, hands up. Out, lad, out." His own hands were wide and ready, his stance a half-crouch, as if expecting the driver to appear in a rugby tackle. "Come on, now."

DI Adams positioned herself ready to help restrain the driver if necessary, and they waited, the two uniformed officers forming a back guard and the techs peering over the wall like nosy neighbours. The driver's door swung open, and the man inside looked at them anxiously. Blood trickled from a cut in his forehead, but otherwise he looked unharmed.

"Are they gone?" he asked timidly.

"Are who gone?" DI Collins asked.

"The – the things. They were following me."

"The things?" Collins repeated, and DI Adams felt her stomach tighten.

"They stopped me. I thought someone was hurt, and they got me to stop, but when I got out, they weren't *people*."

"They weren't?"

"No." He shook his head firmly, and wiped blood off his face. He looked at it without much interest, then took a nervous peek at the sky. "I thought they were going to eat me, but I jumped in the back." He nodded, more to himself than to the police, and glanced at the sky again. "So are they gone?"

"The things, you mean?" DI Collins asked. He'd straightened up, apparently confident that the man might be unbalanced, but he wasn't dangerous.

"Yeah, the – the monsters."

Collins glanced at DI Adams, then said, "Yeah. No monsters here."

"I think they'd have eaten me, if it wasn't for the charcuterie," the driver said, and slid carefully out of the van. His legs seemed to be a bit wobbly, and he clutched the door to keep himself upright.

"I'm sorry?"

"The charcuterie. And the dessert tray." He nodded at the back of the van. "I had a load of platters in there for a function tomorrow. And sandwiches, but they didn't seem so interested in those. I threw the whole lot at them, and legged it while they ate the charcuterie." He looked suddenly worried. "My boss isn't going to be happy."

"I imagine he'll be more worried about the van than the charcuterie," DI Collins said, taking the man's elbow and leading him gently toward the marked car.

"She," the man said, letting himself be put into the back seat. He was shaking, and one of the uniformed officers went to pull a blanket out of the boot. "Oh, no, I'm going to be in *so* much trouble."

DI Adams crouched at the car door before Collins could close it. "Sir, what did the people on the road look like? The ones that got you to stop?"

He chewed his lip. "Like people at first. But then you got closer, and they were just all wrong."

"All wrong?"

"Yeah. Like the proportions were all wrong. Their heads were too big. And they had too many teeth."

DI Adams frowned. She had no idea what that might be, but it didn't sound pleasant. "And the monsters?"

"Oh, big. Well, maybe not that big. But pretty big. And scaly. Wings. Breathing fire." He thought about it for a moment. "Dragons, I guess."

"Thank you, sir," DI Adams said, and closed the door. She looked at Collins, trying to keep her expression neutral. He glared at her as if dragons were her fault, then pulled his phone out.

"Let's find out what my damn aunt's done with these bloody dragons, then."

DI Adams looked up at the sky, waiting, while Collins walked in a circle, shouting into his phone. A moment later he hung up, shaking his head in frustration. He marched back to her.

"Signal's no good. She couldn't hear me."

"Can you track it?"

"Should be able to. Can you call it in?" He headed for the car, and she fell into step with him.

"Where're we going?"

"Well, they went past going that way, didn't they?"

"We don't know if that had anything to do with the dragons."

"Any suggestions, then, on what two ladies of a certain age were doing driving a cat around the Dales at 8 p.m. on a cold December night?"

"I have no idea what the cat's about," DI Adams admitted.

"I don't even like cats."

He pulled away from the lay-by and they headed into the suddenly unfamiliar night as DI Adams called through to the tech department. As long as it had GPS on it, she'd have Miriam's phone as a lovely little red blip in an app on her own mobile in about five minutes. Someone answered, and she gave them the phone number, then hung up and concentrated on not leaving permanent fingernail marks in the door handle as DI Collins flung them around the corners.

17

MORTIMER

Mortimer, Amelia and Gilbert perched shoulder to shoulder on a ledge in a quiet corner of the Grand Cavern, peering out at the High Lord dozing on his Weber.

"He doesn't *look* worried," Gilbert said.

"He's probably not," Mortimer replied. "He has far too much faith in people."

"But what do we do, Mortimer?" Amelia asked. "I mean, if Lord Margery gets in …"

"If Lord Margery gets in, then it's back to hiding in holes and scavenging for food and fuel all year, scared of every picnicker or rambler or loud noise we hear. She won't even let us stay here. She's always saying it's too close to the village. We'll wind up some place worse than the slate quarries."

"She can't do that!" Gilbert said.

"She can if she's High Lord," Mortimer said. He wished Beaufort would *do* something. He didn't know what, but surely there had to be something. Rousing speeches, perhaps, or flags or banners or that sort of thing. It worked for humans.

"Well – well, I'm not living like that," Gilbert declared, rather loudly. He threw his wings wide and caught Mortimer across the snout, making him stagger on the ledge. The small dragon was flushing a furious puce, and Amelia and Mortimer stared at him. "I'm *not!* That's not being a dragon. That's being a mouse or a rabbit or something. Not that there's anything wrong with that, but it's not being a dragon."

"And what do you know about being a dragon?" Amelia asked. "You can't even fly!"

Mortimer winced, even though she did have a point.

Gilbert nodded at the High Lord. "*He* doesn't care that I can't fly. *He* said all you need to be a dragon is to hatch out of a dragon's egg."

"So what do you propose we do then, Gil? Mount a mutiny?" Amelia looked tired, and Mortimer wished he hadn't let them work all night on the baubles. But he hadn't expected the day to turn out like this.

"We have to do *something!* We can't just sit here and watch Lord bloody Margery and a bunch of silly old stuck-in-the-past dragons and rock-headed glory-days-ers like Rockford ruin everything!"

"Gilbert, calm down," Mortimer said. They were starting to attract stares from the dragons already in the cavern.

"No! Why should I? This is *important.*" Gilbert glared at them both. "You don't get it. Beaufort's old, and, well – *really* old. But he's about *living.* That's why he doesn't care that I like swimming instead of flying. That's why he likes trading with humans and sneaking around markets and drinking mulled wine. Because it's *living.* And that's what a dragon should do. That's what *everyone* should do. Creeping about all frightened, and hiding, and holding to old ways just because that's the way it's always been done, and being scared of anything new or different – that's not living. That's existing, and only barely. So we can't let this happen."

Mortimer sighed, and wished it was that simple. He wished *anything* were as simple as Gilbert always seemed to think. "We can't stop it if the vote goes the wrong way. Beaufort will abide by whatever the clan decides."

Gilbert swatted Mortimer with a wing again, and Mortimer was inclined to think it wasn't entirely accidental. "And we're just sitting here. You know what Lord Margery will be doing? She'll be out there talking to all her old clan mates, and all those ridiculous dragons who think she's all about some mythical glory days when dragons ruled the skies or some rubbish like that, as if that was ever even a thing, and we're just *sitting* here. I bet Rockford's out there telling everyone they'll be able to burn villages and raid farms and all sorts of rubbish. Anything to get them to vote Beaufort out."

Mortimer blinked, and sat up straight, feeling suddenly foolish. What was he doing? Why hadn't he thought of this? He was still thinking like an old dragon, as if the fight was just between Beaufort and Lord Margery. It wasn't. It was up to all of them. Every one of them got a vote. Every one of them made a difference. "You're right. We should be doing something."

"I *know.*"

"Come on. We need to do this. We need to remind everyone how much Beaufort has done for them. Because he's not going to."

"What about the baubles?" Amelia asked.

"Bollocks to the baubles. I don't care about the baubles. Ghasts take them." Mortimer was already scrambling down the slope and toward the entrance. "Hurry!"

IT WAS LATE AFTERNOON, the clear sky peppered with low cloud that was turning a cold gold in the early sunset when Mortimer hurried into the Grand Cavern and scrambled up the rocks to join Amelia. The cavern was packed, full of dragons flushing anxious greys and excited reds and half a dozen shades in between, their steam forming a low, multi-coloured cloud that hid the roof from view. Everyone was here, from Lord Walter to the tiny, hysterically excited shapes of Rupert and Josie dashing among the adults, between legs and over tails. Mortimer didn't think he'd ever seen so many Cloverlies gathered like this. There were dragons here who didn't even live in the mount, but who had their own dens and burrows in the high fells, keeping themselves to themselves and scorning even the company of other Cloverly dragons. Their presence made him nervous. It didn't seem very likely to him that such recluses would be voting to make dragons more connected to the outside world.

"Have you seen Gil?" Amelia asked, and he shook his head.

"I haven't seen him since we all left."

"I hope he's alright."

"He'll be fine. I'm sure he's just trying to round up some more votes."

"Should we have let him, though, Mortimer? I mean, I love Gil, but he's kind of – different."

Mortimer settled himself on the ledge. "Of course he is. That's why Beaufort loves him. And he convinced us, didn't he?"

She sighed. "I suppose. But he does get a bit overexcited. And he should be here by now."

Below them, Beaufort uncoiled himself and sat up, his head high and his chest proud. He surveyed the crowd with those old eyes, the gold crackled by the heat of centuries, then gave a cough that was halfway to a roar. The excited chatter died to nothing almost instantly, and all eyes turned to him.

"Dragons of the Cloverly clan," he said, his voice calm and warm, booming across the walls. "This is indeed a historic day. Rather than your leader being dictated by might – or dropping dead – you will choose who you wish to lead you on into the coming age. I won't be making any speeches, and I won't be making any promises, because you have lived with me as your

High Lord for long enough to know me. As I know you, from hatchling to old age. I will say only this: we have lived small for centuries, because it was the safest way to be. But the times have changed around us. Humans have changed. And with that change comes an opportunity for us to live large once again. Because we may be small, but our hearts are not." He paused, looking carefully around the cavern, and Mortimer felt his own heart aching, small or not. He couldn't stand it if Beaufort lost. He couldn't. And not just because of the baubles, or any of that sort of rubbish. Because Beaufort didn't deserve to lose. His heart was too big for any of them.

"Lord Margery," Beaufort said.

She stepped to the edge of a rock outcropping, where everyone had to look up to see her, even Beaufort. Her wings hung heavy above her, a deep indigo blue, and her face was proud and beautiful. "Dragons of Cloverly," she said, "I'll make this brief, because there's little to be said. Beaufort has led us well for many years, but with great age can come certain … idiosyncrasies."

"*Cow*," Amelia hissed, and Mortimer shushed her, although he agreed quite firmly.

"And idiosyncrasies are fine," Lady Margery continued. "Until they get us killed. And, as we all know, that's what humans are best at. Killing anything that's different to them, anything they don't understand. Gods – they even kill each other over it!" She paused to let a ripple of agreement pass through the cavern, and Mortimer swallowed against a tightness in his throat. "And if the humans don't kill us, the Watch will exile us to desert lands, without a rabbit in sight. These are the facts."

"They are *not*—" Amelia began rather loudly, her scales flashing with hectic colour, and Mortimer stomped on her paw. She squeaked and subsided with a hurt look, but she wasn't helping anyone. There was no point making a scene. It wouldn't change anyone's mind. Not in the direction they wanted to, anyway. They

236 | KIM M. WATT

just had to let it play out, be dignified and calm and *dragonish*, just as Beaufort was. The High Lord was sitting on his Weber, looking terribly relaxed, with his wings tucked comfortably against his sides while he nodded agreeably to Lord Margery's words. They had done all they could do.

Lord Margery gave her wings a final, impressive shake ("Show-off," Amelia muttered), and Beaufort inclined his head. "Lovely, Lord Margery, thank you. If you'll just come down and seat yourself over there, please?" He indicated the opposite end of the chamber, rather lower down than her current lofty perch. She scowled but complied, and a titter of laughter rippled around the cavern. Rockford's little group growled and stomped, and the laughter died quickly. The High Lord ignored it all. "Now, my friends. There is no shame in either choice. There will be no repercussions. Move to the side of the chamber where your choice of High Lord sits. Once you are all seated, Lord Margery and I will both count, so there can be no disagreement."

"Wouldn't put it past her to cheat," Amelia grumbled, but this time Mortimer didn't shush her. A rumble of wings and scraping paws was washing around the Grand Cavern, amplified by the high ceiling and hard walls, turning it into a stampede. The Cloverly dragons were making their choice.

❦

MORTIMER WAS COUNTING. They hadn't had to move, and it made a good vantage point, the little ledge on Beaufort's side of the cavern. The big dragon sat below them looking as if he were attending a tea party rather than a vote on his fate. He'd climbed down from his Weber and was leaning against it, exchanging a few words with the dragons closest to him. They were an odd mix. Lord Walter had come to Beaufort's side, muttering that he might not hold with humans, but this voting malarkey was even more ridiculous, and if they were going to have the upheaval of a new High Lord it should be done the traditional way and involve some bodily harm, if not actual death. Lord Pamela was there as well, growling that if Beaufort had kept his silly investigation to his silly self they wouldn't be in this mess. And as for the dragons who had been trading with Amelia – well, Mortimer didn't know what she'd said to them, but they were all firmly on Beaufort's side of the Grand Cavern, and some of the younger ones were wearing rings in their tails or on their ankles, and the older ones had blankets to protect themselves from the hard floor. There seemed to be quite a lot of envious looks coming their way from the firmly blanket-less camp of Lord Margery (although none of them had protested about barbecues, he thought sourly). Even some of the recluses had joined Beaufort's side, and were investigating his Weber with great interest. One, a rather rotund dragon with moss growing on her cheeks, was petting Wendy's kitten blanket and *ooh*-ing in delight.

"*Where* is my brother?" Amelia demanded, peering around the hall. "He's still not here, Mortimer."

"Thirty-eight, thirty-nine. Yes, I gathered that the last time you said it. And the time before that."

"Don't be snotty. We need him here. It's close, isn't it?"

"There's still six dragons down there dithering like ducks, damn them."

"*How close*, Mortimer?"

He sighed. "Thirty-nine to Lord Margery. Thirty-six to Beaufort."

"He's *down?*"

"Yes, and Rockford's lot are down there with the six. They'll be trying to bully them all into going across." Although still not as big as Beaufort, Rockford towered above the other dragons on the floor, and Mortimer could see him leaning over them, using his bulk. He had an inkling that Rockford still did a bit of sheep-stealing when he could get away with it. It was hard to get that big on rabbits. They took too much work to catch.

"That's not right," Amelia said, chewing on a claw anxiously. "He shouldn't be allowed to do that. We should go down there and speak for Beaufort."

"No. We've already done what we can. He wouldn't want us using those sorts of tactics."

"There's being honourable and there's being ridiculous," Amelia growled, but she stayed where she was. Mortimer didn't exactly disagree with her, but he didn't move. Some things were the High Lord's choice, and his alone. And Beaufort always did know best. Well, most of the time. He looked down, realising that he was worrying his tail again, and sighed at the size of the bald patch.

"FORTY," Beaufort said, his voice carrying across the packed dragons.

"Forty-one," Lord Margery said, and she didn't sound as happy as Mortimer thought she might. He supposed she'd been hoping for a clean victory, whereas this was sort of an accidental one – the last two dragons had virtually done eeney-meeny-miney-moe to decide which side to go on.

"*No!*" Amelia wailed. "And where is *Gilbert?* At least we'd have had a tie. Hey! Hey, my brother isn't here!"

Her voice was lost in the chattering of eighty-one dragons – far more dragons than Mortimer still felt had any right to be here. If they had nothing to do with the clan, why should their votes count? But he had to admit that as not all of the recluses had aligned themselves with Lord Margery, maybe it hadn't mattered that much in the end. Wendy's gaudy blanket and purple beanie seemed to have converted quite a few. He covered his face with his paws and took a deep breath, his belly hollow and sick. Okay, so this was terrible. Just awful. But it wasn't a complete disaster, not with such a close call. All Beaufort had to do was agree to an alliance with Lord Margery, then they could get all this bauble thief business sorted and figure the rest out later. Yes. An alliance. The whole situation wasn't anywhere near as bad as it could be.

"Dragons," Beaufort said, and the chattering settled down.

An alliance, Mortimer thought. *That could work.* It might actually be quite helpful. Lord Margery was terribly conservative, but maybe she could balance some of Beaufort's wilder ideas.

"Thank you for attending," Beaufort said, "and thank you for voting. It matters enormously that you have taken responsibility for your own futures like this. This is how we will find our way forward, through cooperation and mutual respect." He looked around, and now Mortimer noticed the droop in his wings, the sad line of his tail.

"Oh, no," he whispered, and Amelia looked at him in alarm.

"What? Mortimer, *what?*"

"It has been my pleasure and my honour to serve as your High Lord, but all things must change."

"No, oh, Beaufort, no …"

"You have spoken, and I will listen. I will step down, and go into exile, as seems only fitting, allowing Lord Margery to take you forward."

"*Dammit,* Beaufort!" Mortimer's exclamation was lost under a sudden babble of alarmed chatter, of protests and uncertain cheers. Even Lord Margery looked more discomfited than triumphant. "Beaufort, what are you *doing?*"

"*Quiet!*" Beaufort's roar cut through the clamour, leaving a wisp of dark smoke hanging above him. All eyes turned to the High Lord.

"This was a vote for the future of the clan. You have spoken, and I will go. This is not up for discussion."

"Beaufort," Lord Margery said, "it was too close. I can't claim this as a majority."

"You'd have claimed it without any majority if I'd just stepped down as you asked me to."

"I thought I had more support." Her voice was level. "This doesn't seem right."

"I'm stepping down, Margery. The seat of the High Lord is yours."

She looked at the Weber dubiously. "I don't think I want it like this."

"Sometimes we don't get to name the way things come to us." He slipped off the rock and trotted toward her with his head high, the crowd shuffling to let him through. On the ledge above, Mortimer rocked back and forth with his paws over his snout. He didn't want to watch this. He hated it. And he wouldn't stay. He couldn't. If Beaufort left, he left.

As if hearing his thoughts, Lord Pamela shouted, "We'll go with you, Beaufort. We'll make our own clan!"

A roar of agreement greeted this, and Beaufort paused, looking back. "I'm going into exile, my friends. I don't know where that may take me."

"South!" someone shouted. "The weather's better!" A ripple of laughter greeted that, then someone else called, "No, north! There's more room!" There was more laughter, and other suggestions were called out, in a wild kind of excitement that had an edge of panic to it.

"Cloverlies," Beaufort said, "What sort of life would that be? Trailing about the countryside, looking for a hole to hide in, cold and wet and hungry? We searched a long time for this place. We worked hard to build it into what it is. Plenty of dragons and hatchlings died before we found it, and the land was much emptier then. I remember. No one should leave this place lightly."

An uneasy silence followed his words. Lord Margery had come forward to meet him, her wings folded down tight to her body. "Neither should you, Beaufort."

"I don't," he said, and placed a paw on her shoulder. "I truly don't."

There was so much sadness in his voice that Mortimer trembled with it, already tasting the loss of long summer days fraught with frustration at the High Lord's stubbornness, and a lingering panic about what he was going to do next, and the utterly bewildering turns of the old dragon's mind, and the way he encouraged everything and everybody, and was both the most infuriating and uplifting creature Mortimer had ever come across.

"I don't go lightly, either," he shouted, before he could think about it too much more. He started scrambling down the slope. "I'm coming with you, Beaufort! I'm coming!"

"Mortimer," Beaufort said sternly. "It's not exile if I have an entourage, is it?" He turned back to Lord Margery, ignoring the young dragon pushing his way through the crowd toward him. "Lord Margery," he said, his paw still on her shoulder. "I, High Lord Beaufort, do—"

"*Stop! Stop!*"

All heads turned toward the entrance as a smallish dragon came tumbling down the tunnel, less flying than ricocheting off the walls. It looked painful, and there was a general intake of breath as he hit an overhang particularly hard, still shouting, then an *oooh* as he spun, apparently out of control, into the centre of the cavern.

"*Gilbert!*" Amelia shrieked. "Gilbert, come down *right now!*"

"*Trying!*" He barrel-rolled across the hall, his wings and legs and tail going in all different directions, hit a wall with a rather solid-sounding thump, and fell to the ground while the dragons below hustled to get out of the way.

"*Gilbert!*" Amelia bellowed, but before she could even leap from the ledge he bounced up again, missing a few scales and bleeding from his snout. He ignored her.

"Everything has to stop," he said, panting.

Lord Margery sighed, and pushed Beaufort's paw off her. "This makes it a draw, I take it."

"A *draw?*" Gilbert squawked. "You *toadstools!*"

"Gilbert," Beaufort said, "That's uncalled for. But to be clear, your vote is for me?"

"It *is* called for. And yes."

A few cheers went up, and Mortimer stopped where he was, not far from Beaufort, feeling himself flushing lilac. He'd just made a complete spectacle of himself, hadn't he?

"It's a draw," Lord Margery said. "So no more of this exile nonsense. I withdraw my challenge."

Beaufort looked thoughtful, but before he could say anything further Gilbert shouted, "That's not important right now anyway!"

"Why not, lad?" the High Lord asked.

"Because I know who's been kidnapping the postmen and stealing the baubles! It is one of us, and I know who!"

A gasp went up around the cavern, and Mortimer forgot to be embarrassed, his eight-chambered heart hammering against his chest as he spun in place, trying to spot the culprit.

18

MIRIAM

Miriam's mobile rang in the warm cocoon of the car, making both her and Alice jump. The cat ignored it. Miriam dug the phone out of her coat and frowned at the display.

"Oh dear. It's Colin. What do I do?"

"Just tell him we've gone out for the night. Dammit. I rather hoped he wasn't at that van back there."

Miriam nodded, and tried to put on her most normal voice as she answered. "Hello, Colin, love."

"… ty Mir …" The reception was bad, his voice cutting in and out, and she let out her breath in a gust of relief.

"Colin? Can you hear me?" *Now* her voice sounded normal. Cheerful, at least.

"… lo?"

"It's no good, dear, we must be out of range. I'll call you later."

"… iam!"

She hung up and looked at Alice. "He sounded a bit agitated."

"Did he? Oh well. Can't be helped." Alice looked at the cat. "Are we on the right track, here, Thompson?"

The cat yawned, exposing neat white teeth, and stared out into the dark.

"I hope he's not taking us anywhere awful," Miriam said. "You know, because of the D-R-A—" She stopped as the cat gave her a look which said, as clearly as if he'd spoken, that he didn't appreciate her doubting his spelling ability. "Sorry." The cat stared at her for a moment longer, then looked back at the road.

"I'm sure we'll find out soon," Alice said.

"WHERE ARE WE?" Miriam asked. The fields stretched long and dark to either side of the car, barely glimpsed beyond the range of the headlights, and they'd left the last houses behind ten minutes ago, turning onto a rutted, unsealed road. The weeds whispered along the flanks and undercarriage, and if she'd opened the window she could have touched the dry-stone walls outside.

"I don't know exactly," Alice said. "I've never been up here before."

"I hope he knows where he's going."

Despite the fact that he was looking up at her, the cat somehow managed to look down his nose at Miriam, his tail twitching. She flushed and rubbed her own nose. Being in such close quarters to him was making her snuffly.

They came to a junction, and Thompson indicated left, paws still steady on the dashboard, taking them up a farm track that headed into open ground, leaving the walls behind them. It didn't need to be marked private. It wasn't the sort of road you'd find by accident, and Miriam didn't even think that that you could call it a road without really stretching the definition. It was nothing more than an ill-defined trail climbing into the fells, a mix of mud and gravel making the wheels slip here and there. Miriam clung to the door and hoped they weren't going to suddenly slide off sideways into a bog.

"You better not get us stuck, Thompson," Alice said. "My poor little car is not made for this sort of thing."

"Well, she's doing better than Bessie would have." Miriam's elderly Beetle probably would have taken one look at their route and expired in shock.

Alice snorted. "That's true enough. I do wish we'd had time for dinner, though."

Miriam dug through her bag, but only found some Tic Tacs. She offered them to Alice and they drove on in silence, surrounded by the scent of mint.

LIGHTS APPEARED UP AHEAD, still a long way off, but Miriam took a deep, relieved breath at the sight. She'd been starting to wonder if the damn cat was going to drive them straight off a cliff, out here in the dark. Or just strand them in the fells to freeze. After all, they still didn't know whose side he was on, if anyone's. She wondered if cats even had sides. But they'd been safe so far. There had been a few dicey moments when the car had started to slide, but Alice had recovered them before they did more than spin a little sideways on the path. The undercarriage had bottomed out on the raised ridge between the wheel tracks rather nastily more than once, and an unpleasant clanking had started up beneath them. Miriam suspected that something had gone wrong with the suspension. Whatever it was, it sounded expensive.

Thompson looked at Alice, and mewled.

"What?" she said, her voice sharp. "What now?"

He pawed the indicators.

"Stop that! It's hard enough to keep on the road without you messing around distracting me."

"I think he wants you to turn the lights out," Miriam said, as Thompson batted the lever again.

The cat mewled approvingly. Or disapprovingly. Who knew what a cat meant, Miriam thought, as Alice brought the car to a stop. It didn't take much. They'd been creeping along in first for the last mile, barely quicker than walking, and the car seemed to shudder with relief as the engine died.

Silence rushed in around them, followed by a thick and hungry darkness as Alice switched off the lights. They were high up in the fells now, and with her eyes unaccustomed to the heavy dark, for a moment all Miriam could see were the distant house lights floating ahead of them, like a deep-sea jellyfish in the far reaches of an abyss.

She swallowed audibly, and Thompson started purring.

"We're here then, are we?" Alice asked, and jumped as the cat walked over her lap to scratch the door. "And you can stop that right now. You've done enough damage to my poor car."

She opened the door to let the cat out, and Miriam followed her lead, the air cold enough on her face to make her gasp as she stepped into the dark. Her back ached after jolting along the rough road, and she stretched the kinks out, waiting for her eyes to adjust to the darkness. The stars were painted in broad, crowded sweeps above them, and the night was still. No traffic noises, no mumbling sheep. Just the wide still sky with a sliver of moon and ahead of them, the distance impossible to gauge, the yellow lights of that desperately lonely house.

She could also just make out the cat, standing in the path ahead of them, waiting.

"You sure about this, Thompson?" Alice asked him, and he turned and started padding toward the lights.

"Are *we* sure about this?" Miriam asked. "There could be anything up there. Those things in the Audi, for a start. And I've still got no phone signal. We can't even call for help."

Alice considered this for a moment. "Even if we had signal," she said, "We've got nothing to tell the police. 'Oh, a cat led us up here'? I hardly think even Detective Inspector Adams would buy that one."

"What about Beaufort?"

"We haven't seen them since they went back for their own investigations, Miriam. We don't know what happened. They might have their own problems. And we have no way of getting in touch with them."

Miriam sighed. "I'm going to get Mortimer a mobile for Christmas."

"Well, wishes and fishes." Alice opened the boot of the car and took out a cricket bat. "Can you swing this?"

"Um. I think so?" Well, she knew she could *swing* it, but Alice probably meant could she hit anything with it. That was another question entirely. She also wasn't sure why Alice just happened to have one in the car, but she supposed it wasn't that important right now.

"Good." Alice handed her the bat, closed the boot and opened the back door, taking a black cane with a silver handle from behind the seat. The cool starlight slid off the silver, revealing the lines of a dragon's head as Alice gave it a couple of experimental swings. "Ah, yes," she said. "There we go."

Miriam tried a couple of moves with the bat, although she wasn't quite sure it had the same style as the cane. Alice locked the car, and they turned up the path after Thompson, still waiting ahead of them with an impatient line to his tail. As soon as they started walking he jumped up and began trotting away.

"Why a cat?" Miriam asked. "Why couldn't it have been a big, scary dog, like a Rottweiler or something?"

Thompson looked over his shoulder and hissed.

THE HOUSE TOOK a long time to get any closer. Alice seemed to be as comfortable as the cat in the dark, following him on light, quiet feet with the cane sometimes resting against her shoulder, sometimes helping her over the rougher ground. Miriam, on the other hand, found herself slipping on loose gravel, suddenly ankle deep in a muddy puddle, and (judging by the smell) she'd also manged to find the only cow pat out here. She tried to carry the cricket bat as casually as Alice was carrying her cane, but eventually resorted to using it for balance, and occasionally as a walking stick.

They staggered – well, Miriam staggered – up a final rise and found the house directly in front of them. It was a big old thing, probably Edwardian, with stern windows and gardens that had likely once been full of topiary and small gravel paths. Now, in the depths of a winter night, the grounds seemed to be mostly populated by skeletal bushes and dead grass, with muddy patches where the rabbits had been at it. There was a light on in one upstairs room, seeping through thin curtains, and another downstairs, where they could see into an empty living room. There were a few ramshackle outbuildings, one with the roof caved in, plus a double garage with a potholed gravel drive leading up to it. Miriam frowned at the drive and squinted into the dark, seeing Alice doing the same.

"That's a road," Alice said, stabbing her cane toward it. "We just about destroyed my car on that damn track, and there's a *road?*"

Thompson shrugged, and headed toward the garden gate.

"Do we have a plan?" Miriam asked.

"Follow the cat. I need to keep an eye on him so when we're done here I can skin him for breaking my car."

Miriam didn't think it sounded like much of a plan, but she fell into step with Alice anyway. What else was she going to do, stay out here on her own?

Up close, the house didn't look much better. The mortar was crumbling between the old bricks, and one of the panes in the front door had been replaced with plywood. There was an old rotary washing line lying on its side in the garden, like the bones of something long-dead, next to a dog house with a wall missing and, thankfully, no occupant. Thompson trotted straight to the front door, but when Alice and Miriam reached him he bared his teeth and pointed his nose to the back of the house.

"That way?" Alice asked, and he purred.

"What're you going to do, cause a distraction?" Miriam demanded.

He gave her a disdainful look and sat down, watching them expectantly.

The side of the house that the cat sent them down was dark, the downstairs windows boarded over and no light coming from above, and Miriam had to admit that the horrible animal had figured out the best way for them to pass unnoticed. She wasn't looking forward to what might happen when they did get noticed. Given the scorched vans and exploding baubles and unpleasant Audi drivers, she wasn't even sure if they were expecting to encounter a *who* or a *what*.

They paused at the back corner of the house, Alice peering into the yard beyond while Miriam peeked over her shoulder. The patchy lawn at the back of the house was washed with yellow light, and Miriam could hear a TV playing inside. It sounded like *Strictly*, and she wished with a sudden, hot fervour that she was home right now, curled up in front of her TV, warm and dry and, most importantly, safe. Because she felt a long way from all those things right now. The drive had been almost surreal, guided through the night by the green-eyed cat, but now all she could think of was Alice's burning door and the scream of the bauble before it exploded. She felt a hiccough-y tightness in her chest and swallowed against it. That was the last thing she needed right now.

Alice leaned in close so she could whisper in Miriam's ear, and

Miriam dragged her attention back to all the cold, damp unsafeness around her.

"Keep against the walls. I'm going to go first and get as close to a window as I can, so we can see what we're dealing with. Do what I do, and for God's sake, *be quiet*." Alice's voice was a hiss in Miriam's ear, and she nodded violently, flattening herself against the wall and bumping it with the cricket bat. There was just enough light for her to see Alice close her eyes and shake her head slightly, then the older woman was gone.

Miriam followed Alice around the corner to the back of the house, holding down the hiccoughs and concentrating on not walking into any shutters, or dropping the bat, or tripping over. Alice eased herself up to the closest window, then peered cautiously around the sill. She stayed there for a moment, then looked back at Miriam, shook her head, and crouched to squat-walk under the frame. Miriam decided that she didn't need to see inside, and after a moment's thought dropped to her hands and knees and crawled after Alice. Dignity be damned – she didn't trust herself not to have the top of her head showing over the sill at the exact moment the bauble thieves walked into the room beyond.

Alice had stopped at the next window, stealing a look inside. She was there for longer this time, and when she looked back at Miriam her mouth was a hard line and her eyes were wider than normal. She beckoned. Miriam, still on her hands and knees, shook her head. She definitely didn't need to see anything that made Alice look alarmed. Alice beckoned again. Miriam shook her head again, and this time Alice grabbed the collar of her coat and hauled her to her feet. Miriam swallowed a whimper as the older woman pressed her to the wall next to the window, then forced her to lean forward until, like it or not, she was peering into a cavernous kitchen.

There was a long wooden table in the centre of the floor, and it was piled with baubles and boats, some of them still in Miriam's packaging. There were other baubles there too, with clumsy designs like the one that had been tearing around Jasmine's house. There were also open cans of sugary drinks and torn packets of sweets, crushed ice cream tubs and empty chocolate wrappers, dirty plates piled anywhere that seemed handy, and drifts of newspaper and dead leaves on the floor. But Miriam registered all that only on the very periphery of her attention. The rest of it was focused on the – the *figures* around the table.

There were three of them, all with heavy broad shoulders and long skinny legs in filthy jeans. One was eating slices of cake and fruit tarts off a huge catering tray, his hard, pale fingers swamping them. Each morsel vanished in a single bite, and he immediately reached for another, exposing broken teeth that crowded his over-large mouth as he chewed. That mouth seemed to wrap halfway around his skull, as if he could flip the whole top of his head open like a cartoon character. His teeth were sharp, too. The ones that weren't broken came to nasty, shark-like points, and his round chin was scarred where he'd bitten it. As Miriam watched, he narrowed bright blue eyes and threw an empty drink can at another creature that was hunched over the baubles. She snarled at him (Miriam decided she was a she, as she was wearing a summer dress as a blouse, her muscular chest stretching the material alarmingly), and her long ears flattened against her bald skull.

"George hungry," the first creature growled, the words deep and phlegmy. "You get George food."

"George eat all sweet things. George idiot. Hazel working."

"Hazel lady goblin. Hazel get George food!"

"Hazel break George head!"

The third creature turned around in his seat, where he had his pointy nose almost touching an old-fashioned TV, and screamed at them both, "Idiot goblins shut up! Clever Sam goblin watching dancy show!" Spittle flew from his mouth, raining merrily down over the table and floor, and Miriam pulled slowly back from the window, the hiccoughs scared into submission, and stared at Alice with horrified eyes. She didn't think she could ever watch *Strictly* again. Not while knowing that *things* like that enjoyed it.

What do we do? she mouthed, and Alice shrugged, then twiddled her thumbs.

Wait.

They waited.

MIRIAM WONDERED how long they were going to be waiting out here. And what the cat was going to do for that matter. *Was* it going to do anything? Or was it just going to lead the goblins out the door to them? You could never tell with cats. He might be an enemy agent.

Her feet were freezing. She was pretty sure one of her boots was leaking, and she just hoped it wasn't the one she'd trod in a cow pat with. At least she hadn't worn her clogs this time. It had been a near thing, but at the last moment she'd remembered the alarming regularity with which they seemed to have unexpected excursions. She was hungry, too. She thought longingly of the curry, now sadly cold on Alice's stove top. Or at least she hoped it was cold. Had she switched it off? It was that cat again, he'd been rushing them. She couldn't remember. She—

An unearthly shriek split the night, jolting her out of her thoughts, and she slapped her hand over her mouth to hold in a scream. What was out here? What was that? Was it a banshee? Oh, God, not a banshee, they were meant to only come before a death. Was one of them going to die? Was it going to be *her*?

Alice grabbed her arm and hauled her forward, not bothering to duck under the window this time, and Miriam gave a *hic* of alarm. What if they were still in there? Those things, those *goblins*, because that's what they'd called themselves, and she supposed they'd know. Miriam couldn't believe she was even thinking that. Goblins. Even the word was scary, never mind those long claw-like nails, and the shark's teeth, and the arms that looked like they could tear your head off. Not that she'd really thought about it, thankfully, but if she had ever thought of goblins, she'd have thought of something like these—

"*Miriam*," Alice hissed in her ear. "Either pull yourself together or I'll leave you out here. *Focus*."

Another one of those terrible screams went up on the other side of the house, and Miriam clutched Alice's jacket. "What – *hicc* – *is* that? Is it a banshee?"

"It's the cat, Miriam. He's got them out of the kitchen, and we need to get in there before they come back."

"I don't want to go in there!"

"I know, but those postmen might be tied up downstairs. I saw one of them go down to the cellar with some chocolate and crisps. We have to find them if we can."

Miriam stared at Alice, wondering if she was going to cry, then thought of the bauble screaming around Jasmine's living room, and the cheerful young DHL man who had been so grateful for his mince pies and Christmas cake. She hiccoughed and nodded. Her legs were shaking, and she was suddenly glad they hadn't eaten the curry. She was pretty sure she'd be throwing it up right now other-wise. "Okay. Yes. You're right."

"Then let's go."

The kitchen door was unlocked, and Alice led the way in. Thompson was still yowling, so Miriam supposed he was holding up his end of the bargain. The mud and chocolate-smeared room stank of wood smoke and stale milk and festering food as they hurried across it, and Alice tried the cellar door. It wasn't locked either. The goblins evidently weren't too worried about anyone escaping. Alice hit the light switch, and they scurried down creaking steps lit by one bleak yellow bulb at the bottom.

"Oh, sugar," Miriam whispered, peering over Alice's shoulder as they arrived on a stone floor covered with a thick wash of mud and dirt. A man and a woman in Royal Mail uniform, the nice DHL driver, and another, older man in a black polo shirt were sat on the floor, heavy chains running from thick iron bands at their waists to heavy rings set in the walls. The woman had a cut on her cheek, and the DHL man had a black eye, but otherwise they seemed unharmed. They stared at the newcomers in astonishment.

"Are you hurt?" Alice asked. "Can you stand?"

"What does it matter?" the woman said. "We can't get out. We're *chained*." She spoke the way people sometimes do when they're overseas, and think over-enunciating will magically make everyone speak English.

Alice frowned as her. "That is not the way to look at things."

"Look, I don't know how you got in, but you should leave now," the Royal Mail man said. "That bloody *thing* that stole my name and goes around calling himself Goblin Sam has the keys. He's the only one."

"We've tried breaking them," the DHL man said. "They won't budge."

"I'm not surprised," Alice said, examining the rings on the wall. "These are old, but they're solid. Driven right into the foundations."

Miriam wasted a moment wondering why anyone would have old chains in their basement, and was just deciding that she didn't really want to know when she realised Alice had said something. "Sorry, what?"

"I said, let's go."

"Are we leaving?"

"No, we're getting the keys."

"What? *How?*"

"We're going to catch a goblin." Alice turned away without waiting for Miriam's response, not that Miriam could come up with anything more coherent than another *hic*. Goblin-catching seemed like a very bad idea in a night that was already full of them. She opened her mouth to try and make some sort of protest as Alice started up the stairs, cane swinging casually in her hand.

Then the light went out and the screams started.

19

MORTIMER

There was a moment of utter stillness following Gilbert's announcement, broken only by the gasps of horrified dragons, while everyone waited for something to happen. Then, with a thunder of wings and panicked growls, Rockford, Lucille, and three other dragons broke for the cavern exit. They launched themselves off the ground in powerful leaps, knocking smaller dragons out of their way and fighting to be the first to get out, colliding with each other in their headlong flight.

"*Them!*" Gilbert shrieked, rather unnecessarily. "*Them! Well, him! Rockford! Stop him!*"

The big dragon was almost at the tunnel mouth, his wings tucking into a dive that would carry him straight through to freedom. Behind him, skirmishes broke out as the dragons recovered from their astonishment and tackled the escapees. Mortimer was shoved unceremoniously sideways as Lord Walter charged past him, creased wings creaking, waving the broken remnants of an old sword. One of Rockford's younger recruits had been knocked out of the air and shoved to the floor by Lucille as she fled, and before he could escape Lord Walter started slapping him about the face with the broken sword, his stentorian voice rising above the melee.

"Bad dragon! You're a disgrace! A dishonour! A bad, bad dragon!"

The young dragon, whose name was Alex, took one horrified look at the old Lord and hunkered down with his paws over his head, trying to keep his wings out of reach of the rusty sword.

Mortimer started to fight his way to Beaufort again, not entirely certain what he should be doing in the middle of what was rapidly descending into a free-for-all. A couple of the recluses were ignoring the current drama entirely and had come to blows over the moral implications of kitten blankets, while Lord Pamela and Wendy had tackled a small male dragon from Rockford's group. They were sitting on him, chortling and taking turns to tweak his tail as he desperately tried to wriggle free, and Mortimer ducked as a young female dragon shot over him, rolling from side to side and barely in control. She was a panicked, hiding grey, and was trying to dislodge Rupert and Josie from her wings. They clung on fiercely, and Mortimer winced. Baby dragon teeth are sharp. Violet just watched in amusement.

"Finally," Mortimer heard her say to Harriet. "Our hatchlings are useful for something. Should keep them amused for ten minutes at least."

Harriet nuzzled her cheek, and said, "I think they're entirely wonderful."

Mortimer looked up in time to see Amelia launch herself from the ledge and throw herself at Lucille. The burly dragon had been circling high above the melee, looking for her moment to escape, and she gave a startled roar as Amelia crashed into her with a clamour of clashing scales and fury.

"Amelia!" Mortimer shouted. The two dragons plunged to the cavern floor, grappling with each other, snapping and growling and spitting little balls of flame. They bounced off the High Lord's seat, sending the Weber flying, and tumbled across the hard

ground, wings flaring and tails snapping while other dragons scrambled out of the way. Mortimer scampered after them, still shouting Amelia's name, and flung himself on top of Lucille, landing between her wings and flailing about wildly with his paws. He hoped that this fighting thing was instinctual, because he'd never actually tried it before.

Lucille threw her head back and smacked him in the snout, sending black spots swimming across his vision. He fell backward, catching her a slap across the jaw with his tail that did absolutely nothing but make her growl furiously. She let go of Amelia and lunged at him, and he stuck his legs out stiffly with the vague idea that one of them might hit her before she got her teeth in his neck.

"Hey!" Amelia bellowed, and tackled Lucille just as she pounced on Mortimer. She took the burly dragon into another roll that ended with her standing on Lucille's belly with her front paws clamped tightly around the other's snout. *"Don't you touch him! He has very! Delicate! Paws!"* She punctuated each of the last three words with a headbutt that made Mortimer's eyes water, the ringing sound of colliding dragon skulls echoing about them. Amelia stopped, took two staggering steps backward, then sat down abruptly. Lucille didn't move, just stayed where she was with her wings flung wide and two of her piercings ripped out. "Good," Amelia said blearily. "And stay down." Then she fell over on her side.

Mortimer stayed where he was for a moment longer, still seeing Lucille's teeth coming at him. She seemed to have far more teeth than anyone had any need for. His heart was beating wildly, and he could see his scales flashing through half a dozen different colours without settling on one. Then he realised that he could see his scales because his legs were still sticking straight out in front of him, so he dropped them hurriedly and scrambled to his feet, rushing to Amelia. She was still conscious, but looked a little cross-eyed.

"Are you okay?" he asked.

"I think so." She pushed herself up to sitting. "*Ooh*. Maybe. Where's Gilbert? Is he okay? Did we get everyone?"

Mortimer looked up. Rockford was the only dragon of the five who was still free, and he was on the ground near the mouth of the tunnel. There were dragons all around him, but no one was approaching him. They all stood back as if waiting to see what would happen next. Mortimer frowned. They could easily all tackle him together, but dragons love the sight of a good fight, and it looked like there was one coming. Beaufort, the only dragon in the clan bigger than Rockford, stood between him and freedom.

"Move, Beaufort," Rockford said, and Mortimer growled at the insolence in his voice. "You can't keep me here."

"Sit down, lad. Take what's coming to you."

"I don't want to fight an old dragon, but I will. Let me go."

"Rockford, I've known for a long time that you were sneaking the odd sheep, but I turned a blind eye. Young dragons need some freedom. This, however, I can not let go. You've endangered us all."

"I have not! *You* did! You did that, hanging out with humans, and going to village fetes, and all your stupid barbecues! That was *you!*"

"We are very lucky to have in our clan some very clever dragons who can see a new way into the future for us. Not one thing has been done that endangers us. I would never risk that."

The entire cavern was silent, except for a few whimpers from the young dragon that was still trying to shake off Josie and Rupert, and the steady *slap, slap* of Lord Walter hitting Alex, interspersed with the odd *bad dragon*. Everyone else was watching Rockford and the High Lord.

"A new future as what?" Rockford demanded. "*Crafters?* Like bloody *dwarfs?* All those stupid baubles, and trading with *humans* like they're our equals. What next, we dress up and give pony rides to children?"

"What would your idea be, then, lad? What were you hoping for?"

"To be *dragons!* To have people fear us again! To be proud again! Destroy this stupid trade thing and be *dragons!*"

Beaufort smiled slightly. "So you think we've become lesser dragons, do you?"

"*Yes!* And it's *your fault! You've* made us lesser! *You!* All I wanted was for us to be real dragons again!" Rockford hulked himself up, flashing with furious purples and reds, his wings wide, and Mortimer prepared himself to probably get quite hurt. If Rockford attacked Beaufort, he was going to have to try this whole fighting thing again, and he didn't expect it to go any better this time around. But he'd do it anyway.

"By kidnapping humans and stealing?" Beaufort asked. "What version of real dragons is that, lad? Because it's none I recognise."

"*Lord Margery would!*" Rockford bellowed, spitting furious purple fire with the words, and rose onto his hind legs with his forepaws hooked into weapons. "*SHE would! She—*" His words became a strangled yelp as someone grabbed his tail and pulled him off his feet and into the air, sparking a chorus of *oohs* from the crowd. He gave a surprised belch of flame, but didn't even have time to flex his wings before he was dropped again. He smacked chin-first into the ground with a distressingly meaty sound, and Mortimer winced, despite thinking that Rockford thoroughly deserved it.

"Lord Margery is utterly disgusted both by your actions and your ideas," the dragon herself said, landing next to Rockford and trapping his tail under one paw to ensure he didn't make a run for it. "Unfortunately, as she is no longer even in the running for High Lord, due to five of her voters being cretins, she can't exile you. But she's going to respectfully ask the current, esteemed High Lord if he'll exile you instead."

"Ow," Rockford mumbled, blood trickling from his mouth.

There were a couple of teeth embedded in the cavern floor by his snout. He shook his head gingerly and peered at Lord Margery. "But you'd have made us into real dragons again," he wailed. "Everything would have been better! None of this stupid human stuff—"

"And what did you think then? That *I'd* let you get away with stealing sheep? Or worse? You have a better life with Beaufort as High Lord than you deserve."

"But you don't like it either! The trading with humans! You said!" Rockford tried to sit up, and Lord Margery let go of his tail to give him a deceptively lazy slap that knocked him back to the floor.

"I may not like it, Rockford, but I know you, and I *detest* what you think a dragon should be. You think dragons are better than anyone else. We're not. No one kind's better than any other. We're all just different. And if you can't see that, you don't even deserve to call yourself Folk."

Rockford gaped at her, looking like he wanted to protest, but she gave his tail a warning tweak and he put his snout back on the ground with a groan.

Beaufort looked at Rockford with his head low. "I thought we were smarter than this."

"Most of us are," Lord Margery said. "Some of us take a little extra convincing, and some are just plain thick." She tweaked Rockford's tail for emphasis, making him squeak. "So what do we do now?"

Mortimer watched Beaufort, his heart painful with fear. What would the old dragon do? He'd almost been ousted, had even volunteered for exile, thinking he was no longer the right dragon to lead them, and then found he'd been betrayed by those he'd spent his life protecting and loving. It was one thing suspecting it, quite another to be confronted with it. And it hadn't even been a dragonish, tooth and claw type betrayal. No, it had been sneaky and underhand and just plain nasty, as nasty as the goals behind it. It was enough to make anyone lose faith.

Beaufort looked over the expectant crowd, his wings low and his forehead furrowed. "I think," he said, and paused, uncharacteristically unsure.

The dragons held their breath.

And Gilbert stood up and shouted, "Beau-*fort*! Beau-*fort*! Beau-FORT!"

Other dragons took up the cry, quietly at first then louder, bellowing it until it shook dust from the walls and even Lord Margery was shouting, her voice fierce and carrying. Beaufort looked around with something like wonder, his wings snapping open behind him and his head rising, until he stood proud and old and unbowed in front of them, the High Lord of the Cloverly dragons.

He sat back on his hind legs and raised his front paws, and the cheers slowly faded away.

"Mortimer?" he said.

"Yes?" Mortimer had managed to get some dust in his eyes from all the shouting and fighting. They were watering horribly.

"Let's go get your baubles back."

The dragons roared in delight.

IT WASN'T SMOOTH GOING, getting out of the cavern. Rockford refused to cooperate and just lay in a corner cradling his injured jaw and whimpering, even after Lydia tweaked his tail and told him to pull himself together. Lord Margery tried shouting at him, but he folded his wings over his head and kept saying (with a slight lisp from the broken teeth), "It was for the good of the dragons. We were going to be *real* dragons again." Eventually they gave up on him.

Alex, on the other hand, agreed to help rather quickly, although it took all of Lord Margery's not inconsiderable powers of persuasion to convince Lord Walter to stop hitting him and calling him a bad dragon. Alex was a very ashamed yellow and wouldn't meet anyone's eyes, and kept mumbling that he'd only done it because Rockford had promised to let him eat a cow, and he'd always wanted to eat a cow, because they looked so *meaty*. Beaufort shook his head and told him that being beaten by Walter was a reasonable start to his punishment, and he'd have to think about what came next. Then he went to check on the other captives.

"It's not that the beating hurt, so much," Alex told Mortimer and Amelia, sitting in the dust with the scales of his nose scattering the floor around him. "It was just really embarrassing. And I couldn't exactly *do* anything. What if I'd hurt him?"

Amelia looked at him with one eye squeezed shut and said, "You deserved it," then tottered off to find her brother, bumping into a few dragons and apologising to a rock along the way.

When Beaufort came back, he stood in front of Alex and stared at him for a long time while the young dragon scuffled uncomfortably on the dusty floor, then said, "I'm quite willing to believe that you were nothing but a pawn in this."

Alex's forehead wrinkled. "Isn't that some sort of fish?"

Beaufort looked almost as puzzled as Alex, and Mortimer thought that the High Lord was quite right about Alex not being the mastermind behind anything.

"Let's not worry about that," Beaufort said. "Can you take us to where the humans are being held?"

"Oh. Yes. Is that what a pawn is? Is it some kind of guide?"

Beaufort squinted at him. "No. Are the humans alright?"

"Yes. Well, they were when I last saw them."

"Who's guarding them?"

"Um." Alex went a nasty shade of yellowish-grey. "Well. Goblins."

A gasp went up around the cavern, and Lord Walter bellowed, "*Bad dragon!*" He took a few more swipes at a cowering Alex, then stomped over to Rockford and started hitting him instead. No one stopped him. Everyone was too busy clamouring to be included in the rescue party, while Beaufort shook his head at Alex and looked at him in a way that had the young dragon sniffling like a hatchling.

Mortimer wished he were slightly more inclined toward violence, because he wouldn't have minded hitting Rockford a few times himself. Goblins! Dragons are no fans of goblins. Dwarfs you could deal with, trade with, even have a beer with, as long as no one makes any jokes about beards or princesses. There's a lot of mutual respect between dwarfs and dragons, no matter what the human stories say. Both species value good craftsperson-ship, and design ability, and honour. Goblins, on the other hand, are interested only in what can get them fast money and the easy rush of sugar, and plenty of dragons had seen hoards stolen and sold off, or even melted down, by a marauding band of the creatures.

Beaufort was attempting to shout the Furnace of dragons to some semblance of order, but everyone was too excited. The idea of having the High Lord's permission to engage in a little goblin-hunting was too good to be missed.

"Dragons!" he bellowed. "*Cloverlies!*"

"I don't think it's going to work," Mortimer shouted over the din. "No one's listening."

"*Cloverlies!*" Beaufort roared one more time, but only succeeded in making Amelia, who'd fought her way back to them through the crowd with Gilbert in tow, fall on her nose. "Sorry," he said, and she nodded unsteadily.

Beaufort put a paw on Mortimer's shoulder. The cavern was heating up rapidly and full of the multi-coloured smoke of dragons spoiling for a fight. "This is no good," he shouted in the younger dragon's ear. "We're going to need to sneak out. We'll never convince everyone to stay back."

Mortimer nodded understanding, and Beaufort leaned in to Lord Margery.

"Can you keep them here?"

She frowned, and replied in a quiet bellow, "I had rather hoped—"

"The smaller the party, the better the chance we have of passing unseen. And of avoiding any mishaps."

"Well, yes. I see your point." She examined his little group critically, Alex still with his paws over his nose and Amelia leaning on Gilbert. "Ah, are you sure you've chosen quite the right dragons for the job, Beaufort?"

"I am quite sure I have the right dragon for the job when it comes to keeping the rest of them here," Beaufort shouted back, and headed down the tunnel to the fresh air, leaving Lord Margery looking a little orange and flustered.

It was crisply cold outside, and they paused on the ledge where the cliff fell away to the lake below, stars captured in it, the fells rolling in deep, rich darkness under the sky. From here, the village was out of sight, and there were no lights, no sign of humans. It was wild and vast and silent, and Mortimer stood next to the High Lord, wondering what he saw out there that made him just so, well, *Beaufort*.

"Thank you, Mortimer," Beaufort said quietly, while behind them Alex was cautiously asking Amelia if she was quite alright to fly, and she was trying to slap him but kept over-balancing.

"I didn't do anything," Mortimer said. "And I'm rubbish at fighting. I tried to help Amelia and she had to save me."

"Fighting's not important," the High Lord replied. "You are, though. You've never doubted me. Even when you had doubts about what I was doing, you never doubted *me*. And that's every-thing." Then he took to the sky with a swirl of his broad wings, a scrap of night wheeling against the stars. Mortimer watched him go, his chest tight and full and that silly dust in his eyes again, then looked at Gilbert and Amelia as they appeared next to him. Amelia was still squinting at things, and Alex was trailing her rather warily.

"Good work, Gilbert," Mortimer said. "How did you figure it out?"

"Oh, I was chasing a turkey, and it ran into Rockford's cave, and he had these basket rigs in there, like yours. One of them still had a bauble in it."

Mortimer considered this for a moment then said, "Why were you chasing a turkey?"

"Long story. Can you help me? I don't think Amelia can fly straight."

"But you can *fly*," Amelia said proudly, and tried to punch her brother's shoulder. She missed and hit Mortimer instead.

"Ow."

"Sorry."

"Gilbert, can *you* fly straight?"

"If I don't think about it too much. Like when I realised it was Rockford, and I knew I had to get back straight away, and I was like, *bam*, flying!"

"About time, too," a raspy voice said behind him. "Baubles and humans and non-flying dragons. The world's a mess."

Alex squeaked, and shoved past Mortimer to take flight.

Mortimer stared at Lord Walter. "Um, sir? Is everything alright?"

"Of course it's not *alright*! There are goblins out there, dammit! Filthy creatures! And everyone seems to think I'm too old to do anything, but do they say that to Beaufort? No. No, of course they don't. It's all Beaufort this, Beaufort that. Well, if *I* had a fancy name …" He flopped off the cavern ledge, still grumbling, and spiralled after the High Lord.

Mortimer licked his lips, and glanced at Gilbert and Amelia, who seemed to be holding each other up. It'd be fine. It'd *all* be fine. As long as Lord Walter didn't eat the postmen.

At least Miriam and Alice were safely out of it all.

☙

THEY WERE HAVING a few technical difficulties.

Amelia couldn't fly in a straight line, and kept crashing into Mortimer and Gilbert. Gilbert was managing admirably, considering he'd never flown before this afternoon, but every now and then he'd forget to use his wings and start falling, while Mortimer and Amelia screamed at him and he tried swimming in a panicked doggy paddle across the sky. So they stayed high.

Mortimer thought that maybe one concussed dragon and one still figuring out the fundamentals of flight, plus one that was grumbling and spitting a furious commentary on every sign of humans that they passed on the way, might not the best team for taking on goblins. But it wasn't as if they could have told any of them to stay. Particularly not Amelia. There was something about the fact that she couldn't actually focus that made her seem terribly formidable.

"How many goblins are there?" Beaufort asked, ignoring Lord Walter's current diatribe regarding the horrors of power lines.

"Three on guard duty," Alex said.

"And they're keeping the humans alive?"

"Yes. I know Rockford doesn't like them, but he wouldn't kill a human for no reason."

"He gave them to goblins," Beaufort said sternly. "It may not be killing them outright, but it is a death sentence."

Alex didn't answer, but he was looking very grey, and after a moment Mortimer called, "Three on guard duty, and how many others?"

"A whole clan in the immediate area. Twenty or so, I suppose."

Mortimer dropped back and watched Gilbert shepherd his sister back toward their route, then somehow get himself turned upside down, yelping that he couldn't see where he was going and flailing his legs wildly. Yes. They possibly could have chosen a slightly better team. He wished he'd watched something about fighting on Miriam's TV, rather than all those dancing shows. Although, if a goblin wanted to foxtrot, he'd be the best dragon for it.

ॐ

"OH," Alex said. "Oh, that doesn't look good." They were coming in fast over the fells, still keeping high so Gilbert didn't crash.

Dragons see in the dark the way cats do, movement sketched stronger and sharper than the background. And there was an awful lot of movement. The house was blazing with light, and all about it scattered shapes were running wildly and apparently without direction, as if someone had kicked over an anthill. There was screaming and shouting, and some of the shapes were waving flaming torches, and here and there groups of them collided and piled up, or raced off in different directions. Mortimer could smell sweat and blood and fear, and the slick stench of goblins.

"*Dragons!*" Beaufort bellowed, all efforts at secrecy abandoned. "Now it starts! Be strong! Be brave! Be *dragon!*" He tucked his wings in on the last word, dropped his head, and roared as he plunged toward the fight. "*To the battle, Cloverlies! Dive!*"

Lord Walter roared back, a savage and joyous sound, and arrowed toward the ground, spitting fire as he went. Alex plunged after them, flushing a furiously excited red.

Mortimer watched them go, and realised this was something he'd never seen. Something probably only Walter and Beaufort had seen, in fact. Dragons in full cry, not hiding, not slipping through the shadows. Dragons in flight, driving back the enemy and taking what was won, and rescuing some princesses along the way. Well, postmen.

He forgot all about Gilbert and Amelia, angled his wings, and dropped. The night air was smooth as ice water across his scales, the stars a high and beautiful roof above, and as he dived he roared, fire flaring across the sky. And for one perfect, endless moment he was nothing but purely, gloriously, dragon.

20

ALICE

The light went out, and the basement was plunged into utter, impossible darkness. Alice dropped into a crouch, and thought she heard a whisper of movement over the chorus of frightened screams.

"Miriam, *down!*" she shouted, and swung the cane in a whistling arc as she straightened up, hoping the other woman had listened. She hit something that snarled in a way that stopped her breath and set the old, clever parts of her brain shrieking about predators and fire. The impact sent a shock jolting up her arms, and she pulled back and swung again, lower this time, hoping to catch whatever it was if it ducked. Nothing but emptiness, and the momentum of her own blow sent her stumbling down a step. One left to the floor. Fourteen above her. She'd counted on the way down as well as the way up. Old habits die hard.

She froze in a crouch, raising the cane over her shoulder, waiting. Her heart was the loudest thing she could hear, and she concentrated on her breathing, slowing it, trying to hear beyond herself. There, now she could hear the panicked chorus of frightened people breathing, and someone crying, and the clink of chains as someone moved. And a strangled *hic*. No footfalls, but the amount of dirt on the floor would render them nearly silent. She waited.

Then white light flared in the darkness, making her flinch, and a phone landed in the centre of the floor, sending up a cone of light like some reverse alien abduction picture. Which meant she not only hadn't hit Miriam, but that Miriam, for all her hiccoughs, wasn't panicking. Alice smiled into the dark and took a careful step onto the floor. She kept low and eased away from the stairs. The phone shed enough light for her to see the bottom step to one side, the feet of one of the prisoners to the other. The rest was nothing but bare dirt. She withdrew deeper into the shadows, cane at the ready, the skin on her back prickling. It felt like someone was stalking her.

They probably were.

She spun, bringing the cane up, and someone caught it, stopping it so short that it jarred her arms. She let go and tried to jump back, but now there was a hard hand curled into the front of her coat, the cloth ripping under sharp nails, and breath on her face that made her gag.

"Naughty, naughty," the goblin whispered, and pulled her a little closer. She balled her hands into fists and slammed them both into his face, and he gave a startled yelp but didn't drop her. She drew back to hit him again, her hands smarting, then there was a soft whistle and a rather final thud. The goblin fell forward, carrying Alice with him, and she tried to push herself free as they crashed to the floor. She managed not to land flat on her back, but her hip hit the ground hard, and she stayed there for a moment with her eyes closed, holding in a little cry of pain. The stone floor wasn't as far under the dirt as it looked. Then someone rolled the goblin off.

"Alice? Alice – *hic* – are you okay?"

"Yes," she said, forcing a smile into her voice. "Nice shot, Miriam."

"Oh, I only finished him off. You got him first."

With the goblin's weight lifted, the pain in her hip was just about bearable, but there was something sharp about it that she didn't like. She climbed slowly to her feet and retrieved her cane in the white light of the phone torch. She wondered if she might actually have to use it in the manner for which it was designed. That would be most disagreeable.

"Which one is it? Is it Goblin Sam?" one of the captives asked eagerly.

"Stop calling him that," the Royal Mail man said. "That's *my* name."

"Well, it's a handy way to know which one we're talking about," Alice said, picking up the phone and using the light to examine the goblin. "No, I think it's the other one. George."

"That's *my* name," another disembodied voice in the dark said, sounding aggrieved.

"Really?" Miriam said. "That's what you're worried about?"

Alice handed her the phone. "Here. Try and light the stairs for me."

"Be – *hic* – careful." Miriam shone the light up into the dark as Alice shouldered her cane again and started up the steps cautiously. The light from the phone was pale and uneven, her shadow a huge block of darkness in front of her. The gaps under the stairs were impenetrable wells, and the kitchen light was nothing more than the thin outline of a door shape above. She couldn't even really tell if there was anyone between her and it. But if it had been her who had sneaked in when the light went out, she wouldn't have lingered on the stairs. No, she'd have waited under them and grabbed the ankles of anyone going up. Quick way to a broken neck. The skin on her back crawled, but she kept going, braced for teeth or claws or just a shove down the stairs, which she was pretty sure would do for her hip entirely. Staying put wasn't going to get them anywhere.

Nothing stopped her, nothing grabbed her, and she jogged the last few steps as quietly as she could, flicking the light back on. It hardly qualified as flooding the cellar with brightness, but after the solid dark of before it still seemed fairly impressive.

There was a chorus of relieved *ooh*s from below and she waved them all to silence, then leaned against the door, listening. She couldn't hear anything. But if one had come back, others might have, too. She surprised herself by hoping Thompson was safe. Damn cat. She wouldn't be here, with her hip sending out little distress flares of pain, if it wasn't for him.

She was still listening when the door was pulled open away from her, and she stared at the two goblins outside with almost as much astonishment as she could see on their faces. For a confused moment no one moved, then she recovered herself, dropped her cane, grabbed the door handle with both hands and jerked it shut again. She braced herself against the door frame, hearing her cane clattering down the stairs, and strained against the goblins tugging on the other side of the door and shouting at her.

"Where Goblin George? Bad human! Goblin George! Goblin *George!*"

Someone was crying down in the cellar again, and someone else was shouting, then there were quick feet on the stairs and Miriam was at Alice's elbow. She was panting, her cheeks flushed, and she had both the cricket bat and Alice's dropped cane in her hands.

Alice smiled at her. "Ready, Miriam?"

"Not – *hic* – really."

"Me neither."

They smiled at each other, then Alice let go of the handle and grabbed her cane. The goblins, still tugging from the outside, went stumbling backward with howls of surprise, and Alice charged toward them, swinging the cane and shouting like she was scolding puppies that had wet the floor.

"Bad goblins! *Bad goblins!*"

Miriam was right behind her, laying about with the cricket bat and doing a banshee impression that would have put Thompson to shame.

ALICE THOUGHT it was rather fortunate that there were only two goblins. Not only were they large beasts, they seemed to have very hard heads, making them difficult to put down and even more troublesome to keep there. Plus Miriam was all enthusiasm, very little accuracy, and Alice counted herself lucky that she hadn't been brained by the cricket bat in the middle of it all.

They came through the door running, and Alice smacked the first goblin, the one calling itself Goblin Sam, right between the eyes with her cane. It was a blow that would have put a grown man on the ground, but Goblin Sam just growled at her, and made a grab for the cane. She jumped back, ignoring the complaints of her hip, and swung again, this time going for the kneecaps. That brought the monster down to her level with a howl, and before she could swing again Miriam gave him four rapid blows to the head, like a tradesman hammering a nail, and Goblin Sam keeled over, his eyes glazing. Alice was already moving, because Goblin Hazel, her sun dress only hanging on by one strap, was getting up off the floor, looking more furious than hurt. Alice hit her on the head with the cane, and she fell back down.

The two women stood perfectly still for a moment, listening. There was no movement in the house, but they could still hear Thompson yowling outside. He was sounding a little hoarse now, but the fact that he was yowling at all suggested that he was still distracting someone. Who, and how many, was the question.

Goblin Sam groaned, and Miriam squeaked, then hit him again. He fell silent.

"Right," Alice said. "Keys." She pointed at Goblin Sam.

"Ugh, do I have to?"

"Please, Miriam." Alice watched her crouch down and start digging through Goblin Sam's pocket with little mutters of disgust. She would have done it herself, but she had a feeling that she wouldn't have got back up again. Goblin Hazel lifted a hand, and Alice rapped her smartly on the forehead with the cane, setting up a hollow ringing sound. No point taking chances.

"Got them!" Miriam held up an old-fashioned ring of iron keys, grinning.

"What is that on your hands?" Alice asked, her stomach rolling over in protest. Miriam looked like she'd been making mud pies.

"Smells like chocolate," Miriam said. "Look, he had chocolate Santas all through his pockets." She pointed at some filthy scraps of foil that might have been wrappers, and Alice shuddered.

"Well, I guess we know why your note was in the state it was, then. And the wonderful writing and spelling." The goblins' hands were cruel and calloused, and ended in nails that were more like claws. It couldn't have been easy writing with them. "Can you go get everyone out of the cellar?"

Miriam bit her lip. "Just me?"

"I'll keep watch up here, in case anyone comes in. Now hurry!" The distress flares in her hip were developing into a bonfire, and there was a thin sweat starting on her forehead.

Miriam picked up her cricket bat without much enthusiasm, and hurried back down into the basement, keys jingling. Alice let her breath out in a series of pained pants, half bent over on her cane, and when Goblin Sam moaned she straightened up and hit him probably a little harder than was entirely necessary. It felt good, though.

There was a shout and a thud from downstairs, and she called, "Miriam? Are you okay?"

"Yes! He was waking up."

"Alright. Hurry up." She could hear clattering chains from downstairs, like a ghost conference getting under way, and before long the captives started appearing on the stairs, looking around blearily and stretching.

"Come on, come on," Alice said, and hit Goblin Hazel again as she opened her bright eyes a sliver. Honestly, it was like playing whack-a-goblin.

"Come on what?" the black polo shirt man grumbled. "We've been chained up here for ages. We need a moment to get our bearings."

"You've only been here a day," Sam the Royal Mail man said. "I was the first one they took. I've been here *forever.*"

"Five days," Miriam said, and the Royal Mail woman glared at her. Miriam shrugged, and Alice smiled. Apparently battering not one, but two goblins into unconsciousness with a cricket bat was very good for Miriam's confidence. And also an excellent cure for nervous hiccoughs.

"Now, then," Alice said, trying to lean on the cane without looking like she was leaning on it. "We need to drag these two goblins down there and chain them all up."

"I'm not touching them," the woman said at once. Alice supposed, given the goblins' affection for stealing names, that her name was Hazel. "They're nasty."

"Yeah. We should just get out of here," the DHL man agreed. He sounded like the one that had said Goblin George had taken his name.

"No one's getting out of here until they're chained up," Alice snapped. "I'm not having them coming after us when they wake up."

"Listen, lady," Polo Shirt said, "I don't know who put you in charge—"

"Just drag the damn things down there!" Miriam hissed at him, the cricket bat brandished over her shoulder. "Don't make us regret everything we've just gone through to get you sorry lot out of here."

Polo Shirt looked at her in alarm, then crouched down and grabbed one of Goblin Sam's legs. The DHL man hurried to grab the other one.

Alice gave Miriam a thumbs up, and Miriam smiled. It was quite a new and interesting smile.

⚜

PUNCTUATED by the occasional thud of Miriam's cricket bat, the two goblins were dragged down the stairs to join Goblin George and locked firmly in the chains. Miriam pulled the cellar door to on faint moans as the creatures started to come around, and Alice looked at the little group as brightly as she could manage.

"Arm yourselves," she said, and they looked at her blankly.

"What with?" the man in the black polo asked, and Alice thought she could end up quite disliking him.

"Saucepans," she said, nodding at the stove. "Brooms. Anything. Use your brains, for heaven's sake." She had a feeling that the pain was making her a little sharper than was necessary, but this was a combat situation, not a school trip.

George found a butcher's knife on the table, and Hazel snatched an egg-encrusted frying pan up before Polo Shirt could grab it. He scowled, but took the smaller saucepan next to it, grimacing at the contents. Sam had the kettle in one hand and a dustpan in the other.

"What on earth are you going to do with that?" Alice asked him.

"They got all the good stuff," he said. His grey hair was sticking up around his head in a matted halo.

Alice sighed. "Take the broom," she said. "The long-handled one there, in the corner. Honestly."

Sam went pink and put the kettle down. He kept the dustpan, though.

With everyone as prepared as they could be, Alice led the little party out the kitchen door into the cold night. Miriam brought up the rear with the cricket bat on her shoulder and a determined look on her face, and they made their way single file along the back of the house and around the corner. Thompson was still yowling somewhere out there in the dark, but it had become more of a harsh squawk than a banshee scream. Alice brought them to a stop before anyone could wander around the corner to the front and be spotted by whatever creatures were running about out there. She leaned against the wall, trying to keep her breathing under control and wondering what the best thing to do was. The delivery drivers stared at her with anxious faces, brandishing their makeshift weapons, and she gave them what she hoped was an encouraging smile.

"Miriam, do you have phone signal?" she asked, palming that irritating sweat off her forehead.

"No," Miriam said with a sigh. "Still nothing."

"Have any of you ever heard cars here? Anything coming or going?"

The delivery drivers looked at each other and shrugged. Alice sighed. If there had been a van in a shed they could have reached, they'd have had a much better chance. But she didn't want to linger here checking the broken-down outbuildings if no one had even heard a car. It was far too risky. They were going to have to attempt a cross-country sprint back to the poor Prius, then some sort of clown car debacle trying to get everyone in, and hope the goblins couldn't run quicker than first gear. If they made it as far as the car, that was. She wasn't at all sure that she could.

She eased herself to the corner and peered around, the

nightscape rendered in deep greys and shades of indigo. Thompson appeared on the road beyond the gate, set up a yowl, then loped away as half a dozen goblins ran down the hill after him. He wasn't rushing, and the goblins were gaining fast. He let the nearest almost touch his tail, then vanished. Alice blinked as the goblins shouted and cursed, wondering if he'd jumped down a rabbit hole or something. Then his raspy yowl rose from a hummock a little further up the hill, on the other side of the house, and the goblins all turned and ran that way. Before they reached it, the yowl stopped, then restarted again just a bit further away. The goblins regrouped and sprinted off.

"Well," Alice said. "That explains a lot." She pushed off the wall and tightened her grip on her cane. "Come on. The cat can only keep them occupied for so long. We need to try and get to the car before they get bored. It's a bit of a hike, and we can't hang around. Everyone ready?"

There were some nervous mutters, then Polo Shirt said, "Why can't we just go down the road? We'll get signal at some point, and we can call the police."

"And if we don't? Or when the goblins realise you're missing? We'll be on foot all the way to the next village, and there's no chance we'll hold them off that long." Alice shook her head. "No, we go to the car."

"I don't like the idea of running off. What if they see us?" Sam said.

"It's true," Hazel said. "They'll catch us."

"If they see us. But if you stay here, they'll definitely catch you." Alice tried to sound patient. She didn't feel very patient.

"We could hide," George suggested. "Then you could go get help and come back."

"We are *all* going," Alice said. "Now shut up, the lot of you." She glared at them, fairly surprised that they had actually subsided into silence, then Miriam said in a small voice, "Oh dear."

Alice spun around and straight into a large and very human chest. She looked up and saw the man from the market stall, the one called Bill, and said, "Dammit." She jumped back, but her hip betrayed her and made her stumble. He grabbed her wrists, squeezing her hand painfully until she cried out and dropped the cane.

"The police are on their way!" Miriam shouted behind her. "Let me go!"

"The police?" the man who had hold of Miriam said. There were four of them, all tall and broad and young, and Alice glared up at Bill.

"Yes, the police. And do you think they'll arrest goblins? Of course not. This is all going to be on you."

He scowled at her. "You're lying."

"Not for a second."

"She's got a point," one of the other men said, the one who had led Bill away from the market. "This is way out of control. What are we meant to do with them all?"

"*We're* not going to do anything, Stu," Bill said. "The goblins are."

"You trust them?" Miriam demanded. "They'll probably eat the lot of you."

"They do drool a lot when they look at us," Hazel said. "It's disturbing."

"One licked my ear," George said. "And not in a nice way."

"I think we should all get out of here," the fourth man said. He was peering around nervously. "You know, we could say we'd rescued you. You'd do that, right?"

"Of course," Alice said quickly, because she could tell without looking at her that Miriam wasn't in the mood to agree to anything. "Have you got a car?"

"Goblin Sam's got the keys," Stu said.

"This is stupid," Bill snapped. "Let's just deal with this lot and

282 | KIM M. WATT

carry on as we said we would. We're not going to see a cent if we run." He released Alice's wrists and bent to pick up the dropped cane.

Alice didn't exactly think. She just knew that her knee and his head were occupying very similar spaces. She grabbed the back of his neck and put them into the same space with as much force as she could muster, feeling a satisfying crunch as Bill cried out and dropped to all fours.

"My *dose!*"

How about that, she thought. *It really does sound like 'dose'.* Then she snatched up her cane and lunged toward Stu, trying to ignore the pain in her hip. He yelped and threw his arms up to protect his head, and the nervous man rushed at her, shouting for her to stop.

Hazel gave a whoop and smacked Miriam's captor with the frying pan, and George shouted something incoherent, waving the butcher's knife wildly as the man released Miriam and staggered away with his hands clasped to his head. Sam and Polo Shirt appeared to be trying to burrow into the wall, and Bill was still on his knees wailing about his dose.

"Let go," Alice told the nervous man, who had managed to wrap his arms around her in some misguided bear hug, making the cane useless. He stared at her with enormous eyes, then Thompson appeared on his shoulder. The cat launched himself at the man's face, hissing and spitting and clawing, and the man let her go, staggering about and yelping in panic. Thompson seemed to have more pointy ends than not.

Miriam had somehow managed to get her captor in a headlock of sorts, and they were both on the ground, rolling wildly about the place with arms and feet going everywhere. Alice turned to Stu. "Now," she said, and he shook his head, looking with wide eyes at the back garden. She turned to follow his gaze, and saw a group of at least a dozen goblins watching the fracas with broad grins. Broad, toothy, *slobbery* grins.

She looked back at Stu. "Bad choice of associates."

He nodded stiffly, not looking at her, as the lead goblin said, "Goblin Lucy like Bill. Bill good name. Now Goblin Lucy be Goblin Bill, and human Bill be Food Bill. Yes?"

Bill looked up at them with his mouth hanging open and blood running down his chin. "What?" he said, although it came out as "Whad?"

"Goblin Jace like Bill too," another goblin said. "Goblin Jace want to be Goblin Bill."

Goblin Lucy shoved Goblin Jace, growling. "No! Goblin Lucy see Bill first!"

Miriam and the man she'd been fighting had stopped struggling, and Thompson had vanished again. Hazel and George were frozen with their weapons raised, and even Sam and Polo Shirt were looking at the goblins.

"Goblin Richard smart goblin," one of the creatures announced. "Goblin Richard decide." He thought for a moment, then said, "Goblin Richard will be Goblin Bill."

Goblins Lucy and Jace looked at each other, then threw themselves at Goblin Richard with their teeth bared and their fists pounding, and within a moment the entire group of goblins were in a pile-up of arms and legs and flying hair and ugly screeches.

Alice looked at the frozen humans, all staring at the brawl.

"Run," she said, as loudly as she dared.

They ran. Miriam stopped just long enough to grab the cricket bat, and they headed for the fells. The delivery drivers bolted like animals released from a cage, each of them racing off in a different direction, and the four men sprinted in a pack for the road. More goblins were swarming out of the shadows, and the fight broke up behind them with howls of fury. There were more of the creatures than Alice wanted to count, far more than had been chasing the cat, and they threw themselves into the chase with utter delight. They cackled gleefully and shouted to each other, hunting in threes and fours and using their long arms to help speed themselves along. Their teeth flashed in the moonlight, and when a quartet of them came charging out of a ditch in front of Alice and Miriam both women yelled something that was not fit for W.I. purposes and waved their weapons wildly. The goblins burst out laughing but swerved away, letting them run on.

They ran in the general direction of the car, trying not to stumble on the rough ground. The cold air tore at Alice's chest, her breathing already ragged from the pain, and she wondered how long she could keep going. Every stride jarred her from jaw to heel, her belly churning with it, and there were tears squeezing out onto her cheeks. She risked a look back and saw the four goblins loping easily after them. There were more coming in from the side. Even if she hadn't been hurt, she wouldn't have been able to outrun them. She doubted anyone could.

She fumbled in her pockets. "Miriam, take the keys."

Miriam slowed, her forehead creased with concern. "Are you okay?"

Alice gasped laughter. "Peachy." She staggered as her hip screamed, and almost fell. Miriam grabbed her arm, pulled her upright, and looked over her shoulder at their pursuers.

"Back to back," she said. "That's how you do it, right?"

Alice shoved her keys at the younger woman. "Run, would you?"

"Oh, Alice. Just shut up for once." Miriam shouldered her bat, ignoring the keys, and Alice snorted.

"Hitting goblins is good for you. But you should still run."

"As if I could." Miriam smiled at her. "Hitting goblins wouldn't be as much fun without you."

Alice laughed, and turned to face the creatures advancing on them. She shouldered her cane and decided she'd just found her second wind.

21

DI ADAMS

Tracking Miriam's phone had proved more difficult than expected. They'd arrived at the bottom of a farm track that looked like it should only be tackled with one of those desert expedition trucks equipped with roll bars, spare water, and a flare gun, and stopped with the nose of the car pointed up the hill. Alice's Prius was nowhere to be seen, but somewhere above them Miriam's phone crawled on at walking pace. DI Collins killed the lights and they got out, staring up at the fells. For a moment DI Adams could see nothing at all, the night rushing in to surround her, swaddling her in high crisp cold, and she tipped her head back to look at the stars, taking quick shallow breaths that hurt her lungs.

The stars steadied her, and once she looked down she found that she could see the heavy folds of the fells hulking away from her like sleeping giants, and the track leading off into the darkness.

"Do you know where it goes?" she asked DI Collins. He was a shadow cut out of the night, rocking on his heels.

"No. But we can't take the car up there. No good to anyone if we get stuck."

She nodded, realised he couldn't see her, and said, "There's light up there every now and then."

There was a pause while he watched, then he said with a note of wonder in his voice, "I don't think that's a torch. I think they're headlights."

DI Adams thought of the Prius speeding past them, and wondered what the hell Alice and Miriam were thinking. They weren't equipped for that road. They were probably stuck in a ditch up there somewhere, freezing to death. And, if not, they were likely to slide straight off a cliff edge at any moment.

"Come on," she said. "Get the GPS up and see if we can come at them from the other side."

THEY HIT the main road in a squall of gravel, sliding almost into the wall on the opposite side before the tyres gripped and they were accelerating rapidly, the headlights cutting the night ahead of them. It was only a main road in the sense that it was bigger than the one they'd just come off, and it had tarmac, and in the wider spots there was occasionally a centre line. Otherwise it was silent and empty and uncluttered with lighting or cats' eyes, and DI Adams just hoped they didn't meet anyone coming the other way.

Miriam's phone was still creeping up the fells, and the GPS had shown them an isolated house up there that they seemed to be heading for.

"I don't understand why they went up that bloody track, though," DI Collins said, not looking away from the road. "The map shows a paved lane right on the other side of the house. Private, but better than that damn death-trap of a trail." He hit fifth gear, and DI Adams braced herself against the dashboard.

"I'm guessing they've not exactly been invited up there."

"But why the hell didn't they tell us what they were up to? Silly old women!"

"Maybe they thought we wouldn't believe them."

DI Collins glanced at her, then back at the road in time to drop into third and spin them around a tight bend, engine and tyres screaming in protest. "You'd have believed them. You're their dragon contact." He sounded vaguely put out.

"True," DI Adams said, letting go of the dashboard to cling to the door. "But I think they may have a slight problem with authority."

DI Collins snorted. "Well, they certainly do now."

DI Adams went back to bracing herself on the dashboard as they hit another straight, and thought that Collins might be being a bit optimistic if he thought that was going to be their only problem.

THE LONG WAY ROUND WAS, well, long. It seemed to take forever to make their way through an impossible maze of back roads and one-car lanes, and in the end they shot straight past the gate to the private road, DI Adams with her eyes on the GPS shouting to Collins to stop. He slammed the brakes on, swearing, and reversed with the back of the car fishtailing wildly. He shoved the nose of the Audi into the lane and the headlights lit a locked gate.

"Got it." DI Adams had her door open before the car had quite stopped moving, running to the boot as Collins popped it open. She grabbed the bolt cutters from the kit that lived in every police car and ran to clip the padlock. It gave way easily enough, and she hauled the gate wide, jumping back in the car as it came through the gap. There was no time to bother about closing it. She just hoped there wouldn't be any more sheep incidents. DI Collins accelerated rapidly, and they barrelled up into the deep dark of the fells, sliding on the odd patch of loose gravel. There were explosions rolling across the sky ahead of them.

DI Adams looked at Collins. He was still driving with the same unaffected confidence, both hands on the wheel, but his eyes kept straying to those flares of hungry light. They were mostly purples and reds, balls of fire tighter and more intense than any fireworks display.

"You said not like *Game of Thrones*, right?" he said suddenly.

"Um, yeah."

"I hope you're right."

They came around a corner and the road straightened out. He floored the accelerator, slapping the lights on. DI Adams doubted anyone was paying any attention. Whatever was up there was probably fairly busy as it was, and the flashing blue was rather less spectacular than the fire above them.

They were almost airborne as they came over the crest of the last hill and into utter chaos. An outbuilding and several trees were burning, lending a terrible red light to the scene, and as DI Collins hit the brakes a man in a DHL shirt ran screaming across the road in front of the car, waving a butcher's knife and being pursued by three snarling *things* that stood roughly on two legs, but otherwise didn't look particularly human. They ignored the car entirely, and were gone into the dark again before DI Adams could get a proper look, but she was sure there had been far too many teeth.

Something roared not far off, and as they got out of the car a fireball bloomed purple-hot to the left of the house, followed by some not very human screaming. Another of the strange bipeds went bolting across the road, hunched over and using its hands to speed it along. It was shrieking, and being pursued by a small cat with a bushed-out tail.

Collins blinked, and looked at DI Adams. She stared back at him. This was not at all the same as the tea-drinking and cake-eating dragons from Toot Hansell. This had shades of London to it, dark spaces under bridges and missing children and feeling like she was swimming against a riptide just to keep the slimmest grip on what was real.

There was a roar that shook her bones, and she ducked as a dragon shot through the sky above them. Somehow they seemed much bigger when they were flying and breathing fire at you. She peered over the bonnet at Collins, who was hunkered down on the other side of the car, and he shouted, "I thought you said not *Game of Thrones*, Adams!"

Another dragon shot overhead, huge green wings buffeting them with a gust of wind, bellowing, "Old Ones take you, Walter! *Just the goblins!*"

DI Adams stood up cautiously and watched the retreating dragons. Walter had banked back over the fells, now on the trail of three of the toothy creatures (she assumed they were the goblins), spitting fire at them happily as they fled, and Beaufort was circling back toward the house. "My understanding is that Walter is a bit of a problem," she said.

"You don't say," DI Collins said, straightening up.

A man ran from the fells toward the house, his arms pumping like a professional sprinter, screaming, and another man ran to meet him, throwing rocks at the goblins closing in on them as he came. One rock caught the sprinter square in the forehead, and he crumpled to the ground without so much as a whimper. The goblins descended into helpless laughter, clutching each other and howling. The rock-thrower stopped where he was, looking confused, then turned and bolted when a woman with familiar curly hair appeared out of the dark and jogged toward him swinging a cricket bat. She was shouting something the inspectors couldn't quite hear, and when one of the goblins popped up next to her from behind a hummock she smacked it unceremoniously in the face with the bat and kept going.

DI Collins pointed. "That's a human, right?"

DI Adams nodded. "Probably your aunt."

"I know that. The other one."

"Looks like it."

"Good," he said. "Let's go arrest someone before they all get eaten."

"They don't—"

"I'm not talking about dragons," he said, and nodded at two goblins who were sprinting through the headlights, wearing scraps of badly fitting human clothing. Their teeth flashed in the light, and they kept their eyes on the inspectors as they ran. One licked its lips. "They look bitey."

"Good point." DI Adams grinned, feeling suddenly that she was at least in the same hemisphere as her element. "Let's go arrest people."

They marched off into the flaming night, while someone above them shrieked, "Pull up, Gilbert! *Pull up!*"

⁊⁊

IT WAS CHRISTMAS EVE, and while Leeds had nothing but some grimy slush on the streets, the fells in the Dales were heavy with snow, the fields white blankets broken by the shadows of trees and the trails made by livestock. The sky was high and pale and thin, and Toot Hansell looked like a picture on a particularly twee card, every roof white-capped, every lawn pocked with disguised bushes and birdbaths and, often, snowmen. The roads were black lines dividing the houses, and the streams had burrowed themselves away under ice and snow as if in hibernation. Chimneys bled smoke that lingered in the still air, and Christmas lights danced in every window, or near enough that the odd grinch could be ignored. Footprints pattered across the crisp surface everywhere – big snow boots and little ones, cat paws and dog paws and the little cross-hatchings of birds.

And, DI Adams was quite sure, if one knew where to look, some rather more unusual footprints. She felt oddly reassured by the fact.

DI Collins stopped the car and they sat looking at Miriam's squat little cottage, the roof heavy with snow, baubles bobbing in the windows.

"I guess we should go in," he said.

"We were invited," DI Adams said. The bandage was off her wrist now, from where the goblin had bitten her, but the scars puckered the skin quite spectacularly. She'd told the paramedics that it had been a particularly big and toothy dog. They'd looked mystified, but patched her up and sent her off to get stitches.

DI Collins took his hat off and ran a hand over his hair. It was starting to grow back. He'd had to take it down to almost a number one, to match the bit that had been scorched off by Lord Walter. The old dragon had apologised and said that he was terribly shortsighted, and had assumed that, based on the inspector's height, he was a goblin. It was a pretty thin excuse, and DI Adams had been able to hear Beaufort chastising him until the dragons were out of sight.

Now she opened her door and got out. "Come on. We've faced goblins. We can face your aunt and Alice."

"As long as it's not the whole bloody W.I. again," Collins muttered, and followed her through the little gate and up the path to the door. She had her hand raised to knock when he said, "Wait."

She turned to look at him. The short hair made his face look round and young, and he was twisting his hat in his hands. "What?"

"It was real, right, Adams? All of it?"

She showed him her wrist. "Real as this."

"And no one else knows."

"Well, other than the whole W.I., but they seem better at keeping secrets than bloody MI6, so, yeah."

"But what do we do about it?"

"We don't do anything, except keep them secret. Dragons seem to be pretty self-governing. I'm not sure we didn't make more of a mess than they did up there." Which was true. They'd arrested the four men, all brothers, but by the time the ambulance arrived the dragons had not only routed the goblins, they'd cleared the house of anything remotely suspicious, and the delivery drivers had suddenly decided that there had been no one involved but the humans. That decision had seemed to coincide with Walter leering at them and drooling into the garden from his perch on top of a fence post. And it was doubtful that the brothers would say much, given that they seemed to have taken most of their injuries from two members of the Women's Institute and a small tabby cat. Even criminals have images to uphold.

DI Collins rubbed his jaw, then shoved the hat in his pocket. "Alright," he said. "Let's have tea with dragons."

DI Adams knocked, taking a deep breath of the calm day, and waited. A moment later the door swung open, and Miriam smiled at them, looking distinctly calmer than she usually did at the sight of the police.

"Come in, come in!" she said, ushering them into the warmth and scent of the house. "We're just having eggnog."

"Pass," DI Adams said with a shudder.

DI Collins looked at her. "We're off-duty, Adams."

"Why would I want to drink custard?"

"Suit yourself. I'll take one."

"Everyone's in here," Miriam said, and led the way into the living room, while Collins gave a very small groan and DI Adams braced herself for the onslaught of the Women's Institute. She should have taken that eggnog after all.

Instead, they discovered four dragons taking up most of the

available floor space and Alice settled in the armchair with the tabby cat on her knee. He opened one eye, examined the inspectors, and shut it again.

DI Adams claimed a spot on the sofa, and Collins hesitated in the doorway, studying the dragons with a rather stern expression. "You're real, aren't you?" he said.

"I should hope so," Beaufort said. He had a book in one paw and a large mug of tea in the other. "I shall feel very disappointed if I find out I'm not real."

"Beaufort Scales, High Lord of the Cloverly dragons," Alice said. "As we didn't really have time for proper introductions the other night. Mortimer next to him, then Amelia and Gilbert are over there." Mortimer had mince pie crumbs on his snout, and he gave an embarrassed sort of wave.

"Right." Collins' serious expression vanished, and he grinned broadly. "Detective Inspector Colin Collins."

"Delighted to meet you, Detective Inspector," Beaufort said, as Gilbert whispered, "Colin Collins?" and Amelia shoved him. Beaufort flourished his book at the inspector. "I've just borrowed this from Miriam. Miss Marple. She seems terribly good at detecting. Have you read it?"

"No," Collins admitted, seating himself next to DI Adams.

"You should. It's excellent. Quite the training manual."

DI Adams wished people would stop giving Beaufort ideas.

"SCONE?" Miriam said. "They're cranberry and orange. Just as a change from mince pies." She glanced at Mortimer, who had three pies still on his plate. "Not that everyone gets bored of them, of course."

"Well, they are compulsory," Alice said. "It's Christmas." The dragon head cane rested next to her chair, the finish looking a little the worse for wear and a couple of new silver bands fitted where the wood had cracked. Not, as she had already pointed out to the inspectors, that she intended on needing it for long. But it was good in the snow.

DI Adams took a scone and decided that it was wiser not to share her opinion about walking in the snow within a couple of weeks of a hip operation.

"Can I have some eggnog?" Amelia asked.

"Me too," Gilbert said immediately. He still had no scales on his chin after his spectacular final fall on the fells. He continued to insist that it had been deliberate, as he'd landed on two goblins and rolled over another three, but Amelia had pointed out to the room that he hadn't been flying since. He'd even walked home after the battle was over.

"So," DI Collins said, balancing a plate stacked with a thick wedge of Christmas cake, four cookies, and three mince pies on his knee. "We booked the men from the house with kidnapping, mail theft, selling stolen goods, you name it. They'd just inherited the house from a great-aunt, and went a bit mad running up credit card bills buying flash cars and clothes and so on, thinking they were rich landowners. Turns out the house is just about falling down and the land's already mortgaged as far as it can go. They claim that they were trying to make enough money from the scam to pay off their bills and were working alone. They also keep asking for the maximum sentence and a cell with no windows. They don't even want to be out on bail." He deliberated, then took a large bite of cake. "So, over to you, um, High Lord? Your Highness?"

"Beaufort," the old dragon said. "I take full responsibility for the involvement of dragons, and they are all being punished. Alex is now Lord Walter's helper, and Rockford has nursery duty for at least the next ninety-three years."

"It wasn't your fault," Mortimer said.

"Yeah," Gilbert said. "Rockford's just a—" He choked on his tea as Amelia elbowed him.

"But it was my fault," Beaufort said. "I rushed ahead into what I saw as a great opportunity for the clan to come out of hiding, and I didn't listen to the voices of others."

"Beaufort," Mortimer protested again, and the High Lord held his paw up.

"I'm working on being more democratic, which will hopefully balance out the needs of those who want to stay hidden and those who are more comfortable being part of the modern world. As to Rockford, he thought that if he ruined the bauble trade in a way that threatened to expose the existence of dragons, I would be ousted and we'd return to a more traditional way of living."

"Hiding," Amelia scoffed, and dunked a piece of Christmas cake in her eggnog.

"Then some goblin got his ear and convinced him that it'd be even better if, rather than just stealing the baubles, they created their own faulty ones. Then they could wreak a little havoc on humans, which Rockford quite liked the idea of. He still fancies himself as a bit of a marauder. Meanwhile the goblins were stock-piling all the stolen baubles to sell later on at a profit."

"I still haven't worked out how the humans came in," DI Adams said.

"The goblins needed someone to post the baubles and help with the internet thingy. Their grasp of English and technology is a little shaky. They're terribly good at sniffing out desperation, though, and they convinced the humans that they'd split the money from the baubles, plus be able to ransom the drivers. Of course, the goblins would've eaten everyone for Christmas dinner, captives and cohorts alike. That's how they usually do things."

DI Adams wrinkled her nose and took a sip of tea. She'd had a nightmare last night in which six of the things had been chasing her while she pelted them with treacle tart, for some reason.

"Well," Collins said thoughtfully. "It puts a new slant on some cases that have been bothering me."

"Me too," DI Adams said. "I wish you'd told me before that there were things other than dragons out there. I can think of half a dozen cases that fit goblins."

Beaufort shook his head. "Most of them will be human, I'm sorry to say. You can be quite nasty enough to each other."

DI Adams sighed. "That's true, unfortunately."

"Not all of you, though." Beaufort raised his mug. "In fact, most of you are entirely wonderful. Just like Folk."

There was peaceful quiet after that, filled with the whisper of the fire and the contented rumbling of the dragons. DI Adams sipped her tea and watched Collins examining them. He looked like he wanted to measure their teeth and look inside their ears, and was only restraining himself due to a combination of cake overload and the memory of Walter's near-scorching.

"What about the silver Audi?" Miriam asked.

"What, mine?" DI Collins asked, glancing out the window as if to make sure it wasn't being taken apart by goblins.

"No, the one that was lurking around the village," Alice said. "There were goblins driving it at least once."

DI Adams supposed that explained the ladies of the W.I.'s impromptu spying session in the village square. Aloud, she said, "Funny, you didn't mention that."

Miriam went very pink and made a little squeaking noise, and Alice gave DI Adams an amused look. "She was doing so well, Inspector."

DI Adams took a scone from the coffee table. "Sorry, Miriam. But as to the car, the brothers got themselves four matching silver Audis for some reason. We found two of them driven off the road around the farm, and another sticking out of the tarn, so maybe the goblins were teaching themselves to drive. I imagine they were hanging around looking for their chance to steal baubles."

"They were planning to kidnap either Alice or Miriam," a new voice said, rich and a little BBC-presenter-ish. "Or both. They thought they'd fetch a rather good ransom from the Cloverlies."

DI Adams pinched the bridge of her nose, wondering if she was ever going to get to grips with Toot Hansell. DI Collins choked on his tea and Alice said something very unbecoming. Miriam made a new sort of squeaking noise.

"That – what?" DI Collins said.

Alice picked the cat up and lifted him to eye level. "All of that nose pointing and wine spilling, and you could have just told me what was going on?" Thompson blinked lazily and yawned at her, and Alice put him on the floor. "I don't think I want you on my lap anymore."

"Suit yourself." He inspected a paw. "But you're lucky even goblins are smart enough to know not to grab humans that the Watch have their eye on. That's why all they did was try and warn you off."

"The Watch?" Beaufort asked.

"Well, I'm Watch, aren't I? But it goes no further. Some things can be kept between friends."

DI Adams wondered if she wanted to know about the Watch, and decided that a talking cat was more than enough for one day. "So you were protecting them?" she said.

The cat looked uncomfortable. "Looking out for them, let's say. Protecting's a bit … you know. Doglike."

"And you did that by taking them straight to the goblins?" Mortimer demanded.

"Yes," Beaufort said. "Why didn't you come to us?"

The cat shrugged. "I can't get anywhere near a dragon hill. Not with those blocking runes you have all about the place. You weren't around, so I thought the *ladies*, as you call them, could take a look and call the police. I didn't expect them to go all commando on me."

Alice scowled at him. "As you call them indeed. And you've not once said thank you for all the tuna."

"I prefer salmon," Thompson said, and sprawled out by the fire.

"I still want to know why you didn't talk," Alice insisted. "It would have been an awful lot easier."

The cat looked at her lazily. "This. Questions, questions, questions. Talk-talk-talk. It would have been the new year by the time we got there." He closed his eyes.

"And that," Beaufort said, "is why most people are better off thinking cats can't talk."

DI Adams glanced at Collins. He was looking at his mince pie as if suspecting it might contain some rather unusual and possibly illegal ingredients. "I'm really not keen on the eggnog idea," she said, "but if you have any Scotch...?"

"AND WHAT ABOUT YOU, Detective Inspector Adams?" Alice asked. "I understand you weren't really meant to be up here."

DI Adams sipped her Scotch. Yes. Turning up with a stitched-up arm from an arrest that wasn't even in her jurisdiction, let alone in her caseload, hadn't exactly put DCI Temple's mind to rest. He was still concerned about her stress levels, although she had told him, quite truthfully, that she felt much better. There had been pursuit, and some good punches, and even a couple of tackles, although technically that had all been with the goblins. The humans had all been fighting to be first in the car. It had done the trick, though. "I'm on probation," she said.

"I keep telling her that if she likes it that much she should just transfer up here," DI Collins said. "I'll put in a good word for her."

"I'd be bored out of my mind. What was your other case? Missing turkeys?"

Gilbert choked on his eggnog, and Amelia patted him on the back affectionately.

"Oh," Mortimer said. "I completely forgot."

"Forgot what?" Beaufort asked.

"Why were you chasing a turkey when you went into Rockford's cave, Gilbert?"

Gilbert mumbled something, and everyone leaned forward.

"Sorry?" Beaufort said. "Speak up, lad, some of us are a bit deaf."

"It got away," Gilbert said.

"Away from where? There's no turkeys living on the hill."

Gilbert took a deep breath, then said, "I took them from the turkey farm and hid them in my cave. I didn't want them to get eaten. I was going to let them go, but then I figured it'd be safer after Christmas."

"Gilbert! Not again," Beaufort said, frowning. "We've talked about this."

"You've got to stop," Amelia said. "What's wrong with you?"

Gilbert glared at her. "They're living creatures!"

"Frank does overcharge terribly," Alice said, "And I don't think he feeds his birds decent food."

"You see? I saved them!"

"You stole them," Beaufort said. "You have to put them back."

"But they'll get eaten! It's so unfair!"

"There's your case solved," DI Adams said to Collins.

"And you thought it'd be boring. Can I just – Gilbert, why don't you want them to get eaten?"

"Because no one needs to eat meat. We should all eat pumpkins," the young dragon said earnestly.

DI Collins looked at DI Adams, then took a large bite of Christmas cake. "I was prepared for dragons," he said. "No one said anything about vegetarian dragons and talking cats."

OUTSIDE, the snow began to fall again, bringing a hush to the soft fields and wild fells, and a full moon hung silver among the stars as Christmas edged quietly closer. Inside, in warm cottages and fire-lit caverns, in cosy dens and sheltered nests, small secret lives were lived and loved and dreamed, on two legs or four, and sometimes on more or less than that. And, for one night at least, magic was as much a part of the world as all the many forms of love, because they are, after all, one and the same thing.

And what a poor world it would be without either.

A BEAUFORT SCALES MYSTERY

THANK YOU

Lovely people, thank you for taking the time to read *Yule Be Sorry*. I hope it's left you feeling suitably festive, if slightly wary of buying baubles at market stalls (you should be safe, but maybe keep an oven tray handy, just in case. Or a cricket bat …).

And because it's always fun to scatter the tinsel of festive cheer a little further (or the mince pie crumbs), I'd appreciate it very much if you could pop a review up on the website of your choice.

Reviews encourage others to step into the world of Toot Hansell, meaning the word of dragons spreads! Plus everyone should be forewarned about the risk of goblins …

If you'd like to share your review with me, let me know your favourite festive treats, or otherwise talk dragons and baked goods, drop me a message at kim@kmwatt.com. I'd love to hear from you!

Thanks again for reading, lovely people.

Read on!

(PS head over the page for more dragonish adventure, and to discover your *free* Toot Hansell recipe collection!)

A SPA WEEKEND WITH A DIFFERENCE ...

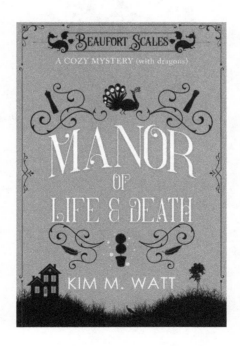

Warring staff. Strange guests. Topiary of dubious intent.

Throw in the full complement of the Toot Hansell Women's Institute and dragons doing yoga on the terrace, and DI Adams is starting to wonder if she might have made a small misjudgement signing up for this particular spa weekend in the country.

And that's before the dead body in the sauna and the storm that cuts them off from the rest of the world ...

Grab A Manor of Life & Death today to catch up with the next instalment in the Beaufort Scales series!

Scan above or head to books2read.com/AManorOfLifeAndDeath to join the adventure today!

DRAGON-FRIENDLY RECIPES
INCLUDED

Your free recipe collection awaits!

Lovely person, I hope you enjoyed chasing goblins and evading police officers throughout the Yorkshire Dales, and that you now appreciate the importance of a well-made mince pie.

And, of course, I have recipes for exactly those in the *Yule Be Sorry* recipe collection!

Plus, if this is your first visit to Toot Hansell and my newsletter, I'm also going to send you some story collections - including one about how that whole barbecue thing started ...

Your festive treats are waiting - grab your free recipes collection now!

Happy baking!

Scan above or head to https://readerlinks.com/l/2351069/ybspb to claim your copy!

ABOUT THE AUTHOR

Hello lovely person. I'm Kim, and in addition to the Beaufort Scales stories I write other funny, magical books that offer a little escape from the serious stuff in the world and hopefully leave you a wee bit happier than you were when you started. Because happiness, like friendship, matters.

I write about baking-obsessed reapers setting up baby ghoul petting cafes, and ladies of a certain age joining the Apocalypse on their Vespas. I write about friendship, and loyalty, and lifting each other up, and the importance of tea and cake.

But mostly I write about how wonderful people (of all species) can really be.

If you'd like to find out the latest on new books in *The Beaufort Scales* series, as well as discover other books and series, giveaways, extra reading, and more, jump on over to www.kmwatt.com and check everything out there.

Read on!

amazon.com/Kim-M-Watt/e/B07JMHRBMC
bookbub.com/authors/kim-m-watt
facebook.com/KimMWatt
instagram.com/kimmwatt
twitter.com/kimmwatt

ACKNOWLEDGMENTS

To you, lovely readers. For reading, for commenting, for sharing, for making Beaufort something more than just a strange conversation with my dad. You are all entirely wonderful.

To my dad, without whom Beaufort would never have come about. Thank you for giving me a sense of the ridiculous, and teaching me to appreciate silliness. And for passing on the odd imagination. I could have done without inheriting your weird feet, though.

To Lynda Dietz at Easy Reader Editing, who is responsible for all the correct grammar, punctuation, and spelling in this book. The mistakes are all mine. She's also responsible for making me really, really look forward to the editing process. Thank you for making what could have been the hardest part fun, easy, and entertaining.

To all my wonderful writer friends. You know who you are. Thank you so much. You're responsible for making me believe in this writing lark. Especially Alison and Anna, who I met at different points, but exactly when I needed to. You are truly amazing, and I kind of want to make a cheesy A-Team joke, but I'll restrain myself.

To Sylvie, Sophie, and my other non-writer friends who manage to not only resist glazing over when I start talking about dragons and tea, but who actually encourage me.

And, of course, to you, new reader who has just taken a gamble on a book about tea-drinking, mystery-solving dragons. You are entirely awesome.

ALSO BY KIM M. WATT

The Beaufort Scales Series (cozy mysteries with dragons)

"The addition of covert dragons to a cozy mystery is perfect...and the dragons are as quirky and entertaining as the rest of the slightly eccentric residents of Toot Hansell."

– Goodreads reviewer

The Gobbelino London, PI series

"This series is a wonderful combination of humor and suspense that won't let you stop until you've finished the book. Fair warning, don't plan on doing anything else until you're done …"

- Goodreads reviewer

Short Story Collections
Oddly Enough: Tales of the Unordinary, Volume One

"The stories are quirky, charming, hilarious, and some are all of the above without a dud amongst the bunch …"

- Goodreads reviewer

The Tales of Beaufort Scales
A collection of dragonish tales from the world of Toot Hansell, as a

welcome gift for joining the newsletter! Just mind the abominable snow porcupine ... (you can head to www.kmwatt.com to find a link to join)

The Cat Did It

Of course the cat did it. Sneaky, snarky, and up to no good - that's the cats in this feline collection which you can grab free via the newsletter (it'll automatically arrive on soft little cat feet in your inbox not long after the *Tales* do). Just remember - if the cat winks, always wink back ...

CPSIA information can be obtained
at www.ICGtesting.com
Printed in the USA
BVHW031116260223
659226BV00005B/108

9 781999 303761